Old Grimes Is Dead

Dennis McFadden

Summerhilll Publishing

Copyright © 2022 Dennis McFadden

All rights reserved.

ISBN: 979-8-798474-81-3

The author gratefully acknowledges the journals that first published short stories excerpted from this novel: "Old Grimes," *The South Carolina Review*, Volume 39, Number 1, Fall 2006; "Little Brier," *New England Review*, vol. 35/number 3, 2014; "Carry Me Home," *Pennsylvania Literary Journal*, Volume XIII, Issue 3, Fall 2021.

Cover Design: Eric Armstrong

This is a work of fiction. Names, characters, places and incidents are products of the author's imagination or are used fictionally. Any resemblance to any real person, living or dead, is purely coincidental.

I lovingly dedicate this novel to my most faithful and devoted reader.

You know who you are.

CONTENTS

	Acknowledgments	i
1	October 30, 1857: The Resurrection	1
2	August 15, 1857: The Unfortunate Miss Eva	18
3	November 3, 1857: The Miracle of Molly	32
4	August 18, 1857: The Luckiest Man in the World	52
5	November 9, 1857: Resurrection Redux	71
6	October 30, 1857: Napoleon Makes a Splash	95
7	November 22, 1857: Grave Consequences	114
8	November 4, 1857: We All Got That Coming	130
9	December 7, 1857: The Trial. And Tribulation	149
10	December 6, 1857: The Last Days of Pompey	173
11	January 14, 1858: The Great Escape	194
12	January 19, 1858: Love, Dirt and Fire	217
13	January 21, 1858: The Price You Must Pay	233
14	January 21, 1858: The Axe Man Cometh	245

1: October 30, 1857: The Resurrection

In 1832—four years before Darling was born—a man named Burke confessed to killing fifteen people in Edinburgh, Scotland, for the purpose of providing dissecting material to medical colleges. He was paid what amounted to two dollars and sixty-seven cents per specimen, and was hanged for his trouble without ever retiring as a wealthy man.

Will Darling had learned about Burke from his preceptor, Cyrus Vasbinder, who at the time of Burke's mischief had been forty years of age, and a doctor for fifteen of those years. Darling could understand why Burke's actions had been considered beyond the pale, no matter the stratum or class from which he may have drawn his specimens, and concluded that Burke had been paid what he'd earned. What he couldn't understand was how the whole business could have failed to lead to the reform of the statutes outlawing the medical use of cadavers, which was still against the law, even to this day. Moreover, he also could not understand why, given the indisputable illegality of the act, even to this day, his preceptor now stood before him, scarcely able to contain his enthusiasm while proposing the resurrection of Fudge Van Pelt for the purpose of scientific dissection. The unfortunate Mr. Van Pelt had expired only the day before.

"You propose to dig the man up?" Darling said.

"That is hardly the proper terminology, my dear," said Vasbinder. "We are proposing his *resurrection*. Of course that shall not be possible until after he is interred tomorrow."

"Cyrus, I—" Stepping from the doorway where he'd greeted Vasbinder, Darling closed the door quietly behind him; his mother was in the kitchen, and little escaped the woman. Glancing conspiratorially up and down the street, he saw nothing but chickens, an old dog sleeping in the dirt, and Vasbinder's fat horse who nickered and pawed impatiently, jostling the shay behind him. Across the street, the Stormer boy was chopping cordwood for his mother, somewhat furiously, Darling noted, against the hint of winter infiltrating the cool air.

"I can assure you, Will, we shall not end up at the end of a rope the likes of which awaited the notorious Mr. Burke. Poor Fudge is already as dead as he can be."

"It's not the end of a rope I fear. It's imprisonment. It's the end of my reputation, such as it is, the end of my prospects. How will a convicted felon go about building a medical practice?"

"Fear not, my dear, word shall never leak out. We shall take every precaution." Vasbinder was a balding man, stocky, with a bushy white mustache and eyes of cloudy gray. He possessed an odd, beseeching way of blinking both of his eyes simultaneously, a symptom of his sincerity, a facial tic, the degree of which indicated the depth of his passion on the subject under discussion. Now, as Darling watched, the tics could not have been more earnest.

"Who are 'we'?" Darling said. "Who are our fellow conspirators?"

"The proposition was brought to me by the Doctors Bullers, and I quickly concurred. This shall be an excellent exclamation point to your education as a physician, standing you in good stead as you assume my field of practice—as I, if it please God and the voters, move on to the legislature." Darling knew of his preceptor's political ambitions, and he also knew the Bullerses. There were but seven practicing doctors in Hartsgrove, and he knew them all. Dr. Alexander Bullers, known as Big Bull, was renowned for the speed of his saw, attributable to his size and strength; he could whip the arm or the leg off a man in no time, then wear his bloody frock into the Peace and Poverty Tavern for a jar of small beer. Dr. Samuel Bullers, Little Bull, was known as man of serious purpose. "Little Bull is particularly enthusiastic," continued Vasbinder. "It is his idea. He harbors ambitions of becoming a surgeon."

One of Vasbinder's oft-repeated dictums came into Darling's mind; just as quickly it came out again: "Ambition is like love—laughs at the law, and takes fearful risks."

As he became acclimated to the idea, it quickly gained supremacy in his mind, and by the time Vasbinder had departed, Darling's enthusiasm was on the rise. He had ridden and read with his preceptor these past three years, and the more he learned, the more he found he no longer blindly agreed with him in all matters. But he whole-heartedly concurred with another of Vasbinder's oft-repeated dictums, that a knowledge of anatomy is the foundation of the healing art.

Moreover, Vasbinder's proposal—and poor Fudge's demise—had occurred at a time when little Molly Plotner had taken a turn for the worse.

Though one of the youngest practicing physicians in the state—at twenty-one—Darling was nevertheless wary of the pitfall of becoming too attached to a patient, which was generally profitable neither emotionally nor financially. But it was too late. Molly Plotner was—or had been—a sturdy little girl of five with an impish grin and inquisitive mind. Watching her bright green eyes turn pale and dull, her thick black hair lose its luster and begin to fall out, had been almost more than he could bear, despite having seen his share of patients fail and die. He did not particularly respect death, but the girl seemed to inhabit a unique niche of innocence, one that infants hadn't yet earned, and adults had long since forfeited.

Was it mere chance, the coincidence of Molly's decline and Fudge's demise? Possibly. Probably. Yet Darling did believe in providence, and this would be his first opportunity to study directly the mysteries of the human anatomy. In his youthful enthusiasm, he did not believe it entirely beyond the realm of possibility that somewhere within the earthly vessel of Fudge Van Pelt, he might find—not a cure, certainly, he was neither naïve nor foolish enough to believe that—but an insight of some sort that could only enhance his understanding, and, in the long run, only be of benefit to Molly.

Van Pelt had been a bootmaker, a friendly man whom everyone, including Darling, had known, and he would have to set aside his fondness for the man and view him objectively, as a specimen, an object of learning. It was Van Pelt himself who seemingly blessed the proposition. He appeared that night in Darling's dream, hovering like an Angel of Enlightenment, his bony black face smiling his gap-toothed smile quite beatifically at the prospect of his humble contribution to the little girl's cure, indeed, to the medical sciences. Using his rasp file like a lecturer's wand, Van Pelt, in the dream, pointed to his own breast, where the first incision would commence, drew it down his abdomen, then effortlessly peeled back his ebony dermis, exposing his musculature like stepping out of a suit. When he began to pry open his rectus abdominus muscles to expose his viscera, a white light emerged, brighter than the sudden flash of a lantern at midnight.

The graveyard was on a hill overlooking Hartsgrove, where the town ended and the forest commenced. Darling kept watch from the corner above the town, crouching like a criminal in the crystal clear moonlight, listening to the shovel and mattock behind him biting at the grave of Fudge Van Pelt with eager little chomps. All the while, a noble resentment festered within him, resentment at *having* to crouch like a criminal (indeed, at now *being* a criminal), resentment at how such a munificent, humane and altruistic enterprise such as the medical use of cadavers could still be illegal, at how such small minds and little laws could still prevail, here, now, in modern-day

Pennsylvania. Half an acre behind him, his colleagues labored, an odd melding of ghouls and coolies. Nothing stirred on the hillsides, though the cool night air was alive with sounds: the *chomp, chomp, chomp* of the digging behind him, the lowing of a curious cow, the barking of a dog, the nickering of a horse, over and over, creeping across the town below as if they were passing the word from yard to yard: *Somebody's digging up Fudge!*

At early candle-lighting, the five conspirators had met at Sandt's Drug Store to finalize their plans for the resurrection. It had been Darling's idea to enlist the aid of his old school chum, Joshua Sandt; though not a doctor, Sandt was a druggist, somewhat educated, and medically-inclined. Darling had been the last to arrive, finding Vasbinder, Sandt and the two Bullers brothers already awaiting. As did every merchant in Hartsgrove, Sandt kept on his counter a pail of pure Monongahela whiskey, clear as amber, smooth as oil, and all but Darling and Vasbinder had dipped repeatedly into it, bracing themselves for the work before them. The plans had been made and remade, every aspect of their roles, their shifts, their contingencies, even their tools, hashed and rehashed. No one had been in a hurry to actually climb the hill to the lonely graveyard by the woods.

Now, keeping watch above the town, Darling suddenly realized that the sounds of the digging had ceased. Looking back, past the sprawling bare skeleton of the chestnut tree, he saw his four companions sitting idle in the moonlight by the grave.

Had they reached Van Pelt? With a final glance down the hill, Darling left his post. At the graveside, Vasbinder was standing, hands on hips. His bushy white mustache shuddered when he clucked his tongue. "They were brave as lions, to a man," he told Darling, "until the whiskey quit. Feeble be the unfortified heart."

"Why the hole's damn near dug," Big Bull said, spitting into the dirt. Overflowing the gravestone on which he sat, he was a large man with a miniature nose and a beard that reached down to his chest. His brother, squatting on his heels beside him, was similar in appearance, though a cut smaller; he spat at the same time: They both took tobacco. "I'm all wore out is all," Little Bull said. "Not enough men for the job. If we'd enlisted Captain Alcorn, as I wanted..."

"Your turn, Will," said Sandt, unfolding himself from the stone upon which he sat. "I'll take watch for a while." Sandt grinned, wispy whiskers clinging to his skinny chin, and draped a gangly arm over Darling's shoulder. Darling felt a flush of impatience break over him; he was finding himself increasingly irritated by his old school chum, and he wondered why on earth he'd recruited him. When Sandt had commenced construction of his new house on North Street, while he, Darling, continued to scrape by with his mother, a reservoir of resentment had opened up within him that he hadn't realized was there. He, Darling, was a physician, a man of learning, who'd labored endless hours to attain that position; Sandt had opened a store and stocked some shelves. Darling tried to remain above the tugs of petty jealousy, keeping them at arm's length where they assumed a vague and guilty aspect. He was not always successful.

Then there was the matter of his lady friend, Kathleen O'Hanlon. Darling considered her his lady friend, had been courting her for several months, though he knew too that his old school chum had similar designs, and was awaiting his opportunity. Darling shrugged free of the arm, and Sandt turned toward the corner of the graveyard, then stopped, hiccupping loudly. "Will, I forgot," he stage-whispered. "Was it one if by land and two if by sea, or the other way around?" He chuckled and winked, then made his way across the graveyard, rustling loudly through the fallen leaves. Stealth did not come easily to him at any time, a lanky man with rusty joints, but with the whiskey, it was all but abandoned.

Vasbinder sighed, his breath spreading out on the moonlight before him. "Then I shall finish the job myself."

"I shall," said Darling, dropping into the grave, setting to work with nervous energy.

"I didn't know they put niggers down so deep," Little Bull said.

"Plant 'em too shallow, they tend to sprout up again," Big Bull explained.

"Gentlemen," said Vasbinder, "perhaps a modicum of respect would be in order. Mr. Van Pelt may have been only a Negro, doomed by nature through no fault of his own to live a useless, no-account life, but he endeavored to rise above his station, indeed becoming a passable craftsman—and in death he shall make an even more valuable contribution to mankind. We do him honor—by the Jew's eye, we bestow something of value upon him in death that he could never have achieved in life."

"Amen," said Darling from the grave. Toiling in the dark, he pictured Vasbinder's facial tics, the symptoms of his sincerity. He agreed that it was unfortunate enough to have been painted black by the Creator without the added burden of abuse, even in death, and he took the thoughtful silence that followed to mean that the company assented.

Little Bull broke the thoughtful silence. "What I can't figure is why it's against the law to dissect niggers in the first place."

"You know the law," his brother said. "Seldom makes a lick of sense. Why, it's perfectly legal to cut up monkeys and mules."

When the shovel shuddered on wood, Little Bull leaped nimbly into the grave, where he and Darling finished clearing the pine box, making room for the ropes. Climbing out again, they hoisted the coffin to the side of the grave, opened it up to a burst of putrid odor, and quickly undressed the dead man—he'd been buried in a new, yellow flannel shirt and corduroy trousers—placing him on the coffin lid. They turned the coffin over, put it back into the ground, tossed in the new clothes and slippers, and quickly refilled the grave.

Taking up the bier, they left, Sandt joining them with a lurch at the edge of the graveyard.

Below, the dark hillsides of the town were dappled by the whitewashed houses in the moonlight, thin streams of chimney smoke trailing up like threads of silver. Darling could see across toward Irishtown, where his lady friend Kathleen would be sleeping, unaware of his nocturnal adventure. The chatter of the cattle, dogs and horses seemed to grow louder, worrying him that Constable McClay would surely be alerted.

Down Prospect Street they marched, bearing Van Pelt like hunters home from the hunt, past Coal Alley, across Jefferson, across Main and the new lumber smell of Kelty's rebuilt blacksmith shed, along the paling fence enclosing his neighbor's back lot, to Vasbinder's house on Water Street. Cyrus was a widower, and childless, his house on a deep wooded lot. In a small bedroom just off the kitchen they laid Fudge Van Pelt to rest again in the dark.

They headed for their homes. It was past two A.M. on Sunday, which would be a day of rest; they planned to meet on Monday night to begin the dissection, using Vasbinder's house as their "school." Taking his leave, Sandt winked absurdly at Darling, irritating him all the more.

Vasbinder walked with Darling down Water Street till they came to the corner, where he took his hand. "My dear Will," he said, "you mustn't fret so. I assure you you'll be amazed at the wonders of the human anatomy, the things you will learn. It is quite apart from the pictures, models and manikins."

"It's not that," Darling said. "I anticipate it eagerly. Maybe too eagerly. It's just that I can't stop thinking about Molly Plotner."

"She's shown no improvement?"

Darling shook his head. "She's failing. The cough has eased, but she's become wan and listless, and now her hair falls out."

"How's her bowels?"

Darling shook his head again in response. "Still costive."

"The fever persists?"

Darling nodded. "Intermitting."

"The poor girl's blood is still over stimulated," Vasbinder declared. He questioned Darling on his course of treatment, then recommended more. The flesh of his face twitched around the intensity of his eyes—a combination of bored and beseeching—as he advocated opening of the little girl's veins, inasmuch as cupping was obviously not up to the task; and the calomel dose must be doubled. Young doctors tend to be too timid in their practice, he said, he'd been young once and timorous himself, but the disease must be looked upon as an entity—indeed, as a devil—which the physician must have the courage to expel by violent means. "Take the unfortunate example of Fudge Van Pelt," Vasbinder said.

"He took the fever, I understand."

"Lingered less than a week. He had the misfortune to fall under the care of Mr. Means who bled him not a drop, treated him with only a boneset infusion—this I know for a fact—and gave him not a single dose of Dover's powder. Less than a week." Darling sighed. Vasbinder continued, "Mr. Means is, unhappily, under the influence of the eclectic school of medicine, not a real doctor at all, not by any reach. Eclecticism, by the Jew's eye, is synonymous with— "

"Ragtag and bobtail?"

"I was about to say humbug and quack."

"I never know which," Darling said.

Vasbinder's mustache trembled as he studied Darling's smooth, white face in the moonlight. "I'm often unsure how to regard your remarks, my dear. Your face betrays nothing. It is clear as a slate."

"It is my bedside face."

Vasbinder nodded, staring. "We are not beside a bed," he said.

In his own bed that night, Darling saw the faces again, staring at him from the amorphous border between thought and dream. Kathleen's face was replaced by Molly's, her eyes bright again, her small face mirroring the pleading tics of Vasbinder's as she stared at him imploringly. And Fudge Van Pelt's dead, black face suddenly opened its yellow eyes; then, somberly, with a hint of collusion, winked at him with Joshua Sandt's wink.

At first light, Darling patted the gray shoulder of his mare, Gertie, who nickered a toothy greeting over her shoulder. He saddled her, secured his pill bags, and led her from the stable; swinging his green legging over top, he set off in an easy canter up Hamilton Street toward Main. In front of Clover's General Store he pulled up to wait as a team hauled a stick of timber across the newly laid, hewed-log bridge over the gully gouged across Main by the August storms over two months before. He nodded to the driver, a man named Coleman.

Moses Clover stood in the doorway in his long white apron. "Morning, Will. I got some oranges in."

Darling had had only a handful of dried hominy for breakfast. He couldn't afford the extravagance of an orange, but purchased one anyway; his credit was still good with Clover. He tucked it into his pill bag, to enjoy the anticipation of it during the unpleasant call before him.

He headed north, out of Hartsgrove. A mile up the Coolbrook Road, he stopped to watch buzzards circling over a copse in the middle of a cleared field. Something was dead within the little patch of woods. Darling counted four buzzards, then suddenly, five, then six, eight. He watched the ease and grace with which they glided, looping lower and lower, yet never alighting. Gertie gave a shiver, anxious to move on.

Darling refused to let the notion of an omen enter his mind: He was on his way to Plotner's. When the first buzzard floated into the woods, he gave his horse a nudge and rode off, thinking about life feeding on death. Past the lane into the Negro settlement along the Little Brier Creek he rode on, thinking about the doctors and Fudge Van Pelt.

Enoch Plotner was a raw-boned, hard-working man, though his farm was far from prosperous. Plotner and his mule were removing a stump from the edge of his field. The morning sun was flush in his face, his squint giving him a bitter aspect. Smelling the sharp scent of fresh earth and broken wood, Darling pulled Gertie up beside them.

"Morning, Enoch," he said.

"Doc," said Plotner. He took a rag from his pocket to wipe his brow.

"Who's winning? You or the stump?"

Plotner harrumphed. "What I need's a ox," he said, "'Stead of this worthless old critter. Or I'd settle for a son, for that matter. Either one."

Darling thought better of resenting the remark, his attachment to Molly notwithstanding. "How is our little girl?" he said.

Replacing the rag in his pocket, Plotner only shook his head.

Darling rode on, following the fence along the field toward the crude cabin the Plotners called home, listening to the mean thumps of Plotner's axe echoing down the hollow.

Plotner's wife Emma greeted him in the doorway, twisting her apron in her hands. Darling trod lightly into Molly's sick room; it was dark, the air dank and fusty. Nearly swallowed by the soft straw tick, the little girl watched him with listless eyes. Opening his bag, he placed his lancet and cup on the faded quilt. Molly clenched her eyes.

"How do you feel, my dear?" He felt her forehead, hot, barely found her pulse, looked at her tongue. Extracting her arm, he laid it on the quilt, then retrieved the other. He inspected them, searching for a vein. Taking up his lancet, he stood beside her, pausing. Behind her clenched eyes, Molly began to hum.

Darling detected the tune; it was an old song, a song that was sung in every household, one he'd often heard his mother sing: "Old Grimes Is Dead." Molly began to sing, eyes shut, small voice off-key, nearly inaudible:

Old Grimes is dead, that good old man, / We ne'er shall see him more; / He used to wear a long black coat, / All buttoned down before...

He marveled that a child of five could master the verse by heart, though her tune was hit and miss. He softly sang another verse, Molly joining him midway through:

He lived in peace with all mankind, / In friendship he was true; / His coat

had pocket-holes behind, / His pantaloons were blue.
Darling smiled. Molly failed to even try.

Riding back into town an hour later, there was no sign of the buzzards. Nevertheless, Darling pulled up, letting Gertie graze, as he pictured the feast within the copse. Hooking his leg across the saddle in front of him, he leaned upon it, drained.

Perhaps he should become a teacher, as his father had been before he'd died. Perhaps he should apprentice to Mr. O'Hanlon, Kathleen's father, and become a cabinet-maker. His confidence in his skills as a physician had never been lower.

What would he say to Cyrus? (What business was it of Cyrus's at all?) He could hardly admit that he'd been unable to bring himself to bleed the little girl again, unable to administer the calomel, even a single blue pill. That he'd offered her no treatment at all, and had in fact acted in a contraindicative manner, if all he'd ever learned at Vasbinder's side were true. Impulsively, he'd drawn the ragged curtain, letting in the light, nearly blinding Molly; he'd thrown up the sash, allowing the cool autumn air to fill the room; then he'd lifted the poor girl from her sickbed wrapped in her thin blanket, and held her on his lap, trying to will the fever away. He'd sang in a whisper verse after verse of "Old Grimes is Dead"—trying to earn a smile. Then he'd peeled his orange, and fed it to her. As the smell of it had filled the room, she'd nearly swooned; her gums were bleeding, and she scarcely had strength enough to chew.

It was contrary to everything he'd been taught, but he couldn't deny it. His confusion easily accommodated his feeling of cowardice, for not having the courage to heal his patient. He'd left without a word to the Plotners, without even mentioning his overdue fees again. He felt too small and unworthy to broach the topic, given his failure to treat the little girl.

Hearing the squawk of a buzzard, he was suddenly hungry. He hadn't even tasted the orange, though the smell had made his stomach rumble. He thought of Garrity's sign on Main Street, *Jumbles & Beer For Sale Here*, his mouth watering. The jumbles were delicious, small, cakes made of New Orleans molasses. He pulled the coins from his pocket: twenty-two cents, his entire fortune at this moment in time. He listened to the grinding of Gertie's chewing. It occurred to him that perhaps it was not cowardice that had stayed his hand. Perhaps it was God, answering the prayer he'd been meaning to pray. Perhaps he was not to act until he'd learned whatever it was that Fudge Van Pelt had to teach him.

Arriving back in town, Darling detoured up the hill to the graveyard. He felt he should survey the land, to assuage his anxieties, to confirm that nothing had been overlooked in the darkness of the night before, that the grave appeared unmolested.

Cresting Prospect Street, he was shaken by the sight of someone kneeling over the grave. He pulled up at the corner of the graveyard by the monument to Eli Hart, a Revolutionary War hero and the town's first settler, where he'd crouched in the moonlight not so many hours before, keeping watch. The kneeler had his back to him. From the ragged warmus, the nappy gray head, Darling recognized Fudge's pal, Henry Westerman, a colored man called Black Hen. Reaching down, Black Hen touched the dirt of the grave—in supplication, or suspicion?

Hearing Darling approach, he scrambled to his feet, clutching his floppy hat to his chest.

"Henry," said Darling, nodding. "Paying your respects?"

Black Hen returned the nod. "Yes sir. Gonna miss this ol' nigger."

"Yes. God rest him. How's his family?"

Black Hen nodded again. He might have been ten or twenty years older than his late friend; Darling couldn't tell. His leathery face was frosted white with whisker stubble, and Darling was surprised when it took a sudden, painful twist. "Mr. Doc, it shoulda been me," he said. "I's the oldest nigger here. It shoulda been me."

Darling felt vaguely guilty at the relief he was feeling: Black Hen was not suspicious. "I know you'll miss him, Henry, but… You must try to remember the good times you had. Recall what a friend he was, and be glad for it."

Black Hen sighed, looking down at the grave. "We had us some good times all right, Mr. Doc, up there on Little Brier Creek."

"Good, Hen. That's what to think of. That's what to remember."

Darling let the silence take root between them. Black Hen turned his back, kneeling again, his hand coming up to his cheek. Darling flicked the reins, turning to go, then stopped at a sudden thought. "Hen," he said. "Did you pay your last respects? Before he died?"

The frosted head shook, never turned. Darling took it upon himself to assuage the man's obviously troubled conscience; it was the least he could do. "Now, you mustn't abuse yourself, Henry," he said. "The fever can be very contagious. It's laid many a brave man low."

Black Hen didn't turn. "Mr. Doc?" he said. "You reckon ol' Fudge can hear me now?"

Darling, his stomach growling, watched the old man, impervious to his altruistic intent, kneeling over the empty grave. "I'm sure of it, Black Hen," he said. "Though you might want to speak a bit louder."

Darling was never pleased when his vague and guilty thoughts began to distil. The vagueness served to mitigate the guilt. He knew they were inversely proportional, the vagueness and the guilt, so he resisted the distillation. Plucking another flea from his calf, he rolled it roughly between his thumb and forefinger, pinning it to the board with his thumbnail. With his bistoury, he sliced it in two. He liked practicing his dissection on these loathsome little creatures, keeping his eyes keen and his instruments sharp.

His belly contented with Garrity's jumbles, his mind kept returning to the image of Molly skipping through a meadow, a perfectly restored little girl; then he imagined riches: a new home on North Street, a new suit of clothes, a phaeton and span of fast horses, means to care for his aging mother. But he imagined they were incompatible. God was forcing him to choose between the two. God was standing here next to him in the kitchen, by the cast iron stove, frowning divinely at Darling's mutilation of His tiny creatures, whose real and beneficent purpose was known only to Him, and telling Darling he must choose. His voice was entirely deep and Biblical: *Take your pick*, He said: *the health of Molly, or the wealth of Sandt. Which will it be?*

Both, answered Darling, with an emphatic slice of flea. He wouldn't speak to the real God in such an impudent manner, but inasmuch as this was only his own mind's God, he felt safe enough. He plucked another flea from his leg. The hunt—which consisted of walking barelegged over the haunts of the dogs and cats—hadn't been all that successful; he'd cut up only six so far, and there were perhaps a dozen still clinging to his calves. The cold nights were killing them off. He'd managed to cut one into four distinct pieces, though he had to admit it had been an inordinately fat flea.

He refused to choose.

His mother came into the kitchen, wrinkling her nose at the sight of her son at the table, trousers rolled up to his knees. She did not approve of this particular practice. Ada Darling was a stern woman, her cool blue eyes—inherited by her son—the only unworn feature on her face. She had about her an air of perpetual weariness, perhaps from her long hours as a seamstress at Mrs. McCurdy's, perhaps from her long years as a widow.

"William Darling," she said—sternly, even for her.

Darling's bistoury froze in mid-flea. "Do not say a word," his mother said, "just listen. You have been out nights. You have gotten yourself into trouble." She paused, letting the words hang heavy. Darling looked out the small window, to the necessary in the back yard.

"You and the other doctors have dug up Fudge Van Pelt. Samuel Bullers told Captain Alcorn about it, and he told his foreman, Claude Pepper. Claude Pepper told his wife, who told Mrs. Libby Stormer, who told me this afternoon. Now you must watch out for yourself. You mark my words, young man. You will be the only one to get into trouble, for you are poor, and the others are all rich and influential gentlemen."

Even after the words had saturated, it took some time for all the implications to be absorbed. The most galling of which was this: that Joshua Sandt was a rich and influential gentleman. And that he, Dr. William

Darling, was not.

He should speak with Kathleen before the rumors reached her. He rode Gertie to Irishtown, on the south side of Hartsgrove, down the dusty street between the shacks and shanties, among the chickens and pigs and dogs and children. Past O'Hanlon's Furniture Factory, silent on a Sunday, he waved to two of Kathleen's brothers rolling a hoop in the yard. Her father was a successful cabinet-maker and undertaker, employing ten men, all Irish immigrants like himself. The Irish had arrived and settled en masse ten years ago, to the chagrin of the Doctors Bullers and much of the town's protestant populace.

Darling continued on to Mrs. McClay's, ostensibly to see how her rheumatism was. When he rode back, Kathleen was waiting by the willow at the edge of town.

"Darlin' Will," she said with a smile. Kathleen's hair was black, full and flowing, framing her pretty face upon which there was no wasted space, highlighting the brightness of her teeth. Her black hair and green eyes were shades similar to Molly Plotner's, but there the resemblance ended; Molly's face was sturdy and plain, Kathleen's delicate and fair. "We must talk, my dear," he said, helping her up behind him.

They rode into the woods, past a stand of beech trees where they'd harvested goldenseal a month earlier, up the side of the hill a short distance to a secluded boulder, one of their spots. "You'll never guess what I did last night," said Darling, helping her down.

She thought for a moment. "Invented a cure for some dreadful disease?"

"Not exactly. We resurrected Fudge Van Pelt—the colored man who died Thursday."

"You dug the man up?"

"That is hardly the proper terminology, my dear. It is called a 'resurrection.'"

"You dug the man up. From the ground."

"Yes," he said impatiently, "from his grave."

"And I suppose you'll be cutting him up into wee pieces."

"Yes, in a manner of speaking. We'd hoped—we still hope—to perform a scientific dissection, but... Word seems to have gotten out."

"This town, they'll think you're nothing but a pack of ghouls. Ignorant, the lot of 'em."

Darling took her hand. "I thought you'd be a bit more shocked."

"Why?" she said. "Once the soul is in God's hands, what becomes of the mortal shell is of little consequence." From her pocket she took a string of beads.

"I suppose." He knew she believed in omens, and told her his feeling that the dissection might somehow benefit Molly Plotner.

"Fudge died of what the little girl has?"

Darling shook his head. "I didn't attend to Fudge, though apparently his fever was not dissimilar. It's certainly not as if I would expect to open up the man and find a cure for the girl. Maybe eventually, with many more dissections, with much more learning, for her grandchildren, or theirs. It's just that…well it's decidedly unscientific. Superstitious almost."

"And what's wrong with that?" said Kathleen, fingering the beads in her lap.

Shifting his weight on the rock, he told her how that morning he'd been unable to treat the little girl; how he'd opened the window and held her instead, fed her his orange, and how the thought had even entered his head afterwards that perhaps it was God who had stayed his hand.

A dead leaf floated down, and a squirrel scurried twisting up the trunk of a nearby tree. Kathleen leaned against him. "When I was a boy," Darling said, "and my father was dying, I found myself playing with a barrel hoop one day—just as your brothers were today. And I said to myself, if I can roll this hoop the entire length of Main Street, from Mill to Valley, without it tipping over once, then my father will be all right." He put his arm around Kathleen. "It's that sort of thing. Decidedly irrational."

"And did the hoop tip before Valley Street?"

"Yes." Darling nodded.

"And did your father die?"

The caucus was convened in Sandt's Drug Store that night, Vasbinder's face a shade redder than usual. Sandt pulled the shutters over his front window and turned down the lamp, the high tin ceiling vanishing in the gloom. On the wall behind the counter, row upon row of gold-labeled glass bottles containing Sandt's tinctures, syrups and powders gleamed like a dull ache. Every man but Darling dipped into the pail of whiskey. Big Bull slid Sandt's spittoon with his foot to a spot between him and his brother, depositing a turnip-sized gob with a splash.

"Whatever possessed you to confide in that blatherskite Alcorn?" Big Bull growled at his little brother. His linen frock coat was rusty with blood.

"I've always known Captain Alcorn to be the soul of discretion," Little Bull said. "Except perhaps when there's drink taken."

"The only time he isn't taking drink is when he's unconscious from the taking of it," said Big Bull, gulping at his whiskey, "particularly since the unfortunate business with his daughter. I wouldn't entrust the pompous old windbag with directions to my shit house."

"The unfortunate business with his daughter, as you put it," Little Bull said, "is all the more reason why we should have engaged the Captain in the first place." Judging by the smug expression on the bearded face, Darling guessed that the words carried a significance beyond that which he could decipher, though no one else in the company seemed inclined to notice.

"Gentlemen," Vasbinder said. "It is an unfortunate fact of history that the hide of many a good man has been nailed upon the Tree of Learning."

"I'd just as soon keep my hide around my bones," Sandt said. "Or, to put it another way, I'd just as soon keep my hide around my bones."

"For five men to keep a secret," Darling observed, "four of them must be dead."

Vasbinder, a Democrat, was engaged in a political feud with the Republican Burgess, James Butterfield. All agreed that the discovery of an illegally resurrected Negro in Vasbinder's home could sound the death knell for his political aspirations. Van Pelt would have to go.

"Maybe we could wax him up and stick some cigars in his hand," Sandt said, nodding toward his wooden Indian. "Old Red Smoke over there, he's getting pretty weather-beat."

"The situation is grave," said Vasbinder, unamused. "Hardly an occasion for flummery and folderol."

"Why don't we stick him up in your ice house?" Big Bull said to Sandt. "He ought to keep up there."

"Surely," said Sandt. "Lay him out next to my butter."

Word was out, Darling assured them, so they must act quickly. Anxious to be gone, he was becoming increasingly agitated in Sandt's store, surrounded by the wealth of the wares on the floor-to-ceiling shelves—the drugs, medicines, dye stuffs, perfumery, soaps, candles, lamps, tobacco—all testament to Sandt's ascendance.

It was agreed to remove Van Pelt to Sandt's ice house. Singly and in pairs, they made their way down to Vasbinder's house.

Vasbinder had participated in a dissection in Harmony Mills four years earlier. The subject had been an Irishman who'd frozen to death, the story went, from drinking too much water in his whiskey. Vasbinder assured them that a proper dissection required fifteen days, that Hartsgrove would not afford them that, and that at any rate Sandt's ice house lacked the necessary amenities. Big Bull offered to ride to Slabtown tomorrow and enlist the aid of Dr. Breakey. Perhaps their school could be removed to the nearby village.

At midnight, Van Pelt was enshrouded in the coffee sack Sandt had provided, and mounted on the coffin lid. In the meantime, Little Bull suggested an additional precaution to prevent the identification of the specimen in the event of discovery: They decided to remove the tell-tale black dermis; they would skin the cadaver.

Old Grimes Is Dead

Darling took no part in the debate, nor cast a vote. He supposed it was a sensible enough precaution, and he was eager to catch his first glimpse of the anatomy of an actual human, yet he couldn't escape the feeling that it was also somehow a desecration, a violation of a man—the color of his skin notwithstanding—of whom he had been fond. At the same time he feared his reluctance was a sign of weakness, of his inability—decidedly unscientific and unprofessional—to cast aside his feelings and act objectively, in a manner beneficial to the greater good, his immature sensibilities and personal qualms notwithstanding. To act, in other words, as a good doctor should. While he took no part in the debate, once the decision had been made, he had no compunction about taking his part in the ensuing removal of the dermis.

The ice house air was cold, the inside walls white with frost gleaming in the lamplight. Van Pelt was divided into five parts for the procedure: Vasbinder took the right arm and side, Big Bull the left, Little Bull the right leg, Darling the left. Sandt was assigned the head. They had skinned large mammals before, yet somehow, to Darling, it was different: The atavistic odor of the flesh seemed more acrid, choking his nostrils; the silky, slithering, ripping sound of the skin peeling from the flesh like skin from an orange seemed somehow sharper.

Within the hour, the job was done. Darling could not look at the skinless cadaver without imagining the tiny musculature of Molly. They gathered the cuticle, toes, fingers and bowels into the coffee sack. Big Bull would bury them in the woods tomorrow on his way to Slabtown.

The gleaming remains of Fudge Van Pelt were laid out on the frozen floor. Vasbinder placed a large lump of ice in the abdominal cavity. Darling was not at all squeamish about the anatomy, nor about the work of dissection, and he noted with a measure of delight the pallor overcoming Sandt's face, his quick trip around back of the ice house. His own light-headedness he was at a loss to explain, finally attributing it to a vague notion—distinctly unscientific—that Molly would somehow survive after all.

The soft plank floor of Darling's room was pockmarked with tiny holes. They'd been put there by a hardwood peg protruding from the sole of his father's boot. Sometimes the holes were invisible; sometimes, depending on how the light played upon them, they were prominent, forming constellations and patterns which Darling might study for signs, like stars or tea leaves or clouds. He'd first examined them fifteen years earlier, as his father had lain dying in the room, his guilty boot abandoned and useless beneath the bed.

A few months before, his mother had noticed the holes, deduced the source, and scolded his father. Anxious as always to please, his father tried hammering the peg back in, to no avail, then fell into the habit of removing his boots inside, when it was warm enough, when he remembered. Thus he encountered the splinter in his great toe one day. The suppurating toe was removed by Dr. Nevers a month later, followed by the foot, then the leg, in successive months. Darling remembered his father's suffering, vaguely, guiltily; he'd never tried to decide whether the crushing dread he'd felt had been empathy for his father, or fear for himself. He remembered his father delirious on his death bed calling for Billy Boo the fiddler to come play a jig, and the smell of putrefaction that smothered the closed little room, the same smell that had burst from the coffin of Fudge Van Pelt.

Darling could discern no meaningful pattern in the holes this night; they were too plentiful, lost in the confusion of one another. He saw the limp hide of Fudge Van Pelt, the falling hair of Molly, and a dozen other traces leading nowhere. He hadn't seen the little girl, though she'd been on his mind all day. He knew the Plotners would call for him if she worsened; he'd debated going this afternoon, had nearly decided not to, when he'd been spared the decision, called away in the opposite direction to repair an axe gash on the leg of Lester Vandevoort. He'd used Balm of Gilead stick plaster spread on muslin strips.

Hearing a knock on the door, Darling hurried downstairs, lest it awaken his mother. In his haste, he absent-mindedly carried with him the book he'd been studying, even though he was expecting Vasbinder. Vasbinder it was; the flesh of his cheeks and brow immediately began bunching around his eyes in earnest tics.

"Will, my dear," he began, "the plan has been laid. I've just left Dr. Bullers, who—what is that you're reading?"

Darling held the book behind him. "Nothing—what is the plan?"

"Let me see the book."

"Never mind the book. What is the plan?"

"Why you're reading Buchan's *Domestic Medicine*."

"Merely leafing through it. I only borrowed it out of curiosity. Now what—"

"By the Jew's eye Will, surely you're not seriously considering these recipes as singular courses of treatment. Why it is all nothing but a bunch of—"

"Poppycock and twaddle?"

"I was about to say stuff and nonsense."

"I never know which." The older man's facial tics diminished. "Cyrus," Darling said, "how can education of any sort be a bad thing? Surely we must learn everything we can, no matter the basis, no matter the philosophy, and make use of the best remedies from any and every source?"

"That sounds quite eclectic, Will."

Old Grimes Is Dead

"Maybe there's something to eclecticism," Darling said, hastening to add, "when combined with the good, solid practice of regular medicine."

"Where did you borrow the book?"

Sweat sprang from Darling's brow. "From Mr. Means."

Mustache quivering, Vasbinder staggered, as if struck. Darling quickly fetched a chair for him to sag upon. "Can I get you some water?"

"No, no thank you, Will," Vasbinder said. "We must act at once. Time is of the essence." Big Bull had made arrangements with Dr. Breakey of Slabtown, who would arrive within the hour to remove Van Pelt. Vasbinder told Darling the plan, then stood to go, quite wearily. He looked as if he'd aged even since he'd arrived.

In the doorway, he took Darling's hand. The neighbor's dog barked, and Vasbinder's fat horse farted in the street. "Will," he said, "the little girl cannot be cured by cooking tubers and grasses and roots. Hear me. Chestnut astringents and boneset tea will not do the job. It is *your* job. *You* must be the hero. Her life is in *your* hands."

The plan was this: Vasbinder would go to the barroom of the American Hotel on Main Street to ensure, through conversation, whiskey or whatever means necessary, that none of the clientele was in the streets come eleven o'clock; Big Bull would do likewise at the Peace and Poverty Tavern. At quarter till, Sandt would go to his ice house and unlock the door. Five minutes later, Darling and Little Bull would enter the ice house to await Dr. Breakey, then lift Van Pelt out to the wagon. It was to be swift and silent, with no crowd, no loitering that might draw attention.

The best laid schemes. What happened (Darling later learned) was this: In his nervous haste, Sandt dropped the key. Unable to find it in the weeds, dirt and darkness (unwilling, Darling suspected, to drop to his knees and soil his fine new trousers), he retreated to his store to fetch a hatchet to open the door by force. Darling and Little Bull arrived as Sandt was halfway down the hill, and, finding the door locked, left as instructed. Returning with his hatchet, Sandt broke open the door, leaving again just as quickly. Dr. Breakey arrived with his wagon and large store box, only to find no one there. After waiting five minutes, he too left, without Van Pelt. On his way out of town, he stopped on the bridge and pushed his empty box into Potters Creek, where it floated away.

At dawn, young John Espy happened by and noticed the ice house door had been smashed. Thinking someone had broken in to steal butter during the night, possibly wondering if the thief had overlooked any, he peeked in.

Screaming, he fled the horror, his breakfast porridge spattered upon his boots.

2: August 15, 1857: The Unfortunate Miss Eva

Near as Hen could recall he'd been eight or nine, maybe ten, when an Indian called Sassy John—whiskey on his breath, blood in his eyes and murder in his heart—had massacred his family back east along the Crooked Creek in Lycoming County over fifty years before. He was still abed when Sassy John had burst into the cabin, his tomahawk bloody from Hen's father in the field, and instantly struck down his mother. His two sisters and brother had scattered in panic, and Sassy John had pursued and dispatched them, one by one. Hen never stirred. Stayed in bed, his eyes tight shut against the world, never opening them again till the man named Yellow Charlie shook his shoulder some minutes or hours later. Thus the legend was born that Hen had escaped by pretending to be dead. Perhaps. Perhaps Sassy John never noticed him there, or perhaps Sassy John, in his high state of blood lust and drunkenness, had seen him as just another stick of furniture in the room, like the rough board table or the peg-legged stool. All Hen knew for sure was that if he'd moved quickly on that day he wouldn't be alive on this one, and so to this one, as a general rule, he avoided haste.

"*Move* it, Hen," Fudge said. "We gonna see what that boy up to, we got to get there before the sun go down." It wasn't much past noon.

Hen had stopped to pee. "What that boy up to," he said, watching his feeble stream trickle into the dirt. "What that boy up to."

His friend Fudge, a good twenty years younger, had pulled ahead by a fair number of paces, and he stopped and turned in the road, staring and waiting. Fudge was worried. Worry was his domain. Like haste, worry was a thing Hen avoided as a general rule. Passing this way earlier, down the Birchwoods Road by the school, Fudge had spotted a horse looking suspiciously like one of Augustus Hamilton's Morgans tethered up behind the schoolhouse, in what looked like attempted concealment. It was hot, a

Old Grimes Is Dead

sweltering August day, and Fudge removed his tattered straw hat and waved it in his face, taking a rag from his back pocket to mop his neck. Hen shook his pizzle, buttoned his britches and resumed his leisurely pace. He caught up to Fudge in his own good time, having barely broken a sweat, his floppy old felt hat still firmly atop his head. Patience was an art, one he feared his younger friend would never master.

"Your mama ever told you you was slower'n a one-legged turtle?" Fudge said.

"Man gotta pee when a man gotta pee."

"Man gotta pee every two minutes whole way down the road?"

"Old man do," said Hen. "You find out one day."

They moved on down the dusty road, tromping their shadows. The cicadas buzzed and droned in the woods by the road where it dipped down into the hollow toward the schoolhouse. Fudge was worried that Augustus, a young man who'd shown up in their settlement, Little Brier, only a year or two before, might be taking liberties with the young white school teacher, Miss Eva. That could only lead to trouble. Fudge had seen him talking to Miss Eva a few days before, up on Hartsgrove's Main Street, right in the middle of the town, in front of God and the whole white world. You didn't have to be a blue-ribbon worrier the likes of Fudge Van Pelt to know the kind of trouble that might spell.

When the schoolhouse came into view, there stood the black Morgan, the older, gentler of the pair, the horse Augustus called Jupiter, the one he used as a saddle horse. Not tethered to the post in front, he was tied suspiciously to a bush out behind the building. Fudge took Hen's arm. "Looky there," he said with a mournful grunt. "We gots to see what that boy up to."

"What that boy up to," agreed Hen, "what that boy up to."

Fudge reconnoitered, finally pointing. "Okay—we run over behind the big oak there, then make us a beeline to the rock on the other side. Make our way over to the corner, we can sneak on up to the window. Ready?" Hen nodded approvingly, then walked straight across the yard toward the window. "*Dang* it, Hen," said Fudge.

Hen walked up to the open window and looked in. "What you up to, boy?" he said.

Inside the schoolroom Augustus looked up, forehead raised in surprise, which did little to raise his eyelids—his eyes were constant slits. A handsome young black man, his burnished skin a perfect fit for the muscles of his face, he was sitting on a children's bench, lanky legs nearly up to his chin, a stub of chalk in his hand, slate on one knee, his hat—a nearly brimless black derby—on the other. The boy had his manners. At the blackboard stood Miss Eva, frowning out from behind the twin curtains of brown hair that tried to hide her face—loose, flowing hair, not piled upon her head as it normally was.

"Learning my A-B-C's," Augustus said, innocently enough.

Miss Eva came toward the two older men in the window, the boards of the floor clicking beneath her airy step. "Not all darkies are shiftless," she said in a voice too high and anxious to carry the authority it wished. "Not all darkies are lazy." And she swung the shutter shut, though not before they saw the flush on her face, nearly hidden behind the curtains of her hair.

Yellow Charlie had founded Little Brier some forty years before, albeit with no intention of doing so. A mongrel, part Chinese, part white, part colored, Yellow Charlie had been something of a hermit, building a shack on the east bank of the Little Brier, near where it flowed into Potters Creek, which flowed into the heart of Hartsgrove, the town that he wished to avoid. He disliked people, engaging with them only when he had to, as when he wheeled his barrow into town to sell the stone coal he picked from the creek beds for money for flour and other items he couldn't grow, kill or steal on his own. Whether Hartsgrove or any other part of western Pennsylvania had been Yellow Charlie's destination all along Hen never knew, though it always struck him as unlikely. More likely it was where he finally wore out, came to roost after wandering through the wilderness with the boy he'd come across in the aftermath of the Crooked Creek massacre. Why Charlie, given his reclusiveness, had taken in an orphan in the first place was anybody's guess, though few believed the goodness of his heart had anything to do with it. From the moment he acquired him, Yellow Charlie never collected another stick of firewood, never toted the heavier pack, never raised the shelter or set the traps, did less and less of the hunting and gathering and picking of coal. Most believed it was Yellow Charlie's hard driving of the boy in his youth that accounted for his laziness as an old man. He'd simply worn him out.

Yellow Charlie had long since passed on to his eternal reward. Feeling poorly one day, weak with the fever, he'd picked up his axe, gone into the woods, never to be seen again.

Fudge Van Pelt had come to Little Brier some twenty-odd years after Yellow Charlie, some twenty-odd years ago, along with his new bride, Lucindy. It was Lucindy Hen had seen first, leaning on his rake, staring. It had taken him a while to notice Fudge, though it was Fudge who was doing all the talking, engaged in an animated discussion—most of Fudge's conversations were animated—with Cornelius Nips, one of Little Brier's elders even then, concerning the site for Fudge's cabin. Lucindy had eclipsed the men in Hen's eye, beautiful in a lopsided way, crooked nose, skinny legs, wide, square shoulders. Fudge had learned Hartsgrove was in need of a bootmaker just as he was nearing the end of his apprenticeship in

Harrisburg, and so he'd moved west, settling for a short time in Hartsgrove itself, before discovering Little Brier—where a number of other colored families had congregated. It was a peaceful place, among the willows along the banks overlooking the creek, a collection of tilting shacks and shanties, an easy trot to Hartsgrove. Fudge found it far more uplifting to be living among his own kind, far easier to hold his head up and not have to look over his shoulder, far easier to look a neighbor in the eye. It was freer. These feelings he shared with his new friend Hen, whereupon Hen recognized the feelings as his own, though he'd never tried to put them into words.

"Aiming to *better himself*," Fudge said, the last two words rolling off his tongue like a cut of bad tobacco. Hen was sitting with Fudge and Lucindy in front of Fudge's cabin in Little Brier shelling corn for the hens, a scattering of which strutted and pecked imperiously around them.

"Can't blame the boy wanting to better himself," said Lucindy.

"You suppose he ain't aiming to better Miss Eva along the way?"

Lucindy looked up from the long slender cob in her hands. "Fudgeon Van Pelt, you hush up that mouth. Ain't all men think like you think, from somewheres down in the ditch."

"That boy is, or I miss my guess," said Fudge. Taking another ear from the basket, he slipped his thumb into a slit in the skin, into the fair silky hair. From the swimming hole came the sounds of whoops and splashes, half the population of Little Brier—including Napoleon and Belle, Fudge's and Lucindy's boy and girl—seeking relief from the swelter in the cool creek waters. Hen was still on his first ear of corn as Fudge twisted his third, kernels rattling into the tin basin on the ground between them. "That boy up to no good."

"What you think, Hen?" said Lucindy.

Hen shrugged, placing his half-peeled cob on his knee to rest.

Fudge said, "Them crackers think Augustus sniffing around a white woman—even one mousy as what Miss Eva is—then they end up sniffing around Little Brier. And that ain't good."

Hen and Lucindy took that into account, listening to kernels peppering tin, the odd splash and shout from the creek. They remembered the last time white folks came sniffing around, remembered it well though it was fifteen years ago, remembered the fires and the wailing, every shack in the settlement burned to the ground. A stolen pig had been found in one of those shacks, and Hen could still feel the heat on his face, watching the flames, watching the red embers shoot and twist out over the black creek waters. High price for a pig, he'd reckoned.

He looked at Lucindy frowning down at the cob in her own hands. She was glowing with sweat in the heat, her indigo work dress drooping between her legs as she leaned over the basin. Hen loved how the red rag tied in her hair made her cheekbones shine.

She said, "What if he just learning his A-B-C's like he say?"

"All's they gots to do is *think* he sniffing around," Fudge said.

"You ain't never like that boy," said Hen.

"No," said Fudge. "I ain't." Augustus Hamilton had shown up in Little Brier the spring before, the warm, wet spring of 1856, building himself a little cabin in no time, purchasing himself a wagon and a brace of fine black Morgans, finding himself work as a teamster. Where he got the capital nobody knew. Fudge had said all along that the boy didn't talk like a Yankee, he'd talked to plenty a Yankee, and so he doubted Augustus' claim to be a free Negro from Connecticut, despite his Certificate of Freedom he kept in a leather pouch strapped to his leg. Where were his family, his friends? But it was the eyes that cinched it for Fudge. Augustus's eyes were constant slits, never seeming to open all the way, obviously, in Fudge's mind, hiding something behind them. And his smile that all the girls loved—including Fudge's own Belle, just nine—the white teeth, the lifted lip, amounted to nothing more, in Fudge's mind, than a sneer.

"Ain't got nothing to do with the wrestling he always beating you at," Lucindy said.

"No," Fudge said. "It ain't."

Hen said, "First time they rassled, never seen a man flat on his back so fast."

"Ain't no joking matter," said Fudge.

"Leas' you handsomer," Lucindy said, and Hen laughed. Nothing slow about Hen when it came to laughing, laugh wrinkles on the back of his neck from years of throwing back his head. Hen's laugh always made Lucindy laugh too.

"Ain't funny," said Fudge, but he smiled a little, aware of his own balding head, skinny chin, bony cheeks, the prodigious gap between his front teeth. Hen continued his laughing even as Lucindy's faded away, and he soon realized he was laughing alone, that Fudge and Lucindy were waiting, and he stopped, and the shelling of corn went on, the kernels bouncing on tin, the children shouting and splashing in Little Brier Creek. The laughter was all used up.

The fretting went on. The fretting wasn't going anywhere. From his bootblack chair in the corridor by Fudge's shop in the back of the American Hotel, Hen stared at the little sign in the shape of a boot hanging above the doorway, and listened to Fudge's incessant hammering, punishing the piece of leather on his lapstone, and he could only shake his head at his friend's industriousness. Hen was a big enough man that he had the capacity to admire industriousness in another man, without dirtying his own hands on it. The bootblack chair had been Fudge's idea, and Hen had agreed. A good way to keep an eye on his friend, to keep an eye on the white folks of Hartsgrove whom he would never trust, and to have a good reason for doing so. The chair was comfortable, he could nap when he pleased, though he seldom more than dozed since the day a year or two ago when he'd been awakened from a deep, pleasant nap when the match in his boot had burned down, threatening to roast his toe, the circle of little dirty white faces standing about, grinning in anticipation—*eeny, meeny, miny, mo, burn the nigger's big black toe!* Hen had casually removed his boot, blown out the flame. Wiggled his toe for good measure, smiled at the boys. No shouting, no yelling, no dancing about in panic and pain, and so the young ones, clearly disappointed, had dashed off in search of better mischief.

Dozing, Hen didn't see Dr. Means walk by, but he heard him greet Fudge in his shop.

Means was a white man, small and friendly, possessed of a red goatee and an infectious enthusiasm which included a habit of thrusting his hands before him, thumbs up. Despite his color, Hen liked the doctor, a Quaker, one of Hartsgrove's few, and a strict abolitionist—one of Hartsgrove's even fewer. He was seldom without his smile, and his smile seemed to be the same for white men or black. Hen heard the doctor and Fudge exchange pleasantries, but what brought him fully alert was when the doctor lowered his voice.

"There's been some talk," said Means.

"I ain't surprised."

"Bad talk."

"Bad talk ain't good," Fudge said.

"I'm concerned about the safe passage of our cargo."

"I been thinking along them same lines. Got my worry up."

"Not just the cargo. I'm worried for that boy, Augustus. And for you and Hen as well. But especially for him."

"Let me have a talk with the boy."

"You talk to him."

"See if I can't straighten this here thing out."

"Cast your magic spell. Use your silver tongue."

At that the two men laughed, though not very convincingly. Hen never opened his eyes as Dr. Means left, hearing his light step go by, down the corridor toward the lobby.

Down in the lobby and barroom of the hotel white voices hummed and chattered. White folks knew about Little Brier, but didn't much care. Couldn't be bothered. They never set foot in the settlement just a little northeast of their town, with the one flaming exception some fifteen years earlier, which had involved only the sheriff and his band of ruffians. White folks were just as pleased to have their black folks out of sight, to have them appear only when needed, to not have to think about them, nor about the problems they'd created, problems like abolitionists and states' rights and the Missouri Compromise and bleeding Kansas. Problems pointing toward a whole lot of trouble brewing. White folks, Hen knew, would be just as pleased if black folks didn't exist at all, except maybe when they needed a boot blacked or a sty mucked out or a spittoon scrubbed. White folks didn't know what went on in Little Brier, didn't want to know.

Fudge had told Hen what he'd seen, a runaway slave run down in Harrisburg, his black skin in shreds and tatters, blood washing the gutter. Hen knew. He was aware of the ways of the world, he'd been a nigger all his life, and he'd seen things with his own eyes, seen the ugly tangle of scars on the back of Solomon McManigle, a Little Brier neighbor and former slave himself, whose manumission papers were always within arm's reach. When Dr. Means had approached them, Hen and Fudge had decided to do something about it. Now more than ever, white folks not wanting to know what went on in Little Brier was a good thing.

Now along came Augustus Hamilton, aiming to spoil a good thing.

Even after sundown, the heat remained. Hen left his airless little shanty and walked up along the creek, watching the half moon climbing the sky through the branches and leaves overhead, to the spot on the bank where the breeze sometimes found its way in over the water, a comfortable place to loaf. Fudge was there when he arrived. Neither man spoke as Hen settled in against the trunk of his hickory tree.

Through the trees they could see the fire Augustus had built in front of his cabin. The boy liked his fires. Big, angry fires. Often, like tonight, the young folks gathered around, laughing and singing—Napoleon and Belle were there—and Hen and Fudge sat in silence for a while, hoping for a breeze, listening to the children, foolish, foolish children, celebrating fire on night so hot. Few of them were old enough to remember the fires on that other hot night, the night of the stolen pig, the fires that had spelled an end to Little Brier as they knew it then, the devil's eyes laughing in those mean and angry flames.

Fudge said, "We going to have to go on over, talk to that boy."

They watched the fire a while longer. "What you gonna tell him?" Hen said.

"You ain't coming with me?" Hen's silence was his answer. After a bit Fudge said, "Tell him he got to quit sniffing around Miss Eva. That's all. Ought to be enough."

Hen listened as the night tightened its grip on Little Brier, the only sounds the ripple of the creek and the odd hoot, snort or bark, yip, yowl or squawk. The occasional snap and pop from Augustus' fire over through the trees grew drowsier, and it grew quieter, the children having all drifted off to their beds. Fudge drifted away as well. Hen looked and saw the half moon high up the sky, a warped reflection wrinkling in the creek, and through the trees he thought he could make out his friend sitting across the fire from Augustus, could see the flash of the firelight off the brim of his old straw hat, and he tipped his own hat, took it off and waved it in his face, admiring the sheer industriousness of his friend. Taking care of business. Up further, Fudge's cabin was dark, no candle in the window. Napoleon and Belle probably asleep. Hen wondered if Lucindy was in her bed as well, hers and Fudge's, or if she was sitting up by the hearth in the kitchen, waiting. He pictured her there, asleep in her bed and unaware, he pictured her sitting in the rocker by the hearth, the faraway look in her eyes the way she sometimes stared at nothing, her long skinny legs and crooked nose, the glaze of sweat on her skin, and the peculiar sensation of floating came over him again.

He opened his eyes when Fudge returned, bringing him back down to earth. The air had cooled a little and the moon was low. Fudge sat down by his rock on the bank and grunted. "That dunderheaded young nigger up and fallen for that white girl. He sweet on her."

After a bit Hen said, "Miss Eva?"

Fudge shook his head. "Miss Eva. What other white girl?"

Clucking his tongue, Hen joined his friend, shake for shake.

"She oughta set him in the corner with the dunce cap on his head," Fudge said.

Hen raised himself up off the ground with a mighty stretch, considered the dunce cap, unbuttoned his britches and peed in the creek. He looked at the moon, then up through the trees to Fudge's dark cabin where Lucindy was. Buttoning up and turning away, he sat back down and said to Fudge, "What you tell him?"

"Told him them crackers'll cut his balls right off, they think he sniffing around Miss Eva," Fudge said.

"What he say?"

Fudge picked up a twig and snapped it in two. "Told me her daddy whips her. Miss Eva's daddy. Whips her bad. Said she knows what it's like to be a nigger, knows what it's like to be owned by somebody else."

Hen nodded. Sometimes a nod was as good as a word.

After a while Fudge said, "And how you suppose Mr. Free Negro from Connecticut knows what's that's like, to be owned by somebody else?"

Yellow Charlie had never aspired to anything fancy, nor had Hen, and so his shanty was among the rudest in Little Brier, a collection of cast-off boards and branches, close to the creek, often invaded by the springtime floods when they lapped up over the banks, one-room, a small fireplace, an old corn-shuck mattress on the dirt floor, a trestle table and stool, a door, a tiny window. After the fire, Hen had rebuilt the same shanty he and Yellow Charlie had constructed all those years before. Kept him warm in the winter without a big fire, but on the hottest nights of summer, air was hard to find. Something woke him early, after only an hour or two, and he went back outside to the air. He seldom slept the whole night through anymore anyway.

What awoke him was the sound of a voice. The voice of a woman, or a girl.

The dawn was lightening the eastern sky over the trees, but the forest itself teemed with fog, heaped high and thick over the creek, spilling out into the woods all around. He couldn't see Fudge's cabin where it ought to be, beyond the nearest trees. Everything was still, but for the fog slyly stirring, lifting, shifting, and Hen felt his blood begin to stir and hurry. Exactly where the sound of the voice had come from he couldn't say. There were no words to the sound, only an exclamation of surprise, maybe, of anger or fear. Augustus' place too was hidden in the fog.

The only sound was of birds trying their best to be heard in the mist. From down in the cluster of cabins came a tentative garble of a crow from Absalom, the Widow Winter's famous rooster, wondering in the fog if his dawn had arrived.

They were expecting a cargo. Dr. Means had told Fudge. Hen walked up creek in the fog, heading to his spot on the bank to sit and doze and wait for morning. It grew quieter, the birds and Absalom the rooster seemingly having abandoned their efforts to be heard in the fog, and he dozed again. Miss Eva appeared. Before she'd been sent away to the Brookside Seminary for Young Ladies, Hen had seldom seen her except in the company of her father, Captain Alcorn, a stern widower with a curled mustache, drunk as often as not, who rode a sorrel horse with a silver mane and a bridle ornamented with leather straps, balls and tassels. He was a man who was proud of his possessions, and Hen had often seen him with his daughter, riding—she beside him in the seat of his one-hoss shay, or behind him on the sorrel horse, her face forever averted, her hands griping the cantle before her—or walking hand in hand on the board sidewalk of Main Street, between his distillery and his foundry. Sometimes he saw them in the hotel, socializing on court day, sometimes at the campground at the annual muster, or picnicking down by the sand spring where the creeks converged. Always Hen was invisible. Always Miss Eva's face wore a sour, pinched and painful aspect—she seemed a most unhappy child.

The sound of a voice brought him back, a different voice, softly calling: the cargo.

Little Brier was situated along the east bank of the creek a mile or so west of the Coolbrook Road, the highway from Hartsgrove to Coolbrook and points north. There was only one road into the settlement from the Coolbrook Road, a narrow lane through the woods scarcely wider than a wagon, and it was a well-travelled lane. A half mile north of that was a little-travelled trail, well hidden, that led to Fudge's cabin at the north end of Little Brier.

Fudge was waiting outside his cabin. They walked without a word around back to the trailhead, where, emerging out of the fog and the woods was Silas McKay, a white man from Harmony Mills, leading two young blacks, a man and his wife, scarcely more than a girl, both dressed in little more than rags. *Two Virginia hams*, the cargo Dr. Means had promised.

McKay, a big man in a baggy blue waist coat, introduced the runaways, Luke and Mary, then took his leave, clasping Fudge's hand warmly, then Hen's, turning and vanishing again into the fog, back up the trail he'd just travelled, to the Coolbrook Road where his wagon would be waiting, hidden in the trees. He seemed to Hen a tolerable white man, and it seemed odd to realize that this spot, the trailhead behind Fudge's cabin, was the only place on the face of the earth where he had ever seen the man, and the only place he likely ever would.

Luke was a lanky young man, possessed of a small nose on a prayerful face, all muscle and bones, no pickings on him at all, and his wife, Mary, was even skinnier, her jaw slack with weariness, her large white eyes and large hands empty and wanting. Fudge said they must be tired, Hen said they must be hungry, and Luke said they were both. Fudge began to lead them toward his cabin where they would sleep, past the dug-out just into the woods, the hiding spot to which they would flee if need be, until after dark when they would transport them north, further north on their journey, deliver them up to the Deer Run station near Sugargrove.

Hen was the first to see her. Motion in the corner of his eye, and there stood Miss Eva, just beyond the trailhead at the edge of the woods, like a ghost in the fog. There was a flash of white, a glimpse of light from behind the curtains of hair hiding her face as she threw back her head, her arm rising, a finger pointing straight at Hen, Fudge, and the two young runaways.

In an instant she was gone, swallowed by the fog.

Hen was the first to give chase. He dashed off toward the spot where Miss Eva had vanished, leaving Fudge frozen in his tracks with Luke and Mary.

The woods were darker than the clearing by the cabin, thicker with the mist as he ran, crashing through the undergrowth, unable to see more than a few trees before him, rushing blindly along the path most likely taken by Miss Eva. A minute or two later, seeing nothing, he stopped to listen. Fudge rushed up behind him with a crash through the thicket.

When he started to speak, Hen held up his hand. "Shush—listen up."

Nothing but silence, their raspy breathing, a slight moaning breeze, the muffled warble of birdsong. No sound of running feet.

"She gone to ground," Hen said.

"Or she faster'n a scalded pussy," said Fudge. They listened for another moment, then, out of breath, he said to Hen, "When you got so quick? Never seen you so quick before."

Hen caught his own breath, gave a solemn nod. "Always been quick."

Footsteps crashing behind them, Augustus bursting out of the mist.

"Where she at?" he said.

Hen shrugged. "Gone," said Fudge.

"What she see?" said Augustus.

Hen shook his head. Fudge said, "Seen something she shouldn't of saw."

Augustus was scarcely breathing hard. He frowned toward the foggy trees.

Fudge said, "You brung her here? After what I done told you? You brung her here?"

"I ain't brung nobody here," said Augustus, frowning down at the two older men.

"Then what she doing here?"

"Running away," Augustus said. "Told me she running away from her papa. She show up, middle of the God damn night—ain't nothing I can do 'bout that."

"Running away?" said Hen.

The three men stood still, the young man, Augustus, the old man, Hen, and Fudge in the middle, looking from one to the other, as the fog seemed to lift, fresh light filtering in. Off through the trees, something crashed through the brush, but they could tell from the sound it was a smaller animal. "Damn," said Fudge, his bony cheeks beginning to lift just a little.

Hen smiled bigger. "Run her up north with the cargo, she want to run away."

Fudge said, "First class fixings for the young white lady—back of a wagon underneath of a load of straw and manure."

Hen threw back his head and laughed. "When she ain't walking down a trail in the black and rain, tripping over roots, shooing off wolfs."

"Getting lost in a swamp whole way up to her bustle."

Augustus stared through his half-closed eyes. "Glad you gentlemens ain't lost your keen sense of humor."

"Gots to laugh, young man," said Hen, his face going sober, "else you just end up crying."

Fudge took a breath, blinked away the last bit of amusement. "Now what?"

"I know where she probably head to," Augustus said. "I'll find her. She listen to me. I can make her see what's right, make sure she don't tell nothing to nobody."

Hen still saw in his mind the raised finger pointing in the mist, a ghostly specter of accusation. Fudge was the one to put his feeling into words: "Cap'n Alcorn bring a whole lot of hurtin' down on this place."

At that they nodded in unison, as if bowing their heads in prayer.

Back in Fudge's cabin, breakfast was a hurried and worrisome thing. Augustus had come back, had met Luke and Mary, then taken off for parts unknown. No one mentioned the apparition that had been Miss Eva, though Lucindy could tell something was wrong. Napoleon and Belle could sense it too, for Fudge wore his worry like a necktie.

Hen watched Lucindy stay busy, pouring mugs of strong coffee, frying up hotcakes on the cook stove, cutting the bread with a steady hand, her lips grim and tight.

He sat at one end of the plank table that Lucindy kept scrubbed white as a bone, for the table was a gift from her mother, the only part of her mother left to her. Fudge sat at the other end, neither man speaking. Hen felt pressed down by the weight of the worry in the room, thick as the fog outside. Luke and Mary leaned together timidly, wearily, on the floor in the corner, and Belle sat holding her husk doll before them, talking to Mary—*How old is you? You sure is pretty. Where you come from? Is it hot like this down there?*—trying to hide the worry from her new pair of friends beneath a cloak of chatter. *What you got on your sleeve there, on the string?* Belle asked; Mary told her it was the foot of a jaybird, and that was what was bringing her luck. Napoleon went outside to pee in the fog with Hen.

By the time the sun had seared away the morning fog, Luke and Mary were sleeping like stones in Napoleon's bed—Belle's bed empty beside it—their bellies full of hotcakes and molasses, unaware that they were in any particular jeopardy beyond that which they faced every day. Fudge had taken precautions. Napoleon, bored, scratching random letters in the dirt with a stick on the Coolbrook Road, wishing he could form them into words, dotting his i's with spit, was watching and listening, his ram's horn under his arm, his sister down the Little Brier Road at the far edge of earshot, equally bored, equally vigilant. Hen and Fudge went to work at Fudge's shop in the back of the American Hotel in Hartsgrove, as usual, trying to follow their normal routine, though their normal routine stubbornly refused to be followed.

Fudge was unable to concentrate on his work, while Hen, his custom scant as usual, had no work to concentrate upon, and dozing was equally elusive. With clockwork regularity, Hen heard the tapping of Fudge's hammer cease, and Fudge would appear in the corridor by Hen's chair, his face damp with sweat—the more he worried, the more he sweated—and neither man spoke, their ears buzzing, straining to sift through the jumble of conversations taking place in the lobby and in the barroom beyond, keen to latch on to words such as *Eva*, or *Alcorn*, or *missing*. Or *Augustus*, or *slave*, or *runaway*.

Fudge went back into his shop. Hen listened to him pace. Reclining in his chair, Hen crossed his hands over his belly, closing his eyes. There was more to it of course, his knack for avoiding worry, than simply letting his friend do it for him. When the would-be cause got really rough, when something as troublesome, for instance, as that young white lady, Miss Eva, spying a forbidden cargo, then a favorite trick of Hen's was to close his eyes and picture Lucindy. The vision of her, her big eyes, her shining cheekbones, her lopsided smile, her hand on Fudge's knee, assigning all worry to him, could do wonders to soothe the state of Hen's mind. Now and then, Hen imagined her hand upon his own knee, instead of on Fudge's.

Nevertheless, he couldn't doze. He went into the shop, and Fudge looked up.

"What that boy up to," Hen said.

"Let's get on out of here," Fudge said.

"Where we going to?"

"We'll know it when we get there."

"What we looking for?"

"We'll know it when we see it."

Grumblings of thunder from out of the west. Low over the horizon, black thunderheads were growing like toadstools on a freshly dug grave, reaching high into the sky that had been overcome by haze, erasing all traces of blue. They walked toward the Birchwoods schoolhouse, Fudge, his face damp and clammy, clenching his fists to keep from breaking into a trot, Hen content in his own laggardly pace. The breezes commenced ahead of the storm. The leaves on the trees began to flip and twist in panic, lifting and falling in unison, and Hen could smell traces of an odor that always put him in mind of the innards of a freshly gutted trout.

Fudge pulled ahead. "*Move* it, Hen. We gonna get wet."

Hen shrugged, his pace unaltered. "Little wet never killed nobody."

"Tell that to Noah," Fudge said.

Around the bend, down through the hollow, the schoolhouse came into view. There stood the black Morgan, Jupiter, tethered to the bush behind the building. They stopped in the road. They stared at the horse, tossing his head and pawing, his long, black tail rolling like a flag in the approaching storm. Neither man spoke.

"You suppose they in there?" Hen said after a minute.

"Ain't likely they anywheres else."

They stared for a minute more, wind picking up, thunder rolling closer.

"We best go on in, see for ourselves," Hen said.

"How come they ain't no noise?" said Fudge.

"What kinda noise?"

"Noise. Voices. Talking. Yelling. Crying."

"Maybe they busy."

Approaching the building, they made no effort to conceal themselves. By the door that was closed, Hen stopped to pee, Fudge tapping his foot and flexing his fists and shaking his head at the sky. They stood and listened. Nothing. No sound but the wind in the branches, the thunder growing louder, more insistent. A small limb snapped free of a tree, flew to the road and tumbled away. When the first fat raindrops began to lash at their backs, Hen pushed open the door.

Miss Eva floated like an angel. They stepped inside to behold her.

She was hanging from a rafter, her face hidden by her hair falling down, graced by a stripe of red ribbon. A gust from the open doorway caught her, riffling her skirts, lifting the ribbon in her hair, making her body begin to sway and turn in the gloom. Across the room on the little bench, nearly unseen in the shadows, sat Augustus, elbows high on his knees, face buried in his hands.

3: November 3, 1857: The Miracle of Molly

Darling was awakened by the uproar in the street. "There's been a murder!" he heard Mrs. Fowler cry. "Mutilation! A man has been skinned alive!"

Hastening up the hill, he could barely make his way to the corner of Prospect Street and Coal Alley, such was the throng. In the thin morning light, the little ice house was lost among the tall pines and milling crowd on the corner of the uncleared lot. Scores of his neighbors had gathered, many going in and out of the ice house as though visiting a museum, the ghastly remains on display. More arrived by the minute, as word spread through the town and outlying vicinity. Darling saw sobbing women shielding children, men's faces flushed with fear and indignation. Rowdy boys raced through the crowd, celebrating the excitement.

Levi Smathers himself, the district's Member of Congress, was there all the way from Bootjack, in command, strutting and gesticulating with polished ease, his great set of muttonchop whiskers burgeoning upon his cheeks, his eyes glistening, his voice booming. At the peak of his fame, he'd been swept into office a year or two before—on a sympathy vote, according to his few detractors, owing to the accidental death of his little daughter—and his very presence lent a gravitas to the incident that might otherwise have been little more than a highly morbid curiosity.

Other dignitaries arrived as well, trying hard not be overshadowed by the presence of the great man, Smathers: The borough burgess, James Butterfield, stood with his hands on his hips; Justice Henry Martz leaned corpulently upon his silver cane, the pained expression on his face no doubt attributable more to his chronic gout than to the grisly discovery at hand. Richard Southerland, a large and gruff old man who was also the court crier, emerged and stood before the ice house door. "Murder most foul!" he bellowed through his beard. Joshua Sandt, owner of the ice house, showed up, escorted by Constable McClay in his suit of drab. Darling made his way through the milling mob toward the spot where the constable and his old school chum stood near the ice house door with Smathers and the burgess and the justice, and others of the county's more well-regarded citizens, figures of authority all. As Darling neared, Sandt made eye contact; to the other esteemed figures, however, Darling was invisible.

None of the other doctors, he noticed, was anywhere to be seen.

"It is obvious by the splintered condition of the door," Sandt was saying, "that someone has broken in and desecrated my ice house. I shall never be able to use it again for its intended purpose, and I can scarcely afford to construct anew."

"You have no clues, no suspicions?" asked Smathers.

"None," said Sandt. He looked at the constable. "That is your job. What has your investigation revealed?"

"There is something," said McClay. Ducking into the ice house, he returned a moment later, carrying that something in his hand, extended before him. "Upon closer inspection, I seen this lying loose near the body."

Darling slipped closer. It appeared to be a heap of curly hair. Smathers poked at it, as though it were alive, as though it might recoil. Butterfield and Martz leaned in, apparently to sniff at it. Sandt looked away, making eye contact again with Darling.

"Why, that is Negro wool," declared Smathers.

The men looked at one another, nodding. Behind him, Darling heard the words, *nigger wool*, echo through the crowd. Constable McClay, nodding most knowingly of all, declared, "I believe these remains to be those of Fudge Van Pelt, the colored man recently deceased."

Within minutes the excited crowd, under the auspices of Constable McClay and the burgess, procured shovels, picks and mattocks and hastened up the hill to the graveyard. Darling allowed himself to be swept along. Remaining as invisible as possible, he observed Sandt watching expectantly as if wondering what might be unearthed. Feeling his own heated face, he both admired and bristled at the calm, natural demeanor of his old school chum, at what a natural-born liar he was, a talent Darling was convinced he could never achieve. Within minutes, the absence of his corpse confirmed the identity of the remains in the ice house to be those of Van Pelt, and another wave of outrage and indignation rippled through the mob.

Disbelief resurfaced as well. "Why?" a young woman behind Darling asked. "Why would anyone do such a horrible thing?" Moses Clover, nearby, repeated the question: "How could anyone possibly commit such a desecration?" and the question itself in its various guises made its way through the crowd, until Levi Smathers, the great Congressman, answered: "Why, probably for money, I would imagine—isn't it always for the money?"

Richard Southerland, the court crier, agreed. "Nowadays," he declared, "men will do anything for money. Why, a good Negro hide will sell for at least five hundred dollars—they are used in the manufacture of razor strops and boot laces. This I know for a fact. It's all for the money!"

Other recent graves were hastily opened to see if other loved ones were missing. If a good Negro hide was worth five hundred dollars, mightn't a well-tanned white one bring at least two or three? Darling watched the tears stream down the round, red cheeks of the widow Fullerton as her nephew and her son dug feverishly at her husband's fresh grave.

Near the chestnut tree, he and Sandt managed a few minutes alone. Darling clucked his tongue—a habit he'd taken from his preceptor—and shook his head. Sandt said in a voice scarcely louder than a whisper, "Smathers has insisted Justice Martz summon the coroner to hold an inquest—he wants it to be held this very afternoon."

"Oh dear," said Darling. "That cannot bode well."

Sandt shrugged his lanky shoulders. From beneath the tree they watched the crowd, now broken out into discrete knots and groupings, around this grave or that, this tombstone or that. They overheard the constable calling for volunteers for night watch over the cemetery.

"It is fortunate for us that they're barking up the wrong tree," Sandt said. "Razor strops and boot laces indeed."

"Fortunate?" Darling said. "Fortunate?"

"Not the slightest hint of suspicion has been directed toward us, or the doctors."

Noting his exclusion from the latter category, Darling opted not take issue. He said instead, "Yes, quite fortunate. We ought to count our blessings. And I've no doubt that our good fortune will last at least as long as Captain Alcorn and Claude Pepper, and his wife, and Mrs. Libby Stormer, and my mother and everyone else they've already related it to refrain from mentioning it to another living soul. At least that long."

Darling felt like a spider on the stove when the fire has only just been lit. Wishing to seek guidance from his preceptor, he headed toward their office on Main Street opposite the Philadelphia Cheap Store—actually Vasbinder's office, he'd recently allowed Will to move in a table and set up shop in a corner until he was established enough to secure space of his own. But the office was dark, the door locked, as was the office of the Doctors Bullers, just down the street from the Peace and Poverty Tavern. He walked down to Water Street, and knocked upon the door of Cyrus's house, to no avail. The stable was deserted as well.

There were always rounds to make, patients to see, though he doubted he could outrun the galloping news. He should visit Plotners first and foremost, to see how Molly was faring, but he couldn't bear to; he feared the worst. Instead, he headed out toward Beechwoods to examine the gash he'd repaired on the leg of Lester Vandevoort, to ensure the dressing had been properly replaced, and from there he proceeded to Weed Run to visit Mrs. Lemon and her gastric complaints. By the time he returned, the afternoon sun of early November was a bright orange ball behind the bare trees over the hill at the west end of Main, and the crowd was calmer, though diminished little in size. It was gathered now near the Courthouse, in and around the barroom of the American Hotel next door, and up and down Prospect Street as far as the little ice house, which remained a curiosity even though the remains had by now been removed. The coroner's inquest had concluded, the jury finding that the body discovered in the ice house was, to the best of their knowledge and belief, that of Fudge Van Pelt, colored, stolen from the grave in which he had recently been interred, and that said body had been disinterred, and the cuticle, toes, fingers and bowels removed, by person or persons unknown. After the verdict was returned, a rope was tied around the neck of Fudge's remains, he was dragged into Coal Alley, thrown into his coffin, carried back up the hill and reburied in his grave, without benefit of coffin lid or clothing. Or skin. Lucindy Van Pelt, widow of the deceased, watched from the edge of the crowd. It was widely reported that she had made information against Fudge's pal, Henry Westerman, and another colored man, Augustus Hamilton. It was reported as well that Black Hen had been seen loitering suspiciously about the grave.

Black Hen and Augustus were brought to the Courthouse in shackles, then taken to the old stone jailhouse next door, there to be held pending a hearing in the morning. Black Hen looked perplexed and fearful, Augustus Hamilton sullen and angry. A taunt or two—*damn niggers!*—was heard from the crowd. Darling clucked his tongue and wagged his head at no one in particular, but as he did so, Black Hen caught his eye; Darling held up his hand, as if to say he was aware of his innocence, but it was too late. Black Hen had already read it as an accusation, and his old frosted face grew all the more bewildered.

Sandt appeared. "Will," he whispered, "we'd best make ourselves scarce. I've just overheard Captain Alcorn talking to Justice Martz. I heard the word *dissection* spoken, distinctly, and the word *doctors* as well. It cannot be long until we fall under suspicion."

No one would think to look for him in Irishtown. Darling spent the night in O'Hanlon's loft, above the old storage shed, where he and Kathleen had brought the flowers and herbs they'd harvested, and hung them to dry from the rafters.

He'd slept in the uncommon potpourri of aromas—the pungent peppermint and camphorous wild ginger overwhelming the medley of odors—that had accounted, he thought, for the uncommon quality of his dreams. He remembered only the last: He and Josh Sandt had been condemned to hang for stealing a fresh-baked whortleberry pie from his mother's sill.

The dawn through the little gable window lit the inside of the cavelike loft, spiny stalks and roots suspended like twisted stalactites. Near the window, a row of bright yellow goldenseal rhizomes and roots looked like dying insects. He heard the voices of Kathleen and her father over the sound of the hammers and saws from his factory. He heard her on the ladder. "Man on the run," she said, green eyes sparkling at the edge of the loft. "I've brung your breakfast."

"Step into my parlor," said Darling, taking the little sack.

"Two hard-cooked eggs," said Kathleen, climbing into the nest beside him, "and a slab of soda bread. I buttered it."

"Your father knows you're up here, with me?"

"He does indeed. He's not concerned. He knows what an honorable gentleman you are." She winked and smiled and squeezed his knee.

He peeled an egg, taking a slippery bite. Had he ever been this alone with Kathleen? He thought not. His heart fluttered, a delicious feeling passing through his stomach and beyond. He said, "Is there any news?"

"The hearing is taking place," she said. "Those two colored fellows are appearing before Justice Martz."

He looked at her, an array of purple coneflowers hanging just behind her shoulder, eavesdropping. "I never ceased to be amazed at the rampant ignorance and prejudice."

"Aye. They're forever blaming the niggers. Or the papists."

He bit into the crusty bread. "It won't be long and they'll be blaming the doctors."

"There's already whispers and rumors aplenty."

He hadn't realized how hungry he was. She watched him finish his egg and the last crumb of the bread, which he lifted from the front of his shirt. She smiled like a mother watching her child. When he was finished, she said, "I stopped at your mam's as well—there's been no word at all from the Plotner's."

He licked a dab of butter from his lip. "I don't know if that's good news or bad."

"Sure, no news is good news, Will Darling."

"I must go out there. I fear the worse now. Now that the dissection shall never happen...now that— "

"Now that the hoop has tipped," she said.

He nodded. "I suppose I must face up to my job." He repeated Vasbinder's assertion, that Molly's life was in his, Darling's, hands, that he must be the hero.

Kathleen bristled. When she was angry, her eyebrows curled into a tiny knot above her nose. "The arrogance of the man to even think such a thought as that. Sure the little girl's life is in nobody's bloody hands at all but God's."

Emerging from the loft, Darling blinked in the sunlight. Mounting Gertie, he rode at an easy walk down South Street, avoiding eye contact with those he passed by. He turned onto Water Street, heading toward Pond and the bridge over Potters Creek, avoiding Main and the prospect of bringing attention to himself. On the other side of the creek, however, he nudged his old horse south on Federal Street, rather than north toward Plotner's on Coolbrook Road.

He turned down the path leading between the pine grove and the laurel thicket to the white sand spring, a pool in the rock near where the creeks converged. When his father was alive, they'd picnicked there, a popular spot in summer, where many a family went on the Sabbath and Fourth of July. He watched the creeks meet and merge, effortlessly changing identity, and he heard in the rippling noise of the water the sound of Fudge's skin lifting from his flesh. This was the spot where not long ago a band of ruffians had stoned Fudge and Black Hen into Potters Creek just to see them take a dunking; the other picnickers, men, women and children all, had laughed at the antics and found them wonderfully amusing. Once he himself had witnessed Kelty, the blacksmith, attack Fudge on Main Street and knock him to the ground, saying, "Take that, you damned nigger!" without any discernible cause, other than meanness. Kelty was an evil man who'd lost his leg to Big Bull's saw after his toe, nearly bitten off in a brawl with Zibion Bowersox, had turned gangrenous. Now Kelty, wooden leg and all, was healthy as a horse. While Fudge was dead and little Molly Plotner, in all her innocence, was on her death bed.

Why? Why did God paint some of His creatures black? Why did He create fleas?

When his ruminations could detain him no longer, Darling headed toward Coolbrook Road and Plotner's, but, arriving at Pond Street, he was ambushed again by indecision. He was sorely tempted to steer Gertie left, toward Main, not straight ahead and out the Coolbrook Road; his curiosity to learn the result of Black Hen's and Augustus' hearing was strong. But he realized his reluctance to visit Molly was equally strong, and he feared that his curiosity about the hearing was only a pretext to avoid doing the right thing. After he'd watched the outcome of a dispute between a rooster and a shaggy old cat beside the house of Marvin Knapp across the way, he steeled himself and headed north, toward Plotner's.

Riding past Cook's Saw Mill, the sounds of commerce faded away behind him, replaced by the plodding clops of Gertie's hooves and the sounds of the birds in the trees. He encountered not another traveler on Coolbrook Road. Fresh fallen leaves lay golden in the morning sun, and the broad blue sky above the copse in the field was buzzard-free. A skein of geese came toward him, honking their way south. Passing the lane into the Negro settlement along the Little Brier, he thought briefly of the black men again, but soon his thoughts returned to Molly Plotner; a mile or so later, he realized with a shudder that he'd been skinning the little girl in his daydream just as they had Van Pelt, peeling away her dermis to expose her wretched illness. "Old Grimes is Dead" commenced in his mind in his mother's singing voice, quiet and tremulous:

His neighbors he did not abuse, / Was sociable and gay; / He wore large buckles on his shoes, / And changed them every day.

Where the woods quit and Plotner's fence line commenced, a layer of fresh earth marked the spot where Plotner had removed the stump on Sunday morning: another patch of dirt signifying the end of a life. He fully expected to see yet another at any moment, as he followed the fence line toward the little cabin. Enoch Plotner was coming from the creek, two pails of water weighing in his opposing arms like the scales of justice. Setting them down in the dirt, he said, "Doc." He wiped his sleeve across his face, his expression there still bitter.

"Enoch," Darling said with a nod. "How's our little girl?"

"See for yourself." Plotner tilted his head toward the meadow. There was Molly, arms waving at the cow she was herding back toward the barn. Long shadows reached vainly for her across the dying green of the meadow. Hooking his leg across the saddle in front of him, Darling leaned upon it, drained.

"That's..."

"That's Molly, Doc," Plotner said. "Still kicking."

"Good Lord," Darling murmured.

They watched her slow, sturdy step. Seeing Darling, she waved and smiled and sang a happy verse, quite off-key:

He modest merit sought to find, / And pay it its desert; / He had no malice in his mind, / No ruffles on his shirt.

Then she giggled, a normal, healthy child of five.

"Good Lord all right," said Plotner. "Give me back another mouth to feed." He picked up his pails, heading for the house. Darling nudged Gertie along behind, his head swimming. The soaring fancy of the gift of healing had suddenly been grounded by the mundane memory of his bill at Sandt's Drug Store—twelve dollars seventy-two cents and counting—and further encumbered by vague and guilty thoughts involving the potential wealth of an unprecedented healer. He needed to procure more Hooper's Pills; he didn't need Sandt's condescension, his letting the bill slide "for old times' sake."

"Enoch," Darling said, "I was wondering if we could address the matter of my fees, please." The unplanned rhyme displeased him, but Plotner owed him one dollar and twenty-five cents for the bleedings of Molly alone, not to mention five cents a mile, and the price of the medications. Exactly what that might amount to in chestnuts, eggs or feathers, Plotner's likely currency, he couldn't be sure, but even those could be bartered to Sandt.

"What fees is that, Doc?" said Plotner without looking back. "Why, you just said the good Lord's the one who cured her. And I figure what I owe Him, I'll be paying soon enough."

The ride back into town seemed to take only moments. Gertie knew the way well, and he allowed her to attend to the details. His own thoughts were in a scramble, the miracle of Molly's cure wrestling with his reluctance to believe in miracles, his earnest desire to know the scientific reasons; his potential worth as a successful physician muddied by his current poverty, and by a course resentment of Plotner's ingratitude—a most puzzling ingratitude at that, seemingly not only toward Darling, for having cured her, but toward God, for having allowed her to be cured.

The plight of Black Hen and Augustus did not occur to him again until the noise from Cook's Saw Mill intruded upon his reveries. He was still curious, but only mildly so; so much had happened since. He felt quite confident and proud, riding up Main Street, boldly.

As it turned out, no inquiries were necessary. He saw the gathering in front of the Courthouse—smaller than the crowds of yesterday, but unusual nevertheless—and he saw Black Hen and Augustus both walking briskly toward him, away from the Courthouse, Black Hen carrying his floppy hat, while the hat of Augustus, a smaller, trimmer derby, remained squarely on his head. There were holes in the knees of Black Hen's britches. Darling pulled up and the two colored men stopped. They looked up at him, both men, with curious frowns.

"Afternoon, Black Hen, Augustus."

"Afternoon, Mr. Doc," said Black Hen. Augustus, a taller, younger, more muscular man in a blue flannel shirt offered no greeting. Neither man smiled.

"Free men, are you?" Darling said.

Black Hen nodded. Augustus said with narrowed eyes, "Seems ol' Fudge he done skinned by somebody else."

"So I believe," said Darling. He noticed the constable and the justice had broken free from the gathering in front of the Courthouse, and, along with a few stragglers, were heading his way. In the back of his mind, the pieces began to click together.

"Mr. Doc," said Black Hen, his hand levitating toward Darling. Constable McClay's pace had grown brisker as he quickly approached. "They saying you done it—they saying it was you dug up ol' Fudge."

Darling shrank. He felt a momentary panic, his heart rising, and he managed only with great restraint to resist the urge to wheel Gertie about and slap her away at a childish gallop.

"Will!" called the constable. "Will Darling! Come with me, sir!"

Darling had passed by the old stone jailhouse hundreds of times, indeed had stepped inside it on many occasions—until he was six years of age, he'd attended Sunday school there, as well as services in the Courthouse, which had been the practice before the Presbyterian church had been built. But he'd never before been inside a cell, which is where he found himself after the hearing before Justice Martz. The reversal of perspective was jarring.

He sat on the narrow plank bunk on the far wall beneath the barred window, his bail set at fifty dollars, a sum beyond his comprehension. His mother came to see him, saying scarcely a word, though her eyes were damp in the middle of the disapproval that seemed permanently imprinted upon her face He thought he detected another wrinkle there, thought her shoulders a bit more bowed, her bearing a bit more stooped and weary, and a great weight of guilt, hardly vague, descended upon him. *Mark my words* never crossed her lips, this time. "I'll make you some jumbles, Will," she said while taking her leave. Apparently she thought he'd be there for a good, long time.

"Thank you, Mother."

She shook her head. "Thank God your father is dead," she said.

The Doctors Bullers visited. Standing in the hallway beyond the bars, they shook their heads collectively toward Darling, then conversed with one another. "Youngsters nowadays," said Big Bull, "always up to some mischief or other."

"Whippersnappers," Little Bull said. "Can't teach 'em no manners."

"Digging up niggers," Big Bull said.

"Skinning the hide right off 'em," said Little Bull.

"Gentlemen, your attempts at good humor are falling well short of the mark."

"I don't know, Will," Little Bull said. "We're fair amused on this side of the bars."

"Let me ask you this," said Darling, standing, walking to the front of the cell where he took hold of the bars, just as both the doctors had, only from the diametrically opposite direction. "Why *are* you still on that side of the bars?"

"When you get right down to it," replied Little Bull, musing, "I suppose it has to do with our innocence, integrity and moral worth—"

"Not to mention the Republican principles we hold near and dear to our hearts," said Big Bull, "with which we vote accordingly."

"We been left out for witnesses," said Little Bull. "Without witnesses, they would be sore-pressed to prove a crime."

Darling didn't take long to think about it. "So you intend to bear witness against me?"

"Maybe we can figure a way around it." Big Bull said.

In the pause that followed, Darling looked into the eyes of one man then the other and back again, hoping to detect a twinkle of bemusement. He could not be certain that he did.

"What is the amount is your bail?" said Big Bull.

"Fifty dollars."

The words seem to freeze them in place. Little Bull looked at his brother. "Why, they mean business," he said.

"Sure as shooting," said Big Bull, his beard bobbing in agreement.

When Vasbinder arrived, he insisted that Constable Jenkins open Will's cell door and allow him to sit with his erstwhile charge. Jenkins was an older man of indefinite disposition and easily persuaded, particularly given that he was under the care of Vasbinder for his periodic episodes of psoriasis. Darling had to admit to himself that Cyrus's hand upon his knee felt reassuring. "You mustn't fret, my dear," said Vasbinder. "We shall have you out of this dreadful place in no time at all."

"And how shall we have that?"

"Congressman Smathers, the great Levi Smathers, has personally taken charge of the prosecution from the District Attorney," Vasbinder said, "and I shall have some words with him. Mr. Smathers and I go back a long way, his abominable Republican principles notwithstanding. His wife was under my care for many, many years—she was a sickly woman, who finally died a year or two ago."

"What about you? Have you been kept out as a witness as well?"

"No, no," Vasbinder said. "I have been arrested too, and charged, like you, with violation of the act of 1855 to protect burial grounds. The difference being that I was released on my own recognizance."

Darling frowned. "Why would I be the only one—"

"Perhaps my long-standing practice, my reputation, my…I don't know, really."

"It is as my Mother predicted. She said I would be the only one to get into trouble, as I was the only one without friends or money."

"You are certainly not without friends, my dear." Vasbinder gave his knee another heartening touch. "It is apparent that they are striking at me through you. They know that you are like a son to me, and that they can hardly throw me in jail, not without taking into account the high esteem in which I am held throughout Paine, Elk and Forest counties, the wide range of my field for the past thirty years. Indeed, I have far too many friends in far too many high places. But they will use the occasion of our trials to attempt to annihilate me."

When he considered it, Darling thought Vasbinder's scenario to be a likely one. His preceptor was getting older, and was turning his field over to his protégé, Darling, withdrawing from practice as much as practicable himself. He intended in his retirement to become more active in politics—his first love, having been a political creature all his life, having already been elected, twice, to the office of coroner, embracing the Democratic philosophy wholeheartedly—and was in fact preparing to run for the state assembly. "Who, exactly, are *they*?" said Darling.

"Why Smathers himself, of course, and the burgess, Butterfield. He himself is preparing to run for the assembly, and he, Smathers and Martz are in lockstep, Republicans all."

"So what is our plan?"

"First and foremost," said Vasbinder, "to secure your release from this place." His eyes blinked simultaneously, earnestly. "I intend to consult with my old friend, John J. Y. Truby; he is a Democrat and an excellent attorney. Then I shall ride this very afternoon over to Bootjack to have an audience with Congressman Smathers. I shall show him exactly where the bear has gone into the buckwheat."

Darling considered it unlikely that he would be released before the morrow, and he resigned himself to his hard plank bunk and tattered blanket as the shadows grew longer across his cell. The three neighboring cells were empty—there was another wing in a different part of the jail for convicted prisoners—and Darling's only company was his morbid reveries. He tried to imagine the scene in the drawing room of Smathers's Bootjack mansion, Smathers and Vasbinder engaged in a heated exchange, and he was in the midst of losing command of his fantasies, picturing his mentor grasping with both hands the muttonchops of Smathers and yanking hard, when his old school chum Joshua Sandt arrived to visit.

With him was Kathleen. It was a coupling that took him aback.

Darling's first reaction was to stand, nonchalantly and unobtrusively sliding his slop bucket into the shadows beneath his bunk with his foot, hoping Kathleen wouldn't notice. The nervous condition of his bowels had rendered concealment imperative. "I'd hardly expected to see your lovely face in a place such as this," he said.

"Thank you," said Sandt. "You just never know where my lovely face might turn up."

Darling glared. "I was speaking to Kathleen."

"You'd hardly expect me to ignore the plight of you, either," Kathleen said with a half-hearted smile. "And leave you to do your hard time all alone."

Darling was silent, unless his heart could be heard.

Sandt took hold of the bars, much as the Doctors Bullers had. "How's the grub?"

Darling said, "Have you been arrested? Released on your own recognizance?"

"No," he said. "Not at all. I seem to have fallen completely through the cracks. No one has approached me regarding the entire escapade, no one at all. Perhaps they mean to target only you and the doctors."

Darling gritted his teeth, absently clenching his fist. "I am feeling ill-used. I sit behind these bars, all alone, as my coconspirators waltz in and out of the place."

"As well you might," Sandt said. "And I propose immediate redress. What is the amount of your bail?"

"Why?"

"I shall pay it. Or, to put it another way, I shall pay it."

"It's fifty dollars," said Darling, meaning to put an end to the discussion once and for all. Kathleen's mouth fell open momentarily and she grasped at her throat.

Sandt reached for his purse. "I wonder if they are able to make change."

Darling gritted his teeth, feeling the blood in his face. "Never mind. Do you think for a moment I cannot pay my own bail?"

Sandt began to reply, but only stammered and looked to Kathleen. Kathleen said, "Will, have you gone daft?"

"I've made my own arrangements. I'm securing my own release, thank you very much."

"Very well," said Sandt with a nod.

"Are you mad?" Kathleen said. "You can walk out of here right now, with us."

"I shall be close behind you."

Kathleen glared. The knot was back above her nose. "Pig-headed man," she muttered.

The look of her temper flashing in her eyes stayed with him even after they were gone. What also stayed with him was the last, lingering glimpse of Sandt's hand, as they were disappearing through the doorway, his hand that was apparently reaching toward the elbow of Kathleen swinging back fiercely.

He'd begun seeing Kathleen last winter, after she'd reached the age of eighteen. He'd been attracted to her ever since he could remember, watching her mature on the other side of the classroom, following him up through the years from three grades behind. He'd watched her grow more comely by the day, but what he'd always noticed foremost was her manner of speaking to the master when called upon: not with her face down or her eyes averted as did most of the girls, and most of the boys for that matter, but with her shoulders back and her chin up, directly and boldly—always only directly and boldly enough to approach the border of impudence, never enough to cross it. She was both beautiful and intelligent, Darling had long-since decided. He'd never had eyes for any other girl.

In the years after school, he'd missed seeing her on a daily basis. He'd expanded his practice, as soon as he was able, to include Irishtown, a place where Vasbinder had no patients and seldom set foot. Darling did not believe Vasbinder to be as anti-Catholic as many in the town, certainly as the brothers Bullers who'd been staunch Know-Nothings until the party had recently crumbled. But he could tell too that Vasbinder did not exactly look upon the Irish with great favor. Darling didn't know if his preceptor was even aware that he was keeping company with Kathleen.

Even his own mother did not approve. She'd never explicitly disapproved, but she'd never whole-heartedly endorsed the courtship either. She was adept at avoiding the subject.

Joshua Sandt, on the other hand, was not at all shy with his comments and inquiries, which sometimes bordered a coarseness Darling found displeasing. *Fine hips for making babies* was perhaps not an inapt description of Betsy Henderson or Abigail Arthurs, girls upon whom Sandt had occasionally called, but when uttered in the same breath as Kathleen's name, it became objectionable. And Darling made certain Sandt was well aware of those objections.

As he lay alone on the hard bunk, the flickering light from the camphene lamp on the little stand in the hallway cast faint dancing shadows across the floor of his cell. The thoughts and images that should have prevented him from sleeping—his very incarceration itself, the miracle of Molly, the glistening, skinless cadaver of Fudge Van Pelt—kept slipping away like water through a sieve. And all that remained was Kathleen.

Had Sandt indeed been reaching for her elbow on the way out the door? And had Kathleen willingly submitted herself to such a touch?

It was Vasbinder, again, who set him to rights—good, old, solid Cyrus. He appeared before mid-morning, Darling's breakfast of watery oatmeal still sitting untouched on the stool in the corner of the cell, his mind in a drowsy stew of anticipation, tedium and dread. Vasbinder's presence alone, whatever words he may or may not utter, seemed sufficient to ground

Darling, the mere sight of his mentor's frumpled and earnest appearance—in the same clothes he'd been wearing the afternoon before—his eyes blinking and bunching in sincerity, his bushy white mustache twitching eagerly. There was a stain of indeterminate origin upon his rose-colored vest.

He had indeed secured his release, and Darling departed beside him, climbing into Vasbinder's shay, scarcely speaking a word of his own, listening as Vasbinder told him about his audience with Congressman Smathers, the learned debate that ensued, his successful entreaties and persuasions concerning the worthiness and necessity of scientific dissection, the knowledge of anatomy being the foundation of the healing art; how that knowledge, how that art, could not fail to someday benefit, if not themselves, then certainly their children or their children's children. The latter topic was of mild concern to Vasbinder when he broached it, he said, though it apparently had its intended effect.

"You were aware the man lost his daughter last year, were you not?"

"I'd heard," Darling said.

"It was widely known, and tragic—her pinafore caught afire when she stood too near the hearth. The poor thing lingered in utmost pain for several days. Not yet seven years of age, an adorable little girl. And that not a year after he'd lost his wife in an equally tragic accident, involving, apparently, a fall from a loft."

"She was aloft? How was it she become aloft?"

"She was *in* a loft."

"I see." Darling shook his head in sympathy, impressed by Vasbinder's capacity for compassion, his scientific, medical and political preoccupations notwithstanding.

Vasbinder said, "If you were to ask me, it was that, in fact, the sympathy vote, that swept him into office. Our man, John J. Y. Truby, was the far more qualified candidate."

Even his resentments were of a loftier nature than Darling's. Vasbinder had persuaded Smathers to quash Darling's bail, arranging for his release on his own recognizance in contemplation of dropping the charges. The charges could hardly be dropped at once, however, given the proximity to election day. Vasbinder clucked his tongue.

Snapping the reins, he urged his old mare down Main Street in the thin, gray light of the early November morning—it appeared as though the fine, warm weather was coming to an end. Noticing the protracted stares of Moses Clover from the porch of his general store and of the other citizens they passed in the street, Darling's reflections in Vasbinder's silence took on their familiar vague and guilty aspect—not at the "crime" of resurrection that he'd committed, but rather at the night he'd wasted wallowing in his own petty concerns and jealousies. He reflected on the overall triviality of money and love in the grand scheme of things, glancing sidelong at his preceptor in his own contemplation, the mustache rising and falling in rumination, and he marveled at the exalted ideals coursing through that neighboring brain.

He awoke in the afternoon at his mother's to a sharp renting of his heart, as if it had been torn in two—as if Kathleen had been torn out of it. His own petty concerns and jealousies were back with a vengeance, the triviality of money and love once again in ascendency. Try as he may, no amount of will could restore his feelings to the erstwhile lofty perch he'd attained under the influence of his mentor. He resolved to live with the hurt, to soldier on in spite of it as he would if it were an aching shoulder or ailing back.

He resolved to return to his work. He had calls to make, some of which were overdue, and the solid establishment of his medical practice would force his focus in the proper direction; as well, it would be his best defense against the political machinations which had him dancing like a puppet at the end of his strings.

And hightailing it out of town couldn't hurt.

Packing his things, he noticed Buchan's *Domestic Medicine* among the other volumes on the wooden plank that served as a shelf above his makeshift desk. He'd borrowed the book from Steven Means over a month ago, and cursed his inconsideration in not having returned it sooner—his reputation was becoming tarnished enough without the added discredit of pilferage. He took the book with him, securing it with his cups and pill bags behind his saddle. He would make the office of Mr. Means his first stop on his way out of town.

Mr. Means, if his shingle were to be believed, was actually Dr. Means. Vasbinder held the eclectic school of medicine in such low regard, however, that he was disinclined to accord Means the more learned title, and Darling had followed his preceptor's lead—perhaps too blindly he was now beginning to believe. For Mr. Dr. Means was not without sound knowledge and solid reason, as Darling had discovered upon talking to the man on several occasions over the past summer when they'd found themselves swimming together in the natatorium beneath the covered bridge on the Red Bank Creek. It was where many of the busy men of Hartsgrove—doctors, lawyers, merchants and mechanics—went to welcome up the moon after a hard day's labor. Means was coming out of his office on Cherry Street as Darling pulled up.

"Will Darling! As I live and breathe!" Smiling above his red goatee, Means held out his hands before him, thumbs up.

"Steven." Darling nodded, smiling only out of contagion. "I'm returning your book. It's long overdue, for which I apologize."

"Shall I quiz you on the contents?"

"I read it with great interest."

"Excellent. I'm on my way to Birchwoods to call upon the McKillips—perhaps we could ride together for a ways?"

"I am heading that way myself."

Together they rode their horses at an easy walk over the Potters Creek bridge, a team of ducks crossing Pond Street before them, and up the Tyrone Road, the long climb east out of town. The streets were quiet, oppressed by the suggestion of winter in the air, smoke from the chimneys laying flat and dispirited above the rooftops of the houses and shops. They fell into easy dialogue, discussing the Indian summer that had been, bemoaning the loss of their swimming holes for the winter—Means had been to the natatorium as recently as two weeks previous, he said. The subject of Darling's recent arrest remained unbroached, whether due to Means's ignorance of it or his manners Darling couldn't guess. Inevitably the conversation turned to their work. Means was on his way to see the McKillip's child, Violet, suffering with a persistent case of the croup, which he meant to treat with a soft onion poultice and a syrup concocted of bloodroot. Darling instantly thought of Molly Plotner, and, in turn, told Means about her mysterious cure, avoiding the term *miraculous*, couching it carefully so as not to appear to be bragging. Darling had little use for braggarts.

"Curious," said Means. "In the end, I suppose, much of the outcome is out of our hands, no matter how learned we may fancy ourselves to be."

Darling thought of Kathleen's remarks, about the hands of God. "As it happened," he said, "it was all the more curious because, in effect, I had neglected to treat her at all on the final day that I saw her in her sick room. I couldn't bring myself to bleed her again, couldn't bear to force another pill down her little throat."

Means said nothing. "I fed her my orange," confessed Darling.

They'd come to the crossroads where they would part, Means to continue eastward to Birchwoods, Darling north toward Burkett Hollow, where Mr. Radaker awaited with his rheumatism. From the crest of the hill where they'd paused, a dull flash from the wheel of a wagon descending the road on the far hillside caught Darling's eye, and he followed it till it disappeared behind the outcropping of a cleared field where the corn stalks stood brown, frayed and abandoned.

"Perhaps," said Means, "the little girl's cure was effected *because* you neglected to treat her that day." Darling said nothing. Means shrugged. "The possibility merely occurs to me."

"Opinions on the practice of medicine are somewhat divided these days," said Darling. "If not downright divisive."

"No offense, Will, but I believe disease to be an impairment of life—not an entity to be eradicated by violent and pernicious means."

Darling felt his face begin to redden. "As do I. To some degree. When gentler means are called for, that is."

Means put his hands upon the pommel of his saddle. "Dr. Vasbinder is, as you know—how shall I say this nicely—of the heroic school of medicine, the old school. He is in fact a hero among heroics." Here, Means's red goatee twitched in something like a smile. "Too often, however, patients of the heroics succumb not to the disease, but to the remedy."

"That is one man's opinion."

"Actually, Will, it is the opinion of a new school of medicine. A school that is growing in size and conviction by the day."

" I have seen Dr. Vasbinder's remedies result in many a positive outcome."

"Yes. In a positive outcome for the undertaker."

Darling was taken aback. "Very well. We shall agree to disagree then."

Means held up his hand. "Will, I don't mean to be impudent or dogmatic. But I hope that you will consider my words. Take calomel, for example. A fine purgative when given in moderate doses, but too often the allopathic school—the heroic, or regular school, as they are pleased to call themselves—passes beyond moderation, simply because they do not know what else to give. In large doses, the result is poison."

Darling sniffed, and broke eye contact with Means. He turned Gertie away, nudging her northward. "Thank you, Steven, for your advice, as well as your concern."

The road to Burkett Hollow was scarcely more than a path through the trees for the first few miles, and Darling, preoccupied, allowed Gertie to make her way at her own pace. He found, somewhat to his surprise as he rode away from Means, that his heart was flailing roughly and he seethed with resentment. He was left with only the conclusion that *Mr.* Means was directly and impudently impugning his mentor; that the allegations being made against Dr. Vasbinder—and indeed against himself by implication!—were of the basest nature, bordering the slanderous. Positive outcomes for the undertaker indeed! Darling stewed and fretted, chewing upon a twig he plucked from a limb beneath which he had to duck (for the path was that narrow in places) and thought of all the responses with which he should have rejoined *Mr.* Means had he had the mental acuity to devise them at the time.

You speak of positive outcomes—the undertaker must have been quite pleased by your effective use of the boneset infusion with Mr. Van Pelt!

And would this new school of medicine of which you speak perchance have Humbug and Quack included in its curriculum?

Had you been a hero, Mr. Means, perhaps Fudge Van Pelt might be alive this day!

These were the bitter ruminations upon which Darling chewed—along with his twig—till he found himself in what seemed like no time at the door of the cabin of Richard Radaker. Gertie had done her job well, and Darling stroked her ears. The sun was low and the shadows long as he dismounted, stretched, tethered the old girl to a log by the cabin where there was grass enough to keep her interested, and loosened her cinch. Radaker's daughter, Daisy, opened the door. "Thank goodness you're here, Doctor—his ankles are so swole up he can't hardly move." A certain pride swelled in Darling's chest as he followed her into the room.

Radaker looked up from the old rocking chair. "Where's the doctor?" he said, deflating the swelling at once.

"Cyrus sends his greetings," Darling said, and set about his work.

By the time the treatment was done—he'd applied his cups, sweated the old man, wiped him off thoroughly with dry flannel and put him into his bed—the sun had set, and Daisy insisted he eat with the family and stay the night.

He was happy to oblige. He made Gertie comfortable in the stable, ate a plate of potatoes and beans with a small bit of bacon, and retired with his blankets to a comfortable mow of hay where he fell asleep listening to the sounds of his fellow creatures rustling and gnawing in the night. He'd gone from a lowly, jailed criminal that morning to a respected and welcomed healer that night, and his thoughts fluttered like a butterfly from this station to that, flitting about randomly in-between. He was not entirely content, though he felt as he drifted off a curious and incongruent relief that the focus of his discontent had turned away from his dispute that afternoon with Mr. Means and back again to Kathleen.

For three days he rode his circuit, north into Forest County, on good roads and bad, over the wooded hills and around them, fording the creek near Penrose where the bridge had fallen in, avoiding the corduroy road between Blue Run and Halton where Gertie was liable to break her leg. Without exception his patients were happy to receive him, whether they were suffering gravely, mildly, or not at all, and he received only one or two more remarks questioning the whereabouts of the doctor—meaning Vasbinder—and those Darling thought harmless enough. He'd begun to believe that word of his arrest was not as wide-spread as he'd supposed, until, at his very northern-most call, the home of Mrs. Minneweiser on the outskirts of Sugargrove, she saw him to the room in which he was staying the night, commenting that the graveyard was just up the road, and she would trust him to stay out of it after midnight. But Darling judged by the gleam in her eye that the remark was intended in good humor, and fell asleep accordingly. His spirits were high, as she had paid him four dollars and seventy-three cents for his fees. In real American money.

Next morning he headed south toward Hartsgrove, much of the journey a straight trek down the Sugargrove Pike, following the Calico Creek. The sunshine had returned, though the air was little warmed by it, and Gertie plodded along briskly, happy to be headed home. The last time he'd traveled this stretch together with his preceptor, in the summer, Vasbinder had been obliged to stop at maddeningly regular intervals—every mile or so it seemed —to relieve himself by the road. *Please pardon an old man, my dear,* he'd said time after time, and Darling had assured him that the pauses were no trouble at all, that indeed Gertie was glad of the rest—even though Gertie was stamping impatiently, annoyed by the delay in her journey toward home. And each time Cyrus had climbed back up on his own horse, a brown mare he was pleased to call Dover, the effort had seemed increasingly difficult, until Darling had thought he might have to dismount himself and help the old man up. Vasbinder was weary from four days in the field, and Darling knew then his days there were numbered.

And he'd swelled with apprehension at the thought of filling the old man's shoes. At every stop, at every cabin and shanty, the welcome had been warm and joyful, the joy proportional to the degree of suffering within. Every stop had been a testament to the esteem in which Vasbinder was held by his patients, far and wide. At each stop, the old doctor was certain in his diagnosis, swift and steady in his treatment.

Eventually, rocking in the saddle to the rhythm of Gertie's gait, Darling's daydreams turned again to Molly Plotner and the mystery of her healing. He had seen his share of patients recover quickly in his days as a doctor, few as they might be, but never so dramatically. Inasmuch as her cure was a singular and unique circumstance, and inasmuch as his treatment of her—or lack thereof—was singular and unique as well, he began to suspect, reluctantly, that Mr. Dr. Means might possibly have been right in his assertion that it was the cessation of bleeding and calomel that helped to bring about her recovery. He had to admit to himself—and to himself alone, at this point—that much of what Means had to say was sound; he could not admit, however, to himself or to anyone else, that his preceptor's lifelong practice of medicine, to which he'd devoted himself so singularly and unselfishly, had been based wholly on error and folly. There had to be a common ground somewhere in the middle. Such was the tenor of his thoughts that when Gertie, headed south toward Hartsgrove on the Sugargrove Pike, turned on her own, with no prompting from Darling, onto the Coolbrook Road, Darling didn't correct her. Gertie was heading toward Plotner's. Darling allowed her, though he was unaware of a good reason to go there. It occurred to him, quite suddenly and without premeditation, that he needed confirmation of Molly's cure. He needed to assure himself that he hadn't merely dreamed it.

Where the woods quit and Plotner's fence line commenced, Darling took note again of the layer of fresh earth covering the spot where Plotner and his mule had removed the stump on that Sunday morning, a very long eight days ago. Such was the state of his mind, his preoccupation with his thoughts, and the degree of his anticipation, that he failed to notice the second fresh layer of earth, a much smaller patch on a little rise beneath an elm tree not a hundred yards further on, a little patch of dirt marked by a little wooden cross.

The first thing Darling noticed was the hulking shadow over by the barn—an ox. It was an ox—somehow, Plotner had procured his coveted ox.

Enoch Plotner himself was at rest, to Darling's surprise; had he ever encountered the man at his ease before? He was seated on a three-legged stool in front of the cabin, his arms on his knees, his hands empty and dangling between them. Above his jeans he wore only a linen shirt in the chilly air. Perhaps it was the ox—perhaps that was why Plotner was at his leisure now, being possessed of a hard-working, labor-saving animal.

When he looked up at Darling—which seemed to take a moment or two too long, for he didn't do so until well after he was aware of Gertie trotting in—the sour aspect was still evident upon his face, perhaps even more so than before.

"Afternoon, Doc," he said. "Come looking for them fees again?"

"Do you have them?" Darling said, regretting it immediately.

Plotner only stared, a bit too bitterly, thought Darling. "In truth, that was not my reason in coming," Darling said. "I merely wished to see Molly again—I was so astonished by her recovery, I wanted to ensure there had been no setback."

In the doorway of the cabin, Darling had failed to notice Plotner's wife, Emma, failed to notice her till he heard the sob and glanced up in time to see her vanish inside.

Plotner stared hard, still squinting and bitter. "Why, you just rode right past her, Doc, right back there at the edge of the field.

"I buried her up there on Saturday."

4: August 18, 1857: The Luckiest Man in the World

Was a word ever spoken? Not so as Hen could recall.

They didn't look again at Miss Eva, not directly. The solid, hovering vision of her in their periphery, ghastly and undeniable, was presence enough. Crossing the room, they stood by Augustus, who didn't stir. His face remained buried beneath his nearly brimless black derby. Hen and Fudge each took an arm. Augustus rose up between them. They made their way to the door and outside, into the blistering rain. Not until then did Augustus, his strong young arms embracing the shoulders of his smaller companions, finally lift up his face, into the wind and the rain. His face was clenched like a fist. As the rain washed it over, Hen wondered if there had been tears there to wash away.

They headed back behind the building to where Jupiter was tied to the post, his head lowered, ears pointing away from the storm. The wide brim of Hen's felt hat yielded to the rain, falling down over his eyes. Fudge took the reins, and, afoot, they headed at a walk back toward Little Brier. Lightning burst and thunder cracked and the rain came crashing down, but they were impervious to the violence. They never looked back to see Miss Eva, the peace and ease with which she rode out the storm.

By the time they reached home, the storm was dying. A stroke of sunshine fell through the clouds in the west as a last grumble of thunder sounded in the east, and Fudge said, of the coincidence, *Looky there, look at that—the ol' devil beating his wife. You see that, 'Gustus—you see that, Hen? Ol' devil beating his wife,* but neither man answered. Augustus went into his shanty, closing the door behind him, without uttering a word. Hen could not tell as he walked away with his friend, up through the trees toward Fudge's place, whether the moan he heard came out of the wind up above or out of the cabin left

Old Grimes Is Dead

behind.

Long after sunset, Hen made his way down to the cabin of Solomon McManigle. He didn't go to the door. He tapped once on the window, and Solomon came and lifted the rag curtain. Hen nodded, Solomon nodded his big, pock-marked black face in return, dropping the curtain. Hen went to the little stable and hitched Solomon's wagon to his old chestnut horse, leading her quietly to the edge of the road. Fudge appeared out of the night with Luke and Mary. When they were aboard, Luke and Mary in the box atop a load of straw, Fudge took the reins and flicked them, saying *haw* to the horse, but before the old mare could move, Augustus appeared, taking hold of her bridle.

"My wagon," he said. In the darkness, they couldn't see his face. "It's quieter. Sturdier. Built for long hauls. We take my wagon."

Whenever Fudge and Hen arrived late and weary for work at the American Hotel on any given morning, no one paid much heed. The white folks of the town thought nothing of the two boys arriving late and weary, for the happening was not out of the ordinary, and was to be expected, the tardiness attributed to the shiftlessness of the Negro character, the tiredness to mere laziness, another natural condition of the race.

On this particular morning, they paid even less heed. More important matters had the town abuzz: Miss Eva had been found.

She'd been discovered in her schoolhouse, a bench tipped over beneath her slippers. Suicide was assumed. Hen and Fudge had little difficulty detecting the tenor of the feelings in the town, as the lobby and barroom of the hotel were more crowded than usual, and the place reverberated with the sound of the voices. The name of Miss Eva and of her father, Captain Alcorn, who was nowhere to be seen, was on every lip. But there were glances too, more than usual, meaner than usual, toward the two black men.

Nodding to Hen as he passed, Dr. Means went into Fudge's shop. Hen rousted himself from his chair and ambled toward the doorway, as the rumble of chatter rolling down the corridor made eavesdropping all the more difficult.

"You're aware of what has happened?" he said. "Regarding the unfortunate Miss Eva?"

"Done heard talk," said Fudge.

There was quiet. Hen, standing beneath the little sign in the shape of a boot, looked in, saw the two men standing facing one another from across the tiny shop, four hands on four hips. "Is there anything," Dr. Means said, "that I ought to know?"

"Ain't they always?" Fudge said. "Ain't they always things a man oughts to know?"

"Absolutely. And foremost among them is any knowledge concerning a threat to the security and safety of one's holy endeavors. I say again: Is there anything I ought to know?"

Fudge shook his head. He looked the doctor in the eye. "No, sir. Ain't nothing."

From the doorway, Hen spoke up. "Anything we oughts to know, Doc?"

The doctor turned and smiled. "Excellent question, Black Hen," he said. "My assessment is that much of the rancor seems to be directed toward Captain Alcorn and his questionable proclivities. Augustus Hamilton, however, has not gone without mention."

As the day wore on, Hen sensed, with a bee's natural instinct for danger, an elevated level of hostility in the whispers, frowns and glances on all the grim white faces. In mid-afternoon, when the tide of chatter had begun to ebb, Fudge closed up his shop—which had not seen a customer all day—and he and Hen headed out. Main Street too was busier than usual. Though it was a cooler afternoon, the sunshine still dazzled, and it took some time for their eyes to adjust to the brightness after the gloom of the American Hotel. A knot of seven or eight men stood on the sidewalk blocking their way, a smell of whiskey in the air. Hen and Fudge stepped into the street to avoid them. Among the men was Jonathan Kelty, the blacksmith, who cast a nasty glance; Hen noticed men watching them pass, and not a glance was friendly. Hen and Fudge looked away. Fudge began to whistle. Just in front of the Philadelphia Cheap Store they heard an angry cry, and turned to see Kelty the blacksmith hobbling toward them on his wooden leg, still wearing his leather apron, his seared red face full of beard and anger. "Take that, you damned nigger!" he cried, striking Fudge a powerful blow to the head.

Fudge staggered and fell, his straw hat rolling away. Hen backed away.

Kelty raised his arm to smite again, but unable to stoop on his wooden leg, his blow missed its mark above the prone man, time and again, Fudge raising his arm before his face. Kelty, even more enraged at his inability to strike another blow, tried to kick the prone man, but his wooden leg was even more of an impediment to this particular act of violence, and he succeeded only in losing his balance and falling to the dirt in the street beside his victim. Hen staggered backwards, torn between his desire to go to the aid of his friend and outright fear. Fear won. On the ground, Kelty now seized Fudge by the shirt and struck again, and Fudge rolled into a shell to protect himself, Kelty swinging his arm again and again, strong blows but ineffectual, as he bellowed in frustration and rage.

A man came forward and pulled them apart. Hen hadn't seen William Darling coming, a young doctor of the town, whose office was there, just across from the Philadelphia Cheap Store.

"Jonathan!" cried Dr. Darling, "Jonathan! Stop!"

Fudge rolled away, scrambling to his feet. The two black men hurried off at a trot, Hen demonstrating again, for the second time in two days, his surprising capacity for something akin to haste. Fudge, this time, failed to notice. Hen saw the bruise beginning to swell above the eye of his friend, the trickle of blood. Fudge never looked back, but Hen did, glancing to see Kelty still bellowing, waving his fist, struggling to stand on his one good leg. Fudge's straw hat lay in the middle of the street, amid a sea of white, glaring faces in the sunlight.

When Lucindy saw Fudge come into their home, trailed by Hen—Hen had removed his own hat, holding it in his hands before him, in deference to Fudge's bony bare head—her first reaction was of anger and accusation.

"Fudgeon Van Pelt, look at you! Where your hat? What devilment you been up to?"

Fudge didn't answer. He sat at the table, touching the cut on his swollen eye.

"Done got attacked by a white man," Hen said. "Kelty, the blacksmith. Done attacked him in the middle of the road, for nothing."

Lucindy caught her breath, her gaze softening. "Fudge Van Pelt," she said.

Fudge looked up at his wife.

"You bleed on my mama's table, I'm gonna kill you."

Fudge looked down. A drop of blood fell from his face, befouling the bone-white surface. He looked up again in anguish.

"How I'm gonna get that out of there?" Lucindy said.

"With a saw?" Fudge said timidly, and Hen threw back his head to laugh.

Lucindy started to laugh too, but her heart wasn't in it. She went to her husband, took his chin in her hand, staring down at his face, at the eye swollen nearly shut. She shook her head. Fudge looked down, bare-headed and shamed. He couldn't look his wife in the eye. Hen looked at the floor. He couldn't look at his friend.

Lucindy fetched a cloth and a bowl of water and brought them to the table, where Fudge still sat with his head bowed down. When she began to dab at his eye, Fudge winced. "Why he attack *you*," she said to Fudge, looking up at Hen, "and not your friend here?"

Because he was old and white-haired and harmless, Hen knew, and because Fudge was not. "Because I's too quick for him," he said.

"You's too scared for him. Run off like a scared ol' rabbit."

"My mama didn't raise no fool."

"What mama?" Fudge said. "You never had no mama."

"Had one for a little while," said Hen.

"Not long enough so's you could say she raised you up."

"If she had of, she wouldn't of raised no fool."

"For Lordy sake," Lucindy said. "If you two don't sound like a old married pair."

That quieted them. Hen watched Lucindy laboring over her husband's eye. The banter was done, and he was suddenly aware of his hat in his hands, wondering why he was here, why he was holding his hat, feeling he didn't belong. Lucindy touched his arm. She understood. "Go on now," she said, her dark eyes reaching into him. "Go on home. Best just leave him be."

After an unsettled day or two—they stayed at home in Little Brier, the shop closed, the chair unattended—the weather turned fine and hot again, and Hen fell asleep on the bank of the creek. He had a line in the water, but was hoping he wouldn't get a nibble until after he'd had his nap. He'd dip the trout in egg white and bread crumbs then fry it up in lard, with a sprinkle of nutmeg. Make sure the fire was good and hot. Hen was an excellent cook. His mouth watered as he drifted off.

The breeze was fair, keeping the gnats away, and the nap was good and he dreamed about his old dog Smoky. Smoky was in a tree, sunshine blazing down through the limbs all around, and he was impatient, turning in a circle, looking down at Hen, waiting for him to climb up and join him, so they could move on together to—where? Hen didn't know where. Where could a dog go in a tree? A fly landed on Hen's cheek, waking him up.

Content with his nap, he didn't open his eyes. He waved away the fly, waited for the dream to come back, but the fly landed again. He waved it away again. When it landed on his cheek once more he opened his eyes, and there was Augustus Hamilton, squatting over him, tickling his cheek with a long piece of grass. Sunshine blazing down through the limbs all around him. "How you sleep so sound like that? Rattlesnakes up in these here woods."

Hen frowned. He hadn't considered rattlesnakes, nor was he pleased to. "You leave 'em be, they leave you be."

"You best be hoping them snakes got the same outlook as what you got."

Hen stood, checked his line, walked over to pee in the creek.

"Just done hauled a load of dry goods down from Lewistown," Augustus said. "Ain't been no more cargos since I been gone?"

"Nary a one," said Hen, buttoning up, sitting down. "Lot of 'em getting shipped up through them New York mountains nowadays is what I heard."

Augustus chewed on the long piece of grass. "Stopped in town, seen the shop closed up. Surprised ol' Fudge ain't in there working at his boots."

"Taking a day of rest. That's all."

"Stopped on up at Fudge's place," Augustus said. "Seen his eye. What happen?"

Hen said, "Leaving work the other day—day after … Miss Eva. Strolling down the street, minding our own business, the blacksmith Kelty come after us. Knocked Fudge down."

Augustus nodded. "Fudge done told me Lucindy whomped him one upside the head."

"He done told you that?"

Augustus nodded again, still watching the creek. "How come Kelty come after him?"

Hen shrugged. "White man don't need no reason."

"Fudge's boy, Napoleon," Augustus said, "he tell me 'bout the night all them white bastards come out here and burn the place down few years back. Whole damn place."

Augustus was staring at the creek. Hen looked at him through his own cloudy eyes, over his own wrinkly, white-frosted cheeks and saw youth and strength gathering, glowing, ready to erupt. Hen had never been that young. "Napoleon, he wasn't but a baby," Hen said. "They all rode out here one night, sheriff and a whole pack of 'em—that blacksmith Kelty probably right in the thick—put the torch to every single shanty. On account of somebody done stole a pig."

Augustus spit in the creek. He plucked another blade of grass. He said, "What become of the man that stole the pig?"

"Elmer Johnson. Run off in the woods that night. Nobody ever see him again."

Augustus clenched his jaw, shook his head, spat on the ground. "Dark things done up in these here woods."

"They is," Hen said. Oddly, he felt compelled to tell the young man about Yellow Charlie, how one day Charlie walked into the woods with his axe and never came out. So he started to tell him about the massacre on Crooked Creek, about how Charlie found him, about how they ended up in Little Brier, all of it. But when he turned around, Augustus was gone.

Sunday afternoon, Hen found Lucindy and Fudge in the yard at their leisure, shelling corn for the hens. He pulled up an old wood crate and joined them, though he didn't reach for an ear in the basket. The hens pecked and strutted in the dirt, and there was a hint of fall in the air, along with the smell of fresh baked bread. Down through the trees, Augustus had brought his Morgans, Jupiter and Lovejoy, around from their stable and was showing Napoleon how to clean Jupiter's hooves with a hoofpick, while Belle, undaunted despite having been chased away twice by Napoleon, sat on a nearby stump, feigning interest. Fudge kept his eye on them.

Hen rubbed his knees. "We heading into town tomorrow?"

"Better, I reckon," Fudge said. "Them boots ain't gonna mend themselves."

Hen said, "That egg on your eye done gone down pretty good."

Fudge looked up, but didn't reply. Lucindy twisted the ear of corn, kernels rattling into the basin. Down through the trees, Belle was stroking Jupiter's muzzle, while Napoleon and Augustus had commenced working on Lovejoy's right rear leg.

"You think that white girl done herself in?" said Fudge, staring down through the trees.

"Course she did," said Lucindy. "She go and fall in love with a nigger—and what girl ain't gonna fall in love with that nigger—ain't nothing else she can do. What else a little white girl can do, 'specially one with a pappy like that?"

"All's I'm saying," said Fudge, "'Gustus, he never say nothing."

Hen said, "Wasn't he crying?"

"I never seen no tears. I never seen nothing but rain."

Lucindy said, "So what you saying? You saying she didn't do herself in, that boy done it for her? Lynch her up like a nigger?"

"I'm just saying," Fudge said.

"Ain't you ask him what took place? You spent that whole night alongside him in that wagon, you ain't never ask him?"

"Never ask him nothing," Fudge said. "Can't go ask a man no question like that."

"Why not?" Lucindy said. "Why you can't ask him that?"

Fudge looked at his friend. "Hen, you tell her why you can't go ask a man no question like that."

Hen shrugged. "Figure the boy talk when he want to. If he want to."

"And what if he don't ever want to?" Lucindy said.

"Then we ain't never gonna know," said Fudge. "Are we?"

They stared down to where Augustus stood with his hands on his hips, Belle beside him mirroring his pose, both watching Napoleon at work, cupping Lovejoy's hoof, holding it close to his leg, picking out manure and dirt without digging in the point of the pick. Lucindy gave a twist and a great shower of kernels rained into the basin. "Course she done herself in," she said.

Fudge and Hen considered the possibility. Finally Fudge offered up his own theory. "Raining like blazes that day," he said. "Maybe 'Gustus just hung her up there to dry."

There was a moment of silence, till Fudge's gap-tooth smile broke through, and Hen threw back his head to laugh. Lucindy frowned. Or tried to frown. Her face twisted into a mass of conflicting wrinkles as the words clawed their way out of it: "Man can't eat no soggy cracker!" and she gave in to a great hysterical laugh herself, louder than either man.

Down by Augustus', the three youngsters all stood frozen, mouths open, staring up through the trees at the three old folks howling with laughter, falling to their knees, slapping the ground in glee.

Monday morning they went back to work. The shop and chair were as they'd left them. The lawyer Truby came in and ordered a new pair of boots and Fudge traced the outline of his feet on the leather, and custom seemed back to normal. The level of hostility in the air might have abated, back to where it had always been, mitigated by the invisibility the two black men had always endured, usually enjoyed. Neither ventured down toward the far end of Main Street, toward Kelty's blacksmith shed. Dr. Darling, a fine-featured young man with light hair who looked as though he had not yet begun to shave, nodded at Hen on his way into Fudge's shop. "Morning, Black Hen." Hen nodded in return. Under Darling's arm was a straw hat.

"Fudge," he heard Darling say, "how are you?"

"Me? Raring to go."

"That's the spirit. Here—I fetched this for you from the street where it fell."

"Thanky, Doctor. Thanky very kindly."

"Let me take a look at that eye. Nasty cut—seems to be healing nicely. Did you apply a sticking plaster?"

"The misses she put something on it. She keep on putting something on it."

"Good. Very good. Well, you seem to be in fine hands."

"Yes sir. Fine hands."

"I am in need of new boots," Darling said. "I shall return to order a pair, as soon as I can afford them." At that, the two men laughed, and Darling left. The word *Kelty* had never been uttered by either.

Thursday morning Kelty was uttered plenty. As they made their way up Pond Street and down Main toward the hotel, it was overcast, a smell of smoke heavy in the sodden air. At the far end of Main, beyond the hotel, they saw a knot of people, men, women and children, milling about. Hen and Fudge, though curious, kept their distance. Soon they learned that Kelty's blacksmith shed had caught fire in the night, burning to the ground.

"Don't God work in some mysterious ways now?" Fudge whispered.

"You suspect it was God done burnt down Kelty's shed?" said Hen.

"I likes to think so."

Augustus came into the shop, his smile like a sneer never broader. "Gentlemens," he said, "anybody know where a man can go and get his horse shod around these parts?"

"What you know about that fire?" Fudge's smile was gone, the black shade of his face going pale.

"Well, it was hot," Augustus said. "And damn angry. Done burnt away purt near everything that white bastard held dear. Heard it might of even burned up a wood leg or two."

Fudge went to the doorway, looked both ways, then turned again toward Augustus. "You had something to do with that fire?"

Augustus' face feigned shock. "Ain't that against the law?"

"Forget the law," Fudge said. "Law don't mean nothing to them white men. Law's the least of it, they think some nigger burning down their property."

Augustus' face changed too, the lightness gone. "You right about that there," he said. "Law be the least of it."

Augustus left. Hen shook his head. "What that boy up to," he said.

A few days went by, a week, then another, summer plodding toward fall. Nothing happened. Whatever they were waiting for, the next humiliation, the next attack in the street, the next fiery raid—the next anything resembling the stuff of their nightmares, the cat-haulings, the whippings and floggings, the lynchings—failed to come to pass. Walking on Pond Street, up and down Main every day, biding his time in his bootblack chair, watching and listening and napping, Hen tried to identify the feeling he felt—or rather, the feeling tried to identify itself, without Hen's active participation—and what came to his mind was the way he felt on the few occasions he'd found himself wading through high weeds in rattlesnake country, waiting for the rattle and hiss, the strike that never came.

That *so far* had never come.

He and Fudge went about business as usual, as did the other denizens of Little Brier who ventured out every day into the homes and fields and factories of the white folks of Hartsgrove and the surrounding Pennsylvania countryside, biding their time, plying their trades, doing their work, living their lives on eggshells. Augustus still found the odd hauling job, usually over the mountains to Lewistown and back, and when he wasn't hauling freight, or spending time at the home of Mrs. Barber, Little Brier's youngest widow, he was teaching Napoleon the finer points about horses. There were mules and pigs aplenty, but horses were rare in Little Brier; neither Hen nor Fudge had ever owned one. Gradually, most of the curious and hostile gazes—most, but not all—of the white folks began to subside, and the mantle of invisibility descended over the black men once more.

Miss Eva Alcorn passed into the collective lore of the town, an unfortunate girl who'd led a short, sorrowful life. Suicide remained the assumption, for the hidden bruises over the years had not gone unobserved, nor had her previous attempts to run away, nor her father's iron fist. Captain Alcorn was diminished by his daughter's death, or at least by the whispers and rumors around it. He fell from favor with the town's elite. Invitations to dances and dinners declined. No longer was he invited to review the local blues on muster day. He spent less time in his foundry, more in his distillery, drinking his product, losing his interest, counting his profits and losses.

Silas McKay delivered another cargo early on a cool September morning. Hen, drifting near sleep, heard a voice and rose, making his way toward Fudge's cabin just as Absalom, the rooster, let loose a mighty crow. In the pre-dawn twilight, color like rust was beginning to appear on the motionless leaves. By the time Hen arrived, McKay was gone and Fudge was rounding the corner of the cabin with a man who appeared to be, at first glance, a rough-cut copy of himself. About the same age, he was the same height and build, only thinner, a balding head like Fudge's, cheeks less bony, jaw only slightly fuller. His pants were torn at the knee and held up with twine, and his shirt was white and roomy, a cast-off from some charitable donor. His feet were bare, and his name was Shepard.

 Lucindy and Belle were still in their beds, and Napoleon was already off helping a farmer by the name of Lemon bring in his corn. After Fudge had started a small fire and put on the coffee to heat, he, Hen and Shepard sat at the bone-white table and watched the morning through the little window begrudgingly grow lighter by degrees.

 Fudge said he was worried.

 "That what you good at," said Hen.

 "What you worried about?" said Shepard. His eyes, weary and wary, were also calm and wise, lacking the kittenish fear Hen had seen so often in runaway eyes.

 "Doings lately hereabouts," Fudge said. "Ain't never know who watching what."

 "Amen," Shepard said. "Ain't *never* know who watching what, when or where."

 Shepard was the first cargo delivery since Miss Eva, since Kelty's shed had burned, and all day long, Hen could feel the tension from Fudge like heat from a fire. Augustus on the other hand was cool as an autumn breeze. Fudge fetched a pair of shoes from the shelf in his shop that he thought would suit Shepard, and after sunset Augustus harnessed Jupiter and Lovejoy, hitched them to his red wagon and they set off, Hen up on the driver's bench beside him, Fudge back in the box beside Shepard. Napoleon had wanted to go too—nearly every delivery, he pleaded with his father to let him come along—but Fudge had instructed him stay at home to watch over his mother and sister.

Augustus and his team knew the way north by now with scarcely a prompt from Fudge or Hen. They travelled as little as possible on the main turnpike, holding their breath as they passed near any cabin and farmhouse along the way. Though it was not implausible that a teamster might be out on an overnight run, the fewer questions asked, the better. They skirted the settlements, wending their way over logging trails and lanes, cow paths and open hillsides, across fields and pastures, fording shallow creeks, bouncing and jouncing along the route scouted out by Fudge years before. They crested a familiar hill where there was just enough moonlight through the clouds to see the wooded hills rolling gently away to the far ridge.

In the back, Fudge told Shepard to take a peek. "Fresh from the mint, and good as gold," he said of the view. He said it every time they came upon that particular view.

Augustus and Hen were as quiet as Shepard and Fudge were talkative, mile after mile of whispering murmur. From beneath the floppy broad brim of his hat, Fudge looked at his young companion, reins loose in his hands, animated only by the occasional flick, the cluck, haw or gee, though the horses seemed to know his intentions as well as he. Augustus' face, nearly invisible in the scant moonlight beneath the brimless black derby, was as sleepy-eyed and inscrutable as ever. Hen found himself wondering. He did not like it. Wondering made him restless. First he wondered about Augustus' speech. He considered his friend Fudge's contention that Augustus did not talk like a Yankee, and could therefore not be the free Negro from Connecticut that he claimed to be. If he was not, then who was he? What was he? Where was he from? And what about the matter of *free*? Could it have been him who burnt Kelty's shed, on the Main Street of a town the size of Hartsgrove, and done so completely invisible? And if he had set the fire, what did that say about the young man? Hen could not decide whether, if Augustus had set the fire, it was a symptom of courage or lunacy.

Miss Eva was next. Miss Eva, floating like an angel, red ribbon a-flutter in her hair, all the fury of the heavens breaking loose around her.

Augustus had been there. What had happened before Hen and Fudge had found them, the quick and the dead, in the schoolhouse? Had Augustus found her there, already hanged, the victim of her own despair? Or could he have had a hand in her death, silenced her to keep her from telling Captain Alcorn, to protect the secrets of Little Brier? Or did he sit and watch, unmoving, unmoved, from across the room, watch her in all her anguish mount the bench, place the rope around her neck and step into eternity? Fudge had concluded the boy had loved her. Hen, judging himself unfit to make such a judgment, would have to take his friend's word for it. Could a man watch a woman he loved end her own life, take away everything she ever was or would be, every thing *they* ever were or would be? And suddenly, in his mind, it was Lucindy. Lucindy in the schoolhouse, Hen sitting on the bench across the room. Lucindy's face etched with anguish as she mounted the children's bench, the rope in her hands.

Hen turned to ask Augustus, and he might have, he might actually have put together a question of some sort if Augustus had not turned to him in the same instant, moonlight on his cheek. Before Hen could ask the unformed question of his own, Augustus said, "What's the matter, old man? You look like you done seen a ghost."

It was mid-morning by the time they arrived back home, and Augustus headed in to his bed. Fudge seemed almost energized by his long journey with the man, whom they'd delivered safely into the hands of Jim Bundy, a Sugargrove Quaker and prosperous white merchant. He found Lucindy at her washing.

"We was both born in the same month of the same year," Fudge said to his wife. "April of '19. Different days, though."

"You and that man, Shepard?" Lucindy said.

Fudge nodded. Hen stood by a hickory stump watching.

"That ain't all. Both born near a place called Albany. Different states, though."

"Lordy be."

"Both had us a dog named Bob. Not at the same time, though."

"My, my." At her tub and washboard she looked back over her shoulder.

"Like talking to my own brother, though I never had a brother. We hit it off. Shame I won't never get to know him no better."

"Umm, um," said Lucindy with a shake of her head.

Hen sat down on the hickory stump to rest. Lucindy looked over Fudge's shoulder—his back was to Hen—straight into Hen's eyes with what seemed to be a question. Off through the trees, leaves drifted down from the tall oak and fell into the creek.

"Both of us gots families," Fudge said. "I still gots mine, though."

"What become of his?" Lucindy said.

Fudge shrugged. "His woman gone, done passed on. Name was Ruth. He talk about her like she still there. They had children too, don't know how many, two, three maybe, but they gone too. Old soul-driver done sold 'em all off."

Lucindy shook her head. She put her hand on her washboard, as if to keep it from running off, smiled and cocked her head. "See how lucky you is?" she said. "We still here."

Hen watched a gust sweep another shower of leaves down to skim the water. He saw the door to Augustus' house breathe open in the breeze, saw old Hiram Appleby hobble into and out of his sight down through the trees toward the cluster of shanties that made up the heart of Little Brier, and he felt content, as though he could see the whole world in the palm of his hand.

He saw the straw hat on Fudge's head bob up and down. "I does see," he heard him say. "I does. I gots to be the luckiest man in the whole world."

The euphoria caused by the revelation that he was the luckiest man in the world stayed with Fudge. Grateful for his lucky life, he took to expressing his gratitude openly and often, often to the annoyance of Hen, or Lucindy, or Augustus, or anyone else he touched in his new-found propensity for physical affection, the hugs and holding of hands, the clapping of shoulders and knees. Such a change in demeanor represented a disruption to the normal flow of their own daily lives, a somewhat suspicious and contrary thing.

He slowed down. Walking into Hartsgrove with Hen, or home again in the afternoon, he no longer pulled ahead. Now he strolled, frequently stopping to stare down a curious deer at the edge of the woods, or to admire the spiral of a hawk on the wind, or to watch the colorful pattern of the leaves afloat in the water, bantering cheerfully all the while. Hen found himself gritting his teeth. He wanted his friend back, his old, often-grumpy friend. There was something irritating about Fudge's façade—for despite his apparent sincerity, that is what it seemed to Hen to be—of blissful appreciation. It was also frightening. Hen had tasted enough delicious cakes in his lifetime, had thumbed up enough crumbs, to know that the only time a body slowed down to savor something the way Fudge had slowed down to savor his life at this moment was when it was almost gone.

One fine Indian summer afternoon, Fudge insisted they take the time on their way home to take in the beauty. Hen, tired from a hard day dozing, wasn't interested. Fudge took him by the hand, insisting. Hen shook his hand free. Fudge led him down the path between the pine grove and the laurel thicket to the white sand spring at the bottom of the town, a great pool in the rock near where Potters Creek met the Sandy Lick to form the Red Bank, a pleasant spot where the families—the white families—often went to picnic, or just to loaf, in fine weather.

The weather could not have been finer, sunshine sparkling off the waters, a breeze rippling the bright leaves of the trees. Overhead, a skein of geese glided gracefully through the sky, honking melodically. Fudge walked past the pool to the spot above the confluence of the creeks, put his hands on his hips, took in a great breath of air, and smiled. Hen had no choice but to follow. He noticed the many white faces staring at them. He joined Fudge, standing on the bank to look out over the creeks, hoping that the next time he looked around all the white faces would have turned back to their blankets and baskets.

"Fresh from the mint, and good as gold," said Fudge, putting his arm around the shoulders of his old friend. Hen shook it off.

A white child, about three, walked up to the two black men. They looked down at the little girl in a pink velvet bonnet. She stared right back up at them, at Fudge in particular, for he was the closest to her. Her eyes were wide. Hesitantly, she reached up and touched Fudge's arm. Then, more boldly now, she rubbed her fingers from his elbow to his wrist, put her hand to her face and sniffed. After a sniff or two, she stuck out her tongue and licked at her fingers.

Hen was the first to laugh. He threw back his head and roared. "She expect you gonna taste like chocolate!"

Fudge looked at his arm, perplexed. A portly young woman, whose only resemblance to the child was her pink velvet bonnet, rushed up and hurried the little girl away, back to a bearded man and boy by a blanket beyond the pool. The man began to laugh. Others among the white families began to point and laugh as well, explaining what had happened to those who hadn't seen as they too joined in the mirth. Hen laughed the loudest, his head thrown back. Belatedly, Fudge began to laugh as well, just as Hen had quit, wiping a tear from his eye. Fudge slapped his thigh and roared, just as the first rock landed.

It landed beside Hen's foot, skipping over the bank and into the creek. Fudge's laugh ended abruptly. The young boy with the family of the pink velvet bonnets, having thrown the first stone, was searching the ground for another, his father pointing toward a likely choice. Other boys and young men followed suit, reaching to the ground, picking up rocks, flinging them at the two black men. A rock struck Hen on the shoulder, another hit Fudge on the back of the head just beneath his hat as he tried to duck. In the steady rain of rocks, Hen and Fudge, arms raised to cover their heads, stumbled down the bank, the only direction available to them, and into the water. Hen felt a rock bounce off his back, another hitting his hip.

The two men sloshed and slid on the slippery creek-bottom rocks away from the mob, up to their knees, up to their waists in the creek, the hail of stones continuing. Those who were not throwing were pointing and laughing now, just as they had when the little girl had tasted Fudge's arm. Hen and Fudge were up to their chests, rocks splashing around them. Some of the throwers had ventured to the very edge of the creek where the supply of rocks was more plentiful, a few actually wading into the shallows, still throwing, with even more urgency, as the laughter and merriment of their audience increased in proportion to the flurry of rocks and stones.

The water was cold, the current was swift, and still the rocks kept pelting down, splashing all around their hat-covered heads, and soon they lost contact with the slippery rocks on the bottom and began to swim, fighting the weight of their clothes and boots. At last the shower of stones dwindled, ceasing as they moved out of range on the far side. They waded, weary, out of the creek, away from the crowd of revelers, still pointing and laughing at the sight of the two drenched darkies collapsed and shivering on the opposite shore.

Hen stood, legs wobbly. Taking Fudge by the shoulder, he pulled him up too. He could feel the throb of welts on his back and hip. They watched the white folks returning to their baskets and blankets, heard one last call—*damn niggers!*—echo across the creek. They stood staring over the water for several minutes, till the scene returned to normal, till the white folks were settled, back to their picnics and pleasant chatter, with scarcely another glance across the water to where Hen and Fudge stood wet, cold and bewildered.

Hen put his arm around the shoulders of his friend. "Fresh from the mint, and good as gold," he said. Fudge shook his arm away.

Hen didn't hurt too badly at first. Walking up Coolbrook Road toward Little Brier, he felt the soreness in the bruises on his body from where the stones had struck, but he knew that pain would go away. His friend Fudge didn't seem all the worse for the wear either, though there was a trickle of blood down the back of his neck, and there was no denying that his blissful mood, along with the rest of him, had been considerably dampened. When it began to hurt Hen the most was afterwards, after they'd made their way back home to Lucindy, after she'd heard what had happened and had kissed the cut on Fudge's head, after she'd began to help him take the wet clothes from his body with a frown toward Hen that told him it was time for him to leave, after he was alone, sore, weary and wet, in his forlorn little shanty.

Fudge Van Pelt was never again to attain the plateau of euphoria associated with being the luckiest man in the world. His haste and impatience soon returned, and Fudge was, in the eyes of his friend Hen, back to normal. But after a week or so of normal, his descent into gloominess inexplicably resumed, past normal, to a place where Hen had never seen him go before. Walking into work on a Tuesday morning when the leaves had gone from glorious colors to brown and dead, fleeing the trees in great numbers, on a morning when a single goose, lost to its skein, honked its lonely way eastward overhead, Fudge kept walking. He'd pulled ahead of Hen as usual, but when he came to the bend a quarter mile before the sawmill, he kept walking, disappearing around it instead of waiting there, as he normally did, watching the workings of the mill while his old friend caught up to him. When Hen reached his bootblack chair in the corridor of the hotel beneath the little sign of the boot, he could hear Fudge already at work in his shop, the tapping of the hammer upon the lapstone.

Hen cooked the meal that evening, fricasseed chicken with parsley and onion, and while Lucindy and Napoleon, and even little Belle, licked their lips and made other sounds of gustatory satisfaction, Fudge only grunted, his head down over his bowl. Afterwards Hen noticed that Fudge seemed to draw himself close to the fire, showing every evidence of feeling a chill in the evening air that was not particularly cold. He grew more listless.

When Hen went to his cabin a few mornings later, Fudge still lay in his bed. Lucindy stood by her bone-white table, a worried look on her face. When Hen looked in, Fudge opened an eye. "Coming down with something," he said. "Backbone aches."

"Want me to go and fetch the widow?" Hen said.

"Just leave me be. Just need me some rest is all."

Elza Winter was the widow. She lived in a shanty patched with canvas in the heart of the cluster of shacks that made up Little Brier, a large-boned and officious old woman known for her cures and for Absalom, her cantankerous old rooster. She sprinkled vinegar around Fudge's bedroom, called for more blankets to be heaped upon the patient, instructed Lucindy to feed him nothing but roasted apples and light bread boiled in water, the occasional boiled prune, and that only sparingly. Starve the fever, she commanded. She also prescribed the smoking of tobacco by the patient, which Fudge obliged. The widow herself was partial to the pipe.

But Fudge failed to show signs of improvement.

On the fourth day, when the chills seemed to be increasing in frequency and intensity, Lucindy insisted they summon Dr. Means. Hen found the doctor just leaving his little office on Cherry Street, and told him of Fudge's affliction. Dr. Means, after querying Hen on the details of the symptoms, and the course of treatment advised by the Widow Winter, did not seem overly concerned. He'd treated hundreds of cases of the fever, he said, usually to satisfactory outcomes.

He called upon Fudge late on a bleak October afternoon. After examining the patient, Dr. Means remained unconcerned. "Keep him in bed," he instructed Lucindy, and Hen as well, for Hen was hovering there at the table with the rest of the family. "As much fresh air as is practicable, no work whatsoever. Keep his diet simple—no pork. Fowl, mutton, wild game are fine—let him eat as his appetite dictates, no more, no less. His body itself is the best prescriber."

"No remedies?" Lucindy said.

"Yes—a cold infusion of boneset three or four times a day. That and a hot foot-bath in the evening should suffice to avert an attack of ague."

Fudge remained restless in the night, his dreams disagreeable. Hen was little motivated to journey into work without his friend, reasoning that the need for his bootblack services was diminished without the accompanying bootmaker to craft the boots to be blacked, and so he sat with Fudge one morning when the sun did not shine, and Fudge told him, again, about his dream.

Last night had been so still, Fudge told him, now that the leaves were gone from the trees, that the waters of the Little Brier seemed to be flowing just beyond his window, even closer, beneath the very ropes of his bed, and in his feverish state he felt the motion of the running water, and found himself floating downstream toward Potters Creek and Hartsgrove. He was quite content at first, watching the green hills gently rising above the creek, the black crows soaring overhead, until, gently drifting, he found himself drawn toward the wheel of Cook's Sawmill, then, splashing in panic, toward the hidden hooks of the fishermen suddenly there on the banks of the creek. White. Every time he dreamed the dream, the faces were turnip white, twisted in grim determination to hook him, land him, flay him, fry him up over the fire. Then a scream from a panther in the woods awoke him. Every time he dreamed the dream something awoke him before the hooks sank into his flesh, sometimes a snore from Lucindy, or Napoleon falling out of his bed, or little Belle coughing, and always when he awoke he could feel the heat on his face, though last night, in his feverish state, the heat was stronger, the sweat on his face even more profuse. "Put me in mind of the night they burnt the place down," Fudge said. "Like I was watching them flames jumping up from the shanties all over again."

Hen sat on the little chair by the bed. Through the small window bare, black branches crisscrossed a blank gray sky. Fudge shivered, his dream related, and Hen nodded, though in truth he failed to understand what dreaming of hidden hooks had to do with the burning of Little Brier years before. He was willing to credit the leap to the high art of worry perfected by his friend, just as he was willing for his own part to feel how the dream had brought him low, how the dream had drained him, somehow, of hope.

Hen had his own dreams. About Yellow Charlie, snippets and shards of dreams flaring and dying in random disorder like sparks from a fire: Charlie piling rough boards from the scrap heap at the sawmill for Hen to tote out to Little Brier to build a shack by the willow on the bank of the creek, a year before their first neighbor arrived, before a single tree or bush had even been cleared; Charley tearing down the shack a year later so Hen could haul the boards and sticks and stones a hundred feet up the creek to reassemble when their first neighbor, Hiram Appleby, built on a spot considered by Charlie too close; Charlie eating roasted rabbit with honey, the grease running down his fingers—for Charlie never held a spoon in his hand all the years of his life—and down his face into his wispy, Chinaman's beard; Charlie's yellow-brown face in his Chinaman's near-grin as a swarm of mosquitoes and gnats torments Hen, up his nose, into his mouth and eyes, while Charlie himself they ignore.

The dreams—half-dreams, daydreams, reveries—about Yellow Charlie took place in the hours before dawn, as Hen lay on his corn mattress on the dirt floor of his shack, the cool fall air creeping into his old bones, hours he'd heretofore spent considering matters of the day: Fudge's condition, Lucindy's very being, the mystery that was Augustus, the abandoned boot shop and bootblack chair—what must Fudge's custom be thinking, arriving day after day to find the shop empty, wondering about the state of their new shoes or old boots in for repair, never about the state of the bootmaker?

At first he had no earthly idea why all the everyday, ordinary objects of his dreams and thoughts had been so suddenly shoved aside by Yellow Charlie, after the many years the man had lingered in his memory as little more than a shadow—until one morning he thought of the odor in Fudge's sick room: the smell of apples too long in the barrel, the smell of the underside of a fallen log in the forest, an odor that drifted down from his nostrils and settled heavy over his tongue, and reminded him of Yellow Charlie.

Fudge continued to fail. At times he shivered so uncontrollably the bed shook down to the floorboards, his nails and lips turning blue, his eyes sunken and the ache in his back unbearable. Dr. Means applied sinapisms—poultices of meal and pulverized mustard seed—to the painful areas, and hot bricks to the feet; Lucindy bathed his head in warm water and fanned it so as to cool it by evaporation. Fudge began to vomit, a new symptom. Dr. Means increased the infusion of boneset and prescribed a compound of Peruvian bark, rhubarb root, gentian root and orange peel, a wineglassful each morning and evening. He further instructed that the patient should have no company. Here he looked at Hen. "Anything that disturbs his imagination feeds the disease," Dr. Means said. "And the air that he breathes must be pure. Nothing spoils the air, or does more harm to the patient, than a multitude of people breathing it. That air loses its spring and is rendered poisonous to the sick."

This was why Hen never saw his friend again, not in a living state.

He stood beside Augustus Hamilton on a Thursday morning, staring at the black wreath on the door of Fudge's cabin. There was still a full moon low in the sky, as the sun tried to break through the clouds on the other side. Of all the birds in song, it was the sound of the mourning dove, the melodic and melancholy coos, that Hen kept hearing to the exclusion of any others, even Absalom's mean crow. Though irony was not something Hen normally considered, it was not lost on him that his friend had passed away only a month or so after declaring himself to be the luckiest man in the world, and the briefest of wonders flickered through his mind as to whether or not the God about which he was only vaguely aware, and vaguely unsure, might indeed be a cruel and fickle being. Or had the fault been entirely Fudge's for daring to declare such a foolish and boastful thing? Hen had thought it unwise the moment Fudge had spoken the words, though he hadn't imagined the penalty for being prideful might be so severe. Hen knew instinctively that the safest place to be was hidden within the folds of the multitude.

The last week of Fudge's life had passed in loneliness, the only faces he saw those of his wife and his doctor, and the turnip white faces of the fishermen in his dreams. This Hen had to guess. No thoughts would set firm in his mind, only an ache and a muddle of black images, among them the stones and the water. He and Augustus watched as Lucindy left the cabin wearing her widow's weed, and walked up into the shadows of the woods to be alone. Many of their friends and neighbors had connected the dots from the stoning and the dunking in the creek to Fudge's last illness, Augustus chief among them.

"Who throwed that first rock?" was what Augustus wanted to know.

5: November 9, 1857: Resurrection Redux

"The loss of a patient is never easy, my dear."

Through the wavy glass in the window Darling watched the long shadows moving on Main Street, shadows of the chickens and horses and dogs, the occasional hog, shadows of customers going in and out of the Philadelphia Cheap Store across the street. The oily smell of medicines permeated the air, from the table along the far wall with its assortment of bowls and mortars and pestles, and other of Vasbinder's implements, above which were three shelves laden with various bottles, boxes, tins, pots and jars. On the opposite wall, bookshelves groaned beneath Vasbinder's medical library, volume after leather-bound volume. Darling listened to the quiet voices of his preceptor and his preceptor's old friend, John J. Y. Truby, whom the doctor was examining in the room behind the closed door at the rear of the outer office. Truby coughed once, a little bark, Vasbinder murmured, and Truby coughed again. Darling sat across from Vasbinder's stately roll-top desk, leaning back in his chair, listening to the weary ticking of the grandfather clock in the corner, and staring through the window at the Philadelphia Cheap Store, wondering if it were too late for him to consider going into retail.

Truby emerged before Vasbinder, his bald head wearing a frown, a neatly curled mustache, and a yellowish hue. He plucked at the bottom of his waistcoat. Shaking the doctor's hand and nodding to Darling, he took his leave, clutching the parcel of pills that Vasbinder had thrust upon him. From the doorway, Vasbinder watched him walk away, then turned to stare at Darling. His hands were in his pockets—seldom were they so concealed—and the look on his face was somber, placid and tic-free. He shook his head.

"The loss of a patient is never easy, my dear," he said again, resuming their conversation as though they'd never been interrupted by Truby's arrival, "particularly one to whom we've grown attached, and especially one so young. Each of us must learn to deal with it in his own particular way. My way was learned decades ago. Your way will come to you in time."

"It's not the youth so much," Darling said. "Had her death come a week before it did, I was quite prepared to accept it. But the last time I saw her—she was *well*, Cyrus. She seemed to be perfectly whole. That's what bedevils me."

"A false recovery, my dear. Not uncommon. Many a young physician has been flamfoozled by a false recovery."

"Flamfoozled? Or would *honey-fuggled* be closer to the mark?"

Vasbinder stared. "I'm often unsure how to regard your remarks, my dear."

"In the best way possible, Cyrus."

Vasbinder's mustache twitched. "Carrying on is the best remedy. Get on with the business of healing your patients, bury yourself in your work. With the exception, that is, of the Plotners—I shall be happy to assume their care once more, should it please you, as I entirely sympathize with the reluctance you must feel to visit them again. An occasional jaunt out to Coolbrook will be a fine tonic to keep me from growing too stagnant. Just what the doctor ordered," he added with a chuckle.

"I appreciate the offer, Cyrus. But I couldn't help but feel that that would somehow be a dereliction of my duties."

"Not at all, my dear, not at all. If anything, you're being too conscientious. In fact, I shall insist: the Plotners once again are my patients. There. Upon my authority, consider it done. No dereliction on your part whatsoever."

Clover Hill, above South Street between Irishtown and Hartsgrove proper, was the unlikely site where Darling's courtship of Kathleen O'Hanlon had begun some nine months before, almost to Darling's surprise. It had been an evening of moonlight, new-fallen snow and tolerable temperatures, and the young people had gathered on the hill to ride their sleds and sliding-boards down its lengthy slope, a well established Hartsgrove tradition on evenings as rare as that. Darling had spent a long day in the presence of smoke—from the woodstove in the office he shared with Vasbinder, from the cigars of Vasbinder and his patients, and then, in the early evening, from the drafty fireplace in his mother's home—and the fresh air of that moonlit night was like a dive into the pool by the Red Bank on a hot summer day.

Arriving with Joshua Sandt, Darling didn't spot Kathleen amongst the moonlit crowd until she was almost upon him, having spotted him first, running with a shriek of delight to leap into his arms—this before they'd ever even danced. "Will Darlin'!" she cried, as they tumbled to the snow, laughing like children; Darling was immediately infected by the joy. Then she hugged Sandt, and insisted they share their first ride down the hill together.

Darling could still recall at will the memory of her body—though their coats had been bulky—pressing into his, though he would be the first to admit that the memory was undoubtedly augmented by his imagination. Riding down the hill together—laughing, flying!—the three of them crowded onto a sliding-board made for two, Darling was in the front, Kathleen clinging as closely as she could, another embrace he could bring to mind at will.

Now, passing by Clover Hill on his way to Irishtown, where the green of the grass on the hillside had gone to brown, he remembered the moonlight glistening on the crest of the snow that evening, and the question occurred to him for the very first time: If Kathleen had been clinging so tightly to him, to what—to whom—to what part of whom—had Joshua Sandt, behind them on the sliding-board, been clinging? And just how tightly?

The melancholy of Molly's demise had thoroughly tainted his heart.

Had he indeed been flamfoozled by a false recovery? Had his neglecting to administer treatment on his penultimate visit contributed to the little girl's death? Or was Mr. Dr. Means correct in his beliefs and assertions, that Darling had ceased his erroneous heroics too late? Or was there somehow more to it, more yet to be revealed? And what additional degree of fault or blame might those new revelations assign him? He needed to unburden his heart to Kathleen; talking to Vasbinder was of little use, given the man's pragmatism and empiricism. Darling required a spirited and passionate defense. Passing by O'Hanlon's Furniture Factory on his way to Mrs. McClay's, he waved and nodded to Kathleen in the window of the office, where she kept the accounts for her father. The left-handed wave was their sign that she should meet him by the willow. They could talk by their boulder in the woods past the stand of beech trees.

But when he returned, no one was waiting by the willow. Puzzled, he rode the short distance up into the woods to their boulder. Kathleen was not there, either.

Disconsolate, he dismounted. Breathing in the thin November air, he fought off the cloud of melancholy that threatened to swallow him. He should go and wait by the willow; perhaps she'd simply been detained. Perhaps it was only temporary. Perhaps Joshua Sandt was not in the office with her at all, purchasing great quantities of furniture for his store and his new house, impressing her father with his feeble witticisms. Darling clenched his fists and punched violently at the air. Sighing, bereft, he patted Gertie's muzzle with his hand, and she nipped affectionately at his fingers. Was she his only friend? He embraced her neck, nuzzling the old horse with his face, thankful for solid, dependable presence of her, at least, if no one else. Gertie nickered back over her shoulder, stamping her foot tenderly. Stroking her shoulder, he glanced around the woods, down to the road that was visible through the trees, thankful that no one was there to see him acting the fool with his horse.

A giggle came from the tree above his head. He looked up.

Kathleen sat above him on a branch of the nearly leafless hickory tree. She began to laugh aloud and even so, even though she was laughing at him, she appeared immensely like an angel on high. She was wearing a long, pink linen skirt and white blouse beneath a dark blue hooded cloak. Her legs were crossed at the ankles, swinging freely beneath the branch, which she clung to with both of her hands by her sides.

"Come down here at once, young lady," he said looking up with a grin.

"No," she said, her legs still swinging. "You come up here."

He assessed the situation and quickly commenced an ascent, an assault, his brogans slipping on the bark—it was as though there were a magnet in the tree, and he was the iron, drawn irresistibly upward. She laughed again watching him climb nearer. "Just exactly what is it you find so amusing?"

"You hugging your horse—if only your patients could see their stern doctor!"

Darling settled on the closest branch he could find, slightly lower than Kathleen, looking up. "Have you no shame, spying on your beau like an old spinster aunt?"

"And who says you're my beau?"

He slapped the bark. "*I* do."

"You and you alone?"

"Not at all," he said, nodding down. "Gertie there will attest to it as well."

She laughed again. "Gertie must know how partial I am to jailbirds."

They fell into an easy silence, the hint of awkwardness fitting quite comfortably. Kathleen swung her legs. Darling leaned against the trunk of the tree. "I have bad news," he said after a few moments. "About little Molly Plotner."

"Oh, dear." Kathleen made the sign of the cross.

The story was not a short one, for he hadn't yet told her about Molly's apparent recovery, prior to her demise, which he had to relate in order for Kathleen to appreciate the utter shock of her death. He told her as well about the arguments of Steven Means, summarizing his own guilt and confusion: Dr. Vasbinder would hold him to blame for the girl's death, for treating her suitably but insufficiently, while Dr. Means would do likewise, for essentially the same reasons, albeit from the opposite course. Either judgment rendered him a poor facsimile of a physician.

Kathleen shook her head. "You doctors are all the same. Forever taking the credit that rightly belongs to God, whatever the outcome, for good or for ill."

This was not the spirited and passionate defense he'd hoped for. "So what are you saying? The course of treatment is of no consequence? That we might as well treat every patient with ice cream and oysters?"

She sighed, her eyes softening, and Darling was prepared at last for his well deserved sympathy and concern. "Not a'tall," she said, "not a'tall. What I'm saying is that arrogance seems to be a precondition to entering the medical profession."

He felt as though he'd been slapped. "And do you find me so arrogant as well?"

Kathleen stared, her face neutral. At that moment, a horse passed by on the road below and she pointed. "Look—why, it's Josh."

He did; it was. Darling's finger was halfway to his lips, where the shushing noise was just beginning to leak out, when Kathleen called, "Josh! Josh! Up here, in the woods!"

Sandt wheeled his horse about and headed up the path. Pulling up beside Gertie, he stared up at the pair of them in the tree, wispy whiskers clinging to his skinny chin, resplendent and ridiculous in his blue velvet waistcoat. To Darling, from his perch, Sandt looked the perfect fool. "What have we here?" said Sandt. "A new custom of sparking?"

Kathleen giggled again, to Darling's chagrin. "What brings you out here?" Darling said.

"You do," said Sandt. "Wait until you've heard the latest."

"I'll be right down," said Darling.

"Nonsense," Sandt said. "I'll be right up." He dismounted, his lanky frame covering the short distance between his horse and the tree in three strides. His climb was awkward but quick, and he was soon settled on the next branch above Darling, slightly higher than Kathleen as well, between the two of them. Darling seethed at the look of pleasant amusement on Kathleen's face.

"Yes?" said Darling.

Sandt put his hand to his brow, like a visor, staring out beyond the road down below. "I believe I can see clear to Bootjack from here," he said.

Kathleen laughed. Darling did not. He said, "So what is the latest?"

"The latest is this: There's a rumor afoot, that would have it that Fudge Van Pelt was intentionally done in by the doctors in order to provide themselves dissecting material."

A moment passed while the rumor sank in, during which a sparrow landed on an adjacent limb, squawked in displeasure and flew away. "Such twaddle," Kathleen said.

"And how exactly would the rumor have it that Fudge was done in?" said Darling.

"Cleverly," Sandt said. "With poison undetected—perhaps in his whiskey."

"Nonsense," Darling said. "I never knew the man to be fond of the drop."

"Aren't all niggers fond of the drop?"

"Fiddle-faddle," Kathleen said. "No one in their right mind could possibly give any credence to it." She thought it over. "Could they?"

"Well," Sandt said, pausing for effect, "I don't wish to go out on a limb here, but—" Darling endured the burst of laughter from Kathleen, in which Sandt fairly glowed. "But I wouldn't be so sure. Eventually it will be proven fallacious no doubt, but in the meantime, if I were Will Darling, I'd remain out of sight."

"Will Darling specifically?" said Will Darling.

"Your name was foremost and most frequent."

"Darlin' Will," sighed Kathleen.

Darling sighed as well, though the sighing was as much the result of an unfounded infusion of pride as it was of the added burden of another nuisance. The mere fact that his name was being bandied about foremost and most frequent was significant and reassuring to him, implying that he had assumed a leadership role of sorts among an older, more established and learned group of men, at least in the eyes of gossipers and rumor-mongers. They sat in silence for a few moments more, the occasional chirped criticism of the odd sparrow notwithstanding. Below them near the boulder, Gertie and Sandt's horse, a young blue roan, nudged aside fallen leaves in search of edible undergrowth, as a clopping sound of hooves came near, and another horseman passed by on the road down below. It was Constable McClay, on his way to work in his suit of drab. Not a word was uttered from the tree. Darling looked out beyond the road as McClay disappeared, out over the trees behind which the Sandy Lick Creek flowed beneath the gray slate of November clouds. He felt the urge to spit upon the ground, to try and hit the small rock protruding from the carpet of leaves near the hickory tree. Kathleen beat him to it, a pearl of spittle falling from her ruby lips to the ground.

The two men exchanged glances of bemused surprise. Kathleen said, "Will—have you told Josh about Molly yet?"

"Told me what about Molly?" Sandt said. "Molly who?"

"Little Molly Plotner," Kathleen said. "Has he told you nothing?"

"Less than that," Sandt said.

"She died," Darling said.

They waited for him to expound. Darling was silent.

"Of what?" said Sandt.

Darling shifted his weight, having decided to depart the tree. "That I do not know," he said, commencing his descent. It was the simplest answer. And the most truthful.

As soon as he was down, he looked up to see Sandt hurriedly following behind him. When the two of them were standing on the ground, looking up at Kathleen still sitting on her limb, the reason for Sandt's urgency began to dawn on Darling. Kathleen leaned over and spit again. She watched the droplet hit the ground, then glanced briefly and sternly at the two young men beneath her, took a breath and began her own descent. They watched. They should not have, Darling knew, but they did; they both watched as her long, pink skirt became entangled here and there on the bark and branches, and her ankles and calves—in one glorious instant, the back of her knee—became exposed in one tantalizing glimpse after another. Darling felt the blood rushing to his face, as well as to other parts of his body. Sandt's face was equally red, Darling resisting the urge to smite it.

On the ground, she stood with her back to them for a moment or two, bending and smoothing her skirt, straightening her clothing that had become disarranged. Then she turned, a flush upon her own stern face, an angry flash in the green of her eyes. She glanced at Sandt, daring him to comment, then she looked at Darling in much the same manner. "Then why don't you find out?" she said.

Darling drew a blank. "Find out what?"

Her foot in her slipper stamped impatiently at the leaves. "Find out what caused the death of that poor little girl."

"How would I find that out?"

"By an autopsy," she said, looking at him with something like disdain. "How else?"

"In order to perform an autopsy, I would have to—"

"Yes," said Kathleen, "you would."

Sandt filled the ensuing lull. "Well, we've had a fine rehearsal," he said. "*Hearse* being the operative part of the word."

"Practice makes perfect," said Kathleen.

In an instant the image came to Darling: him lifting Molly's lifeless little body from the ground, and it seemed to him, in that instant, like a rescue, the courageous act of a hero, all the sorrow and difficulty, the ghastliness, notwithstanding. "You people are ghouls," said Darling, his smooth, glowing face wistful. "Delightful, delightful ghouls."

At the dominoes table, Vasbinder sat in fierce concentration, stroking his bushy white mustache with a thoughtful finger. Across the table, his opponent, Samuel Bullers, took another gulp of his whiskey, sat back and crossed his arms over his keg of a chest, silent till he could no longer bear it. "Cyrus," Little Bull said, "either you have a five or you do not. It is not a science."

"That is where you are wrong, dear fellow," said Vasbinder. "Perhaps I have two fives. Perhaps one of them is joined with a four, the other with a two. Just perhaps, mind you. Then one would have to calculate the odds of the other remaining fours—for only one has thus far been revealed—being in the boneyard, or in your pile. And so on with the twos. It is very much a science indeed."

Everyone came to court, whether or not they had business there, to see and to be seen. Court having been in session, having just recessed, the barroom of the American Hotel was full to overflowing, a jovial rumble of noise in the air, along with the smoke from a hundred cigars. Will Darling was there, though he did not particularly wish to see or be seen; he sat watching the dominoes contest, awaiting the opportunity to steer the conversation toward relevant matters. Black Hen passed by, shuffling slowly through the throng, a wooden box filled with shoes and forms and casts and tools in his hands. His old tired eyes made contact with Darling's and he might have nodded in greeting, but Darling couldn't be sure. His face was a quiet accusation. Behind him, carrying a similarly laden box, came an old Negro man, bald, stocky and righteous—Darling thought he knew the man to be Cornelius Nips, prominent in the Negro community on the Little Brier—and the younger black man, Augustus Hamilton, carrying rolls of leather over his shoulder. Augustus was the only Negro still wearing his hat, looking narrow-eyed, sullen and handsome. And *dangerous;* the word popped suddenly into Darling's mind, but he let it pass again just as quickly as the Negroes passed. They were vacating the premises of the dead man's boot shop.

A sad business, but Darling considered it for only a moment, brushing away just as quickly the hint of vague guilt, before his mind turned back again to the business at hand. He'd wanted to speak with Vasbinder, but the presence of Little Bull might only be of benefit. When Big Bull strolled over from the bar to join them, the majority of the learned ghouls who had participated in the resurrection of Fudge Van Pelt were present, all but Joshua Sandt.

The significance of the gathering was not lost on Congressman Levi Smathers, as he entered the crowded room with an entourage of dignitaries including Burgess Butterfield, Justice Martz and several others. He paused with his assembly by the dominoes table. "See here, gentlemen," he cried, loudly enough for the whole barroom to hear in the hush caused by his grand entrance. "It would seem that the doctors have gathered once again at the boneyard!"

Clever enough, Darling supposed, though not enough to account for the ensuing tidal wave of laughter rollicking through the room, which he could attribute only to the added lubrication of small beer and Monongahela whiskey. Vasbinder said, "I am pleased to see that your sense of humor has returned with such a vengeance, Levi."

Scanning his audience at Vasbinder's table, Smathers's beaming face stopped short at Darling's. "Who is this?" he said, still loud enough for the all to hear. "Is this the young man whose case you've been pleading so earnestly?"

"Yes, indeed," Vasbinder said. "This is William Darling. My protégé."

Smathers leaned close to Darling's face, rudely close, examining him, sizing him up, as he might a cock before a cock fight—and dismissing him, Darling could see, as far too scrawny to scrap. Darling could also see iron-gray eyes burning coldly and acne-scarred skin hidden beneath the muttonchop whiskers. "I was so sorry to hear about your daughter," Darling said. Exactly why he said this, why he'd felt a pang of sympathy for this man upon whom it would seem to be wasted, he was at a loss to say. Perhaps it was only for the lost little girl.

"My what? Oh, yes, my daughter." Suspicion creasing his brow, Smathers stood, turning again toward Vasbinder. "Cyrus—have you been expounding your ersatz sympathy vote theory to this young man? Is that what this is about?"

Cheeks flushing, eyebrows fluttering, Vasbinder said, "Sympathy vote?"

Smathers laughed a hearty imitation of a laugh, clapping Vasbinder good-naturedly on the shoulder. "Never mind, Cyrus, never mind! All is right with the world once again—all is right!"

As Smathers made his way off through the crowd, shaking hands, clapping other shoulders, Vasbinder muttered to the doctors alone, "Pompous ass." Darling was uneasy. Something about the man, Smathers, struck him as far worse than pompous, far more dangerous, and though he was at a loss as to what its exact name might be, a viper slithered into his mind.

The word *evil* slithered with it.

"Without a doubt," Big Bull said, "although it does beg the question of the prosecution—where does that stand?"

Vasbinder sat up, having abandoned his concentration upon the game at hand. "It stands somewhere between limbo and Bootjack," he said, nodding reassuringly toward Darling. "I have made arrangements with Smathers, and have every reason to believe that the worst is behind us."

"Of course when you say 'we,'" said Little Bull, "you mean 'you,'

Alexander and I being mere witnesses, innocent as babes in the woods."

Darling was unsure of the degree of jest in Little Bull's remarks, delivered as they were with a somber countenance. Both of the brothers were generously partaking of their tumblers of whiskey. "And what of the newest rumors?" Darling said.

"To which rumors do you refer, my dear?" Vasbinder said.

"Josh told me there's a new rumor afoot alleging that we—the doctors—intentionally did away with Fudge in order to obtain his cadaver for dissecting material."

"Can you imagine," said Little Bull. "Actually doing away with a nigger merely to advance the cause of medical science?"

Darling looked up to see that the Negroes, passing by, might have overheard.

"Preposterous," said Big Bull.

"What was it you said, Cyrus?" said Little Bull, "'By the Jew's eye'—here his voice took on a somber tone, which Darling supposed was meant to ape Vasbinder's—'we bestow something of value upon this nigger in death that he could never have done in life.' Something of that nature, was it not?"

" Something approximate," said Vasbinder.

"The very idea," said Big Bull, with another gulp of his whiskey.

"The very idea indeed," Little Bull said. "Why on earth would we require dissecting material when there is already such an abundance of fleas available in the world to practice upon?" Here he looked at Darling, a mischievous grin beneath his beard.

Darling felt his face darken. He looked at his preceptor, who looked away sheepishly; he'd been unaware that Vasbinder had shared Darling's flea-slicing proclivity with the other doctors, and he wondered how widely his practice was known. Undaunted, he said, "I have achieved the dissection of a single flea into four distinct and equal parts."

"I much prefer their carriers," said Big Bull. "The dogs and the cats of the world."

"Nonsense," Little Bull said. "Give me a good ol' nigger any day!"

The exclamation came out quite loudly, as did the Bullers's subsequent laughter, and Darling glanced up again. Black Hen's and Cornelius's faces were downcast, staring at their burdens, but Augustus Hamilton's was not. His eyes were locked upon the doctors, and Darling glanced across the table to see Little Bull returning the stare in kind.

"Here's a toast," Big Bull said, "to brighter days." Only he and his brother lifted their tumblers. "Next time we shall not be so careless as to be discovered. And I propose that next time might be nearer than you think— niggers are, after all, dying everyday."

"Dying to become our specimens!" said Little Bull. At that the two brothers laughed, quite hardily, tears upon their bearded cheeks.

Darling and Vasbinder sat silently, watching as the antics of the brothers grew more farcical and inane; Vasbinder had given up on his dominoes game, Darling on his desire for serious conversation. The Negroes carried a final load outside, Augustus Hamilton casting one last glance over his shoulder toward the dominoes table, and they were gone.

Darling and his preceptor soon quit the crowded room as well. "We must forgive them their excesses, my dear," said Vasbinder, taking Darling's arm as they walked down Main Street. "The Bullers are good men, but too predisposed to the drink. God help us when the demon whiskey has taken them by the knees." He hiccupped, which caused a little lurch.

"I shall see you to your home, Cyrus," Darling said. Vasbinder did not object. Another of his dictums, *moderation in all things*, he still practiced, but Darling had noticed that whiskey, even in moderation now, made more of a mark than it formerly had. They left behind the raucous overflow from the hotel, fidgeting horses all tethered to the rail in a row, strolling past the shuttered windows of the stores, the only light in the street coming from the lamps and candles in the windows of the houses they passed. Turning down the hill toward Water Street, Darling saw a fur-bearing creature of moderate size scurry from the street and into the brush by the side of Silas Breakey's house; whether cat, fox, possum or skunk, he couldn't venture to guess. Vasbinder didn't notice.

They made their way down Water Street, aiming for the lamplight in the window of Vasbinder's parlor. "You're rather quiet tonight, Will," Vasbinder said.

"I have much on my mind."

"You may put your mind at ease, my dear, at least insofar as your arrest is concerned."

"Yes," said Darling. "My first arrest, at any rate."

"I beg your pardon?"

"I came to talk to you tonight seeking reassurances that the rumor about the doctors having done away with Van Pelt was totally baseless. After hearing the banter of the Bullerses, however, I find myself with more doubts than ever."

Vasbinder's step seemed to falter, if only for an instant. "Not at all," he said, his pace regaining its purpose. "Consider this: as you know, the Bullerses were leading Know-Nothings. The state of their bigotry is such that it would preclude either man from ever being in the proximity of a Negro long enough to administer him any harm."

"A twisted alibi if ever there was one."

"But an alibi nevertheless," said Vasbinder. At the top of his porch steps—Vasbinder's house was well appointed, a wide front porch with a rocking chair, vines and a trellis—Vasbinder paused to catch his breath.

"Thank you, my dear," he said to Darling, laying his hand on his arm.

"Cyrus, there is something else."

The old man looked up, his eyes bunching in a beseeching tic. "What is it?"

Darling sighed, choosing his words. "The thought has entered my mind, and will not leave, it's nagging there like an itch. It's something I feel I must do, only—"

"What?" Vasbinder said with a touch of exasperation.

"Little Molly Plotner. I must know the cause of her death. I must perform an autopsy."

"You mean, resurrect—"

Darling nodded. Vasbinder sagged as though struck, his knees seemed to wobble and he staggered backwards. Darling held tight to his arm, guiding him to the rocking chair in front of the window, into which he crumbled. Darling was taken aback. He'd expected disapproval perhaps, a mild admonition maybe—but nothing to this extreme.

"Out of the question," said Vasbinder.

"I'd hoped you might be willing to help. It's not as though I'm proposing to dissect the poor girl. I merely thought an autopsy was called for, given the mysterious circumstance—"

"No, no, no, no, no," said Vasbinder, his voice regaining its strength.

"Why?"

"First of all, Enoch Plotner will never agree to it. He's a simple and strong-minded man, with little use for the medical sciences. Second, the cause of her death is in no way mysterious; it is already known—the little girl died of the fever. Pure and simple. There is nothing mysterious about it, Will, you've merely been—honey-fuggled, if you will—by her apparent recovery, which, as I believe I've already explained to you, is not at all a rare occurrence. Many a false recovery have I seen; many a young physician have I seen flamfoozled. It's the calm before the storm, the eye of the hurricane. There is simply no need for autopsy, no need for resurrection. The little girl must be left to rest in peace. I repeat, *must* be."

Darling said nothing. The call of an owl from a nearby tree, the squeak of the rocker, as his preceptor looked up, his face earnest in the nighttime shadows, the bushy white mustache gray as a ghost. Vasbinder clung to his arm. "Should you be foolish enough to spurn my good offerings and proceed regardless," he said, "and should you again be apprehended—and I have no doubt that that would be the result, given the climate of the day—there would be no holding Smathers back. No amount of negotiation or persuasion would keep him from persecuting you with singular tenacity. The consequences would be quite grave. No pun intended."

Vasbinder went quiet, but didn't release his grip; Darling realized a response was expected. "A powerful case," he said.

"Powerful is the least of it," said Vasbinder. "Promise me, Will. Promise me you won't make such a imprudent error of judgment. I couldn't bear to watch you squander your future, full of such shining promise as it is. I think it would kill me."

Darling made his way home in the cool night air, wrapping his roundabout tighter to ward off the chill. From Water Street to Pine was not a long distance, and it seemed as though he were passing through it soundlessly, invisibly, the black shadows of houses and trees, the occasional bark of a dog, the glimmer on the dirt of the street from the odd lamp in the window, all unimpressed by his presence. Everything of the world was permanent and unmoving; all would exist, with or without him.

His mother was still up. She sat by the hearth, staring into the dying fire, a blanket across her knees. "Mother," he said from the doorway, "it's past your bedtime."

"Sleep eludes me," she said, glancing at her son, then back to the fire. "After what Libby Stormer told me today."

Weariness weighed down upon him, forcing out a sigh. "And what did Libby Stormer tell you today?"

She didn't answer. Darling took off his roundabout; he wanted his bed. After a few moments more, she said, "Do you remember how your father loved his oysters? I had seen him eat two dozen at a sitting at the Red Lion Hotel up in Halton."

"He loved them boiled," said Darling.

"Boiled, broiled, deviled or stewed—he loved them all the same."

"Oysters are good." His mother said nothing. Dare he retire?

"That awful rumor isn't true, is it Will? You did no harm to that Negro, did you?"

"No, Mother. I did not. We did not."

"It would kill me to see you in jail again."

On the precipice, apparently, of killing both his mentor and his mother, Darling felt wearier than ever. "Fear not, Mother. I shall behave myself. I shall be a good son."

She tucked her blanket more tightly about her knees. Even in the dim light from the oil lamp turned low, he could see the gray of her hair, how it seemed to shine as he'd never noticed before. Darling was about to take his leave when at last his mother looked up at him once more. "Thank heavens your father is dead," she said.

The plan was this: to depart Hartsgrove at midnight on three good horses—they ruled out the use of Sandt's Dearborn wagon as too cumbersome—trusting in God to provide them with suitable conditions beneath the quarter moon which was due within the week. Clouds few enough to allow them adequate visibility to navigate the road at night, yet sufficient to prevent them being recognized by a farmer or his wife making use of the necessary, would be ideal. They did not expect to encounter another traveler at that hour, not along the lonely Coolbrook Road. Sandt took charge of the scheming: should they be seen, should suspicions be aroused for any reason, he devised an alternate route, a logging trail used by his uncle and cousins which entered the woods from the Coolbrook Road near Enoch Plotner's farm and ran across the Muddy Bottom Creek, emerging on Jimtown Road a few miles north of Hartsgrove. Sandt had purchased a map from Moses Clover, that he rolled out along the counter top, upon which he pointed out various routes and rendezvous, detailing each contingency with a possible scenario. Darling's mind, however, was elsewhere.

They were again in Sandt's Drug Store, shutters again drawn, lamp again low, rows of gold-labeled glass bottles again gleaming, but there the similarities with the earlier caucuses came to an end. Now there were no gruff, contentious voices, no repugnant deposits into the spittoon, no dipping into the whiskey pail, for it was only him, Sandt and Kathleen. Molly's meetings may well have been on a separate planet from Fudge's, and Darling spent his time entirely within Kathleen's orbit.

Her eyes gleaming green in the light from the candle that Sandt held close over the map were distraction enough, that and the way she swept her black hair back, holding it fast to her head with her pinkie finger sticking out, the better to lean over the map on the counter. Her eyebrows curled into the tiny knot above her nose as she concentrated with all the curiosity and wonder of a child studying the workings of a grasshopper.

"How shall we carry her?" he asked Kathleen. "I can't bring myself to sling the little girl over Gertie's rump like a sack of flour."

"We can make a little bier," Kathleen said, "sure, there's plenty of old boards laying about my father's factory." She took his arm. They were walking down Main Street from Sandt's to the Peace and Poverty, where her father had business; she would accompany him back to Irishtown. "What I can't understand is how you can ever bring yourself to put the knife to her a'tall—such a ghastly business."

"That is where, as Cyrus might put it, one has to employ one's powers of disassociation—it was the same with Fudge Van Pelt, of whom I was very fond. The physician must step outside the mere man and do what must be done."

"Oh, I understand the theory. But the practice is another story—I have to admire you so."

Darling hoped to remain humble. "Any physician would do the

same."

"What do you expect to find?"

"God only knows. I merely hope I possess the skills to know it when I see it. Something obvious would be a blessing, a defect or degenerative condition of some sort, perhaps of the heart, or even the brain." *Something which would indicate beyond a trace of a doubt that my treatment—or lack thereof—was not the cause of her death.* This he did not add.

"I have all faith in the world in you," she said.

"Perhaps, when the time is right, I can convince Cyrus to participate. He is very much against the resurrection—I was quite taken aback by how adamantly he opposes it—but, after the fact, after the girl is already on the table, perhaps he'll be amenable to taking part in the autopsy. He has performed more than I've even read about. His opinion would be invaluable."

"Would Josh be of any help?"

A grunt of disdain escaped from Darling.

Kathleen didn't respond. Across the street in the shadows, barely discernible in the light from the lantern of a stage in front of the American Hotel, stood Constable McClay in his suit of drab. Darling nodded; from across the street, he couldn't tell if the constable returned the nod, but Darling kept walking, resisting an unreasonable urge to quicken his pace. Kathleen didn't seem to notice. Although he'd heard nothing more about the rumor of Fudge's demise in the past few days, it was still much on his mind.

Kathleen said, "Perhaps he'll surprise you."

"Who?" said Darling.

"Why, Josh, of course. Despite all his joking and flummery, he's a real concern over the cause of her death. He's not always the flibbertigibbet."

"And how would you know about Josh's concerns?"

"He's after telling me. He told me he had a dream about the little girl that he was walking down by the sand spring one afternoon, and doesn't he come across her there, lying on her side in the pine needles holding her raggedy doll, and the sun shining in on her shoulder. And she says to him, in the dream, "Joshua—when are we going away together?"

"Josh told you that?"

"Yes. 'When are we going away together?' Isn't it lovely?"

"He said he dreamed about Molly Plotner?"

"Yes."

"I wasn't aware that he had ever set eyes on the girl." Darling felt a bile rising in his throat; a dream such as that should by all rights be his.

"Such a lovely dream regardless. And fitting so perfect."

They'd arrived at the Peace and Poverty Tavern. Darling turned to

Kathleen, her face half in shadows. "When was this?" he said.

"When was what?"

"When did Josh tell you about his dream? When were you talking to Josh?"

"Why, Will Darlin'—are you jealous?"

"Jealous? Jealous?" Darling tried to scoff. "The very notion. Have I reason to be?"

Even in the thin, pale light from the window of the tavern, he could see a small spark in the green of her eyes, though the smile he would have expected to see beneath it was absent. Her face was a blank, flat mirror throwing the question back at him. Her father emerged from the tavern, a fleshy man in a leather vest, a red array of hair and whiskers coming toward them with purpose.

Darling's eyes never left Kathleen.

"For such a learned man, you have so much to learn," she said.

Early afternoon of the next day he rode Gertie at a slow walk up Pond Street and onto Main. While the fog had lifted from the town itself, it had not lifted a great distance, and still it hovered in the air just over the hills, a gray ceiling barring any hint of sun. He headed to his office. He'd had no intention of stopping there on this day—no patient visits were scheduled—but he assumed Vasbinder would be in, and he felt an almost childlike need to turn to him. At each step in his education and maturation as a physician, it had been Vasbinder, his preceptor and mentor, who had, through humor, guile, reason, or force of personality, lent Darling whatever impetus he needed to accomplish whatever he needed to do, at the time when he needed it most.

Precisely how he hoped Vasbinder might lend him the gumption to carry on with the resurrection and autopsy of Molly Plotner was far from known to him, given Vasbinder's adamant opposition. He was hesitant to even mention the little girl's name.

Vasbinder was with a patient in the room beyond the outer office. Darling soon recognized the voice of the patient to be that of the burgess, James Butterfield, a recognition facilitated by the escalating volume of the voices. He was befuddled at first by the words he was able to make out, words such as *liberty, Kansas, free soil* and *Catholic,* in heated tones, jumbled into a variety of equally heated exclamations and, he was able to deduce after a time, accusations. Dread politics had erupted during the medical examination. The door burst open and the two men made their way through the room, faces flushed, fingers pointing.

"Had you had your way, sir, Mr. Van Pelt should have been enslaved rather than resurrected!" said Butterfield.

"Had you had your way, sir, we should be at war by now with the southern states!" said Vasbinder.

With a vehement gesture of disgust, Butterfield departed the office, huffing past the front window down Main. "He forgot his hat," said Darling, noticing the top hat on the cloak rack in the corner. Vasbinder seized the thing, flung it to the floor, and stomped it flat.

"There!" he said. "Now his hat stands as high as his virtues!" He walked in a huff of his own back into the examination room so hurriedly vacated. After a slam and a thump, a series of diminishing clunks, all became quiet again. Presently, Vasbinder emerged once more at a much slower step, looking older than when he'd gone in, making his way to the hat flat on the floor. He picked it up, poked it out and brushed it off.

"Having second thoughts?" Darling asked.

"Not at all," said Vasbinder. "Butterfield was not wearing his hat. This is my hat."

Placing his deformed hat back upon the cloak rack, Vasbinder made his way at a painfully slow pace around his desk, where he gingerly sank to his chair. From his own chair behind his little oak table, Darling watched his mentor. Vasbinder's bushy white mustache seemed to droop, and the flush that had failed to leave his face was tinged with a pale hue, the residue of sweat and heat. The old man, staring vacantly at the window in the front of the office, looked older than ever. His heart went out to him, ensnared as he seemed to be in an undeniable decline, the unrelenting grip of mortality.

As he seemed to be at his lowest, Darling decided the moment opportune. "I was thinking again about little Molly Plot—"

The end of her name was lost to Vasbinder's eruption. "Stop!" he cried, slapping his desk. "Stop thinking at all! Molly Plotner is dead! The Plotners are no longer your concern! None, in any shape or manner! Stop thinking! Your thinking—or your muddled attempts at it—has gotten you into more trouble than you're worth! Perhaps you should consider retiring from the practice of it altogether, until you cultivate the necessary skills! By the Jew's eye, *stop thinking*!" On his feet—sprightly as a youth—Vasbinder slammed the palm of his hand upon the high top of his roll-top desk, several times, exclamation points to his tirade. After the last slap, he stomped again into the examination room in back, slamming the door behind him.

Clutching his wounds, Darling walked meekly out to the street, where Gertie seemed to shy from his touch.

When next he saw him, the following afternoon at the door of his mother's home, the old man was back. Vasbinder stood with his hat in his hand—the same marred and misshapen hat he'd errantly stomped flat—contrite and apologetic. "I don't know what came over me, Will. Can you forgive an old man?"

"Certainly, Cyrus," said Darling, not at all pleased by his sibilance.

"It's just that I was…I was angry at Butterfield, and my anger and frustration became misdirected. I should know better by now, but there's no fool like an old fool, I suppose. James and I go back many years, long before our politics came between us… At any rate, can you forgive me?" He brushed at the hat in his hand, trying to wipe away the unmistakable boot print thereon.

Vasbinder's fat horse shook at his harness, jostling the shay behind him. "Of course. It was my fault as well, I never should have brought up…the little girl again."

"No, you should not have. You *must* leave the Plotner matter behind you."

"Yes. I am aware of your feelings."

"You have to move on. It is imperative. It's a part of your growth as a physician."

"Yes, Cyrus. On I shall move."

"Promise me, Will? Promise me it is behind you."

Darling looked his mentor in the eye, where the familiar tic of unabashed sincerity reappeared as he awaited the younger man's response. Noticing a smudge of indeterminate origin upon the collar of Vasbinder's shirt, Darling at that moment grew as a physician, matured as a man. He said, "Cross my heart and hope to die."

Retiring to his room that evening, Darling did not remove his shirt or his pantaloons, only his boots. Blowing out the candle, he waited. Across the street, Stormer's dog gave a howl of despair. He heard his mother, already in her bed, as she began softly singing a familiar verse, singing herself to sleep, and he wondered if it were an omen:

But poor old Grimes is now at rest, / Nor fears misfortune's frown. / He had a double-breasted vest— / The stripes ran up and down.

When he arrived at midnight at the twin oaks on the Coolbrook Road, Sandt and Kathleen were already awaiting, emerging slowly from the fog as he approached. They sat beside one another on their horses, Kathleen's with its head down, exploring the weeds by the road, Sandt's sniffing the air, so that from Darling's angle, the apparition of a two-headed horse materialized out of mist, to which the hidden moon lent a ghostly luminosity.

"I'm concerned that we shall end up lost in this soup," Sandt said.

"You would find misfortune in a four-leaf clover," said Darling. "I expect the fog will be to our advantage."

Kathleen agreed. "God is on our side," she said.

With a nudge of his heels, Darling kept Gertie walking, past his companions who fell into place behind him. They appeared to be in need of leading. "Do we have everything?"

"Three shovels, one pick," said Sandt.

"And one little bier," Kathleen said.

"And one little flask of Monongahela," said Sandt.

"Which you would do well to keep to your pocket," Darling said.

"Which I would do well to put in my stomach," muttered Sandt.

They rode in silence, the fog muffling the clops and clacks of the hooves, the occasional scurry, squawk and hoot from the woods along the way. Darling slowed, so that he was beside Kathleen, Sandt bringing up the rear. Glancing at her, Darling tried to assess her mood—was she frightened? Was she thrilled? Was she bothered, bored?—but he was largely unsuccessful, unable to discern the expression on her face, hidden as it was in the shadows by the cowl she wore over her head. Her shoulders were back and her spine was straight, however, and Darling concluded that she was not the slightest bit undecided. Sandt he didn't bother to assess.

Sandt said, "This is quite unlike our last resurrection, Will. I suppose no two shall ever be the same. Like snowflakes."

The attempt at wryness sounded to Darling like the ramblings of a man in need of reassurance, but he was not overly concerned about providing it. "That is because, Josh, unlike our previous resurrection, you are half-way sober."

"I have the perfect remedy for that," Sandt said, fishing for his flask in the pocket beneath his cloak.

It *was* quite unlike the last resurrection. On that occasion, he'd been at the periphery, an afterthought, practically a spectator; on this he was the leader, the instigator, the one upon whom the whole endeavor depended. On that occasion, beneath the full moon at the edge of the town, it seemed in his memory as though the air had been full of light and sound, and the mood, despite the banter, one of scientific investigation. This occasion was entirely spookier, eminently riskier, marked by loss and wonder.

On this occasion, the love of his life rode beside him. Was she the love of his life?

On this occasion, the bane of his existence rode behind him. Of that he had little doubt.

Leading them steadily through the fog, Darling fell into a trance of contemplation: This was a moment unlike any he had ever lived before, and unlike any he would ever live again. The singularity of the occasion struck him, leaving him feeling light-headed and quite ephemeral. A bat darted through the air not far from his ear, a black sailing object that appeared and vanished again just as swiftly; it was gone, and Darling had no empirical evidence that it had ever existed—only the uncertain chemicals that constitute memory. He had ridden down this road—where it curved through the hollow not far from the Wonderling farm—tens of times before, but never before and never again like this. The fog and the moonlight combined to lend the familiar fences and trees by the side of the road a one-dimensional, artificial quality, as though they were the ersatz scenery behind the stage upon which he was play-acting this imagined drama. He looked at his companions, neither of whom acknowledged his glance, both plodding on, lost, like him, in a singular world of his own.

A sudden flash of light; Sandt had lighted his lantern, revealing the eerie eyes of a possum glowering from the side of the road. "Josh," said Darling, "are you mad? Put that out!"

"I have no idea where we are," Sandt said. "Or *if* we are, for that matter."

In the darkness, Darling thought he detected the rolling of Kathleen's eyes.

"Put it *out*," Darling said.

Sandt shuttered his lantern. In the blackness after the light he said, "Now how do I know if I'm here?"

No one answered. Darling imagined Kathleen's head shaking in time with his own. Their eyes again accommodating the moonlit fog, they rode a while longer in silence, nearing the Plotner farm. Darling hoped his old school chum was not losing his grip. When they turned off Coolbrook Road toward Plotner's, where the woods quit and the fence line commenced, Sandt rode up and squeezed between them. Glancing, Darling saw a face too white, a flask too empty.

"Will," Sandt said in a husky whisper, "do you love me?"

"Of course," said Darling, unenthusiastically. "You're my fondest chum."

"Kathleen?" said Sandt. Kathleen didn't answer. Darling saw her shoulders shift in what he took to be a sigh. "Kathleen, do you love me?"

"Of course," she said, far more airily than Darling's response had been. They rode a few paces more, toward the grave of Molly Plotner on the rise beneath the elm tree. "You're my fondest chum as well."

Sandt leaned across to embrace Darling. Darling submitted. Then Sandt leaned across to hug Kathleen as well, but she failed to reciprocate, remaining upright and unaccommodating on her saddle, and Sandt, leaning too far, tumbled from his horse, who hopped in confusion. The other two horses joined the dance with sidling hops and prances of their own, as Sandt landed on the hard dirt of the lane with a thump and a grunt in a tangle of limbs.

Looking down, Kathleen's hand rose to her face too late to stifle the laugh that slipped out. Darling laughed as well, as Sandt tried to rein in his galloping limbs, finally wobbling to a standing position, dazed and confused. Darling dismounted, Kathleen followed suit, still laughing, each grasping for their companions, Darling attempting to shush through the laughter, as Sandt, thoroughly infected, began to laugh as well. The three leaned into one another, arms clasping shoulders, heads together, laughing as heartily and silently as they could.

The embrace slowly disassembled, the laughter ebbing away. No one remounted. Following Darling, they led their horses, finally reaching the rise and the elm and the small wooden cross, then tethering the horses in the trees behind the grave, hidden from sight. The outburst had altered the atmosphere, to Darling's mind. Now it was real. Less frightening and mysterious, more mundane and necessary, a job that had to be done, and for all the proper reasons. They stood above the patch of dirt, staring down.

With scarcely a word, they set to work. As they took their shifts with their shovels—two digging, one resting at any given time—the quality of the light seemed constantly changing, the fog thin and wispy one moment, heavy and damp the next, the moonlight going from clear to diffused and back again. He could taste the fog, like sweat without the salt. The sounds inside the silence were constant, the occasional grunt and sigh of a digger, the hoot of an owl in the woods, the never-ending bites of shovels in dirt. Darling could not take his eyes off Kathleen. With every shovelful he tossed, his glance then fell to her.

Two or three feet down, she said, "Josh—did you tell Will about your dream?"

"I did not," Sandt said. He was resting, sitting on a stump at the edge of the trees.

"Do tell him," Kathleen said.

He did. The same as Kathleen had related, Molly Plotner lying on her side by the spring, holding her doll, the sun behind her, asking Sandt, "When are you going to take me away?"

"I was not aware that you had ever seen her," Darling said.

"I had not," said Sandt. "That marked the very first time."

When Kathleen had first told him about Sandt's dream, Darling had been prepared to conclude that his chum was a liar, devising the dream to win her affection. Now he considered that Sandt was incapable of lying in a circumstance such as this. Darling considered the dream, the likelihood, the meaning, and he felt a gathering of sorts. He sensed the three of them being drawn toward the little girl; he sensed the four of them being drawn together.

"And now we shall take her away," Kathleen said.

Darling's shovel was the first to touch wood, not four feet down. He and Sandt cleared the coffin quickly. He was not surprised at the shallowness of the grave, which the smallness of the wooden box seemed naturally to follow. When it was clear, when it was ready to open, they hesitated, climbing from the hole to join Kathleen by the side of the grave where they caught their breath, and, without premeditation, bowed their heads. Then Darling went into the trees and stroked Gertie's neck, took her reins and led her out, carrying with him the little bier.

Sandt said, "What's that?"

"Why, it's the bier," Darling said.

"No," said Sandt, pointing, "not that—*that*."

What it was was clear: the light of a lantern, approaching from the direction of Plotner's farmhouse.

Approaching rapidly. Then the shout, "Who's there?" It was Plotner.

"To the trees!" said Darling.

Beyond the possible routes, an escape plan had not been formulated. Nor was one now; there was no time. Darling didn't act, he reacted; he didn't think, he yielded to instinct. As his companions were concealing themselves in the trees, he mounted Gertie, setting off.

Down the rise, the mist parting before him, he saw Plotner, quite close and also mounted, the lantern held before him at arm's length. "Stop!" cried Plotner. "Who's there?"

Darling dashed down the lane into the gathering fog.

"Stop!" Plotner's voice was farther behind him. "Stop, or I'll shoot!"

A clutch of chills took hold of his back, as he crouched low over Gertie's neck. Cracking her reins, jabbing his heels, he urged her on to a gallop. He relied on their memory, his and Gertie's, for the lane was thick with fog, the light faint and diffused, only a few yards visible before him.

The sound of a blast behind him. Darling imagined—heard?—the ball streaking through the mist by his ear, as he willed himself the size of a flea.

Gertie flew. Where the fence line ended, he turned onto Coolbrook Road, slowing for a moment to gauge the pursuit. He heard a rattle of hooves not far behind, then another blast. In an instant Gertie was off with scarcely a nudge from Darling, galloping down the road. Not two hundred yards on, he pulled her reins, steering her onto the logging trail Sandt had pointed out on his map. The trees and fog were thicker off the road, and the trail was little more than a suggestion. Darling slowed, unfamiliar with the path. He wondered if he'd lost Plotner, if perhaps he was still galloping down the Coolbrook Road, in pursuit of a shadow.

He heard the sound of hooves: Plotner had followed. Darling set off again, rushing maddeningly slowly, the alien terrain visible scarcely farther than Gertie's nose in the mist that was thickening. His teeth were clenched, his skin and clothing soaked with fog and sweat, his hands cramped and aching from gripping so fiercely the reins. Now and then he hesitated, turning an ear behind him, where inevitably he heard the sound of hooves still following, though never, it seemed, growing closer. The trail was just as foreign to Plotner.

The path grew more haphazard, through terrain that was heading downhill, till finally he heard the rippling waters of Muddy Bottom Creek, and found himself in the midst of random trees, in the forest itself, the trail having vanished. He pulled Gertie up in the midst of a cluster of evergreens in the fog, and waited. He listened for the sounds of pursuit; he waited.

After what must have been a quarter hour, he was prepared to conclude that he'd lost his pursuer, or vice versa. Though the thought occurred and wouldn't let go that perhaps Plotner was waiting as well, nearby, waiting him out, waiting for Gertie and him to make their move.

So he continued to wait. As he did so, his blood gradually cooled, the pounding in his temples gradually abated, and the chill in his bones gradually spread. His thoughts began to move beyond mere survival. They moved beyond the image of himself lying torn asunder and dead in the road, to less deadly consequences. Had he been seen clearly enough by Plotner to be recognized? With the little girl's body missing—he assumed his companions had finished the job they came to do—how quickly, if at all, would suspicion be directed toward him?

The suspicion, especially, of Levi Smathers?

Finally, he led Gertie out of the evergreens, stopping in a little clearing to listen once more. He heard nothing but the whisper of the running creek waters. Slowly he led her through the trees and the fog, wandering uphill on the path of least resistance, the logging trail still nowhere apparent. He was cautious and wary, his breath coming shallow, expecting at any instant the blast of the musket, the sudden and violent appearance of Plotner.

Eventually, he mounted Gertie again, riding her at a slow walk. His path of least resistance grew straighter and wider, and he realized that he had found the logging trail again, or the trail had somehow found him.

On the Coolbrook Road he exhorted his horse to a brisker canter, feeling utterly exposed and precarious. In this way he rode into town. The journey was over in what seemed like an instant, which was quite odd, given that it had seemed to take a lifetime while he was living it. He rode straight to the willow at the edge of Irishtown.

His companions awaited, both of them.

"Thank God," said Kathleen, her face a mask of worry and concern.

Dismounting, Darling embraced her. Then he clasped Sandt's shoulder. Then he looked around, seeing only their two horses tied to the bush. "Where is she?"

"That," said Sandt, "is the question of the hour."

"What do you mean?"

"She was not there," said Kathleen. "Her coffin was entirely empty."

"Empty?"

"Or, to put it another way," said Sandt, "her coffin was entirely empty."

He met his mother in the doorway just before dawn, leaving the house as he was entering. She was an early riser and had business at the rectory. Darling, weary and bleary, frayed and disheveled, prayed she'd conclude that he'd been called away for medical reasons. He had frozen all the facts at his disposal, all the urgent wonder, in his mind, and preserved them there in a block, ready for thawing and careful dissection later, after he'd slept and was thoroughly restored. He said not a word to his mother, and she only five to him.

"Church is in one hour," she said, sternly, even for her.

Thus, it was nearly four hours before he was finally able to sleep. When next he awoke, however, he was only moderately rested and restored, far from thoroughly, for where he next awoke was on the hard plank bunk in his familiar cell in the old stone jailhouse, having been arrested as he walked from the church.

6: October 30, 1857: Napoleon Makes a Splash

When Hen walked into town on Friday, the day after Fudge died, a clear new day when the air felt washed and unfamiliar, he didn't know why he was going, and he didn't know what he would do when he got there. He didn't know how fast he should walk. *Move it, Hen*—the words kept shouting in his head, and his tendency each time was to hurry, as had never been his tendency before, when Fudge had actually been alive to utter the words. The absence of the utterer seemed to lend an urgency to the imaginary words that had never accompanied them in real life. So much so, so much his actual hurry, that by the time he reached his bootblack chair in the back corridor of the American Hotel beneath the little sign of the boot, by the half door that was closed beneath the note chalked on Fudge's board in Fudge's hand—*Closed Up Shop – Back In A Jiffy*—he was so weary he sat in his chair to nap.

Though napping was his intent, it was met with some difficulty. What would become of Fudge's boot shop, all his tools, all the boots and shoes lined up neatly on the shelves, the leather and lapstone and cobbler's bench all idle and waiting? He wondered what would become of him and his bootblack chair—after all, the same reasoning applied now as before, namely, what need of a bootblack with no bootmaker to craft the boots to be blacked? He wondered too if Lucindy was all right, if her and the Widow Winter and the other ladies of Little Brier—Irene Plato and Esther Nips and Ophelia McManigle—could do Fudge proud in preparing him for the ground. And he wondered about Augustus, if that boy might go off and do some fool thing, try to find out who had stoned him and Fudge, and burn down a barn or a house or two, bring the wrath of the white world down on Little Brier. And what about the next cargo? Who would handle that, without Fudge? It struck Hen then, an unfamiliar flash of recognition that he didn't particularly relish, like lightning too close, that all of his fresh wondering amounted to downright *Worry*. Through the years, Fudge had done all the worrying that needed to be done, as had Yellow Charlie before him, but now they were both gone, worried no more, and someone was obliged to pick up the fallen colors. Hen wondered—worried—if that burden had fallen to him. Such was the nature of his wondering—his worrying—that when he finally slipped into his nap, it was fitful and troubled and far from refreshing.

What would become of Lucindy and Napoleon and Belle, all alone now, with no man? That was cause for worry, he suspected, if anything was. Lucindy, sitting by the hearth with Fudge, her hand on his knee as she told the story—any story, every story, about her father, a big man, the only man who could stack three barrels of flour on top of one another at the Harrisburg grocery store where such stacking was done for sport, about her mother's buttermilk chicken, or Cornelius Nips taking a tumble into the creek, Belle's first words, anything—always with her hand on Fudge's knee just as natural as can be. Though five times—Hen, close to dozing, remembered each time over the years—five times it had been him, Hen, who'd ended up beside her when her story had commenced, and each time her hand had fallen to his knee, just as natural as it had ever fallen to Fudge's. Sitting back in his chair, eyes closed, hands clasped over his belly, Hen could feel a warmth on the top of his knee where Lucindy's hand had touched. And he saw Fudge's gap-tooth smile disappear, saw him staring down at the hand on the knee.

Fudge's gap-tooth smile was nowhere to be seen after the ladies had laid him out. He was a handsome corpse, considering the raw material they'd had to work with, his countenance stately and proud, and everyone agreed the ladies had done a fine job putting his best foot forward. Lucindy purchased new clothes, a yellow flannel shirt, a bow tie and corduroy trousers, and they placed a pair of his softest leather slippers on his feet to bury him in, and he was pronounced altogether fit for eternity. He was to be buried in Hartsgrove, in the old graveyard on top of the hill, where the founders and leading white citizens of the town were interred, and where few of the denizens of Little Brier had ever been able to afford the price of a plot in the back of the lot. Lucindy, however, insisted. Fudge had worked hard at his craft, she said, and lived a dignified life; he would be buried with dignity, in a dignified place.

And in a dignified manner. Black plumes were mounted on the sides of Solomon McManigle's wagon, Fudge's pine coffin was taken up and nearly all of the citizens of Little Brier followed from the cluster of shacks out Little Brier lane, down Coolbrook Road and into Hartsgrove. Up Pond Street, down Main, up Prospect toward the graveyard, the white folks of the town watched with various manners and attitudes, some barely noticing, some glancing with frowns, some doffing their hats in respect. Dr. Means, and Dr. Means alone of the white population, took his place in the procession behind the wagon bearing Fudge.

Hen remained not far behind Lucindy in her long, black veil, holding the hands of Napoleon and Belle on either side, just behind the wagon. Augustus made his way to Hen's side, and nudged him on Main Street. "You see anyone was throwing them stones? You see any them bastards, you point 'em out."

"Listen to me, boy," Hen said. "Never mind 'bout who throwing them stones. You let me worry 'bout who throwing them stones." What would Fudge say? "We got crackers enough sniffing around our business already, we don't need no more."

Augustus regarded him askance, eyebrows nearly high enough to pry his eyes open. Fudge's words coming from Hen's mouth had taken him aback, much as they had taken aback Hen himself. Neither man was sure where they'd come from.

The procession climbed the steep slope of Prospect Street to the graveyard, carved from the forest at the north edge of town, then past the monument to Eli Hart, the town's founder, past the monuments and mausoleums, beneath the sprawling chestnut tree, to the plot where the freshly dug grave awaited. Cornelius Nips, a stocky man of substance, his head as bald as Fudge's boot leather, was Little Brier's preacher, presiding over a service every Sunday at the old barn on the Lemon farm which served as their Praise House. When the congregation was settled, he took his place by the grave and raised his face toward the sky. "The Lord is my shepherd," he said, in words that resounded, "I shall not want!"

By the time the second line commenced, "He maketh me to lie down in green pastures," every man, woman and child, including Dr. Means, was speaking or mouthing the words—"he leadeth me beside the still waters." By the time the psalm concluded—"Surely goodness and mercy shall follow me all the days of my life, and I will dwell in the house of the Lord forever"—the rocky harmony was as soothing to Hen's ears as the babble of the Little Brier's waters. Cornelius Nips's face by then was bowed reverently, his voice still loud and strong. After the psalm was over he paused, and Hen could hear a pebble fall into the grave.

"I knowed this man," Cornelius said then, his face rising up. "I knowed this man, Brother Fudge Van Pelt, and I loved him. Oh, I didn't love him because he was a religious man—why, even Brother Fudge would not of claimed he was no religious man. Seldom was he seen at our meeting come a Sunday, seldom was his head seen bowed down in prayer, but I can tell you this, brothers and sisters, I *can* tell you this—the Lord dwelled in Brother Fudge's heart. How is it I knows this? Because Brother Fudge, he told me so. Oh, he didn't tell me so in no words, no sir, Brother Fudge, he too bashful a man to go bragging 'bout the Lord dwelling up there in his own heart, he too modest to go blowing on his own horn 'bout where the Lord be dwelling. Brother Fudge, he done told me this by the way he lived his life. Never was a man work harder for his family than what ol' Brother Fudge done, and I know what you saying, I know what you thinking, how hard a man can work anyways setting all the day long up there in that shop, not out in no field with his hoe or his rake, not out in no woods with his axe or his saw. But I seen him sweat aplenty over his hammer and his stone, I seen him sweat aplenty trying to poke a long needle through a piece of leather harder'n iron, trying to get them long shears of his to cutting through a piece of leather harder'n a white man's heart"—here Hen and a few others glanced toward Dr. Means, whose face remained passive—"jus' to make a nice soft shoe for somebody po' aching foot. He ain't gots to work in no fields or no woods, cause he got a skill, brothers and sisters, a *skill*, and that skill was the Lord dwelling up there in his heart and making His way out Brother Fudge's hands."

Cornelius's praise of Brother Fudge continued, the fine craftsman he'd been, the hard worker and earnest provider, the dignified citizen, the lover of the Lord, but Hen's focus had begun to fade, and he found his eyes wandering again to Lucindy, standing with her children, staring not at the rough coffin lying there holding her man, but down into the hole in the earth that soon would have him. He looked at others in the congregation as well, at Hiram Appleby, old and feeble, leaning on his stick, his spectacles glinting on his face, hiding his eyes from the world, much as Augustus's eyes were hidden, and he looked at Solomon McManigle, the scars on his back hidden by his best threadbare brown suit, his big black, pock-marked face bowed down. But always his gaze returned to Lucindy.

Cornelius spoke of the glory of Brother Van Pelt, who now, even as they sang his praises, was walking down golden streets, in a new white suit of clothes, wearing a starry crown on his head, silver slippers on his feet, feasting on milk and honey and chattering with the angels. Hen was watching a pair of crows watching from the dead limb of an oak tree high above the graveyard. His mind was called back to the funeral when Cornelius broke into song, for when Cornelius broke into song, everyone was called to notice. The man had an awful singing voice that had been compared to the caw of a crow in pain, but what he lacked in tone, he accounted for in vigor. *Jordan River, I'm bound to go*, he sang, or attempted to sing, an old, familiar hymn, and everyone sang the next line, instinctively, reflexively, the words coming clear and strong, perhaps, Hen suspected, in a great gush of relief that the sermon was finally over, *Bound to go, bound to go*, and Cornelius cried out again, *Jordan River, I'm bound to go*, and the congregation concluded the verse, *And bid 'em fare ye well.*

Then Cornelius commenced the next verse, *My Brother Hiram, I'm*

bound to go—
  And all the voices boomed back, *Bound to go, bound to go—*
  My Brother Hiram, I'm bound to go, bawled Cornelius.
  And bid 'em fare ye well, came the response.
  Brother Henry was next, and Hen shifted nervously on his feet, mouthing the words of the chorus as all eyes turned to him, and then came *Brother Solomon, Brother Marcus,* and on and on they went, until every man in the gathering had been singled out by Cornelius in his song, every man but Dr. Means. Hen wondered if Cornelius purposely passed over the white man because he was a white man, or because he didn't know his first name—which Hen suspected was Steven. Hen thought he saw Lucindy cringe, but whether it was the omission of Dr. Means, the quality of Cornelius's voice, or some other pang, he couldn't be sure.
  When the hymn was exhausted, Cornelius nodded toward Hiram Appleby. Hiram was Little Brier's elder, having settled there not long after Yellow Charlie, and he'd known every citizen. He hobbled on his stick over to coffin. He coughed and spat and cleared his throat and spat again, then said as loud as his creaking throat would allow, "I too knowed Brother Fudge. Knowed him well. He was my friend. Why, I knowed Brother Fudge since he was no bigger'n the hind leg of a jackrabbit, and I watched him grow up into the fine man he become." Hen noticed in the corner of his eye Augustus looking at him. Hiram went on, "Never was a finer man, never a more Christian man neither. Once, back in the winter of '36, back when I was laid up with a bad croup and couldn't get my family nothing to eat, Brother Fudge done borrow—some would say stole, but a good Christian like Brother Fudge done borrow—three chickens from the farmer he work for over by Coolbrook and brang 'em to me and the chil'en."
  Augustus nudged Hen. "Thought Fudge come here after he was already growed."
  "He did," whispered Hen.
  "Then what the hell ol' Hiram talking about?"
  "He talking about Tom Hunt, I expect, a Indian died couple years back. Ol' Hiram, he get confused sometime."
  Augustus nodded his head and chewed on his cheek.
  Hiram went on about how Brother Fudge had taught his youngest son to track and to hunt with a bow and arrow, and when Hiram was done with his praise, Cornelius and several others in the congregation cried out, "Amen, brother!"
  Then Cornelius nodded at Hen.
  Hen pretended he didn't see him.
  When Cornelius nodded again and Hen still feigned unawareness, Cornelius called, "Brother Henry—come up here, say a few words in praise of Brother Fudge—your best friend."

Slowly, Hen made his way to the coffin, to the spot Brother Hiram had vacated moments before. He cleared his throat as if to speak, but his mind was a tumult of emptiness, and nothing would come. He saw the faces of the congregation, one by one, each expectant, each awaiting his words. Finally, he said, "Ol' Fudge—never was a better man," and the words calmed him a bit. Taking a breath, he said, "Never was a better friend, neither. Me and ol' Fudge—Brother Fudge—we was pals. Ol' Fudge always in a hurry. Always telling me get a move on. Every time I stop to make some water"—here Hen hesitated, wondering if that had been a proper thing to mention with women and children present, but by then there was no turning back—"every time I stop to do what a man gotta do, only he gotta do it more and more oftener older he get, Fudge always stomping his foot down and telling me to hurry on up, we ain't gots all day. And I tell him, hold your horses, boy—you be a old man one of these days."

The congregation shuffled and shifted and smiled, waiting for the next anecdote from Fudge's great pal. "Guess I was wrong 'bout that," Hen said, and he turned and shuffled back to where he'd been standing.

There was a long silence, Cornelius staring after him with a frown until finally he nodded to Solomon McManigle, and Brother Solomon took his place by the coffin and began to praise Brother Fudge. Hen couldn't hear. His mind was too busy raking over and sorting through all the things he could have said—all the things he *should* have said. It dawned on him he'd not earned a single *Amen, brother*, and he realized how lacking his words had been, and he looked at Lucindy, still downcast, and wondered what she must be thinking of her husband's friend, an old fool incapable of uttering proper praise. The churning raged on in his brain, oblivious to the words of Solomon, to the words of Marcus Swan that followed and to all the rest.

When the last hymn ended, there were cries of *Amen*, and Cornelius with a nod of his head and a grand, waving gesture, signified the service was over, and folks began to drift away. Some lingered in separate clusters, some watching Lucindy watching the men who were filling the grave. Hen sidled away to stand by himself. Napoleon drifted over to Augustus and several of the younger men and boys, while Belle stood holding the hand of Ophelia McManigle. Lucindy lingered alone by the side of the grave. The late October air was cold, the sun behind thin clouds of little use, and Hen saw her shiver, the black veil over her black dress of little more use than the sun. What would Fudge do? Hen took off his old warmus, walked over to Lucindy and placed it over her shoulders. She shook it off. Or did it fall? Hen picked it up and began to place it on her shoulders again.

Lucindy shrugged away, turning angrily, slapping at Hen's arm. "Stop it, Hen," she said. "Just stop!"—her voice rising—"Go! Just leave me be!"

Next day he walked again to the American Hotel. The place was nearly empty. He stood in the back corridor beside his bootblack chair, hand on his hips, nothing on his mind. Nothing would come to his mind, nothing but a vague, humming thing he supposed was called worry. He stared at the chair, at the half door beneath Fudge's hand-lettered sign, at the little sign of the boot. He turned and walked away.

He climbed Prospect Street toward the graveyard, beneath the chestnut tree, shuffling through fallen, dead leaves, to the freshly filled grave. He took off his floppy hat and knelt, his face stinging with the memory of his failure to properly praise his friend, with Lucindy lashing out at him. There was no marker yet. He didn't know what Lucindy intended. She hadn't shared her plans with him. He didn't know what to do. He'd forgotten what grief was. Hearing the stamp of a hoof, he turned and saw Dr. Darling, mounted, riding toward him at a walk.

"Henry," said Darling, nodding. "Paying your respects?"

Standing, Hen returned the nod. "I am. Gonna miss this ol' nigger."

"Yes. God rest him. How's his family?"

Hen kept nodding. His next words took him by surprise. "Mr. Doc, I reckon it shoulda been me," he said. "I's the oldest nigger here. It should rightly a been me."

"I know, Henry, you'll miss him, but… You must try to remember the good times you had. Recall what a friend he was, and be glad for it."

He looked away from the doctor, down at the grave. "We had us some good times all right, Mr. Doc, up there on Little Brier Creek."

"Good, Hen. That's what to think of. That's what to remember."

Hen shook his head. He turned his back to the doctor, kneeling again.

"Hen," said Darling. "Did you pay your last respects? Before he died?"

Of course he hadn't. Dr. Means had forbidden it. Hen just shook his head.

"Now, you mustn't abuse yourself, Henry. The fever can be very contagious. It's laid many a brave man low."

Hen allowed the words to settle in. Dr. Darling thought it had been cowardice, not another doctor's orders, that had kept Hen from his dying friend's bedside. You'd think white doctors could get their stories straight. But it didn't pay to contradict one, even one as harmless as Darling, and so Hen only said, "Mr. Doc? You reckon ol' Fudge can hear me now?"

Darling hesitated a moment before answering. "I'm sure of it, Black Hen," he said. "Although you might want to speak a bit louder."

Hen listened to Darling ride away. He shook his head at the foolish young doctor.

Then he spoke to his friend. "Fudge? Fudge Van Pelt? Can you hear me down there?"

It wasn't long before Fudge answered. *Course I can hear you. Ain't nothing wrong with my ears. My heart done stop beating, but my ears is working just fine.*

This made sense to Hen. After a while he said, "Listen. I know I's the oldest and I should of died before you did and all. But they ain't nothing I can do 'bout that now."

Don't be a dunderheaded nigger, Fudge said. *Oldest gots nothing to do with it.*

Hen thought about it a while. He supposed Fudge was right. Next, he told him he was sorry he messed up his praise yesterday, and he told him about trying to throw his warmus around Lucindy when she seemed to be shivering. He told Fudge how she shook it off, then yelled at him and told him to get away from her. "In case you wasn't watching," he added.

Women, was all Fudge said.

"I didn't mean nothing by it." Fudge didn't say anything for a while. Hen hoped he wasn't thinking about Lucindy's hand on Hen's knee, or the way Hen always got all tongue-tied and light-headed whenever he got too close to Lucindy.

Then Fudge said, *You ain't never gonna understand a woman if you live to be a hundred years old. No sense even trying.*

Hen felt relieved. "I reckon."

A minute later Fudge spoke again. He said, *Listen. I wants you to watch after her. Ain't nobody else gonna do it now, ol' Solomon, Cornelius, Hiram, they gots their own families to watch after. And 'Gustus. You keep that nigger the hell away from her, or they be hell to pay. You mark my words. Don't trust that young buck nigger. And he too young for her to boot. Course you too old for her. But watch on over her. You do that. You hear?*

Hours later, heading back home to Little Brier, Hen carried with him an orange from Clover's General Store. He'd had to clean floors, scrub spittoons and muck stalls all afternoon to earn the orange, and it was after dark by the time he got back to Little Brier, and he was bone weary. He carried the orange in his hand all the way, not entrusting it to his pockets, which had proved themselves untrustworthy any number of times. Lucindy loved oranges.

The dwellings of Little Brier sat hushed and tilted among the trees in the shadows of a hidden moon. Beyond the main cluster of shacks, Hen heard the sounds of voices and laughter, coming from Fudge's house—Lucindy's house now—and he headed in that direction, orange in hand.

The door was open, folks going in and out, some congregated in front of the house. Sam Cash, a blacksmith, standing with his powerful arms crossed, swapped nods with Hen, as did Hiram Appleby and Marcus Swan. Augustus Hamilton came through with his own arms full of firewood, Napoleon trailing behind with another load. "Hen—where you been?" Augustus said.

"Been working," Hen said.

Augustus stopped for a moment and regarded him suspiciously. "I thought you done broke yourself of that habit years ago."

Hen threw back his head and laughed. It felt good. Others laughed as well, and Augustus set the logs by the hearth, throwing another on the fire, though the fire was already roaring.

Lucindy inched her chair back from the hearthside. "Enough, 'Gustus—no more logs. You like to burn Fudge's place down around my ears, and I ain't got no place else to go." She fanned herself, staring at the flames. Beside her sat Irene Plato, fat and homely, with a lump on her cheek, and lips like the rim of a jug.

Lucindy's bone-white table was laden with crocks and pots and platters—biscuits and gravy, pies and Johnnycake, hog and hominy, a rich jumble of aromas that set Hen's stomach to growling. Spotting a speck of gravy on her table, he tried to wipe it away with his thumb, but it wouldn't be wiped, and Hen realized then it was the stain from the drop of blood that Fudge had dripped there. He looked at the orange in his hand, walked over and handed it to Lucindy.

She took it, looked up at Hen, then back to the orange, without a word.

Irene looked at the orange and frowned suspiciously. "Where you get that from?"

Augustus' narrow eyes narrowed even more. "You steal that there orange?"

"I ain't steal no orange." Hen, for the most part, had given up stealing. He'd never been a serious practitioner, but he'd more or less given up the practice altogether after the time he'd tried to filch three eggs off J. Eberly in his grocery stall at the American Hotel. Eberly turned his back to measure out flour for a farmer, and when he came back he must have noticed his basket of eggs was lighter. Hen had stuck them under his floppy hat. Eberly came over and clapped him on the head, hard, saying, "Black Hen, a man ought to take off his hat in the company of ladies," breaking every egg, slime and bits of shell running down Hen's face. Eberly laughed, as did everybody else. Hen said to Augustus, "Done worked all afternoon for Moses Clover for that orange, mucking out his stalls and such."

"That white son of a bitch sure know how to drive a bargain," Augustus said. "And you figure a afternoon hard labor a fair price for one piddly little orange?"

"That orange for Lucindy," Hen said.

Lucindy looked up at Hen, but Hen was incapable of reading anything her face might be saying. She looked again into the fire, cradling the orange in her lap with both hands.

Smoke began to drift into the room, hanging low, the chatter growing louder as everybody went about the business of remembering Fudge. Hen was hungry but he couldn't bring himself to eat. Solomon McManigle told the same story he told at every funeral, the story about the time Jack, his old dog, had carried a shovel up and dropped it at his feet, then laid down on the ground and died. He'd brought the shovel for Solomon to bury him with, the story went, as it went every time. Hen stared at the orange in Lucindy's hand, the orange nobody seemed to notice any more. It sat there, rising and falling in her lap with the rocking of the chair, as if floating on the sea. Hen stared, spellbound. The orange bobbed gently, then suddenly pitched up as Lucindy made a gesture, speaking a word to Irene Plato that Hen didn't hear. Hen, the spell broken, grew too hot, and went outside. There he grew too cold. Now that November was here he was cold all the time, except when he was inside by a fire too big. His warmus was tattered and didn't keep the heat in well or the cold out well, and there were holes in the knees of his britches. November brought in the cold, no doubt about that. October a man could manage. He imagined his chimney would need some repair before he could risk a fire.

He imagined it was God clapping him on the head, breaking all the eggs up under his hat, and all the egg running down his face, and all the angels laughing.

He might have been sleeping, or maybe not, it was difficult to tell nowadays, his mind busy with thoughts or dreams of Lucindy, the roaring fire and the table full of food. His heart was aching, his body cold, his stomach hungry. What woke him up—if indeed he'd been asleep—was the sound of the leather hinge on his door giving a sleepy squeak. He saw a dark figure enter, pause, then cross the dirt floor coming toward him. Lucindy.

He struggled to free himself from the nest of bags and blankets into which he'd burrowed. He sat up as Lucindy sat down beside him, on the far end of his corn-shuck mattress.

Leaning forward, she handed him something that turned out to be a piece of cold mutton on a warm biscuit. "Here," she said. "Man oughtn't sleep on a empty stomach."

He only nodded, though he supposed she couldn't see.

"Ain't you going to eat it?"

"In a little bit," he said.

"I brung this too." She held up a round object that gradually assumed the color of orange in his eye. "We gonna share this together."

His stomach grumbled. Finally, when it seemed the only thing left to do, he took a bite of biscuit and mutton and chewed slowly, gratefully. His teeth weren't good any more. She began to peel the orange, the smell of it quickly filling the little shanty.

After a while, she said, "Well." He swallowed. She said, "Gonna have to get along without him now," and there was a glimmer on her cheeks in the darkness.

"We manage," he said. "We get by."

"How you gonna get by, ol' Hen? How *you* gonna get by now?"

"Me? Like I always done," he said, feeling free to frown, knowing she couldn't see his face anyhow. "You the widow, not me. You gots the family, not me."

Her shoulders moved in what he took to be a shrug. "Fudge, he saved up a little. We gots that. Napoleon, he can work. I can sew. Go into town, get some work."

"What about all them boots?" he wondered. "All them tools and such."

She didn't answer right away. It was impossible to think of the tools and the boots without thinking of Fudge sitting there in the shop, hammering, nails in his mouth, cutting, sewing, the long needle popping through the leather, the grinding snip of the shears, the dull tap of the hammer on the leather-clad stone. Fudge in command, master of his craft, bony head, gap-tooth smile and all. "Got to look into selling the trade," she said. "Don't know who to, though. Don't got no idea."

"'Gustus, he might know somebody," he said, then thought better of it. "I find out. You let that up to me." He could talk to Cornelius. Not Augustus.

She handed him a piece of the orange, and they ate in the quiet. He wondered how late it was. It seemed a shade lighter, the paper-covered window a shade brighter. Over the gurgling creek waters he heard the call of an owl, and Lucindy said, "I thought it was a real nice service yesterday, didn't you?"

Hen froze, unsure of her real meaning. "I's sorry," he said.

"Sorry? What you sorry 'bout?"

"Sorry I couldn't think of nothing when it come to praising Fudge."

Lucindy was quiet a moment. Then she seemed to jiggle. Then the giggle escaped. "Oh Lordy, Hen," she said, slapping her leg, "I never heard such praise like that in all my born days, all 'bout making water and stamping foots and hurrying up—oh, Lordy." And she laughed, and Hen laughed too, or tried.

Just as quickly she quit, wiping at her cheeks in the dark. She said, "Don't know what I's going to do 'bout a marker for his grave. Gots to do something. What you think, Hen?"

"Why don't you let that up to me? Let me take care of that."

"You take care of that by your own self?"

"Course I can. You just let that up to me."

She sighed. "You do him proud. You hear?"

"I hear," he said. "Don't you worry none."

"Something with some dignity," she said. "Dignified man need a dignified marker. Something stone'd be nice. Though I don't know how we gonna pay for that."

"You let me figure that out." Sweat broke out on his forehead and palms, trickling down his neck. He hadn't the least idea how to go about it, what he was getting into, where to turn.

Birds commenced their morning songs and he listened to them, the birds, the wolf, the scurrying creatures, and all of their voices and noises seemed to have something to say about Fudge. Fudge and the marker for his grave. Fudge, the man in a hurry, the man standing in the middle of the road in all his idle, impatient industriousness, tapping his foot, waiting for Hen to catch up to him, and just as quickly it was Fudge in his coffin, in the ground, tapping his foot, drumming his fingers, waiting for Hen to catch up. Some while later there came a call, soft and urgent, a call that brought Hen straight around, and Lucindy too, the unmistakable call of Silas McKay.

The cool air carried a scent of rotting pumpkin. They made their way in the early gloaming to Fudge's cabin, around to the trailhead in back. There stood McKay with a man, a woman and a child, so black as to be nearly invisible in the shadows of the trees, were it not for the colors of their clothing. The man was tall and skinny, the woman small with bony shoulders, a dress hanging from her as though from a scarecrow. The child, a little girl maybe two, hung from her daddy's neck, face buried beneath his chin. McKay nodded, smiled. "Some folks here I'd like you to meet."

Augustus appeared around the corner of the cabin.

"Ah," said McKay, still smiling. "Welcome, young man. This is Jemmy"—he gestured toward the tall, skinny man, who nodded jerkily—"this is Liza and the baby is Lulu. And these folks are Henry—Black Hen we call him, with much affection—this young man is Augustus, and Lucindy is the wife of the man I've been telling you about, Fudge Van Pelt." At that McKay raised the eyebrows of his big, red face in a question. "Where is the man himself?"

Lucindy pointed her jaw. "My husband done gone and passed away. Four days ago."

McKay staggered, shaking his head as though at a buzzing fly. "Fudge? How?"

"Fever," said Lucindy.

From the top of a tall pine nearby came the mean caw of an early crow, to which Absalom responded down the way, equally mean. "Why, he was never sick a day in his life," McKay said.

"Amen, brother," said Augustus, the first words he'd uttered.

"I can't believe it," said McKay. "No wonder Jacob couldn't find him yesterday—couldn't find Dr. Means, either." When a cargo was on the way, McKay sent his oldest son, Jacob, to alert the next station.

"You tell him look for me next time," Augustus said. "Me and ol' Hen."

McKay stared for a moment at Augustus, then at Hen. "Will any changes be forthcoming? Any new arrangements? I wasn't aware…"

"No changes," Augustus said. "Leave them folks with me and Hen, same as you always done. They in good hands."

Jemmy shifted the baby, Lulu, to his other arm and took the hand of his wife, Liza. The big white man shifted his considerable weight to his other foot. "Are you sure there's…"

"They in good hands now," Augustus repeated. "Ain't they, Hen?"

Hen looked at his hands and he nodded. Sometimes a nod was as good as a word.

The runaways fed and sleeping, Hen and Augustus rode into town, Jupiter hitched solo to the sturdy red wagon where Augustus had swapped the pole for shafts. The horse plodded along very much on his own until they reached the top of Pond Street, where Augustus pulled him away from Main, down Cherry. Pulling up in front of Dr. Means's office, the two men stepped down.

The bell on the front door jangled, and Means, wearing a white apron, stepped out of the back room. "Gentlemen," said the little man, his red goatee bobbing, "please, join me." He gestured with the small instrument in his hand, a club-shaped pestle. Returning to his station behind a high table, he inserted the pestle into a container, a mortar, and continued to grind whatever ingredients he'd been grinding when they'd arrived. "Let me just finish this business," he said. "It mustn't be exposed too long to the air." Elbow high, he ground away. Hen and Augustus looked around the little room. There was scarcely a free inch available, the floors and walls filled with the high table, with cabinets and shelves holding mortars and pestles, scales, clear and amber glass jars and bottles, jugs of every description, boxes, books and tins. There were two high stools, row upon row of small drawers with labels and shiny white knobs, and, hanging from twine strung between the wall boards and the single tall window, a variety of plants and herbs in various stages of drying. Hen saw marigold, dandelion and goldenseal, but most of the others, some familiar, some foreign, were a mystery. A medley of scents filled the air.

"Making up a magic potion, Doc?" Augustus said.

Means made a scoffing sound. "Magic indeed. If only."

Hen noticed that he could actually see the whites of Augustus' eyes, they were that wide, scanning every inch of the room, every bottle, plant and root. "Quite a harvest you got in here—how do you keep tabs of which ones does what?"

"Experience, know-how, superior intellect," Means said with a smile. "That, and of course the *Materia Medica* there." He nodded toward the dog-eared volume laying open on the table near the mortar.

Hen grunted. "Ain't nothing in there for the fever?"

Means looked up sharply, before his face softened again, and he shook his head. "A most confounding case, Fudge's. Many a man, woman and child in far worse condition than he have I treated with the same prescription, almost universally with positive results. I'm still at a loss. We in the medical arts and sciences still have so much more to learn."

They watched him scrape off the pestle with a long, slender spoon, then spoon the yellowish compound from the mortar into an amber glass jar and seal it. "I've been meaning to talk to you both," he said, removing his apron, hanging it on the hook affixed to the side of the cabinet. He sighed, examining his hands on the table between him and the two black men. Hen shuffled his feet. "Life goes on," Means said. "Alas, we loved Fudge dearly, and we shall miss him, but life does go on. So I must ask: Will the two of you be following in his footsteps as far as our business is concerned, our mutual business?"

"Already in them footsteps," Hen said.

Means cocked his head.

"McKay delivered another cargo this morning, Doc," said Augustus.

Means's face opened in surprise. "He did? I was unaware...of course, I was called out of town for the better part of the day yesterday, a tragic carriage accident down in Blue Run. I had conveyed the news—equally tragic, of course—about Fudge, but it looks as though word must not yet have traveled down the line."

"That what you wanted to see us about?" Augustus said.

"That's it exactly," the doctor said, flashing his smile, holding his thumbs up before him. "I'm delighted it's settled. I'm delighted the Little Brier station is still in good hands."

"Good hands," Hen said.

As they were taking their leave, Augustus hesitated, examining the door, swinging it back and forth, jangling the bell. "Got a lock for his here door, Doc?"

"Why, no," said Means. "I don't consider it necessary—there's nothing of value here to anyone but me."

"So anybody could walk on in here any ol' time?"

"They could—and a good thing if they're ill."

"Walk on in here any ol' time, take a stroll in back?"

"I suppose," Means said. "Why do you ask?"

"No particular reason," Augustus said, and the two black men left, followed by the doctor's frown. Augustus worked on his own frown, deep in thought, and Hen didn't pay much heed till halfway home, passing out of earshot of the sawmill, when Augustus spat over the side and said, "You trust them damn white bastards, them doctors?"

Hen didn't answer. He didn't think the question was his to answer.

They set off well after sunset, Augustus driving, Hen on the bench up beside him, Napoleon back in the box with the runaways, and the boards and rags. When Hen had told Napoleon to get ready, Lucindy had frowned, but that had been the extent of her protest. "You ready to fill up them shoes of your pappy's?" Hen had asked.

The boy had smiled with his whole face. He had big, bony cheeks and a high forehead like his pappy's, so there was plenty of face to smile. "All the way up to the top," he'd said.

Hen had seen Lucindy's frown. "One day I's gonna be gone," he'd said.

Out the narrow lane through the woods, then north on the course set by Fudge years ago, Augustus kept Jupiter and Lovejoy stepping along at a lively clip. The journey commenced in silence, and stayed so, only the rattles and thumps of the wagon, the clop of the horses' hooves. Behind him in the box, Hen saw Napoleon and Jemmy grim and alert, Liza and the child quietly amusing themselves. For the longest time Hen felt the presence of Fudge. It was wrong without him. When at last they crested the familiar hill where there was just enough moonlight left between the clouds to see over to the far ridge, to see the hills rolling gently away, Augustus, looking out over the valley, said, "Fresh from the mint, and good as gold," quietly and without heart, yet loud enough to send a jolt through Hen.

Hearing his pappy's words on Augustus' lips let the stopper out of Napoleon. "Where 'bouts this Deer Run Station at, anyways?"

"North," Augustus said, a puff of frost accompanying the word out of his mouth. It was clear and chilly.

"How far?" Napoleon said.

"Far enough."

"When we gonna get there?"

"When we get there."

Napoleon was quiet for another minute or two. "What we suppose to do if we run across somebody? What we suppose to tell 'em?"

"Who we gonna run across?" asked Jemmy.

Hen turned around. "Hush up back there, boy."

Napoleon hushed. Lulu grew restless and began to fuss and squall. Hen turned and watched. The child wished to venture freely about the box of the wagon, but her mother held her close, which Lulu found highly displeasing. Jemmy and Liza were trying without success to placate her with pats and coos, Augustus was about to intervene, when Napoleon took the child from her mother, lifting her several times into the air which caused a quiet giggle, holding her on his lap and bouncing her—when the wagon itself wasn't doing the job—showing her the buttons on his warmus. The new friendship seemed to delight, and quiet, the little girl. Hen nodded. He was always on edge when a woman and child were part of the cargo—it lengthened the stops when he had to pee, a woman in the wagon, causing him to have to find a tree to pee behind, trying the already thin patience of Fudge. Augustus now. But a child too was even worse. He looked in the back again; Napoleon was showing the little girl tricks with a piece of string, a cat's cradle, other nonsense. He was glad he'd brought him along. It was how Fudge might have handled it. Was Hen not watching over them? This was his job now. Thinking of Fudge, the procuring of a grave marker rudely imposed itself on his mind, and he commenced the task of worrying again. Lucindy was depending on him. She'd put the matter in his hands, left it up to him. As Hen worried, they passed by a cabin, a shed, a barn, all in ruin, the surrounding fields reclaimed by scrub brush and saplings on the way back to forest, a place where a farmer and his family had run out of luck, or life, or both. He shivered in the chilly night air. Thinking of luck and life and Lucindy, Lucindy alone with no man, Lucindy in anguish, allowed Miss Eva to creep into his mind once more. Miss Eva and the mystery of her hanging.

Hen, without turning his head, shifted his gaze to Augustus. Fudge was gone. Things were different. He whispered to Augustus. "What happen to the young white girl, Miss Eva? What happen to her? How she end up at the end of that rope?"

Augustus looked at him. The boy was impossible to read. "I ain't been around near as many years as you," he said, looking back at his team, "but I done learn one thing. That is, you gots to travel light. Can't go packing too much load on your back, or on your mind."

Hen nodded, and nodded again. "So what happen to Miss Eva?" he said.

"Who?" said Augustus.

The last leg of the journey meant fording a creek just south of Sugargrove.

The cargo, Napoleon too, had been sleeping as best they could, till they reached the creek and started across, and they smelled the water and woke up. Nobody was paying much mind to the baby, who'd been asleep as well, everyone sticking their heads over the sides to see how far up the wheels the water was rising, when halfway in the middle Augustus rolled over a rock too big too fast, a mighty thump and bounce, and the baby was gone. Liza gave a yelp, and Napoleon was in the water quick as black lightning. The moon had set, and it was too dark to see anything but a flurry of splashes slipping downstream to a chorus of cries and shouts. It went quiet for a moment or two, the splashing faded from view. Augustus stopped the wagon in the middle of the rushing water, everyone craning their necks to peer downstream in the dark, Jemmy going over the side himself, up to his hips in the cold creek.

Over the rush of the water they heard the squalling of the child, getting louder, coming closer, and the first thing they saw was the smile on Napoleon's face, then the wet, loud and miserable child he handed over to her father.

They climbed aboard and the child kept bawling, Liza trying to hush her through her own sobs and tears, and Augustus snapped the reins and clucked at Jupiter and Lovejoy who made their way up the bank and out of the creek, the big, iron-sheathed wheels of the wagon slipping and sliding on the creek-bottom rocks. "Hush, hush, hush up the child," Augustus said, "she going to wake up the dead—or the law." Everyone cooed and clucked and patted and shushed and Lulu began to quiet down as the shivers overtook her. They dried the wet ones, wrapped them in the rags for warmth, and when Hen looked up, the smile on Napoleon's shivering face was still shining as bright as the moon had been an hour earlier.

"You been proud of that boy," Hen told Lucindy. Napoleon sat drinking coffee at the bone-white table, beaming while Hen told his mama how he'd rescued the baby.

Weak sunshine diluted the early morning air of November. Wasn't it cold, Lucindy wanted to know, and Napoleon replied that it sure enough was, cold enough to freeze the ears off a jackrabbit, but that didn't slow him down any. Nobody else was going after the child, so he had to. "You all growed up," Lucindy said, beaming.

The smile grew bigger still. "I's still too worked up for shut-eye," Napoleon said.

"Good thing," his mama said. "Cause you going on up to Farmer Lemon's. He got some late hay he need you to start raking in."

"Farmer Lemon's?" Napoleon said, smile gone, eyes big. "I been up all night working. I been saving babies."

"Now you gonna be up all day too," Lucindy said. "Saving hay."

Napoleon protested only mildly—he knew better than to press the issue—and Lucindy fed him his breakfast and sent him on his way. When he was gone, Hen sat down at the table himself. "I could use me some of that young," he said.

"You ain't going into no work, is you?" Lucindy said.

"Don't see no point. Gonna catch me some of Napoleon's shut-eye."

"You can use his bed, then," she said, "if you gonna use his sleep. Go on in. I'm gonna take Belle into town, start looking for some work."

Hen looked around the inside of the cabin, snug and warm, frost on the wrinkled window, the doors to the bedrooms open and inviting. "Obliged," he said. "But I gots my own bed, down in my own place. Ain't nothing wrong with my own bed."

"Suit your self," said Lucindy, sweeping a crumb from her table. "Stubborn old coot."

Hen slept well, his heart light. The old corn mattress on the ground was no more comfortable than ever, but it might have been Napoleon's bed, in Fudge's cabin—it might have been Fudge's own bed, he allowed himself to dream. He might well be looking after the family, just as Fudge always had, and he felt at ease, comfortable in spite of the draft on the ground and the smell of soot from his fireplace. He didn't know when he finally awoke, but he sensed he'd probably slept through for three, four, maybe even five hours straight, itself a cause for joy nowadays, and so he lay abed, lingering as long as he could savoring the feeling of well being, a feeling as rare and precious as a coin of gold. Fresh from the mint. He listened to the sounds of the creek waters and thought about Napoleon's shivering smile. He didn't even have to pee, at least not too badly, another rare and joyful thing. He heard the chatter of voices from down toward the heart of Little Brier, a clamor growing louder, more excited than usual, and he wondered what the occasion was—a birthday, maybe, maybe somebody finding work. The worry about the marker for Fudge's grave came into his mind, and he let it slip out again just as quickly. The chatter grew louder. He heard an exclamation or two, Hiram Appleby, Sam Cash, then a wail from a woman, maybe Irene Plato. He heard Cornelius Nips arguing, but he couldn't make out the words to the argument, only the tone. He was rising from his mattress on the ground—his old bones failed to share in his mind's sense of well being—when he heard a clatter of footsteps coming near, then the pounding on the boards of his door.

"Henry Westerman!" A white man's voice, unfamiliar.

The door flew open before he'd achieved a standing wobble. There in the doorway stood Sheriff Mills, looking official and brutish and blocking the sun. "Come with me, Black Hen."

Hen came forward, squinting in the sudden light, placing his hand on the splinters of the door jamb to brace himself. Lucindy was there behind the sheriff, her eyes as big as bowls, tracks of tears streaking her face. Augustus was there too, between two deputies, his slit-eyed face carved from stone. Hen saw the shackles on his wrists. Cornelius Nips was among the crowd that surrounded his doorway on the bank of the creek.

"You're under arrest, boy," said the sheriff, the cleft in his chin bobbing meanly.

"Arrest?"

"Come with me."

"What for?" He thought he knew—the runaways. But he was wrong.

"Why, for digging up Fudge Van Pelt."

Hen squinted more severely into the light, trying to see. He cocked his head. The words wouldn't come in, wouldn't make sense, like trying to watch a fish fly through the sky, a bird swim under the water. He saw the sheriff nod toward a deputy, saw him approach, felt his arms roughly handled, cold iron on his wrists. "For digging up..."

"For digging up the body of Fudge Van Pelt," the sheriff said. "For digging him up, for skinning the hide off his body, for selling the hide for the manufacture of boot laces and razor strops. Or for some other nefarious purpose which will come to light at a later date."

Lucindy collapsed to her knees. She commenced to wail, her mouth in an awful O, but no sound would come out, and nobody could hear it. Nobody, Hen thought, but Fudge.

.

7: November 22, 1857: Grave Consequences

The day following the failed resurrection of Molly Plotner, Darling awoke on the hard plank bunk in his former cell in the old stone jailhouse, having been arrested leaving church.

He was scarcely rested after his weary night. The other three cells were vacant. He was alone and abandoned. It was a silent Sunday afternoon in late November, the only sound that of a mouse gnawing somewhere in the vicinity; he could detect no other sounds or signs of human existence. Somewhere life was progressing, people were going about their Sunday business in the normal order, but he had been excised from those scenes, isolated, excluded. He looked down at himself at rest, at his legs and arms and torso in all their manufactured immobility, and he was convinced they could never have been through what they were alleged to have been through on the previous night, the digging up of a grave, the pell-mell chase through woods and moonlit fog. There must be some mistake. It must have been someone else. From his cell window he could see no trace of the fog that had lingered so, and in fact, there was a suggestion of sunshine behind the high clouds in the sky over Hartsgrove.

Concentration, thorough examination of the facts at his disposal, eluded him. He tried to round up his stampeding thoughts, which consisted of these: Molly Plotner's body was not in her grave. He was being held without bail, having been arrested for a second offense, similar to the one for which he'd been released on his own recognizance. His companions and co-conspirators, Kathleen and Sandt, were apparently not implicated. Where was the body of Molly? What were Sandt and Kathleen doing at this very moment? Were they doing it together? His mother was suffering from severe mortification. Thank God his father was dead. Did Vasbinder know?

Of course. By now the whole town would know. Vasbinder would certainly wash his hands of him, after having secured his release the first time, after having warned him quite vehemently not to attempt the resurrection of the little girl. How long would he remain imprisoned? How long would Kathleen wait for him? What were Sandt and Kathleen doing at this very moment? What was it Vasbinder had said? No amount of persuasion could keep Smathers from persecuting him with singular tenacity. *The consequences would be quite grave.* Grave consequences. No pun intended. The Bullerses. Little Bull had said that people were dying to become their specimens. He harbored ambitions to become a surgeon. What would mother be making for supper? Succotash? *Ambition is like love—laughs at the law, and takes fearful risks.* How he loved succotash. How he loved Kathleen and ice cream. Molly Plotner's body was not in her grave. Could the Bullerses have poisoned Fudge Van Pelt? How had Enoch Plotner managed to recognize him in the fog? Violation of the 1855 Act to Protect Burial Grounds carried a term of one to three years in jail, a fine of not less than one hundred dollars. Not *less* than one hundred dollars. One to three *years* in jail. If he did not turn over to the court the body of Molly Plotner, which he did not possess, he might be charged with more serious crimes. *Three years.* Molly Plotner's body was not in her grave. Where was it? What were Sandt and Kathleen doing at this very moment? Were they doing it together? Could Little Bull have poisoned Fudge Van Pelt?

How he loved succotash.

Shortly after Constable Jenkins brought him his supper, dry biscuits and watery broth, Kathleen arrived. Close behind her was Sandt. Ever so close behind.

She clutched the bars in the front of the cell. Sandt remained a step or two in arrears, glancing this way and that, as though fearful of being apprehended and thrust into the cell next to Darling's. As soon as Darling had clasped his hands upon Kathleen's on the bars, the expression on her face went from worry to fury.

"This is the height of balderdash," she said, stomping her foot. "You resurrected no one. There was no one there to be resurrected."

"You know that, I know that, Josh knows that. No one else knows that."

"*Tell* them."

"In order to tell them, I would have to confess that I went there and dug up her coffin. I've sworn I was home in my bed, fast asleep."

"That is foolishness," said Kathleen. "We, the three of us, Josh, you and I, must go to Justice Martz and swear that we were all there and that the coffin was empty. Sure, just digging up an old empty box can't rise up to the level of a crime."

"I wouldn't be so certain," said Sandt, stepping forward. "Nor so hasty."

"Far better you remain uninvolved," Darling said.

"In numbers there is strength. Sure, they'd have to believe the three of us."

"They would not—tell her, Josh."

"Believe me, I already have," Sandt said.

Darling said, "There are forces at work here beyond those apparent to us. The wheels are grinding, and they mean to grind me to dust. You shall not be subject to that."

"Then what will we do?" Dampness had appeared in her eyes.

"Simple. We shall find out what happened to Molly's body. The truth."

"The truth will set you free?" said Sandt.

"How will we find that out?" said Kathleen.

"That," said Darling, "is an excellent question."

Sandt grasped at the bars to give them a shake. To the surprise of all, the door swung open. Jenkins had neglected to lock it. Sandt said, "Care to take a stroll with us?"

Though sorely tempted, Darling let caution prevail.

Vasbinder arrived after candle-lighting, again browbeating Constable Jenkins into unlocking the door of the cell and letting him inside, as he had at the time of Darling's previous incarceration. When Jenkins inserted the key, Darling saw the flush take root on the old gentleman's face as he realized his error, but he mimed the unlocking anyway, keeping his gaffe to himself. When he shut the door again behind Vasbinder, Darling saw the key twist, heard the hard lock click.

Vasbinder slumped to the bunk beside Darling. His collar was smudged and loose, and in his eyes Darling detected weariness more than anything else, more than indictment or blame, more than anger. "So," he said, and let it go at that. "I've spoken with Esquire Truby. He will represent you. He will not come today, however, as it is the occasion of his wife's birthday."

"Please give her my best," said Darling.

"I was young once," said Vasbinder, "and foolish." An undertone of anger, of accusation. "Will, this is possibly the most—never mind. It is done."

"It is indeed," said Darling.

"Tell me what happened. How have you gotten yourself into this soup?"

Darling told him how he rode out to Plotner's after midnight and dug open the grave, only to find the coffin empty, and how Plotner appeared and he fled, losing him in the fog. He told him the lie he'd told the authorities, that he was home in bed asleep. He told him everything except for the fact of his two companions; that, he felt Vasbinder had no need to know. "I'm sorry, Cyrus," he said. Here he was not lying. He was sorry he was in jail, sorry that Molly was not in her coffin, and especially sorry that he would be unable to perform her autopsy. If Vasbinder took the words as an apology for ignoring his advice—indeed, his pleadings and dire warnings—not to attempt the resurrection in the first place, there was little harm in that.

"The coffin was empty, you say?"

"Entirely."

"Extraordinary," Vasbinder said, settling himself with a sigh and a soft, grumbling fart that was nearly inaudible. "So you would have me believe that the real mystery is not only the whereabouts of the little girl, but the identity of the real culprit. If what you say is true, someone else would have had to have been committed to the same folly. Someone else would have had to have already resurrected the child."

"You must believe me."

"I do."

"You do?"

"Of course—why would I not? Are you not telling me the truth?"

"Certainly I am," Darling said. "I was merely surprised at the ease with which you believed me. I had far more persuasive arguments marshaled in my mind."

Vasbinder put his hand upon his charge's knee. He gazed at Darling down his nose, over his bushy white mustache. "How long have I known you, my dear? Do you not think I would recognize a falsehood from your lips the moment it escaped them?"

Cyrus Vasbinder was woven into the tapestry of Darling's entire memory, images of Vasbinder and Darling's father, and a host of other men, huddled around this table or that, in this kitchen or that, this schoolroom, that jury room, or this storeroom with the shutters shut, planning this political campaign or that, with earnestness and fervor. His father and Vasbinder had each been elected to the office of borough school director when Darling was a boy, an office which his father had held when he died. Vasbinder had been reelected to one or two more terms, until his political horizons had broadened. He'd been elected coroner twice, and now he was preparing a run for state assembly, which would all but complete his transition from medicine to politics.

One specific image he could summon at any time, of his father and Cyrus laughing, slapping their knees as they sat in a semi-circle with several other laughing men, cigar smoke encircling their heads at the front of the room in the brick schoolhouse, before the master's desk. The source of their amusement was long since lost to him, if indeed it had ever been his in the first place; as a general rule, most of the sources of adult bemusement were a mystery to him at the time. What he remembered was Vasbinder's thick, bountiful, bushy black mustache, and the matching thatch of black hair upon his head; exactly how and when it had turned to white was a mystery. It was as though Vasbinder had aged behind his back, wholly unannounced to him.

Was it because his father had not? Sometimes he wondered.

On Darling's eighteenth birthday, Vasbinder had arrived at his house riding a handsome gray mare. Though he normally was on foot when he visited—they were neighbors of a medium distance—Darling never bothered to wonder why he was mounted on this occasion. It was his birthday. Libby Stormer was there with her boy as well, as were Josh Sandt and several other friends and neighbors, celebrating Darling's maturity. Under his arm, Vasbinder carried a book, a fine, leather-bound volume, *A Manual of General Anatomy of the Human Body*, by S.D. Gross, M.D., which he, with great ceremony, presented to Darling.

"It is yours to keep, my dear," he said. "It is also your first reading assignment, a fine introduction to the medical arts, of which a knowledge of anatomy is the foundation."

The leather felt like gold to Darling. He entered eagerly, becoming absorbed in the drawings, leafing through the pages. After a while, his mother scolded him. "Will," she said. "Put down that book and talk to your company. Pass around some of your cake."

"Let him read," Vasbinder said. He was sitting by Darling's mother at the table watching Libby Stormer attempting to tame her son who was trying to climb the stairway from outside the banister railing. By the tone of her voice, it was not the first taming of the day. Vasbinder said quietly, "By the Jew's eye, how could one survive in such bedlam? It is my firm conviction that eighteen marks the perfect age to begin the care of a youngster. That is why my wife and I—God rest her soul—never had children of our own. We could not imagine a way to pass over the years between infancy and maturity without the intervening chaos."

Within the hour, Vasbinder arose to take his leave. His supply of idle chatter on topics other than medicine and politics was limited at best, and no one among the gathering was especially disposed to either topic. In the doorway he announced, "Come with me, Will. I have something outside I would like to show you."

It was early dusk of a warm May evening, the chorus of peepers down by the creek beginning their evening serenade. Darling looked around, but there was nothing there except Vasbinder's horse, which he'd tethered to the sapling in front of the house. He noticed that his mother had followed him outside; Mrs. Stormer followed then, as did Josh and a few of the others. Vasbinder patted his horse's flank. "What do you think of her, Will?"

"She's a beauty," said Darling, perplexed by the question.

"She's yours," Vasbinder said.

In the moment it took for the words to sink in, Darling saw the horse anew, with the eyes of a child, her solid, sturdy sleekness, her gentle eyes: she *was* a beauty. "Mine?"

"If you're going to be riding the circuit with me, my dear, you're going to need a more dependable mode of transport than poor old Jethro." Jethro, the retired plow horse belonging to Darling's Uncle Jacob.

"I shall pay you for her."

Vasbinder laughed. "That shall take some time, I fear, with the wages you'll earn riding with me." The audience laughed as well. "I'm afraid she'll have long since been put out to pasture by then. We both shall have been, for that matter."

"What's her name?" said Darling.

"Why, I gave her no name—she's your horse. That's your job."

Darling thought for a moment. "I will call her Gertie."

"Gertie," Vasbinder said thoughtfully. He looked at his charge with an odd blending of curiosity, suspicion and bemusement. "Why Gertie?"

"I have no idea. The name just popped into my head. I think it fits her up and down—does she not look exactly like a Gertie?

"Indeed," Vasbinder said, the bemusement gone from his expression. "What's in a name after all?"

Two hours later, after the company had departed, after he'd fetched a bail of hay and a barrow of straw from Mr. Horner, after he'd cleaned out the little stable in back and had come back inside, his own horse comfortably ensconced in his own backyard stable, his mother said to him, "Why on earth would you name the horse Gertie?"

Darling shrugged. "The name simply popped into my head. As I told Cyrus."

"From whence did it pop?" said his mother. "You are aware that Gertie was the name of Cyrus's wife, are you not?"

"Mrs. Vasbinder?" said Darling, perplexed.

"Gertrude Vasbinder, nee Schoffner."

"I did *not* know that. I swear. Do you think Cyrus is displeased?"

"No, not at all," said Ada Darling. "I'm certain he found naming a dumb animal after his late, lamented wife quite a loving and fitting tribute."

The ease with which his preceptor was willing to believe him was in stark contrast to his mother's reaction the following morning. The tears behind her eyes were held in check by the angry flush on her face as she pleaded with her son from beyond the bars.

"Tell them where she is. Take them to her."

"I don't know where she is. Why won't you believe me?"

"Mr. Martz visited. He and Mr. Butterfield both. They sat in our kitchen. If you tell them what you've done with her, it will go much easier for you—they will convince Judge Hulse, first of all, to set a bail amount so that you may be released pending your trial."

"Mother, you have to believe me. The little girl's coffin was empty."

She sighed, sternly. "But you admit you were there? That you dug her up?"

Darling looked up and down the corridor to ensure no one was listening. "As it turned out, there was no her to dig up. Yes, Mother—although I've told the authorities I was nowhere near Plotner's last night, the truth is I went there with every intention of digging her up—merely for an autopsy, mind you, not for dissection. I *had* to know why she died in my care. I dug down to the coffin, opened it and found it empty—then Enoch Plotner came upon the scene, and I had to flee. I had to flee for my life, as he had his musket, and he meant to use it. As a matter of fact, he did. Use it, that is."

His mother was unimpressed by his purported brush with death. "How can I believe you?" she said, sternly even for her. The tears had by now been totally checked, and the anger etched on her face showed evidence of the aging there. "You admit you intended to dig her up. You admit you went to her grave in the middle of the night, that you dug all the way down to her coffin, lifted the lid, and somehow, some way, she'd been magically transported from her coffin. Please tell me how any sane person possessing the sense that the good Lord gave him could possibly believe you."

"Cyrus believed me."

"I said any *sane* person," she said. "No, I didn't mean that. Cyrus is fine, I suppose, but the man would believe anything you say."

"Someone else must have dug her up first," Darling said. "I can't imagine any other explanation."

His mother sighed and shook her head. "All I can say is thank heavens your father is dead," she said as she turned to leave.

She vanished through the doorway at the end of the hall where the little wood stove emitted a white glow, a hint of smoke and scant heat. Darling shivered. The silence of the cells filled his head where the twin images remained, his mother's stern, disbelieving face contrasted with that of Vasbinder, his preceptor's, so kindly, trusting and believing.

John Jameson Ypsilanti Truby, Esquire, was possessed of a curled mustache, a head as bald as a wagon wheel, and eyebrows that hooded his eyes, giving him an errantly omniscient visage. Only slightly younger than Vasbinder, or than Darling's father would have been, Truby had served as justice of the peace, and had been elected a number of times the county prothonotary. He had run unsuccessfully against Levi Smathers to represent the district in Congress when Smathers had been swept into office on the sympathy vote, according to Vasbinder, owing to the death of his precious daughter.

Truby arrived with Vasbinder to interview his client in mid-afternoon, showing no lingering effects of the illness that had brought him to the doctors' office two weeks prior, when he'd interrupted the conversation between Darling and his mentor concerning the demise of Molly Plotner. The bustle of Monday commerce on Hartsgrove's Main Street, the calls of friends, the clops of hoofs, the barks of dogs, the squeaks, thumps and groans of the traps and buggies, the horn of the butcher, could be heard through the window of the cell. "What have you told them?" said Truby.

"That I was home in my bed fast asleep."

"And were you?"

Darling hesitated, glancing at his mentor. "Tell him the truth," Vasbinder said.

"And the truth shall set me free?"

"Only the law shall set you free," said Truby. "Unfortunately, the law and the truth are oft times at odds."

"Sad but true," said Vasbinder.

"And, therefore, oft times unlawful," Darling said.

He detected a certain synchronicity in the shaking of the two older men's heads. "Will, this is serious business," Vasbinder said. "Hardly a time for flummery."

"Do you think I'm unaware of that, Cyrus? It is I, after all, who is sitting behind these bars, not you."

"Had you heeded my advice, dear boy, you would not be sitting here at all."

Ignoring the comment, Darling told Truby the truth, most of it, the same version of the truth he'd offered to Vasbinder and his mother, how he'd gone to Plotner's, dug, found the coffin empty, then fled when Plotner appeared. Again, he omitted his companions.

After Truby had questioned him on this detail or that, fixing the facts in his mind, he mulled them over in silence for a few moments. "It is clear," he said, "that you stand innocent of the crime of which you are charged. You cannot be guilty of the violation of a burial ground if no one is buried in that ground. If no one is buried in that ground it is, ergo, not a burial ground subject to violation. Violation of ground is, in itself, not yet a crime on the books, so far as I am aware.

"Besides which," added Truby, "I'd like to know how in perdition Plotner could claim to identify you, after only a glimpse on a dark and foggy night on a fast horse at a good distance."

"Indeed," said Darling.

"So how, exactly, do you intend to proceed?" Vasbinder said.

"With every faith in the wheels of justice," said Truby. "Smathers and Sloan"—here he referred to Ira Sloan, the District Attorney—"are summoning a grand jury. Twenty-four citizens of the county shall hear the testimony of Enoch Plotner and shall learn that the body of Molly Plotner was nowhere to be found. They shall also learn that her body was not in young Darling's possession, nor discovered in a place where it could have been presumed to have been in his possession. I submit that even without casting Plotner's identification of Will into doubt—which we can easily do—it would be impossible to presume guilt in the matter of violation of a burial ground without proof positive that the body of the little girl was removed. Violation requires removal of the body, or at least of a part thereof. Mere digging does not constitute violation. They shall be hard pressed to indict."

"Unless of course they were to discover a body," Truby added.

"And how would they discover a body?" Darling said.

"God, the devil and Levi Smathers work in mysterious ways," said Vasbinder, "—the latter two, indeed, in collusion. Even as we speak, the search is underway for the body."

"And we pray," said Truby, his hooded eyes narrowing, "that they do not find her hastily buried along the logging trail."

"They shall not," was Darling's assurance.

"Then they shall not return a true bill," was Truby's.

The resentment of the populace, the anger and the indignation that had been ignited by the resurrection of Fudge Van Pelt, was further inflamed by the attempted resurrection of Molly Plotner. Even though only Darling had been implicated in the latter, the anger was directed at the doctors as a whole, Darling learned from his visitors. He was also able to witness it himself, first hand, on his daily, hour-long excursions to the exercise yard, the site between the jailhouse and the Courthouse, where he walked under close supervision. There he could see his neighbors and acquaintances passing by on Main Street, going about their business, and their greetings, if proffered at all, were seldom more than perfunctory. Upon more than one occasion he was able to detect thinly veiled hostility upon this visage or that.

Kathleen told him her theory. "They see the doctors playing God, and they resent it. They see the doctors as the only thing standing between them and dying, and they resent that too. They're too ignorant, the lot of 'em, to know that dying's nothing to be scared of, and, what's more, they all want their doctor to be just as scared of it as they are."

"I'm sorry, but I have some difficulty comparing myself to God," Darling said.

"Now Cyrus, he's another story," Sandt said. Sandt was present; he seemingly was never far from Kathleen's side. "I can indeed picture God with a prominent thatch beneath his nose."

"Or perhaps Alexander Bullers," said Darling. "God, a roaring, belching, farting Being."

Kathleen was not amused. "Mark my word," she said. "It's the arrogance. Why, even the very name of the act—*resurrection*—sounds as if you're trying to make yourselves holy."

"Next thing you know," Sandt said, "you'll be walking on water."

"I have already accomplished that," said Darling. "Of course, the water in question was, at the time, quite frozen."

The flames of the common anger were further fueled by the persistent rumors that the doctors had been responsible for the death of Fudge Van Pelt. Inevitably, the flames crept further: How exactly had little Molly Plotner died?

Where exactly might she be?

From his visitors Darling heard about the search. At the behest of Levi Smathers and the prosecution, the Sheriff, William Mills from Slabtown, a clean-shaven man with a cleft in his chin and a reputation for diligence, took charge. A posse of Plotner's neighbors and citizens from as far away as Hartsgrove gathered on the Coolbrook Road not far from the scene of the crime, near the spot where the logging trail went into the woods. The search party, each man wearing thick woolen stockings or buckskin breeches, swept through the rattlesnake-infested woods, leaving no stone unturned, no part of the terrain unexamined, no fallen log uninspected, making their way steadily through the sloping woods, the entire three miles down to Muddy Bottom Creek, and back up again to the Coolbrook Road in ever-widening swaths. They were looking for signs of freshly overturned earth, a disturbance on the forest floor, crumpled undergrowth, dead leaves in disarray, where the body of a little girl might have been hastily concealed. It was a chilly afternoon in late November despite the brilliant, cloudless sky, and the sunlight slashing down through the bare tree limbs, while lending little heat, cast an unusual brightness to the interior of the forest, which some took as a sign that God was illuminating the woods just for them, for Molly, to expedite her return to her grieving family. They were to be disappointed.

Nothing was found. Many of the search party returned to the

woods the following day and spread out even further to resume the search. Still nothing was found. After three days, the search was called off.

Enoch Plotner took no part in the search.

Many faulted him as heartless. Many did not. They sympathized with the man, unwilling to blame him for being too despairing to participate, for being too unwilling to risk the chance of coming across the body of his beloved little girl lying moldering in the woods like the discarded carcass of a dog.

The Grand Jury was not to be rushed. Alone in his cell every day, seldom able to concentrate on the medical texts that his mentor had brought him to read, to improve his mind while passing what surely would be a brief interlude before his freedom and reputation were restored, Darling thought of the twenty-four men convened in the building next door, whose identities were unknown to him but who would for the most part be his neighbors and acquaintances, perhaps even a patient or two, men whom he passed in the street every day and with whom he exchanged pleasantries. His fate was in the hands of those men. In theirs and in the hands of Levi Smathers. Darling imagined the Congressman, and the District Attorney Ira Sloan, before them, painting Darling with a villainous brush, Smathers with his convex bushy muttonchops and brimstone voice, going about his job in dead earnest, his job being to see that he, Darling, remained behind these bars, deprived of the basic human right to feel sunshine upon his face.

His noble resentment at the injustice of the law continued to fester within him. It was a resentment that inhabited him always, nagging, cohabitating with his longing for Kathleen, with his wonder at the mystery of the whereabouts of Molly, with any number of other worries, urges and desires, for, his body confined, his life was lived now entirely within the realm of his mind, and in the darkest, loneliest hours of the early morning, he feared sometimes for his sanity.

He isolated himself from the other prisoners who were housed separately, in the other wing of the jailhouse. He was not a criminal. The other prisoners—four men whom he knew, one of whom, Arad Butler, jailed for larceny, indeed having been a schoolmate—were serving set sentences at "hard labor," which consisted mostly of making broomsticks. Darling avoided them on the occasions their exercise overlapped, fearful of contamination, of somehow beginning to accept his status as one of them, as a criminal.

Only one other prisoner appeared in his holding area during the early days of his incarceration. Late one night, well after Darling had fallen into fitful sleep, he heard the door open, heard the rustle of garments and shuffling of feet as Constable McClay deposited Howard Kunselman, an old, decrepit gentleman insensible from drink, into the cell beside Darling's.

McClay did not bother to lock, nor even close, the door to Kunselman's cell, departing as fast as he could. Darling soon understood why. He did his best to fall asleep again to the overwhelming aroma emanating from next door, an odor rife with elements of ammonia, manure, vomit and whiskey. When Darling awoke at first light, *why* he awoke at first light, Kunselman's hollow white wrinkled face was turned toward him, watching, eyes full of phlegm, wonder and accusation. Not a word was spoken.

Darling was not the same person who was arrested. Not only was he not the same, he knew with certainty that he never would be again. The part of him that had been a boy, the part that he had allowed to remain and accompany him on his journey to maturity, was gone forever.

Vasbinder continued to reassure him. "Things may look bleak, my dear, but in a year it will all be forgotten. It will be nothing but a brief, albeit unpleasant, memory."

"I would like to believe that," Darling said.

"Believe it, my dear." They were seated beside one another on the bunk—Vasbinder seldom used the chair—in postures of repose, slouched untidily against the stone wall behind them. It had been a cloudy day, and the near dark of the late afternoon remained unilluminated. Jenkins had yet to light the wick of the camphene lamp in the hallway. They discussed for a while the state of several of Darling's patients, patients whom he believed needed attention, and whom he'd asked Vasbinder to visit in his absence.

After an interlude of quiet, Darling said, "I feel so utterly helpless. If I were out, I could go about the job of attempting to find out the whereabouts of Molly—of solving this mystery and proving my innocence."

"It is a mystery that may never be solved," Vasbinder said, hastening to add, "Which in no way of course would diminish your innocence."

"Have you spoken with the Bullerses? I've not seen their faces."

"They've expressed their concern for your plight."

"Have they? Has it occurred to you, Cyrus, that the resurrection of Fudge was prompted by Little Bull, by his ambition to become a surgeon? And that he gleefully boasted—perhaps while drunk, but nevertheless—that men, women and children were dying everyday to become his specimens? Does that not cast a certain amount of suspicion his way?"

"As to the demise of Fudge? Or the disappearance of Molly Plotner's body?

"Either. Both."

"Not really," Vasbinder said. "I sincerely doubt that he could be either wily or subtle enough to have to have done harm to Fudge. Moreover, I have strong doubts that the Bullerses, either of them, would be motivated enough to travel halfway to Coolbrook, and engage in the necessary manual labor to carry out the resurrection on their own.

Ambitious they may be, but that ambition is tempered by a good measure of old-fashioned sloth as well."

"Still," said Darling. "'Ambition is like love—laughs at the law, and takes fearful risks.'"

"A more likely scenario is the Washington Medical College in Greensville—I've been told that dissection is a common practice in the course of study there, which begs the question: From where does their material come?"

"Is that not rather far to travel?"

"Not at all. One day at most, for a determined brute bent on profit."

They sat silent for a while in the gathering gloom, Darling pondering the possibility till at last his mind strayed elsewhere. He said, "Cyrus, are you not concerned about the length of time the Grand Jury has been out?"

"Not at all. They are, after all, ignorant men engaged in a difficult intellectual exercise, under the direction of an incompetent booby."

Darling looked at him. Staring vacantly toward the front of the cell to the lamp on the little stand in the hallway, Vasbinder rested his arm nonchalantly upon his knee, raised into the air by his foot upon the bunk. Seldom was his preceptor so at ease, and it occurred to him that it was *not* a façade for his benefit, that Vasbinder was honestly not overly concerned. But a part—a large part—of him wondered if Vasbinder's lack of concern was born entirely of his conviction that Darling would soon be cleared and released and his reputation restored, or from his belief that Darling had brought this predicament upon himself, and was being not unjustly punished for attempting the resurrection, for disobeying his mentor in the first place.

His mother visited him at five o'clock in the afternoon, every afternoon, with a regularity Darling found distressing. As soon as her day at Mrs. McCurdy's was done, she detoured down Main Street to the jailhouse, where, having taken a page from Cyrus Vasbinder's book, she required the Constable on duty to open the cell door and allow her to avail herself of the chair therein. There, after the obligatory scolding—had he come to his senses yet? Was he ready to tell them where the little girl was? How had things come to such a pass? Wasn't it a blessing his father was not alive to see it?—she would ask if he'd heard any word yet on the deliberations of the Grand Jury, and then fill him in on her long and weary day, how Mrs. McCurdy was rapidly losing her eyesight, and how she, Ada Darling, was more and more obliged to pick up the slack. But otherwise all was well.

Darling loved his mother. But he found that more and more, as he left behind the boy he had been, tolerance was replacing fear in his regard of her. He found the regularity of her visits distressing, because of the permanence it implied.

He never saw Kathleen except in the presence of Sandt. It was maddening, and with each visit it became more so. They were always together, never one without the other, a pair, like lancet and cups. One day when Sandt excused himself to visit the necessary (Darling offered the use of his slop bucket, which Sandt graciously declined), Darling and Kathleen argued.

"How else can I see you?" Kathleen said, her brow knotting, her green eyes flaring. "My father has forbidden me to visit the jailhouse on my own. You should be thankful to Josh for bringing me often."

"How does it look that you're always in the company of another man?"

"Why should I not be? You and I are not engaged."

"Not officially perhaps…"

"I have not heard a proposal from your lips."

"Well, I've been meaning—"

"Nor do I see a ring on my finger."

"As soon as I—"

"Would you prefer I did not visit you at all then?"

"That's not what I'm saying—I merely—"

"What are you saying?"

"I don't know what I'm saying, *that's* what I'm saying."

They sulked, on either side of the bars, hands grasping the same bar, inches apart. Sandt returned, taking hold of the bars himself, interpreting the cold silence to be one of despair. "'Stone walls do not a prison make,'" he said, "'nor iron bars a cage.'"

"My word," Darling said. "He's quoting the Elizabethans again."

"Not Elizabethan," Sandt said. "Lovelace was a Cavalier."

"Elizabethan, Cavalier, whatever—the only time he quotes poetry is in the pursuit of a lady's favor."

"Untrue," said Sandt.

"He memorized 'She Walks in Beauty' in its entirety to impress Betsy Henderson."

"And what of it?" said Kathleen. "I think it's romantic."

"'She walks in beauty like the night,'" said Sandt, "'Of cloudless climes and starry skies…'"

"Would you recite Byron to me alone, Josh, if Kathleen were not here as well?"

"'And all that's best of dark and bright,'" Sandt said, "'Meet in her aspect and her eyes.'"

They were interrupted by the arrival of Vasbinder and Truby, accompanied by Constable Jenkins, who paused in the doorway to take in the sight of the three young people standing there, to consider the scent of resentment in the air. Behind them, over their shoulders and through the open doorway, Darling saw an office flooded with bright sunlight, sunlight that had not ventured to invade his dim and dreary cell. "A full house," remarked Vasbinder.

"A captive audience," said Truby.

"George," said Vasbinder to Constable Jenkins, "open the door, fetch more chairs. We shall all go in to visit poor Will, and we shall all do so sitting."

Grumbling, the old Constable did as he was asked, bringing chairs from the office, unlocking the door of the cell, waiting till the party was inside before locking it again.

The barrier between him and Kathleen having been removed for the first time in nearly two weeks, an odd sensation of nakedness came over Darling. As she passed within inches they never touched, and his urge to reach out was mingled with a fear of doing so. Kathleen sat proper and upright in the little chair in the corner, Sandt remained standing, as Vasbinder and Truby settled themselves as if before the hearth in the comfort of their homes. Darling sat stiffly on the edge of the bunk.

"It can only be good news, my dear," Vasbinder said, at his ease on the bunk beside Darling. "It's well that your friends are here to share it."

"Let's not be premature, Cyrus," Truby said. "*Promising*, is all I said."

"What is it?" said Darling.

"The Grand Jury is on the precipice of rebellion," said Truby. "Word has it that they are becoming more and more impatient with the length of time that Smathers and Sloan are drawing out the proceedings—"

"They have timber to harvest," Vasbinder said. "Livestock to tend, whiskey to sell."

"What exactly *is* taking so long?" said Sandt.

"I believe that Smathers is overreaching his grasp," said Truby, giving his curled mustache a thoughtful twist. "He is so lacking in confidence that the jury will return a true bill in the matter of the violation of a burial ground—without proof that the body had been removed, it would be all but impossible—that he has been searching the statutes for obscure arcanum, hoping for an indictment on some other grounds, anything at all. It would seem he is extracting tedious testimony from anyone who has ever known Will Darling during this lifetime, particularly anyone who's familiar with the resurrection of Fudge Van Pelt, which matter is entirely inadmissible at any rate. The jurors shall not tolerate it much longer."

"They have not subpoenaed me," Sandt said.

"Because they know you to be a friend," said Truby. "They know you would be entirely sympathetic to him." At that, Darling snorted, albeit mildly.

Kathleen remained silent. Darling could not take his eyes off her. She leaned forward, on the edge of her seat, following the conversation in earnest, her hands grasping her chair.

"How much longer can he hold them?" said Darling.

Truby never answered. The door opened and Jenkins appeared in a bright burst of sunshine. Walking slowly, as if across the stage, he stopped at the door of the cell, composing himself beside the lamp on the little stand. "Gentlemen," he said, adding quickly, "and young lady—I've just been informed that the Grand Jury has returned a verdict." Here he paused for appropriate effect; Constable Jenkins seldom had the opportunity to command an audience, and he intended to make the most of it.

"They have handed down a true bill," he said. "Young Dr. Darling is to be arraigned come first thing Monday morning."

8: November 4, 1857: We All Got That Coming

The night after he and Hen had been released from jail, the day after the mutilated remains of Fudge had been discovered, Augustus Hamilton built a fire in Little Brier. Hen suspected that when Augustus was angry, he liked to burn things. And this was a very big fire.

Too big for his yard. Augustus constructed it on the flat down by the creek, near the swimming hole of summer, between the willow that dipped down to the water and the old chestnut that stretched its limbs across the creek. As the early darkness gathered, Augustus and Napoleon and the other young men and boys of Little Brier gathered armful after armful of dead branches, heaping them in the pile that Augustus soon lit. Some of the girls pitched in, including little Belle, who tried to carry as big a load as Napoleon, dropping most of it, arriving with one big branch and a handful of twigs. Soon the fire was snapping, leaping hungrily up through the pile, a mountain of flame, the oak and the willow shying away from the heat, from the flames nipping and snatching at the branches.

Nearly all of the denizens of Little Brier came out of their shanties and cabins to watch, gathered in silence at first, as the woods and the sky grew blacker and the fire before them grew more fierce and brilliant. Augustus and Napoleon continued to feed it, Augustus snapping limbs in half with his bare hands that other men would have to take over their knee. The cold air of November was beat back. The heat forced them time after time to retreat. They stared at it, quietly at first, mesmerized, Solomon and Ophelia McManigle standing shoulder to shoulder near where Cornelius Nips sat on a stump, his wife, Esther, behind him, her hand on his neck. Sam Cash, the blacksmith, his fists on his hips, stood close, nearly as close as Augustus, nearly as close as Mrs. Barber, the young widow who could not take her eyes off Augustus. Old Hiram Appleby brought out a chair to sit on, his wife fetched a stool, while others availed themselves of a handy rock or pile of leaves. Many remained standing. The Widow Winter watched from the yard of her shanty through the trees. Hen spotted Lucindy standing by a laurel bush, Irene Plato a few feet away, and he moved closer to her, and they stood and stared, the three of them in a row.

They stared into the fire, at Augustus and Napoleon breaking and flinging the branches that were quickly devoured. Hen could still feel the coldness on his wrists, even in the heat from the fire, where the shackles had been fastened. He could still feel the cold iron of the bars in his hands where he'd gripped them. Still hear the deep, gruff voice of Justice Martz grumbling through his white, piggish face, and his mind still could not keep itself from trying to imagine the unimaginable, the desecrated, mutilated, lifeless, skinless mass of muscle and bones that had been his friend.

What if he had *seen* it as Lucindy had? What must she feel?

He turned his head slyly to look at her, her face tight and dry and quite composed, gleaming in the firelight. Was she thinking about it? Was she seeing it still? In the quiet conversations around the roaring fire, he heard the word Fudge surface time after time—*po' Fudge, what they done to that man, po' Fudge, a downright evil sin.*

Sam Cash picked up a shovel. Frustrated, angry like Augustus, he began to beat on a hollow log with the handle. A tap-tap-tapping at first, but then it gathered force, and hands began to clap, feet began to stomp, as Sam Cash flexed his powerful arms, put his back into it, until Hen could feel it like a heartbeat outside his chest.

He felt uneasy. Heartbeats belonged inside your chest. Glancing again, he saw Irene Plato had begun to clap her hands as well, but Lucindy stood still, her arms at her sides, her fists clenched. Down close to the fire, Belle and some of the other children had begun to dance about, clapping their hands in time to the beat.

Cornelius Nips stood up from his stump, walking closer to the fire. He began to sing, or try. The man's voice had not improved since Fudge's funeral. *Take down the silver trumpet!* he sang in his eager, off-key voice, and several voices sang back, *Fare you well, fare you well!*

Cornelius bawled, *Blow your trumpet, Gabriel!*

Fare you well, fare you well! sang a gathering force of voices.

Lord, how loud shall I blow it? Fare you well, fare you well!

Loud as seven peals of thunder! Fare you well, fare you well!

Wake the living nations! Fare you well, fare you well!

Irene Plato was singing the farewell chorus with most of the others. Lucindy and Hen were not. The chorus grew louder still. The dancers grew more numerous.

Then you'll see the coffins bursting! Cornelius sang in an awful howl.

Fare you well, fare you well! was a rumble by now, nearly all the voices joining in.

See them dry bones come a-creeping! Fare you well, fare you well!

Augustus stomped around the fire, the children dancing, some of the older ones joining in, even Mrs. Barber, the young widow, black shadows all, from where Hen stood quiet and anxious. It was a hurried, hasteful scene, not at all to his liking. He felt out of place. He looked behind and all around, at how the dancing shadows played off the tilting shacks and shanties, making them come to glowing life, nervous and hurried.

See the moon a-bleeding! Cornelius, at a fever pitch, reached for the note, his voice quaking and cracking. *Fare you well, fare you well!*

See the stars a-falling! Fare you well, fare you well!

Even the fire roared and popped along.

There's a better day a-coming! Fare you well, fare you well!

A shiver of self-consciousness clutching his back, Hen looked again at Lucindy and saw her shoulders quake. Looking closer, he realized it was a sob. Her cheeks were wet. He didn't know what to do. He moved closer to her. Recalling the warmus at the funeral, he nevertheless dared to put his hand on her shoulder. She stiffened, not having seen him coming, then sobbed again, wiped at her cheek and allowed his hand to stay.

For the judgment day is coming! Fare you well, fare you well!

"Oh, Lord," she murmured, "oh, Lordy, oh Lordy. I never, never, never..."

"I knows," he whispered, "I knows."

Lucindy looked at him, tried to smile, wiped her eyes again. "You neither?"

"Me neither," Hen said, not sure what she meant, not sure what he meant. He could never imagine Fudge and what they'd done to him was what he thought he meant.

Hear the rumble of the thunder! Fare you well, fare you well!

"I never," Lucindy said, "*never* heard such God-awful caterwauling in all my born days. Who done told that man he could *sing*?"

Hen threw back his head and laughed, and Lucindy caught it at once, helpless to do anything but follow, and they clutched one another in great silent, sobbing peals of glee.

The earth shall reel and totter! Cornelius sang in an uncharted, uncertain melody.

Fare you well, fare you well! came the fractured response, the choir's attention having been drawn away to the curiosity of the old man and the new widow clinging together, heaving and clutching by the laurel bush.

Even after the fire, for days after Fudge was gone, the odor that had filled his sick room stayed with Hen, the smell of the underside of a fallen log in the forest, and so too did the dreams and thoughts and memories of Yellow Charlie that it seemed to conjure up.

The first time he saw Charlie's face, when his eyes finally opened, his shoulders being shaken, shaken too long to ignore—*You dead, boy? You dead, boy?*—and there was the face, dirty, brown and yellow, but nothing like an Indian's, nothing like Sassy John's. Eyes specked with green, living and shining. And he was out of the cabin, past the blood-drenched forms heaped here and there, all things seen and heard an incomprehensible jumble, so his eyes fixed on whatever they could, one thing at a time: the peg on the wall where a yellow rag hung ready to slip to the floor, a pail tipped over in the yard, its contents having left a brown stain upon the earth, the freckle on the back of Charlie's buckskin vest, at which he stared as he was transported away in the saddle behind Charlie. He could hear Charlie talking to the man, what man he didn't know, but a peek around Charlie had revealed a large white man with a long, black beard and a long, black coat. Had there been a badge upon his chest? Other men as well, rifles and muskets and horses and hats, shadows with sun slicing in, a congregation of Gods. *Sassy John* was spoken, and *drowned like a polecat in the creek*. The man with a voice like easy, rumbling thunder said, "They was just a bunch of niggers, but they didn't have that coming."

And Charlie's voice, more felt than heard, "Shit, we all got that coming."

Afterward, Hen had ridden forever behind Yellow Charlie, bouncing and aching, staring at the freckle on the back of the vest, unable to see anything of where they were going, anything at all of what lay ahead.

He was staring at the freckle on the back of Yellow Charlie's vest still. The same freckle on the back of the same vest he watched disappear for the last time into the woods so many years after, so many years before, Charlie's shoulders slumped by then, his spine not as straight as before, the axe drooping from his hand.

Shit, we all got that coming.

From Fudge's yard—Lucindy's yard—the heart of Little Brier could be seen down through the bare tree skeletons, the tipped and tilting shanties of unpainted boards, rough shingles and canvas patches, the six-hole communal privy over by the woods. Hen sat outside in the cool air of a cloudy afternoon helping Lucindy make soap. Every autumn she made the soap. This one would be no different, except this autumn Fudge would not be there to help, as he always had, and it seemed to Hen odd but apt to be taking Fudge's place, filling his shoes. Fudge had always insisted on handling the lye, owing to the strength of it; once he'd splashed a bit over the edge of the leach-barrel, burning his leg through the wool of his britches, leaving a white scar on his black knee in the shape of a bell. Hen wondered where that bell had ended up. He insisted on handling the lye this time, letting it leach from the barrel of ashes and water, pouring it into the kettle to be boiled with the grease that he added. Lucindy stirred the mixture over the fire, Belle adding sticks to keep the kettle boiling, sticks she gathered from across the yard where Napoleon was chopping and stacking fire wood for winter. From down across the settlement came the ring of other axes, the flash of other blades, other neighbors readying for winter. His contribution complete, Hen was content to sit back against a stump and follow the industry, the scent of the wood smoke pleasant in his nostrils—for there was a fire on every hearth as well as beneath Lucindy's soap kettle—and wonder what had become of the bell-shaped scar on Fudge's knee.

Lucindy told Belle to begin raking leaves to pack around the bottom of the cabin against the upcoming winter winds. The rake was half again as tall as the girl, and not much thinner. She wore around her neck a string with a chicken foot attached for good luck, having taking an interest in conjuration since seeing the jaybird foot carried by the runaway Mary—she'd been unable to kill a jaybird, however, though she'd tried her best to do so. Napoleon had laughed and teased. Hen watched as she tried to maneuver the rake, awkward as a fawn, tried to herd the dead leaves into a proper array, her bonnet cock-eyed and twisted. Nearby, Napoleon, sweating in the cool air, had removed his shirt and was chopping like a man, fresh muscles beginning to bulge and glisten. Hen's gaze kept returning to their mother, however, her back bent over the fire, stirring carefully, one way only, with the long sassafras stick she kept in the corner of the kitchen for just that purpose, staring into the kettle at the alchemy taking place, the accumulated grease of the year combining with the fresh lye—from the accumulated ashes of the year—magically making the sleek, slippery soft soap. Hen sighed, feeling more relaxed than he had in days. There was something about the proximity of good, hard honest work that always put him at ease.

From over by the cabin came a wail, and there was Belle, the rake at her feet, head down, arms hanging helplessly at her sides, sob after sob wracking her skinny shoulders. Lucindy looked up from the kettle. "What happened?" she said, and Napoleon, planting his axe with a whack in the stump, only shrugged. "Maybe she step on the rake?" he said.

"What's the matter, baby?" Lucindy said, but Belle only kept crying.

Placing the paddle aside, Lucindy went to her little girl, pulling her close, but she didn't return the embrace, arms still hanging at her sides, tears unchecked. "Goodness, goodness," Lucindy said, patting the child.

"Baby!" called Napoleon. "Little cry-baby!"

"You hush," Lucindy said to Napoleon. Then to Belle, "Did you hurt your toe, baby?"

Still sobbing, Belle bobbed her head.

"She hurt her toe," Lucindy said to Napoleon. "You just hush your mouth."

"Baby!" said Napoleon, and it was then that Hen noticed Napoleon's eyes were wet.

"You crying your own self, boy," Hen said.

"No I ain't!" At that he grabbed the axe and commenced to chop with a flurry, and Hen could see drops of sweat flying even from across the yard, drops of sweat or tears, or both.

Lucindy brought Belle back to the fire with her, luring her with the promise of letting her stir. She watched closely over her little girl's shoulder, instructing, making sure she stirred smooth and even, in one direction only. Hen's rest was spoiled. Napoleon chopped away, more furious than before, and the chop-chop-chop that had soothed Hen before like a heartbeat, now just set his nerves on edge like a jagged drumbeat, like a call to battle.

And Augustus, as though called, came walking up through the trees.

"Afternoon, ladies." Lucindy returned the greeting pleasantly enough, as Belle's smile came beaming out from under her bonnet, her tears quite forgotten. She began to stir with added vigor, full of herself, and Lucindy had to reach down and tame the wild stroke. "Any luck with the soap?" Augustus said.

"Too early to say," said Lucindy.

After greeting Napoleon, who wiped his brow, puffed out his chest and flexed, Augustus sat on the ground beside Hen. "Damn old jailbird."

"Damn young jailbird," muttered Hen. "What you up to."

"Just down from Lewistown," Augustus said. "Hauled in a load of pickles."

"Pickles?"

"Pickles. Twenty barrels for Moses Clover. Pickles."

"Man must go through a mess of pickles," Hen said.

"*Mess* of pickles," Augustus agreed.

Augustus leaned closer to Hen, his voice lower. "Tell me 'bout that Darling boy."

"What darling boy is that?" said Hen.

"That there boy. That young man. Supposed to be a doctor. Name Darling."

"Oh, young Doc Darling. Him."

"Yeah," Augustus said. "Him."

"Nice enough young white boy. Don't go putting on no airs. Don't go acting like he own this nigger, if that's what you means."

"Maybe he don't. But I tell you what he did do—he done dug up our friend and skinned the hide right off him."

"That's what they saying, all right," Hen had to admit. "Maybe. Maybe he fell in with a bunch of them other doctors, and they the ones led him to it." Augustus frowned beneath the little brim of his derby.

Belle had tired, and Lucindy had resumed stirring the kettle, Belle perched on a little log behind the fire, touching the chicken foot on the string around her neck, still peeking over at Augustus. Napoleon chopped on, slow and steady. Finally, Augustus leaned close to Hen, speaking even lower. "I been thinking," he said.

What Augustus had been thinking: The doctors were mighty anxious to get a hold of Fudge's body, to use it for whatever it was doctors used bodies for. Their friend wasn't even cold in the ground before they dug him up. Augustus was thinking that maybe, just maybe, the doctors were too anxious to wait for Fudge—or any other nigger—to lie down and die in his own good time, and maybe, just maybe, they had a hand in hurrying that dying along. He didn't think it was Means himself. Means was helping runaways, Means seemed to care about black folk some. Somebody else could have slipped in and messed with his medicine, the bark compound he gave Fudge. Means never locked his door. Always out making his calls. Anybody could go slipping in there to his kitchen. Anybody could mix in a little wolfsbane or night-shade or hemlock with it—wasn't Fudge vomiting just before he died? Didn't Means say folks don't generally vomit when all they got is the fever?

"Lordy, Lordy," said Hen.

"And guess what, old man," Augustus said, "guess what else. Guess who I seen up at Means's place the other day, chewing the fat with the man just like they was long-lost brothers. Guess who I seen there on the very same day he got sprung out of jail?"

"Dr. Darling?"

"You pretty smart for an old feller," Augustus said. "That boy Darling, all right. Maybe he ain't quite such a nice white boy as what you think."

Before he left, Augustus told them about a chance meeting with a man at the general store out past Schoffner's Corner, a man who knew another man up in Rasselton looking to open himself up a boot business, and willing to pay a good dollar for the tools and such in Fudge's shop. A great wave of relief passed over Lucindy's face, but it was Hen who could have kissed the angry young man, a great worry—one of his new-found worries—having been lifted off his shoulders.

Later, after supper—Hen made Lucindy rest, taking it upon himself to conjure up a mess of pan bread and pease porridge—Napoleon and Belle, done in from their hard day's work, were already in bed and dead to the world even before Lucindy had finished clearing the dishes. Hen hung around. He sat at one end of the bone-white table, at his ease, Lucindy at the other. For a while they sat in companionable silence, staring at the fire. Hen noticed she was rubbing at the top of the table, rubbing her thumb in a regular rhythm, as if trying to burrow a groove on the surface. He watched for a while, until he noticed the spot beneath her thumb.

"That Fudge's blood drop?" he said.

Lucindy looked up, as if awoken. As if caught in the act. She nodded.

He said nothing else, and she remained quiet as well. Her thumb was stilled too, though it stayed at rest over the stain from her husband's blood. The candle on the table began to sputter.

She said, "I best be making more candles. Hope I me got tallow enough saved."

He leaned up and blew the candle out. He made no move to leave. It didn't seem right to leave yet. They sat in the darkness illuminated only by the little blaze left dying in the fireplace. He could see, faintly, Lucindy's thumb begin to move again, under cover of darkness, stroking, stroking, stroking the stain left by her dead husband.

They sat that way in the quiet darkness so long that when he finally broke the silence, his voice came out loud and alarming. "How you holding up?" he said.

"I don't know, Hen," she said. "Not so good, maybe. I think... I think if he just passed away on account of the fever, and that was that, and there was nothing else in it, maybe I can deal with it a little bit better. But this other business..."

"This other business," he said. "This other business sure enough."

"I can't stand it. I can't stand thinking 'bout it at all. I try not to, try not to remember what I seen, but..." Her voice was fragile as thin ice. "But...I can't get it out of my head. I want to just take and pull my brain right out of my skull and put it in a pail and scrub it off clean." She stared down at the stain. "I feel like he died twice," she said. "Like he done left me twice. Like he was *took away* from me twice." Her thumb was digging furiously.

Hen said, "'Gustus, that boy seem to have vengeance in his heart."

Her thumb stopped. "Vengeance?" she said, her voice no longer fragile. "Me, I don't feel no need for vengeance, no sir, no vengeance in me. I just like to skin the lot of 'em, is all. I just like to take and pull the sickly, white hide right off 'em, every one of 'em, pull it off slow."

They loaded up the boxes by the guttering yellow light of the lamp on the boot shop wall. Hen felt a heaviness in his chest as they dismantled the place—dismantled the life of his great friend, removing him from living memory, from history. Soon the place would become a barber shop or a confectionery or an oyster saloon, and soon no one would recall that a man called Fudge Van Pelt had spent half his life within these walls, touching the feet and the lives of half the white population in town, displaying for each his bony, gap-toothed smile. For a long time Hen held and studied the sign, the sign written by Fudge's hand long ago, the one he couldn't read—a skill he'd never acquired—but which he'd been assured said *Closed Up Shop – Back In A Jiffy*, staring it up and down and down and up as Augustus and Cornelius busily packed. It was this of course, the remembering, the great sadness, the weight in his chest, that made him move so slowly, not his general aversion to haste, but to Augustus and Cornelius, it was a fine line.

"*Move* it, Hen," said Augustus. "We ain't got all night."

"What *he* say," said Cornelius. "All them white folks making me awful fritterous."

It was court night and the barroom of the American Hotel was packed with white men drinking and swearing and smoking cigars. Hen spotted the doctors on his first trip out to Augustus' wagon. He hadn't noticed them at first, when the crowd had been a rowdy confusion of white faces, smoke and noise. At a dominoes table not far from the door sat young Dr. Darling and an elderly man with a bushy white mustache; Vasbinder, maybe, Hen wasn't sure, but he knew the old man was a doctor as well, the doctor teaching Darling how to doctor. Hen looked at Darling's young face, smooth, white and fresh as new snow, but he could unearth no trace of meanness in it at all, though that didn't mean it wasn't there, he supposed. When Darling made eye contact, Hen looked away. At the same table sat the two brothers, doctors too, named Bullers, Big Bull and Little Bull. The big one looked drunk. The little one looked drunk and mean. Little Bull was watching them, him, Cornelius and Augustus, moving through the crowd with their boxes, watching them meanly.

Hen saw Augustus staring right back at Little Bull, not batting an eye. And he saw Cornelius seeing Augustus staring Little Bull down. And he saw Cornelius, a light brown black man, turn a shade or two lighter.

Back in the shop, Cornelius said, "'Gustus Hamilton—Lordy, boy, what you *thinking*?"

"What you mean, what I'm thinking?"

"You don't go giving no evil eye to no white man setting there drinking. In amongst a crowd of other white men setting there drinking. You look a white man in the eye, you just praying for trouble. And your hat—what that hat of yours still doing up on your head?"

Augustus took off his hat, looking it over with narrow eyes. Then he put it back on. "Man take off his hat as a sign of respect. I ain't got none of that for them white sons of bitches.

Cornelius shook his head. "*You* tell him, Hen. Tell him what they does to niggers."

Hen didn't answer. He had nothing to say and no time to say it, Augustus responding immediately: "Oh, believe me, I knows what they does to niggers. I already knows that. And they gonna keep on doing it to niggers, till niggers starts doing it right back to 'em."

He seized up another box, and headed out into the crowd, hat high, shoulders back. Cornelius's head was still shaking. "Lordy, Hen. I just don't know 'bout them young bucks. Hot-headed. They's bound and determined to bring down the wrath of God on us all."

"Ain't so sure it be the wrath of God," Hen said, "so much as the wrath of them crackers."

Cornelius looked at him, his head in an odd bob, his round face still several shades lighter. "Wrath of God, wrath of them crackers—you see a whole lot of difference from where we be sitting?"

They left the load in the wagon for Augustus to deliver to Rasselton the following day, and Hen and Cornelius waited outside the stable behind his cabin while Augustus unhitched Jupiter and Lovejoy. When Augustus came out, he and Cornelius said, in unison, "We gots to talk."

Then they said, in unison, "'Bout what?"

Augustus, quicker, said, "Quit that," as they started down the path.

Cornelius said, "What I wants to talk 'bout, boy, is 'bout how you gots to treat them white folks with some respect, even if you ain't got none. And if you can't muster up nothing close, just don't treat 'em with no disrespect. Else you just praying for trouble."

Augustus waved his hand dismissively. "Here's what I wants to talk about," he said. "I suspect them white bastards not only dug Fudge up out of his grave, I suspect they done put him down in it in the first place." Cornelius stopped in his tracks.

"You saying they done killed him on purpose?" he said. "It wasn't no fever?"

"I'm saying that's exactly what they done. Too much a coincidence otherwise, and I don't put all that much stock in coincidence."

"Thought you was saying the stoning and the dunking was what done him in."

"That was before I seen Means's place, where he mixes up his remedies—anybody sashay right on in there and mess with 'em. That was before I seen Darling all up friendly with Means, and that was before I heard that white son of a bitch Little Bull in there a while ago going on about killing niggers and digging 'em up to cut up they bodies."

"He was saying that?" Cornelius said. "Watch your cussing, I don't like no cussing."

"That's zactly what he was saying."

"All the years I spent serving that man his whiskey,"—Cornelius had been a servant at the American Hotel—"he never once laid his eyes on me. Never thought he took enough notice of a nigger to want to kill him, *or* cut him up. Even so, he always keen on healing, though. Always talking 'bout how to do this or how to go about that to try and heal somebody up."

"So long as that somebody a white man," Augustus said.

"Never trust a man eats his steak burnt. What you think, Hen?"

Hen shook his head. "I think we oughts to see what ol' Solomon think."

Cornelius nodded. "Wisdom of Solomon."

"I think we oughts to see what ol' Hiram think too. And ol' Marcus," Hen said.

"Hell," said Augustus. "Why don't we see what ol' Fred Douglass gots to say too?"

The addled nature of his memory notwithstanding, Hiram Appleby was Little Brier's eldest citizen, and the seeking of his counsel on any noteworthy topic was a given. They found him sitting at his table behind his foggy spectacles rolling bones from a cup by the light of a single candle. When Cornelius explained the reason for the late call, Hiram stood up, nodded, puffed up his chest, and headed out. On the way to Soloman's, Hiram hobbling along in the lead on his walking stick, they stopped at Marcus Swan's shack, where a light still burned. Marcus, young and officious, was curious, and eager to join in the talk.

Solomon McManigle, an old man now, had been a slave at one time, so it stood to reason he might possess insights into the hostile white mind. He was in bed, his shanty dark, but he answered quickly when Cornelius tapped; he was a famously light sleeper. His wife Ophelia, on the other hand, could be heard snoring, even before the door came open. Solomon lit a candle. His broad, black face, ravaged with pock marks, wore a puzzled expression beneath his nightcap. "We needs the wisdom of Solomon," Cornelius explained, and they all filed in and sat around the old trestle table worn smooth by a thousand elbows.

Cornelius took the floor, relating Augustus's suspicions about the doctors, though tempered by his own concern that Augustus's disrespect of everything white could only lead to trouble for Little Brier. When Cornelius was done, Augustus spoke his piece again, feeling that Cornelius had not done justice to his suspicions. Solomon nodded wisely, scratching up under his woolen nightcap. On the floor his old dog, Young Jack, scratched his ear in his sleep, as Ophelia's snoring railed unabated from the bedroom.

"That ain't really proof," Marcus said. "Suspicions ain't really proof." Marcus always sat with his hands on his knees, Hen had long since observed, as if he was afraid his knees would try to escape. When he spoke, he gripped them harder.

"What I wants to know is why they didn't dig up no white man and skin him," Augustus said. "Hell, a white man name of Fullerton just buried up there a week before Fudge."

"I knowed Fullerton," Hiram said. "Man was a son of a bitch."

"Suppose them suspicions is true," Solomon said. "What you proposing we does 'bout it anyways?"

Augustus shrugged and squinted. "Bible says a eye for a eye."

Cornelius said, "Don't go quoting no Bible on me. Bible *my* business. Bible also says love your enemies—do good to them that hates you."

"Bible says a time to kill, too," said Augustus.

"Says a time to heal," Cornelius said. "Says a time for peace."

"Says a time for war, too," Augustus said.

"Say a time to keep silence, too," said Hen.

"You can read your Bible any way you please," said Marcus, squeezing his knees.

"So what you saying?" Hiram said to Augustus. He thumped his stick on the plank of the floor, clearing his throat in an attempt to make his voice squeak less. "Make war on white folk? You some kind a crazy nigger?"

"Ain't saying make no war—I ain't plumb crazy. All's I'm saying is a eye for a eye—one of them for one of us. That's all I'm saying. Quiet like. Do it right, nobody knows what happen, but maybe they starts to think about it."

"You from Connecticut you say—ain't you from Connecticut?" Solomon said. "Don't know 'bout up in them parts, but everywhere else it's a white man's world. Specially where I comes from, believe me, it's a white man's world. That's what you gots to understand. Ain't right, but it is on account of it is, that's all. You gots to understand we walking around in a lion's den, all the days of our lives. And you be walking around in a lion's den, you best be tip-toeing."

"So," said Augustus. "Just turn the other cheek, let it be?"

"Ain't that in the Bible?" Hen said.

"What I wants to know," Augustus said, thumping the table, "what happen to all that mad, all that yelling and thumping and jumping took place the other night around that fire?"

There was quiet around the table. Ophelia snored on unseen as they talked. She snored on throughout. Solomon threw another stick on the fire, and Young Jack roused himself to crawl over closer to the hearth, his eyes never opening all the way up, reminding Hen of Augustus.

Hiram said, "Pass me that jug over here."

Solomon said, "Way I sees it, even if they didn't kill him, they sure enough dug him up and skinned the hide right off him. That don't seem right. Don't seem right to just let that be."

"We might just as well sign a petition asking 'em to please come on out here and burn the place down for us again," Cornelius said.

"They done it once, they do it again," Hiram said. Shaking his head, he took off his glasses and rubbed them. "Take and sell a few niggers up the river, too, far as that be."

Marcus said, "Why don't we go to the sheriff? They is such a thing as the law."

"That's where you wrong," said Augustus. "White man's law ain't nothing for a nigger." The argument commenced in earnest as Ophelia snored on. Young Jack stood on his shaky legs and walked from the hearth toward the bedroom. Solomon, in his wisdom, thought it couldn't hurt to make their suspicions known to the law—even a broke clock was right twice a day, he reasoned—while still not ruling out anything else. Cornelius believed that, in an instance this famous, they could trust in the powers that be to at least make a show of looking into it, and who knew what might turn up then? It might never lead to the arrest of a white man, but it might serve to keep it from taking place again. Marcus pointed out that they'd already arrested somebody for digging up Fudge, so they might be likely to take seriously the idea somebody could have done him in as well. Hiram, for his part, had seen a crow that very afternoon shit high in the sky and it had landed smack dab in the middle of a barrel head, a sure sign if ever there was one—he hadn't known what the sign was for till this very moment, but now it was clear it meant the authorities would take their case to heart. They should go to the sheriff. Augustus on the other hand remained adamant that it was a bad idea, and could only prove harmful if they tipped their hand. The arguments swung back and forth, this way and that. Finally Cornelius turned to Hen, who had spoken not a word. "What you think, Hen?"

What Hen was thinking had little to do with whether or not they should go to the law. He'd been unable to muster up much of an opinion one way or the other on the issue, and his mind had moved on. He was seldom able to decide where to come down when it came to a good argument, usually finding himself entirely in favor of the side of the man giving the argument at any given moment, and then finding himself entirely swayed to the other side as soon as it was presented. He was cursed with a fair, open mind, was the way he looked at it. Having wearied of swaying this way and that, getting dizzy, his thoughts had moved on to Lucindy. All the talk about Fudge had made him think about her, for he could never think about Fudge and what had happened to him without thinking about Lucindy and what might happen to her. But the string didn't end there. He found he could seldom think about Fudge and Lucindy without thinking about the other one as well, the white girl, and he could still see her face lit by the lightning flashes, peaceful and puzzled, serene and troubled.

"What about Miss Eva?" he said. "What happen to that child?"

All present looked at Augustus, who cocked his head in a slit-eyed stare.

When Yellow Charlie marched out of the shadows of Hen's mind and into his living memory, so too did the night the band of white ruffians burned down the settlement, when the stolen pig had been repossessed from Elmer Johnson's shanty, and Elmer himself had vanished into the woods. That was the night when Lucindy had sought out Hen.

Most of the black folks had scattered. The raid had been sudden, without warning, the thunder of hoofs in the lane before they'd burst into the settlement, on horseback and buckboard, some with faces half-heartedly hidden, torches flaring, pistols and muskets blazing, voices whooping and shouting: *Any nigger don't want shot or burnt, better clear on out!* was echoed over and over. *Clear on out for good! And don't come back!* Not that the citizens of Little Brier needed much persuasion, most taking flight as soon as the shooting and torching commenced, some watching from behind the trees, others fleeing deep into the woods.

Hen hadn't fled far. Even back then, he was too old to flee far. He'd watched from just up the bank of the creek, not far from his shack. Though it seemed forever, the raid was over in minutes, not hours, but it was much longer, not until the fires were nearly spent, before folks began to drift back in to assess the devastation. Not a building had been left unscathed, only a charred remnant still standing here and there, part of a wall, a post, a clothes line. Hen to this day could bring the black, acrid odor to his mind, to his nose, to his tongue.

What could they do? There was nothing that could be done. Anger, sorrow, fear, despair, grief—cursing, crying, wailing—all to no useful purpose. What could be done? The men failed to congregate as they usually did, as no good could come of their rants and curses, had they even felt worthy of ranting and cursing. No use as well for their sorrow. There was nowhere even to sleep, nowhere to go, nowhere to turn, nothing that could be done.

Sparks and flares still erupted from the smoldering debris, so they couldn't settle next to where their homes had been. Bitter smoke lingered. Some gathered leaves, twigs or hay, whatever they could find, and nested as close as they could, to rest, to try to sleep, to wait and see what new light the new day would bring.

Some wandered among the ruins all through the night.

Hen settled himself against the trunk of his tree in the spot on the bank where the breeze sometimes found its way in over the water, an especially welcome breeze on this night, washing away the bitter smoke and smell of destruction. He might have even slept, dozed at least, though mostly he watched in a daze as the sky lightened, as a clear summer morning emerged.

That was where Lucindy found him. He heard her—heard someone—approaching, but didn't turn. She didn't speak at first, just placed her hand on his shoulder, and when he looked up from under his floppy hat to see who it was, she said, "Po' ol' Hen—how you doing?"

"Where Fudge at?" Hen straightened his hat.

"Baby finally fall asleep. He sitting with him." Napoleon was an infant then.

"Everything gone," Hen said.

Lucindy sat beside him, closer than she ever had before. She placed her hand on his knee. "I seen what you done," she said.

Hen didn't say anything. He stared at the moving creek waters.

"Why you done that?" she said.

Still, Hen didn't answer. He couldn't. He stared at the waters.

"They done left your shack be," she said. "Your shack still standing. I seen you pick up that torch and light it on fire yourself."

Now the shaking of his head twisted into a nod. "Sure enough," he said.

"Why you done that?"

"Anybody else see?"

"Not that I knows of. Fudge, I knows he didn't see nothing, he too busy watching them crackers burning and shooting and leaping around like fools. I was watching—I was looking after you." She squeezed his knee. "Why you *done* that?"

"Seem like something needed done." To the best of his knowledge, he *had* done it because it seemed to be something that needed to be done, and for no other reason. To be the only man with a place still standing wasn't right. It wouldn't have made any sense.

Surely, that was the only reason.

She let go of his knee, he let go of his breath, and he looked at her: she was crying, smiling as tears ran down her face beside her crooked nose, and she snuffled and said, "You put the torch to my place, I probably run a pitchfork right through your black ol' heart," and that made Hen laugh, throw back his head and laugh.

Lucindy had begun to laugh as well, though it didn't stop the tears.

When they'd emptied Fudge's shop, they'd left Hen's chair behind. Hen didn't know what to do with it. It had begun to dawn on him that maybe some of his custom would return, that maybe white folks might still need their boots blacked and polished and shined. Even though Fudge wasn't there to build their boots and shoes anymore, they would still have to get them from somewhere—they weren't about to start prancing around barefoot—and no matter where they got them from, it stood to reason they might still want them blacked. But it hadn't been much of a custom to start with, and Hen was not at all sure he could spend the whole day, day after day, without Fudge there, without hearing the tap-tap-tapping of his hammer, the snip of his shears, the snap of the awl, without Fudge's head popping out of his shop at regular intervals to make this or that observation to his pal Hen. Without Fudge to keep an eye on.

He didn't know what to do. It turned out that he didn't have to decide.

When he walked into town, up Pond, down Main, into the American Hotel, the corridor was wide and empty. He stood staring at the spot where his chair had been, white folks passing by, many of whom he knew, none greeting him with more than a nod, none mentioning the absence or whereabouts of his chair. A carpenter, a man he didn't know, was fashioning shelves in Fudge's old shop, preparing it for its next life. Hen noticed the little sign in the shape of a boot still hanging there, overlooked, above the door. He stared at the sign for some time.

His chair was in the alley behind the hotel. The jars of polish were gone, the brushes and rags missing. The chair itself was wrecked, a pile of broken boards and splinters.

Augustus found him upstream on the bank of the creek with a line in the water, shivering in his ragged old warmus. Augustus nodded and sat with a sigh. "What you up to, ol' jailbird?"

"Ain't up to no good."

"No more cargos? No more word from McKay?"

Hen pursed his lips, shook his head.

"Cornelius and them, they ever go to the law?"

Hen shrugged. "Ain't told me if they did."

It was a November morning, a Sunday. There was little commotion from the settlement down through the trees, most attending Cornelius's service at the Praise House up the road in Farmer Lemon's barn. Clouds boiled up gray and gloomy over the creek. Augustus said, "You heard 'bout that Darling boy?"

"What darling boy is that?"

Augustus frowned. "*Doc* Darling. Your pal. He done been arrested."

"I knows he been arrested. For digging up Fudge. Been let out of jail too."

"Done been arrested again."

"Again? For what?"

"For digging up somebody else out of the grave. Again."

"Again? Somebody else?"

"Little girl this time," Augustus said. "Still think your darling lily white boy so damn innocent now?"

"Little girl?" said Hen. "You ain't saying he done in a little girl—"

"Naw," Augustus said. "This one probably die natural. She white."

Napoleon saved the day. Again. It was in early December that Silas McKay's son had sought out Hen to tell him another cargo was coming. Silas's son, Jacob, not much younger than Napoleon, found Hen in the late afternoon, after darkness was already settling over Little Brier, at Fudge's cabin. Napoleon was there, in from a long day at Lemon's where he was helping the old farmer build a tannery shed, and Hen was baking biscuits, allowing Lucindy a rare moment of leisure, knitting in the rocker by the hearth. Hen had merely nodded in response to the boy's news and asked him if he'd like a biscuit. It was Napoleon who had quizzed Jacob: how many in the cargo? What ages? Men or women, sickly or healthy, warm dressed or in rags? Jacob knew little. Hen had noticed a change in Napoleon in the weeks since the death of his father. Almost overnight, he'd assumed Fudge's old place at the head of the bone-white table.

Much of the change was due to Augustus. He'd taken the boy in, teaching him the finer points of horsemanship, about harnessing and bridling, about the driving of wagons and the handling of teams, and now he was instructing him how to saddle and ride a horse, how to move forward to show Jupiter who was boss when the beast began to root, how to squeeze him with his legs to keep him from bucking. All Hen had ever ridden was a mule, and he didn't miss that much. He preferred his own two feet on the ground.

The cargo was two men. Randall had run off when his master had sold his bride away to a slave-producing farm in Virginia, from which Randall dreamed of someday purchasing her back. His skin was a light reddish-brown, the color of muddy water, and he was still strapping and healthy, despite having been a common field hand; he hadn't yet attained the permanent, bent-over, clumsy carriage of many other runaways they'd encountered. He wore around his neck a string of mole-paws for good luck, which Hen saw Belle eyeing curiously. The other man, Hubbard, black as midnight, was older and thicker, with sickly yellow eyes. He'd escaped when his old master had died, and his son, master now, had banished him from the big house to the fields. A house nigger all his life, accustomed to the best left-overs and exposed to a modicum of learning, he'd taken the affront bitterly, unearthing his hatred of everything white. Inside his right sleeve, he wore the right eye of a wolf to ward off all injury. Hen hoped Belle wouldn't notice.

It was cold, a clear night in early December, and Augustus loaded more rags in the box, as the runaways were not especially well suited for the colder climes, outfitted only in threadbare denim and wool. Every snort from Jupiter and Lovejoy was accompanied by a frosty blossom. There was no moon, but as they cleared the trees and crested the familiar hill the view still spread out before them, the wooded hills rolling gently over to the far ridge, darkly lit by a magnificent sky full of stars. "Fresh from the mint, and good as gold," Napoleon said.

"Looky there," Augustus said, pointing, "that the North Star."

"Hallelujah," said Hubbard.

"Amen, brother," said Randall.

Following the North Star, admiring the view, the exhilaration of escape rose up again in their blood. Randall began to sing, softly: *Swing low, sweet chariot, coming for to carry me home.* He had a fine, sweet voice, and the others listened for a while, before Hubbard began to grumble along with him, his voice brusque and unmelodic, as immune to a tune as Cornelius's: *…A band of angels coming after me, Coming for to carry me home.* The runaways shivered in quiet satisfaction, nestling into the load of rags. They were cold, which meant they were in the north, which meant they were free, which meant they were alive.

Hen turned in the seat to see the singing. Napoleon, upright and eager, was singing along whatever words he happened to know, while Augustus stared out at the road ahead.

Then Hubbard recited a song, Randall joining in, trying to lend a little tune to the words. Napoleon was quiet, having never heard it before.

We raise the wheat, they give us the corn, / We sift the meal, they give us the husk, / We peel the meat, they give us the skin, / And that's the way they take us in.

When that song had ended, Napoleon, not to be outdone, began to sing one he'd learned around the fires in Augustus' yard:

O Freedom, O Freedom! / And I rather be a slave than be buried in my grave, / And go home to my Lord and be free.

Augustus groaned. Randall jerked his head around to look at the boy, and Hubbard sat up from his nest in the rags. "What you say, boy?" said Hubbard.

Napoleon quit in mid-verse, perplexed.

"*That* ain't the way it goes," Hubbard said. "The words is *before* I be a slave, I be buried in my grave."

"Not I *rather* be a slave," Randall added.

Napoleon said, "That ain't how I sung it!"

"Yes," Hubbard said, "it sure enough is!"

"It ain't!"

"Is too," said Randall. "Ain't that right, Henry?"

Hen said nothing. Both he and Augustus had turned in the driver's seat to take in the argument, Hubbard growing hostile. "You ain't nothing but a little white nigger, what you even singing 'bout, you got no idea what it like!"

"Maybe not," Napoleon said, "but I knows what it's like to be risking life and limb trying to get 'em free!"

"Only thing you risking is your mama tucking you in your bed!"

"I swear, you ain't nothing but a ignorant nigger—don't know why we helping your hide anyways!"

"Pampered little prissy nigger boy. You never last a day down there."

Augustus said, "Enough! Shut the hell up, all of you, right now."

The three took to sulking back in the box. They were still glowering at one another in the starlight when Napoleon cocked his head at the distant whinny of a horse on the cold night air and allowed that there was something about it that didn't quite suit a horse in a pen. Then the clatter of hoofs that followed he reckoned was too rapid to be a commonplace midnight traveler, and he persuaded Augustus to pull behind the boulder in the trees, and him and Hen to stand beside Jupiter and Lovejoy and stroke their muzzles and keep them quiet. Thus Napoleon was the reason the marshal and his deputies passed them by on the road to Sugargrove that night, thereby saving them from certain arrest, thereby saving the arrogant and ungrateful and ignorant niggers in spite of themselves.

9: December 7, 1857: The Trial. And Tribulation

Snow flurries fluttered in the gray of the early morning light, vanishing the instant they landed upon the dirt of the road or the brown and dead grass in the yard. Darling felt them touching his cheeks and nose as he was led by Constable McClay from the jailhouse to the Courthouse on Monday morning, accompanied by his counsel, John J. Y. Truby, Esquire. Within, the courtroom was large and high-ceilinged, the air filled with the acrid odor of smoldering coal from the round iron stove; vapor clung to the panes of the tall, ornate windows, obscuring the view of the bleak morning beyond. Darling's mother sat with Mrs. McCurdy in the crowded gallery behind the railing; there also were Vasbinder, Kathleen and her father, and Sandt—always Sandt. In the back, the face of Black Hen stood out, weathered and weary, frosted with white stubble, the only black face in the pack, looking out of place, and Darling tried, without success, to adjudge sympathy or accusation, any emotion at all, upon its features. Samuel Bullers was there too, marking the first time Darling had seen him since his incarceration.

Behind a long, polished table of dark mahogany awaited Levi Smathers. He and Ira Sloan, the assisting prosecutor, stared intently at Darling as he and Truby took their places behind a twin table. Richard Southerland, the gruff old man, appearing for all the world to be annoyed by the nuisance of Darling's arraignment, stood behind his little table to the right of the bench and called out, "All rise! The Court of Quarter Sessions, Paine County, Commonwealth of Pennsylvania, is now in session, the Honorable Phineas Hulse presiding!"

Judge Hulse entered through the door behind the bench and climbed the dais, mouth set grimly beneath his hawkish nose. His eyebrows were gray and unruly, in opposition to his whiskers, which were neatly trimmed. Arranging his black robe with a practiced flourish, he seated himself at his pulpit and shuffled through a stack of papers before picking one up. He called for the defendant and his counsel to step forward. After Darling and Truby had taken their places before the bench, Judge Hulse commenced the reading of the criminal charge.

"William J. Darling, you are charged with violation of the 1855 Act to Protect Burial Grounds, to wit: If any person shall open a tomb or grave in any cemetery, graveyard or any grounds set apart for burial purposes, either private or public, held by individuals for their own use, or in trust for others, or for any church or institution, whether incorporated or not, without the consent of the owners or trustees of such grounds, and clandestinely or unlawfully remove, or attempt to remove, any human body, or part thereof, therefrom, such person, upon conviction thereof, shall be sentenced to undergo an imprisonment in the county jail or penitentiary for a term of not less than one year, nor more than three years, and pay a fine not less than one hundred dollars, at the discretion of the proper court." Here Hulse paused to look out over his spectacles at the defendant, then to the silent gallery. Darling heard a pop and a hiss from the coal stove glowing against the wall, and smelled the sour smoke.

Picking up another paper, Hulse continued. "In the matter of the charge of violation of the 1855 Act to Protect Burial Grounds, the grand inquest of the Commonwealth of Pennsylvania, inquiring for the body of the county upon their oaths and affirmations respectfully do present that William J. Darling, of the County of Paine, on the twenty-second day of November, in the year of our Lord one thousand eight hundred and fifty-seven, with force and arms at the County of Paine, at the burial ground of the family of Enoch Plotner in Laurel Township there situate, unlawfully and clandestinely did enter and the grave there in which the body of one Molly Plotner, deceased, had lately before been interred; and the said William J. Darling, with force and arms, unlawfully, wantonly, willfully and indecently, did dig open, and afterwards, to wit, on the same day and year aforesaid, with force and arms, the body of her, the said Molly Plotner, out of the grave aforesaid, clandestinely, unlawfully and indecently, did take and carry away, against the peace and dignity of the Commonwealth of Pennsylvania, and contrary to the form of the statue in such case made and provided."

The Judge shuffled the papers, set them down, and removed his eyeglasses, the better to stare down at the defendant and his counsel. "How do you plead?"

"Not guilty, your Honor!" said Truby in a strong and quavering voice.

"Very well," Hulse said. "Plea is duly noted, recorded and entered.

Defendant shall be bound over for trial. As to the trial date—" Hulse sifted through the papers again, apparently in vain. "Richard," he said in a lower voice, "have you seen my docket?"

Southerland approached the bench, papers in hand, as a murmur crept through the gallery. "Quiet in the Court!" said Hulse with a tap of his mallet, the murmur dying a quick and painless death. He and Southerland exchanged broad whispers, "Why, that's only four days before Christmas, that will never do," and another exchange ensued. An accommodation was reached, Southerland retreated, and the Judge rapped his mallet once again.

"The trial of the defendant, William J. Darling, on the criminal complaint of violation of the 1855 Act to Protect Burial Grounds shall commence at eight o'clock in the morning on the twenty-eighth day of December, three weeks hence. Now. I shall hear arguments regarding the matter of bail."

"Your Honor," said Truby. "We respectfully submit that Dr. Darling be released on his own recognizance pending his trial—or, at the very least, on a token bail."

Smathers arose hastily. "Your honor!" he said.

"Yes, Levi—shall I record your objection?"

"Indeed, your Honor," Smathers said. "This is a serious offense, made all the more so in that it is not the first time this defendant has been charged with this offense. He is a young man, unmarried, without family or significant ties to the area, he is practiced in the medical arts as a physician, and he could easily remove himself from the court's jurisdiction and set up practice in Ohio. Or in Ypsilanti, Michigan, for that matter," he said with glance toward Truby not unlike a sneer. "This defendant is a serious risk of flight, and must be remanded without bail."

"Preposterous," responded Truby. "Will Darling is widely known and respected in Paine County and beyond. He lives in this borough with his aging mother for whom he must care, in the home where he has lived his entire life, he is a God-fearing member of the Presbyterian church, and a stalwart officer in the Young Pioneers."

"Should Dr. Darling be released, your Honor," Smathers said, "not a burial ground in the county shall be safe from violation. Bereaved families shall be at risk for the utmost despair."

"Preposterous," repeated Truby.

"I tend to agree with the prosecution in this matter, John," Hulse said. "And there is also the matter of allegations of more serious offenses circulating in the common knowledge."

"They have not been brought before this court, your Honor," Truby said.

"I shall decide what is or is not before this court," said the Judge. "The request for bail is denied. The defendant will be remanded to the county jail, there to await trial."

The judge rapped his mallet and Southerland cried, "All rise!" as Hulse took his leave.

Darling stood bewildered. Turning, he saw a glimmer of tears on the cheeks of his mother, a red blush of anger on Kathleen's. He saw the bushy white mustache of his mentor twitch in contemplation, saw the eyes of Black Hen transfixed upon him as though upon a ogre, and he saw the back of Samuel Bullers as he made his way to the door at the rear of the courtroom. When he took a step, he found that his knees were weak.

"The Young Pioneers?" he said to Truby.

"What?" said Truby, his hooded eyes conveying a false impression of wisdom. "Oh ... the Young Pioneers. I have no idea. But if it's not a wholesome and nurturing society for the youth of Hartsgrove, it ought to be."

Alone in his cell later that day, Darling succumbed to a growing feeling of quiet panic. The three weeks until his trial stretched before him like a vast and endless ocean, and he thought he could not bear the monotony and despair of the same mindless routine day after day, hour after hour, minute after minute, those intractable bars between him and the world. He found his mind would not permit him to read his medical texts, nor to exercise in any activity beyond remembering all the routines and exercises in which he'd engaged as a free man, and longing for them to be his once again

Truby insisted he would be acquitted at trial. He insisted that without the body of the little girl, and with the identity of Darling himself indeed in doubt, twelve honest men would be hard-pressed to return any other verdict. Darling pointed out a phrase he remembered from the judge's reading of the indictment, one of the few phrases he'd heard or retained in the whole of Hulse's mind-numbing recitation. It was, *attempt to remove*. The charge had read, "unlawfully remove, *or attempt to remove,* any human body, or part thereof." He saw those words as sealing his doom.

"You cannot attempt to remove what is not there to begin with," Truby said.

The words were scant consolation at the time, but as the hours wore on—as the days wore on—their potency gathered some substance and became a lifeline in a vast, cold ocean.

Vasbinder visited daily, his demeanor forever reassuring, if never completely cheerful. His visits were not a cause for joy, but Darling realized that without them his despair would be absolute. Vasbinder kept him abreast of the condition of many of his patients—most of them Vasbinder's former patients whom he'd taken to treating again, in Darling's absence— the bleeding of this one, the blistering of that, the various prescriptions and doses dispensed, the tartar emetic, the Dover's Powder, the little blue calomel pills—forever the little blue calomel pills. Listening to his preceptor's chosen courses of treatment, their aspect assumed a certain quality of heavy-handedness that Darling had never before assigned to them. He found more and more his thoughts wandering back to his last exchange with Dr. Means, an exchange that had taken place little more than a month before, though it seemed eons ago, a heated exchange on the side of a hill concerning Means' contention that patients of the heroic school of medicine succumbed more often than not to the remedy, not to the disease.

Vasbinder also discussed politics, which had become, Darling sensed, his true love. Vasbinder meant to turn the tables on Smathers and company. Smathers intended to discredit Vasbinder—indeed to blackmail him—and destroy his campaign for the state assembly by associating him with Darling, thereby implicating him in the recent resurrections, portraying him in the process as an outlaw, a villain and a ghoul. But Vasbinder's platform would call for the legalization of medical dissection in Pennsylvania, thereby obviating the need for illegal resurrections. While the people of Hartsgrove and vicinity were alarmed by the recent incidents, he would propose to frame an act to prevent the traffic in human bodies and the desecration of graves by legalizing the use of unclaimed human cadavers. He would make use of the resurrections, just as Smathers intended to do, only to the opposite effect. He would use them to *gain* popularity, and votes. He would argue that while dissection may appear inhumane, the opposite was in fact true: it is in the best interests of humanity itself to do so, for how else could a young doctor repair the broken body of a working man, a man injured in the forest, in the field or in the foundry, if he did not possess a knowledge of that man's anatomy, a knowledge that could be learned only through repeated dissections?

A wonderful tactic, Darling said. But what good did do him? he thought. He had difficulty focusing on the best interests of humanity when his own best interests were under such grievous assault.

Kathleen's father was keeping a closer eye on her, suspicious of her activities, fearful of her involvement with a man accused of such a morbid act. He was even more adamant in his refusal to allow her to visit the jailhouse unescorted, and in his refusal to accompany her. With Sandt, she could go. He seemed in fact to be encouraging her to see Joshua Sandt at every opportunity, but Sandt had been busy of late; in addition to construction of his new house, his biannual shipment of medicines, oils, perfumeries, paints, glass and dyes had arrived from Philadelphia, and he was occupied stocking his shelves and rotating his stock.

"He's encouraging you to spend more time with Josh?" said Darling, indignant.

"I'm standing right here," said Sandt. "Or to put it another way, I'm standing right here."

"Please go and stand somewhere else," Darling said.

"Perhaps you don't realize the nuisance it is to accommodate daily visits to the jailhouse. Perhaps a bit more appreciation might be in order."

"Perhaps you've forgotten who drew the pursuit of Plotner away—perhaps you've forgotten that were it not for me, you would be sitting in the cell alongside me."

"Perhaps you've forgotten whose idea it was in the first place to attempt that asinine resurrection," Sandt said. "It certainly was not mine."

"No," said Kathleen. "It was mine."

The woodstove in the hallway popped and sizzled, partaking in the argument. Darling took hold of the bars between them. The bars that were always between them.

He missed his horse. It occurred to him that Gertie was more a part of him than any other living creature, and he missed the sturdy, solid, dependable presence of her, the sound of her nicker and whinny, the kindness of her eyes, her musky smell. He hoped his mother was keeping her well, keeping the straw fresh and clean in her little stable. He hoped Gertie understood that his detention was involuntary, his absence enforced, that he had not abandoned her, that she, Gertie, had done nothing wrong. He hoped she was not blaming herself for the ache in her heart, and hoped so with such empathy that a tear came to his eye, and he buried his face in the thin feather pillow on his bunk and wept, feeling very, very foolish. After all, he was a learned man, a physician, and she was only a horse, a pitiful creature, enslaved by her own limitations.

A week before Christmas, Darling acquired a neighbor when Jonathan Kelty, the blacksmith, was arrested for assault. Perhaps as drunk as Kunselman—who'd since returned to the neighboring cell for yet another visit beside Darling—though not nearly as insensible, Kelty sat slumped for a long period, his knuckles bruised and bleeding, his face brooding and mean, staring through the bars at Darling. Darling had begun to assume he was incapable of speech, which he suspected was a challenge to the man at any level of sobriety, but he was wrong.

After a while, Kelty said, "Ain't you some pumpkins now."

Darling looked up from his book. "Pumpkins?"

"How you like it, doc?"

"Not in the least, to be honest."

"Ain't riding around on no high horse now, are you?"

"Actually, Gertie is only of average height."

"You got a smart mouth on you, you know it, doc?"

"Shall I take that as a compliment?" said Darling.

"Somebody like to knock it in someday."

"Jonathan, what is your problem? I have never wronged you. I am not your enemy. My father in fact used to be among your custom."

"You and all them almighty doctors. Digging up dead folks. Cutting off people's legs."

"I see. Resurrections and amputations are your bones of contention."

"You got a smart mouth on you, you know it, doc?"

"Shall I take that as a compliment?" said Darling.

"Hope to hell I get sat on your jury."

Kelty was fined and gone in a day, and Christmas season came, largely resented by Darling. Hearing the occasional salute of good cheer called out on Main Street, or listening to one of the constables engage in seasonal well wishes with a visitor, Darling felt the sting of his deprivation all the more. None of his visitors wished him a Happy Christmas. All of his visitors knew the folly of the very idea. He realized he was feeling sorry for himself, a practice for which he normally had little patience, but now he allowed himself the luxury. In fact he allowed himself to wallow in it, wholeheartedly.

On Christmas Day, his mother arrived, shaking snow from her bonnet and shawl. The snowfall had begun in the morning, continuing through the afternoon in earnest. She brought him a cold turkey leg and a plate of pudding, which he said he would save to have later. She sat visiting patiently with her son, but Darling sensed her restlessness to leave his cold cell behind—she was invited to a small gathering at the McCurdy's. He couldn't blame her for wanting to be beside the McCurdy's hearth, enjoying good company, a crackling fire, the mantle and sills decorated with sprigs of holly and hemlock, so he encouraged her to leave when Vasbinder arrived, less than a half hour into her visit. The resentment he felt was a generalized resentment aimed at injustice in general, perhaps at Smathers in particular, but certainly not at his mother.

Vasbinder had no other plans. He'd always preferred a quiet Christmas, a day to be spent in contemplation and rest—a day to restore his body and spirit, as he'd told Darling often. For years he and his wife had celebrated the holiday with a simple, quiet sleigh ride over Clover Hill to take stock of their time and place on the earth, the sound of the sleigh bells the extent of their festivities. For the past few years he'd visited the Darlings on Christmas, and his stay had always been brief, only long enough to bring Will and his mother a small gift, and to sit with them for a while by the fire. One year he'd given Darling a mortar and pestle, another year a medical text. Last year he'd given him the uncharacteristic gift of a novel, something by Anthony Trollope, which Darling suspected had been given to Vasbinder, and which Vasbinder had never opened. It looked new. Darling had yet to open it himself.

After his mother had left, Vasbinder pulled a parcel from the pocket of his greatcoat and handed it to his charge. "It's nothing," he said.

Darling accepted it sheepishly. "I have nothing to give you in return."

"But you do, my dear—you can give me a promise. Promise me that you won't give up, that you'll continue to hope, that you'll continue to trust in God to see us through this trying time. Continue to trust that right will prevail. That's all the gift I ask."

"I shall try, Cyrus."

"Do more than try, my dear. Promise me."

Darling nodded in assent. He opened the parcel, removing the yellow silk bow, and beheld seven small wooden blocks, each painted brightly—red, blue, green and yellow—fastened together by thin strands of ribbon. "A Jacob's Ladder," he said.

"I thought you could use a toy." A smile lifted the bushy mustache.

Darling engaged in a reluctant smile of his own. He could not deny the childish sense of joy he felt. "Thank you, Cyrus. It's a work of art. I shall keep myself occupied with it many an hour—many an hour when I should be studying my texts, bettering myself."

"That's precisely what it's for, my dear."

He let it fall and twisted it, both men watching the bright, multicolored waterfall of wood, then he put it back in its parcel and placed it on the shelf by the wall where his toiletries where kept. The snow continued to fall, and they stood by the window of the cell to watch the white coming down, to see how it clung to the trees and shanties along Cherry Alley, which ran behind the jail. Engaging in idle gossip, Vasbinder mentioned that Sheriff Mills and a United States Marshal up from Pittsburgh had conducted a raid out in Little Brier that very afternoon. There was talk of runaway slaves being secreted through the area.

"This area? Here? In Hartsgrove? Little Brier?"

Vasbinder shrugged solemnly.

"Difficult to credit," said Darling. "What did they hope to find?"

"I can only imagine. Word is they found nothing."

"Black Hen harboring fugitive slaves in his shack?" Both men had to chuckle at the thought. The chuckles died as Darling recalled Black Hen's gaze at his arraignment.

"Still," said Vasbinder, "What's the name of that young buck? Augustus, is it?"

"Yes, Augustus. I suppose. He does have a strut about him."

"He certainly doesn't seem to know his place."

"I can't believe these matters are beginning to strike so close to home."

"Would that they should enforce the Bloodhound Act where it needs to be enforced, instead of paying lip service to it, giving hope and motive to those engaged in sedition and abolition, it would never come this far. Do not get me started."

Darling didn't. They talked about anything but the impending trial, the case itself, the mystery of Molly or the political imbroglio behind the whole affair, no more runaway slaves, discussing instead this medical case or that, this neighbor or that, a conversation they might have had passing time in their office, or strolling down by the springs. Darling sensed that his mentor, unlike his mother, was reluctant to leave him alone on this day. He launched into the lengthy story about meeting and courting his wife—*Gertrude*, though Vasbinder never referred to her in Darling's presence by her given name, for what Darling thought to be the obvious reason—leading to the anecdote about the time her mother had opened the cupboard, only to encounter a rattlesnake as long as her arm curled comfortably in the corner and rattling menacingly at the disruption of its nap. Her father, a stocky German butcher, had been obliged to quell the panic and use his tongs to capture the thing, which he dispatched by feeding to his hogs. Though Darling had heard the story many times before, both men pretended he hadn't.

Vasbinder fell asleep on the bunk. From the chair Darling watched the snow drifting down beyond the window. It was not the first time Vasbinder had dozed off during a quiet visit; sometimes the old man—for, increasingly, this was how Darling thought of him—merely nodded for a few minutes, though once he'd slept, even snored, for a good half hour. Darling covered him with a blanket and left him to his rest. Retrieving his Jacob's Ladder from the shelf, he examined it closely, each brightly painted block, each colorful silk ribbon. He folded it and let it fall several times, twisting it to watch the blocks cascade down the ribbons. As the snow fell, as his mentor slept, as the world shut him out and went quietly about its business, Will Darling was content to sit and play with his wonderful new toy.

It took less than two days to pull a jury, after which Darling's trial commenced. Truby came not long after first light and went over again the tactics he anticipated from the prosecution, the unkindnesses to which Darling should expect to be subjected, the demeanor his client should endeavor to display at all times—the essence of youth and innocence, the look of hopeful expectation and confidence upon his clean-shaven face—and the strategy the defense would deploy, which, in addition to portraying the defendant as a dedicated and self-sacrificing healer, was two-fold. Truby intended to cast doubt into the minds of the jurors as to the ability of Plotner to recognize Darling on a dark night at high gallop, and he intended to induce the same doubt as to whether or not the grave was even occupied in the first place. You cannot attempt to remove what is not there, he reiterated. You cannot violate a burial ground in which no one is buried.

He and Truby were escorted to the Courthouse by both constables for the occasion, McClay and Jenkins, in their uniforms of drab, young McClay's tight and bursting, old Jenkins's sagging and soiled. A spell of warm weather had vanquished the last vestiges of the snow that had brightened the Christmas for some, and the yard was soft and muddy. The air had an almost spring-like quality to it, rays of sun prying through the layers of pinkish clouds.

As they entered the courtroom and made their way to the defense table, Darling assessed the crowded gallery. Kathleen's wistful smile stood out, and he mouthed a greeting to her, exchanging nods and waves with Sandt, with his mentor, his mother and others; Darling noticed that Black Hen was not among them. And that not all of the faces were friendly.

The jury filed into the courtroom. Darling was surprised to see that two or three were unknown to him, though he knew all the rest, at least by sight, and he was relieved to see that Jonathan Kelty was not among them. Smathers and Sloan had seen to it that none of his or Vasbinder's patients, no one close to him, was seated. When the jurors were settled into their box—two rows of six chairs behind a railing like that defining the gallery—they quickly homed in on Darling and stared, studying him as if deciding at that moment his guilt or innocence, as if forming the verdict then and there, into which they would subsequently fold and fondle the testimony to fit. One juror whom Darling didn't know, a farmer in rough woolen garb, had a disfigured face, his left cheek having been injured—by the kick of a mule, perhaps, or a wayward axe head—which left him with half a beard and a cruel gaze, as if he blamed the world in general for his deformity, and was prepared to assign that blame more specifically to Darling. Darling stared back to the extent that he could, displaying his forthrightness, his innocence; but he was outnumbered and overwhelmed, and found himself the first to break eye contact and look away, convinced that in so doing he was displaying every evidence of guilt.

Presently, Southerland called for all to rise and Judge Hulse entered from behind the bench, his unruly eyebrows faltering beneath the gravity of the proceedings. After he'd seated himself at his pulpit and rapped the trial to order with his mallet, the opening arguments commenced. Levi Smathers, the great man himself, presented for the prosecution, going first, his voice rippling and reverberant, and to Darling, entirely ominous.

"Gentlemen," boomed Smathers, studying the men of the jury, his muttonchops bristling, "there sits before you"—here a sweeping gesture toward the defense table behind him—"not a young man, nor a young doctor, but a wolf in the guise of a lamb, a blood-thirsty wolf who would violate the sanctity of the grave, who would trespass upon the bereavement of a mourning family, and who would trample into the mire everything that's decent, God-fearing men like you and I cherish and hold dear. For it is in the burial of our dearly departed that we distinguish ourselves from the base, soulless animals; it is that act that gives us our very humanity, and to breach the inviolability of the final chamber of respite of a little girl, the purest of innocents, is an act of depravity, the act of a monster, an act of the most indecent, unimaginable and unforgivable kind." Darling listened raptly, following Smathers in all his meanderings, pacings and posturings in the open arena before the jury, in all his pronouncements, announcements, persuasions and pleas. He could feel the stares of the jurors. He tried not to look away from Smathers as the vilification inched endlessly onward, tried not to challenge the jury, hoping that his expression conveyed only confidence and innocence, not a hint of disrespect or arrogance. It was a fine line, he'd been tutored by Truby. Had he believed Smathers to be an honest man, a man of integrity, a man without a hidden political agenda—which many if not all of the jurors quite possibly believed—Darling was forced to conclude that he'd have little choice but to despise himself.

Fortunately he found his reputation and spirits quickly restored by the glowing and aggrieved summary subsequently presented by Truby. "May it please the court," he began, and Darling hoped that it would. It turned out he was not such a bad fellow after all, neither fiend nor ghoul, only a penniless young doctor who with great dedication and sacrifice traveled the length and breadth of Paine County and beyond in the service of the poor, sick and injured working man, their wives and children, striving to the utmost of his ability, and with little remuneration, to prevent them from joining the ranks of those dearly departed who needed to be buried and grieved for. "The illegality of the resurrection of a human cadaver is not subject to debate—it is in fact illegal, the purpose or reason for that resurrection notwithstanding. The morality, and the necessity, of such a resurrection for the purpose of scientific dissection is, on the other hand, subject to debate—but it is not the subject of our debate at this time and this place. The subject of our debate, gentlemen, the only subject, is whether or not the accused, Will Darling, did in fact commit this resurrection. We shall prove, beyond a doubt, that he did not."

To no one's surprise, Smathers's first witness was Enoch Plotner. For most of the day he occupied the stand, as Smathers began his interrogation of the witness with the day that Molly was born and from thence crept forward through every birthday and illness the child had ever celebrated and suffered—painting a portrait of an entirely adorable angel—through her treatment by Dr. Vasbinder, her later treatment by Dr. Darling, the defendant, through her demise and death. Plotner recounted how he made the tiny coffin and buried the child himself, with little ceremony, only his wife and he to mourn. Smathers homed in on the events that transpired in the early morning hours of Sunday, November 22, 1857, a foggy night illuminated by moonlight: Plotner, a light sleeper, was awakened by the sound of a voice, then, after he'd thrown open his window, by the distinct sounds of a shovel digging at earth, coming from the direction of the rise by the woods where he'd buried his little angel. When he approached and called out, a man fled on horseback. "Is that man in this courtroom?" said Smathers in a loud and sonorous voice.

"Yes, sir," said Plotner.

"Would you point him out, sir?" Plotner pointed at Darling, making eye contact for the first time since he'd taken the stand. Darling was dismayed to find himself staring back at a man who still owed him one dollar and twenty-five cents for the bleedings of Molly alone, not to mention five cents a mile, and the price of the medications; the tendency for his mercenary instincts to prevail at a time when his very freedom was in jeopardy he found troubling. "It was the middle of the night, Mr. Plotner—how can you be sure it was the defendant whom you saw?"

"There was some moon," Plotner said. "I got close enough, I seen him and his horse, a gray mare—I know 'em both pretty good, as many times as they been out to my place to doctor Molly. For all the more good that done."

Smathers asked him what happened next. Darling had fled, and he'd given chase, said Plotner. He'd quickly guessed the nature of the young doctor's business, having heard about the resurrection of Fudge Van Pelt, and he feared the worst. He'd lost Darling in the fog along the logging trail near Muddy Bottom Creek, finally giving up and returning to the scene of the crime, where his worst fears were confirmed: the coffin lay open and empty, the body of his little girl nowhere to be found. He'd ridden that very morning, before daybreak, to the sheriff.

Darling's heart went out to the man, his own jeopardy notwithstanding. He could empathize with Plotner, could feel the anguish he must have felt upon losing first his little girl, and then her very body, to what he could perceive only as a ghoulish and gristly fate. He studied the faces of the jurors which for the most part were staid, although one young man who clerked, he thought, for Moses Clover, did seem to exhibit a pained and sympathetic arch to his eyebrow. The farmer with half a beard glared in Darling's direction.

Truby commenced his cross-examination. He commiserated with Plotner, unable to even imagine the anguish he must be suffering over the loss of a darling daughter; Truby knew from experience how the little packages of joy gave such meaning to our humdrum lives. Darling wondered if the jurors knew, as he did, that Truby had no children.

Truby commenced: how far from the horse and rider was Plotner?

Plotner shrugged. "Purt near close enough to hit with stick," he said.

"As close as from here to, say, the stove in the far corner of the courtroom there?"

"About that close I'd say."

"And it was night."

"Middle of the night, yes sir. Already said it was the middle of the night."

"And does it generally get dark at night out toward Coolbrook?"

"Objection, your honor," said Smathers, rising greatly from his chair.

"Let me rephrase the question," said Truby. "Was it dark that night?"

"There was some moon," Plotner said. "Already said there was some moon."

"And was there some fog?"

"A little."

"So it was in *a little* fog that you lost Dr. Darling—or whomever it was that you say you were pursuing. In other words, the fog was thick enough to lose track of an entire horse and rider, but not so thick that you cannot positively identify that same horse and rider—is that correct?"

"It was thicker'n some places than others," Plotner said.

"And in which places were you? And, allegedly, Dr. Darling."

"Wasn't too foggy to see him clear up by the grave. Him and the horse he rode off on."

"And you're positive, absolutely positive, it was Dr. Darling you saw."

"Ain't a doubt about it in my mind, no sir."

"Very well," Truby said. He paused, picked up a paper from the table, appeared to study it for a moment. Then, dropping it, he said, "And you saw Molly's body?"

Plotner's brow dipped. "No—like I said, when I got back there to her grave, the coffin was open and—"

"No, no," said Truby. "Not then. Not afterwards. Did you see the body of your daughter in the possession of Dr. Darling—if indeed it was Dr. Darling—as he rode off?"

"I—I mighta seen her. He mighta had something tied up in there behind his saddle."

"He *might have*."

"Yes sir. Matter of fact the more I think about it, I'm pretty sure he did."

"Do I have this correct, Mr. Plotner? You're absolutely, one-hundred percent certain you saw Dr. Darling and his horse, quite clearly, but you *might have* seen the body of your daughter. Now, looking back and thinking about it for the first time, you *might* be *pretty sure* you did."

Plotner didn't respond.

"Very well," Truby said. "Let's see if you can be more certain about this. You testified that you heard a voice, as well as the sound of digging, which alerted you to the presence of someone at Molly's grave. Now, I've been to your place, Mr. Plotner, and I'd say the grave site is a good quarter mile or so from your home—is that about right?"

"Close enough, I reckon."

"Yet you could hear a voice—not a shout or a call, mind you, just a voice talking in a normal tone, if not a whisper—and you could hear the sound of a shovel digging into the earth."

"Like I said, it was real still that night. Real quiet."

"Stiller and quieter than most nights?"

"Yes, sir. Why, I could hear the chickens laying eggs out in the coop." A chuckle or two from the gallery.

"And on the other nights," said Truby, "the nights that weren't so quiet. Did you camp out by Molly's grave and keep watch there?"

Plotner's brow dipped again. "No—"

"No. You didn't keep watch over her grave. You'd heard about the violation of the grave of Fudge Van Pelt, about his resurrection, yet you did not keep watch over Molly's grave?"

"Why, I never—"

"Then how can you be certain that Molly had not already been dug up and removed prior to the morning of November 22? Did you inspect her grave every morning?"

"Your Honor," said Smathers, rising once again. "This is pure speculation. Or, more precisely, this is pure hogwash."

"Is there an objection in there somewhere, Levi?"

"I object most vigorously, your Honor."

"Overruled. Mr. Truby is establishing a possible alternative scenario for the crime, and I shall allow it."

"I have just one or two questions more, your Honor," said Truby. "Mr. Plotner, have you ever heard of the Washington Medical College in Greensville?"

"No, sir."

"No? So you're unaware then that the Washington Medical College is famous for its curriculum, which includes the dissection of human cadavers, and that the demand of that college for human cadavers is large and growing, and that some unscrupulous hooligans among the population have taken it upon themselves to supply, by nocturnal and nefarious means, the human cadavers that college requires for study?"

"Objection!" cried a rising Smathers.

"You are wandering very far afield here, John—I believe I shall sustain Mr. Smathers's objection."

"I have no more questions, Judge," said Truby. "I believe we're done here."

Darling found himself sustained as well, by what he took to be the successful cross-examination by his counsel of the principal witness for the prosecution. In Darling's mind, reasonable doubt had been established, and he was reasonably optimistic that such doubt had been raised in the minds of at least some of the jurors as well. And only some would be needed.

The days of the trial passed more quickly than the days preceding it had, those days he'd spent alone in his cell, black-hearted days without hope, solitary days when his mind had had entirely too much time to concoct its own disheartening scenarios. Smathers questioned witness after witness—every doctor in town, every family member and close friend of the defendant, trying to establish motive and opportunity. Had the defendant ever expressed a desire to take part in a medical dissection? Did he believe the practice of dissection to be a necessary part of the education of a physician? Had he ever mentioned his part in the resurrection and dissection of Mr. Van Pelt? Had he ever expressed regret or disappointment at its outcome? Had he ever spoken of Molly Plotner in particular? However, no response seemed, to Darling, surprising or incriminating. Truby, in his mind, successfully parried every thrust by Smathers.

On a Sunday afternoon both frigid and bleak, Dr. Means visited. Darling was not expecting the man, nor had he any reason to be, but he was nevertheless pleased. He valued his visitors all, but especially a new face, a departure from the ordinary. "Steven," Darling said when the smiling red goatee appeared in the corridor, "what a pleasant surprise."

"I've been meaning to visit, but you know how it is," Means said, giving his customary thumbs-up. In his other hand he carried a book. "Never enough hours in the day."

"Idle hands are the devil's workshop, as my mother would have me believe."

"Yes. It seems as though I can scarcely keep apace anymore."

"Spreading the Gospel of Eclecticism, no doubt."

"Indeed," said Means. "That and other matters as well."

Darling immediately began to regret his Gospel remark, remembering their last conversation on the side of a hill over two months before, when they'd argued about schools of medicine; Means's assertion that Vasbinder's heroic approach—and, by implication, Darling's—resulted in a positive outcome for the undertaker more often than for the patient had caused hard feelings, at least on Darling's part, and he was not particularly anxious to alienate a precious visitor now. In addition, he felt a genuine fondness for the man.

Means took the opportunity to proffer the book in his hand. "Speaking of idle hands, I've brought you a little reading material."

Darling took the volume: *The American Eclectic Practice of Medicine*, by I. G. Jones, M.D. "If I didn't know better, Steven, I'd think you were trying to convert me."

Means gave a chuckle. "Not at all, not at all—just hoping you'll keep an open mind."

"Open, certainly. Actually, I'm just hoping at this point to keep a sane mind."

"I can only imagine," said Means.

A lull ensued, quite different from their free-flowing conversations in the natatoriums of summer. Both men said, "Well—" at the same moment. Then Means expressed his dismay that Darling should even be sitting in jail in the first place, it was surely all politics, the confounding absence of the little girl's body notwithstanding. Darling agreed, and then they talked about the cold, and then an unfortunate lull took hold once again.

"See here," Darling said, "I've meaning to ask you something for some time."

"Oh?" Means said. "And I you. A mutual intention."

"Fudge Van Pelt," Darling said. "As I understand, he was under your care."

"He was."

"How shall I put this? Was there a chance, any chance whatsoever…that it was not entirely a case of the disease taking its natural course? There have been rumors. Was there ever an opportunity during that time, about which you are aware, for anyone to do him harm? Not to imply in the slightest any malfeasance or malpractice on your part. You must have heard the rumors, they've been abroad now for some time."

"I have," Means said. "And I'd given them no credence whatever—until lately. Some of Fudge's friends have been quite persistent in their suspicions, and it's gotten me thinking. I can say that I believe that no one—I presume we're talking primarily about the Doctors Bullers here—no one could have tampered with my remedies and done the man harm in that regard. Which brings me to the question I had for you: had anyone—Little Bull, for example—had an opportunity to strike out at Fudge in any other way, shape or form? His demise and the desire for the dissection do seem to have coincided most unfortunately."

"No," said Darling. "No such opportunity about which I am aware. Of course, it has been occurring to me the longer I sit here how very little I seem to be aware of."

The lull that ensued this time was different, more comfortable, contemplative rather than awkward. Darling sensed a mutual interest, a growing notion of camaraderie. Means began to elaborate on Fudge's last illness, on the symptoms displayed and the treatment administered, admitting that while there were anomalies—the vomiting, for instance—as in every individual illness, they seemed well within the median range of a case of the fever. Darling for his part related that the Bullerses, Little Bull in particular, had never, at the time of the resurrection, hinted that they might be aware that Fudge's demise had been anything other than natural, let alone that they might have had a hand in it. Though afterwards, while in their cups, a hint or two might have surfaced, but that he'd attributed mostly to the whiskey, that and the Bullerses' innate racialism. They had been staunch Know-Nothings, and were, for that matter, every bit as biased against the Irish.

Means sighed, and Darling saw what might have been a gleam in his eye. "Then I suppose we can rule out Dr. Vasbinder as well," he said.

"Cyrus?" Darling said. "Why on earth would we rule him in?"

"It simply occurred to me that perhaps he might have driven his shay out to Little Brier in my absence and assumed treatment of Fudge. That surely would have killed him."

Darling allowed a smile at the joke, though he nevertheless felt obligated to object to the implication. "I can assure you, Steven, you will be hard-pressed to find a single patient of Cyrus who would accuse him of less than satisfactory treatment."

When Means responded, "Why, of course not—dead men tell no tales," Darling was later to rather regret the paroxysms of laughter into which he and Means were mutually thrown, the great relief at his first such outburst in months, feeling it must have been somehow a betrayal of his long-suffering preceptor. But he thought, in the end, he could live with it.

When the prosecution called Kathleen O'Hanlon to the stand, Smathers sought to put her at ease, perhaps to unnerve her. "Upon my word, Miss," he said as soon as she was sworn and settled in the witness chair, "you are very pretty."

"I would return the compliment, sir," said Kathleen, "if I were not under oath."

A thundercloud darkened Smathers's brow as the gallery tittered. Gruffly, he asked Kathleen to state her name and occupation, and, after she had, asked her how long she'd known the defendant.

"Most all of my life," she said.

"And how well do you know him?"

Kathleen looked at Darling. "Quite well."

"Quite well. Very well," Smathers said. After Kathleen had confirmed her awareness that the defendant was a practicing physician and that he had an abiding interest in the dissection of human cadavers, Smathers asked if she was also aware that he was disposed to the resurrection of cadavers from their burial places for the purpose of dissection. Kathleen said she was.

"Have you ever heard the defendant mention the name of Molly Plotner?"

"I have. The little girl was his patient. He became quite attached to her—I understand she was a lovely child. Will was surprised when she died—he thought she'd recovered from the illness he'd been treating her for."

"And did he ever mention, in the course of your conversations, an interest in resurrecting the little girl to dissect her?"

"No," said Kathleen. "He could never have dissected her, such a grisly business it is—he was much too fond of her. He did want to perform an autopsy, though—I understand there's a grand difference between dissection and autopsy."

"So," Smathers said, "he said he wanted to perform an autopsy on the child?"

"He did." Darling watched the sincerity on the pretty face he adored, a sincerity that might be killing him. Beside him Truby tensed, gripping the pen in his hand.

"And did he, to your knowledge, act upon that desire?"

"He did."

A murmur passed through the courtroom, causing Judge Hulse to rap his mallet.

"Precisely how did he act upon that desire?"

"He went out to Plotner's to dig her up."

"He did!" cried Smathers. "And this he told you himself?"

"There was need to tell me a'tall," Kathleen said. "Sure, I was with him at the time."

Hulse leaned into his mallet to quell the eruption in the courtroom. "Quiet! Order in this courtroom!" When peace had been restored, he peered down at the witness. "Miss," he said, "are you aware that you may be incriminating yourself?"

"Yes, your Honor."

"I would advise you to seek counsel before you utter another word."

"There's no need, your Honor. I want to get it on the record, once and for all, so it's clear, that the body of the little girl was not there."

Truby stood, he and Smathers crying out as one, "Objection, your Honor."

"Mr. Smathers," said the judge, "you cannot object to your own line of questioning; Mr. Truby, your objection is overruled. I want to hear what this witness has to say." Truby sat, his chair groaning in the hush of the courtroom.

Kathleen continued. "I opened her coffin myself, sir, and it was entirely empty, there was no trace of the little girl at all. Will couldn't have resurrected her, because there was no one there to be resurrected, and so he can't be guilty of violating a burial ground." Her last few words were nearly lost in another gathering rumble of voices in the courtroom. Again the judge took to his mallet, his hawkish nose growing red.

"Kathleen, Kathleen, Kathleen," murmured Darling.

"Kathleen indeed," muttered Truby.

After conferring with Sloan, Smathers continued his questioning of Kathleen, but no new ground was broken; she had told her story. The prosecution seized upon half a loaf: Having now established that Darling had indeed intended to resurrect the little girl, had indeed dug open her grave, Smathers pounded away at Kathleen's claims about the missing body. Of course Molly had been there, of course her little body had been removed by the defendant and his recently unmasked partner in crime. Where else could she have been? What else could possibly have become of her? But Kathleen was adamant.

Truby, in his cross-examination, seized upon the other half of the loaf: the absence of the little girl's body. He asked Kathleen if she had any suspicion as to how, when or where the little girl's body might have been removed and disposed of. Moreover, did she think that Enoch Plotner might be anxious to cast suspicion upon Dr. Darling, with his known interest in resurrection and his known association with Molly, for some other reason? Perhaps because Plotner knew already what had really happened to the body? Here Smathers objected, and the judge sustained. But Truby had planted the seed, and he withdrew the question, knowing that the fact essential to the defense had now been corroborated: There had been no body there to resurrect.

Afterwards, Kathleen again visited him in his cell, again accompanied by Sandt.

"What were you thinking?" Darling said, somewhat intolerantly.

"For God's sake, Will, you and Truby—you can't have it both ways! You can't have your cake and eat it too! Either you were there or you were not—either the body was there or it was not. You weaken your defense trying to have it both ways. Best to choose the one track—best to choose the truth."

"And the truth shall set you free," said Sandt, a vacant expression upon his face.

Darling ignored his old school chum. "Perhaps," he said to

Kathleen. "But I was not referring to that—I was referring to your incrimination of yourself. You might well end up in the cell next door to mine."

"And wouldn't that be grand?" said Kathleen. "Together at last."

Darling fairly glowed. He had not glowed in some time. Putting his hand upon hers, which was clasping the bar, he said, "I love you, Kathleen O'Hanlon."

Kathleen blushed.

"I'm standing right here," said Sandt. "Or, to put it another way, I'm standing right here."

"Please go and stand somewhere else," Darling said.

The euphoria that had infected him from the most recent turn of events sustained him throughout the night and into the trial next morning. He scarcely felt the floor beneath his feet. Which was the more sustaining? His outright declaration of love for Kathleen, or the strategy for the defense she'd unilaterally imposed—which Truby begrudgingly conceded might be as effective as the defense he'd planned. That no body had been there was now corroborated, and more and more Darling trusted his counsel and his mentor—and now the love of his life—that without a body the prosecution had little hope of securing a conviction. As he came into the courtroom, he saw Kathleen sitting expectantly in the front row in a pretty gingham dress, her hat placed primly in her lap, her black hair framing the perfect symmetry of her face. As the proceedings were coming to order, he and Kathleen stared lovingly at one another.

The prosecution called Samuel Bullers. Little Bull was the penultimate witness on the prosecution's roster; his brother would be the final witness before it rested. Little Bull took the oath, standing stout and sturdy in his frayed waistcoat, his twill trousers stuffed into his boots, then turned and looked at Darling with a smile. It was a warm smile, and as Darling returned it, Little Bull winked. Darling felt another rush of well-being, a rush of happiness, a feeling of gratitude for the friendship he felt between him and Bullers, and wonder at its sudden revelation.

Little Bull stated his name and occupation for the record, and after a few preliminary questions, Smathers asked him how well he knew the defendant.

"We been acquainted a number of years," Little Bull said. "And here a little while back, we had some business together, young Dr. Darling and me."

"Would that business have had to do with the resurrection of Fudge Van Pelt?"

"It would, yes sir."

"Dr. Darling was anxious to perform a dissection upon the remains of Mr. Van Pelt?"

"He was. Then again, we all were. He feels dissection is the best way to learn anatomy, and, as he's fond of saying, a knowledge of anatomy is the foundation of the healing art."

"And was the defendant disappointed when that dissection was ultimately thwarted?"

"He surely was. Of course, we all were."

"How did he intend to remedy that disappointment?"

"Well, you know how it is when you're young and stubborn and full of yourself."

"I scarcely remember," said Smathers, smiling for the jurors and gallery. Darling, his spirits still aloft, could not quite contain his own smile, though he noticed a certain reserve on the part of Truby at his elbow. "How is it when you're young and stubborn? And full of yourself?"

"I can barely remember my own self," said Little Bull with a humble chuckle, "but as for young Will Darling, he said there'd be plenty of other chances to get us a body for dissecting. He said people were dying to become our specimens—that was his little joke."

Darling felt a queasiness in his stomach.

"And what was his reaction then to the death of his patient, Molly Plotner?"

"He said she'd be perfect. Said she was no more'n a little hooter he could tuck in his back pocket. Said she'd be a cinch to dig up and move and hide, and the dissection itself wouldn't take near as long—the longer it takes, the more likely you are to get found out. He said she wasn't much bigger than the fleas he's partial to dissecting on his mother's supper table."

His face burning, his stomach in full revolt, Darling felt his mind emptying, spinning. He didn't hear Smathers's next question, rejoining Little Bull's response midway through.

"…he never mentioned any company. I got the impression he was all alone."

Smathers said, "And did he tell you that the coffin was empty?"

"No sir—he said he got her body up all right, and then along came Plotner."

"A pack of lies!" Kathleen cried from the gallery.

The rumble that had been gathering in the courtroom erupted at Kathleen's outcry. Judge Hulse pounded his mallet, his eyebrows in full disarray, his face stern and red. "Restrain yourself young lady, or I shall have you removed and placed into custody! Order in this courtroom!"

Darling could only observe, as if from a great remove.

Smathers continued. "And what did Dr. Darling tell you what became of the body of Molly Plotner?"

"Said he had to bury her again. When he couldn't shake loose of

Plotner, he buried her shallow down by a logging trail not too far off from Muddy Bottom. Said he meant to go back out and dig her up again, only he ended up in jail. If the wolfs ain't dug her up, I'd imagine she'd be out there yet."

Smathers ordered Sheriff Mills to renew the search for Molly. The early January thaw had melted the snow cover. Not nearly as many men turned out for the second search, perhaps out of a pessimism it would bear no more fruit than the first, or perhaps out of a reluctance to endure the frigid January temperatures, a far cry from the moderate weather of November.

The renewal of the search didn't greatly concern the brain trust for the defense. If Levi Smathers and the Sheriff felt obliged to waste the time and toil of a posse of the area's citizens, that was their business; Truby, Darling and Vasbinder intended to spend their time and toil more wisely. They discussed the setback late into the night in Darling's drafty cell.

Over and over they rehashed the testimony of Little Bull: what would possess a man to perjure himself so blatantly? They concluded it to be unlikely it was out of a personal vendetta against Darling. The lack of acrimony between them in the past—the absence of grudge—would seem sufficient to rule it out, leaving them to conclude that the only possible motivation was a desire by Little Bull to throw the authorities off the scent. But off the scent of what? Darling and Truby speculated that by pointing the finger at Darling, Little Bull's own likely hand in the disappearance of Molly's body would remain concealed. He was not likely to be charged with a crime for which another man had been convicted.

Vasbinder, however, dismissed this theory, that Little Bull had taken the body of Molly, and was now diverting attention to Darling. He suspected a more complex scenario, a grander conspiracy involving, at a minimum, Congressman Smathers, the Doctors Bullers and District Attorney Sloan, a conspiracy aimed solely at disgracing Darling in order to destroy the reputation of Vasbinder by association—for everyone was aware of the close bond between the two men—thereby effectively removing him from the political arena. Eliminating him as a candidate for the Assembly would clear the way once and for all for Butterfield. Who else might be involved? Butterfield, of course. Justice Martz? Sheriff Mills? Judge Hulse? The whole of the Paine County Republican apparatus? Where did it end? In Vasbinder's estimation, nothing was beyond the Republicans. In his view, they would gladly sacrifice three years of a young man's life, and the reputations of him and his mentor, in order to prevail at the ballot box.

This had been the intent of Smathers and the Republican cabal all along, argued Vasbinder, beginning with the matter of the resurrection of Fudge Van Pelt. At that time, he'd been able to prevail upon Smathers's sense of decency to persuade him to drop the prosecution, but the second offense had proved too tempting an opportunity for Smathers to ignore—here Darling withered beneath the scolding frown cast his way by his mentor—and decency had given way to political expediency.

In court the next day, Truby was unable to discredit Samuel Bullers's version of events in his cross-examination, and when his brother, Alexander, testified next, corroborating his brother's story, he was equally steadfast.

All day, Darling's daydreams carried him to barren places. As the trial dragged on, the number of spectators had dwindled, not because of waning interest, for the case was still the foremost topic of discussion in taverns and kitchens and sitting rooms, anywhere a hearth could be found, but because the spectators were working men and women, with little time for leisure. Kathleen was absent, her father growing more and more impatient with her neglect of his books, and his old school chum Sandt was minding his drug store. Darling's mother was busy at Mrs. McCurdy's, where, according to her, Fudge's widow, Lucindy, was now employed as well. In a daydream, Darling saw Lucindy standing in the ice house doorway watching the doctors skin her husband, her black face the color of curdled milk. Even though his mentor was present, sitting in the first row, Vasbinder seldom looked Darling's way, and seemed to be daydreaming himself, his expression tic-free and placid, his bushy white mustache immobile. In Darling's reverie, he found himself in the Hartsgrove Cemetery, gazing down at the weed-infested grave of Cyrus Vasbinder, his tombstone cold and unadorned. Next he found himself watching Kathleen and Sandt strolling into a dance together, her hand reaching for his, their fingers intertwining.

It was late, past the nine o'clock hour when he heard the door in the corridor open and saw Jenkins enter. Behind him was Kathleen. The pale yellow glow of the lamp on the hallway stand cast shadows on her face, and Darling thought it was that, the shadows alone, that accounted for the stricken look there, but as she came closer, he realized that was not the case.

He looked to the doorway for Sandt, but Sandt never appeared.

"Kathleen—what's wrong? Where's Josh?"

"I don't know," she said, shaking her head as if trying to banish a thought. "I've not seen him today at all. I came on my own."

"Then why—how—what about your father?"

"My father?" Kathleen looked at him as though she didn't know to whom he referred. She'd grasped the bars, and Darling had grasped her hands. "Have you not heard, Will? Has no one told you yet?"

"Has no one told me what?"

"They found her today—Molly Plotner."

"They—" Shock seized him. "But that's not possible."

"By the logging trail," she said. "Where they say she was buried."

For a time Darling and Kathleen paced, together, the bars between them, back and forth along the front of the cell, angry gestures and exclamations, fists clenched in outrage and despair. They were *lying*, all of them. There could not have been a body. If there was, it could not have been Molly Plotner. What was going on? Who was responsible? Did they know who they were trifling with? Did *who* know who they were trifling with? This would not be suffered meekly.

Soon the helplessness, the hopelessness, overcame the anger, and, for an even longer time, they stood talking in whispers, plotting far-flung and unlikely strategies, reassuring one another that this too would somehow pass. Somehow they would make it through. The truth would come out. Then, weary both inside and out, they sat on the floor. They whispered, sinking lower. When Jenkins finally returned, he looked in to see them sleeping, on the floor on either side of the bars, facing each other, the thin pillow from his bunk beneath her head, their hands touching between the bars. Darling feigned sleep. Jenkins on tiptoe placed a blanket over Kathleen. He turned down the wick of the camphene lamp. Through squinted eyes, Darling watched him stand for a moment looking down at them, his head shaking in the shadows before he turned and tiptoed away again, closing the door softly behind him.

He looked at Kathleen, at the speck on her cheek where the last tear had dried. For the longest time his thoughts continued weakly to rail and rage, refusing to give in to rest. Gradually the storm subsided. Gradually he gave in, surrendering, allowing himself to drift to the place where Kathleen already was. Against all odds he felt strangely safe there, unaccountably filled with hope. Squeezing her hand, he pressed his face as close to hers as possible, his forehead touching the bar, and mouthed the words more than said them, to the sleeping love of his life: "Kathleen—will you marry me?"

"Yes," she murmured aloud, her eyes never opening, her hands clutching his.

10: December 6, 1857: The Last Days of Pompey

Brilliant morning sunlight sliced through the cracks between the boards of the barn, shining on the miniscule motes drifting lazily in the air. On four rude plank benches sat a dozen or two worshipers from Little Brier, Cornelius Nips at a barrelhead pulpit before them, imploring them toward great holiness. Hen and Augustus, just back from delivering Hubbard and Randall, sat weary on a stool and a bucket in the back by the big, wide door. Augustus had never been to the Praise House, otherwise known as John Lemon's barn. Hen had, years before.

It was not for worship they'd come. They'd come to ask about the law.

Cornelius paused his sermon as the congregation turned to take in the two latecomers. "Brothers and sisters, say welcome and hallelujah to Brother Henry and Brother 'Gustus, who just done snuck in the back. Welcome, Brothers!" Members of the congregation, every man, woman and child, nodded deeply. Cornelius continued. "We been talking about belief, before you come in, Brothers, *belief!* And I was telling what I believes—I believes in the heavenly Kingdom of God Almighty. And I believes that the next world ain't going to be nothing like this here world, I believes the next world, God's world, ain't nothing like this here world, the white man's world." From the corner of his eye, Hen saw Augustus shake his head, contrary to the nodding congregation. "Not only does I believe in the Kingdom of God, up there awaiting on us all, awaiting on all us believers, I believes that the Kingdom of God make the kingdom of the white man down here on this dirt like nothing more than a spit in the mighty ocean! A little bitty ant hill you smash underneath your heel!"

"Amen, Brother," cried Marcus Swan, and others followed suit.

"Looky here, brethren, looky here! Looky here, here it is,"—here Cornelius crouched, pointing grandly toward a dark spot high in the rafters of the barn, just above where the horizon would be in the sky—"here's that vast army of angels gathered up there on the white plains of Canaan, singing songs of glory, harps in they hands, feasting on milk and honey, a starry crown on every head—and they all gathered round the Great White Throne where sits the King in his royal garments! And they all singing and calling, 'Where's Brother Cornelius? Where's Brother Cornelius? Brother Cornelius, come on up here and join us!' And when I gets there, they gonna hand me my starry crown, they gonna say, 'Try this one on, Brother Cornelius—that one too big? Try this one on instead'—and, 'Here, Brother Cornelius, here's your harp and your new white suit of clothes! Try them on, see how they fits!'" All the while, Cornelius, sprightly despite his stocky build, hopped about behind the pulpit, sweat glistening on his bald head as the *Amens* and cries poured out of the congregation.

He paused, waiting till the cries had trickled off and the silence was good and thick. Then he started off low. "Ain't no terror in ol' man Death. Ol' man Death done lost his sting—my Lord and Master Jesus done walked up to ol' man Death, done spit in his face, done struck down his colors of terror, done broke his sword over his own knee, done told ol' man Death, 'You through, Death, you through terrorizing my childrens!'"—here Cornelius's voice again ascended in a mighty arc—"my Lord and Master Jesus done blazed the way smooth and easy for to lead his people through, just like ol' Moses done when he brung the children of Israel through the wilderness to the Promised Land!" More *Amens* and moans from the believers. "I believes," Cornelius said quietly again, "does you?

"I believes, thanks be to God, I believes! I got the faith! I believes my Lord and my Master Jesus, he done built me a house up yonder inside them Pearly Gates, a sweet house alongside the avenue where the children of God dwells, and that house be right next door to the house he done built for my mama when she go up there them many years ago, and I can tell it's the house of my mama, I can tell, ain't no mistaking, cause I can see the posies she done planted in her yard alongside that little white fence. And there—there she is in the doorway, there's my mama, fixing to throw her loving arms around me one more time!"

Cornelius paused till the room grew quiet, then started off in a whisper. "All it takes is faith, brethren, faith enough to fill a mustard seed, one bitty little mustard seed—that's all the more faith it takes, brothers and sisters." He paused again, looking about the room, past the dust motes floating in the slices of sunshine, staring at the members of his congregation one by one, settling at last on old Hiram Appleby in front. "Brother Hiram—does you belief in ghosts?"

Hiram, who had not been among the clappers or shouters or moaners, looked up in surprise, peering perplexed over his foggy spectacles. He cupped a hand to his ear. "Does I believe in what, Brother?"

"I say, does you believe in ghosts?"

"Does I believe in *goats*?"

"*Ghosts*, Brother Hiram, *ghosts*—does you belief in ghosts?"

"Ghosts. Oh. Well, hear tell there's a spook haunts the shanty by the injun burial ground up past Mortimer's Pool."

Cornelius nodded. "So, Brother Hiram, he believe a injun spook dwell in that little ruint shanty out by Mortimer's Pool," he said, raising his hands. "If Brother Hiram believe in a injun ghost, then it ain't too big a jump for Brother Hiram to believe in the Holy Ghost! And if Brother Hiram believe in the Holy Ghost, then we all, brothers and sisters, every one of us, all God's childrens, we can believe in the Holy Ghost, in our Lord and Master Jesus Christ, and in Great God almighty Himself, sitting right up there on his Great White Throne, waiting on all his little childrens come a-calling! Hallelujah, brethren!"

Hen leaned over to whisper to Augustus. "I believe I'm going to take my leave, 'fore the man bust into song." Augustus nodded knowingly.

Hen slipped outside, unnoticed by the congregation in the hubbub of glory, and stood in the bright sunshine by the door of the barn. He was numb. It was the fervor of the sermon, the lack of sleep, the echo of the blood racing through his body from last night's narrow escape, the tense after-journey, the disharmony and arguments, it was the brilliance of the morning that made the memory of that black night seem more dreamed than real. The numbness was such that it took him a moment to realize how badly he had to pee. He walked down the little slope of the barnyard, behind the new tannery shed that smelled of fresh-sawn boards. Despite the urgency, relief came only in trickles and spurts, and Hen had plenty of time to contemplate the beauty, the icy surface of the ooze-pit by the tannery glistening in the sun, the expanse of meadow sweeping over to the tree line, the warm sunlight burning off the white frost, mist rising up. Hen could barely button his pants, his hands were trembling so. His heart was scrambling in his throat, trying to flee his chest, and he remembered why he never went to Cornelius's services at the Praise House. He looked up into the sky, so clear and blue and pure he could see forever—where, then, was this kingdom of Heaven, the Pearly Gates, the avenues along which dwelt the children of God? Hen could see no place where it could possibly be hiding. On and on he could see. He could see to eternity. And eternity was empty.

He made his way slowly, his legs like straw, back up the barn door, as the service was concluding. Augustus was first out. "Lordy, Lordy," he said, shaking his head, "that man can't sing worth a lick." Other worshipers emerged, nodding to the two men sitting on the crate and the stump not far from the door of the barn. Cornelius was the last one out. Augustus went to him, Hen not far behind.

"Brother 'Gustus," Cornelius said, smiling broadly, "did you enjoy our service?"

Augustus didn't return the smile or answer the question. "Tell me something—you and Marcus and them—you ever end up going to the law?"

"Going to the law?" Cornelius frowned.

"Like we was talking 'bout the other night, couple weeks ago. 'Bout whether or not them doctors might of done Fudge in."

Cornelius's brow remained furrowed, though his expression shifted from confusion to consideration. "Why you asking, Brother?"

"The law be sniffing around. We seen 'em, me and Hen, sniffing around."

Cornelius nodded. "We didn't go to no law—the law done come to us."

"Say what?" Augustus said.

"Me and Marcus was in at Clover's," Cornelius said. "Sheriff Mills and a couple other big bugs stopped us, asking us questions." Cornelius said the sheriff had wanted to know if they were aware of any activity regarding runaway slaves, that there had been rumors that certain members of the Little Brier community had been involved in illegal behavior, and he went on to ask if, for that matter, either of them had seen the late Miss Eva Alcorn in or around the vicinity of Little Brier. He was accusing no one, the sheriff said, only making necessary inquiries, and expressed his hope that Hartsgrove's niggers, the residents of Little Brier, were not taking it in their heads to become engaged in any criminal behavior, that the citizens of Hartsgrove had always been pleased with the way their niggers had always been well-behaved, never the cause of any mischief, no cause for concern whatsoever. He hoped it would stay that way.

"So me and Marcus, we tells him no, no, we ain't' never seen any of them goings-on, not none of it. But then we says *we* wants to know what happen to our brother, Fudge Van Pelt. We understand them doctors want to dig him up and use his body for cutting up or something, but how come ol' Fudge just happen to die just when they happen to be looking for some body to cut up—we was wondering if somebody might of just helped him get dead ahead of his time."

"And what he say 'bout that?" Augustus said.

"He ain't say nothing. Start smirking. Him and them other big bugs, they all seem to think something funny, like me and Marcus is making some kind of joke."

"Funny, huh? Smirking, huh? What you think 'bout them biscuits, Hen?"

But Hen wasn't listening. He was staring into the sky again, seeing the emptiness again.

They rode back to Little Brier in quiet, Augustus deep in thought, Hen's head as empty as he could make it. As they pulled up by his cabin, Augustus said, "I thought the man done said *goats* too. I was wondering—hell, I believes in goats. Me and ol' Hiram." He gave a little chuckle.

"I believes in pigs."

"Brother Cornelius should of asked me," Augustus said. "I heard tell 'bout a spook suppose to live up in the ol' Smathers mansion up in Bootjack—say it's the ghost of his little girl, Levi Smathers' little girl, got killed in a fire. Hear tell she cries and wails and carries on every time the moon gets big. Sometimes when it ain't no moon at all."

Hen nodded. "Reckon I believes in sheeps, too."

Hen had patched up his chimney with mud, but hadn't yet tried it out. When he did that night, he kept the fire small, and still he scarcely slept the whole night through, but then that was nothing out of the ordinary even on the warmest, most fireless of nights. He fretted and sweated, too hot or too cold, in and out of his blankets and rags, afraid to sleep and afraid not to, having little choice either way, and he arose around dawn—or so he guessed, as the clouds had crept in during the night, gray snow flurries troubling the air, and Absalom had not uttered his crow—and limbered up his tired old bones, broke the ice in his bucket and splashed water on his face.

Mornings he walked into town, passing the saw mill, the mournful loud whine of saws making lumber, the rumble and roar of white men making money, and he kept walking, up to Main to try to earn a penny of his own. Clover usually had an odd job or two, the Peace and Poverty Tavern usually had spittoons to be scrubbed out, sawdust to be swept, Northey the butcher had a bloody trough to slop, though the discarded hides never failed to remind him of Fudge, and so he avoided Northey's whenever he could. He avoided the American Hotel as well, and stayed away from Kelty's new blacksmith shed on the lower end of Main.

One such morning Hen chanced to see a commotion at the Courthouse and strolled on over. Men and women milled about in Sunday finery—although it was a Monday morning—silk bonnets, tasseled shawls, black frock coats, polished boots and shoes walking into the building alongside farmers and mechanics in their denim and flannel and old, scuffed leather. It was, Hen discovered, the arraignment of young Dr. Darling. Hen decided it would be a fine place to sit for a spell. The room was big and warm, Hen amazed at the height of the tin ceiling and all the wasted space it held, frost clinging to the windows that were taller than him. Darling came into the room through a door in the front and the first thing Hen noticed was the lack of shackles—no manacles or chains for the young, white doctor. The second thing he noticed was the man behind a table in the front, across from Darling, a man with great patches of black whiskers on his cheeks, a man he recognized after a moment as Smathers, Levi Smathers, the fancy congressman who lived with—if the rumors Augustus had heard were true—the ghost of his little girl.

For a long time he couldn't pry his eyes off the man, looking for evidence of a ghost on his shoulder. Smathers looked higher than the other high white men Hen had seen in his life, slicker, slyer than a rattlesnake, and this one, this Smathers, looked even more dangerous.

Because of the little girl's ghost?

Then he looked at Darling. The day after Fudge's funeral came to mind, when he'd been kneeling at his friend's grave and Darling had ridden up. It occurred to Hen now, for the first time, that Darling had known then Hen was kneeling over an empty grave, that his friend had been dug up and skinned and laid out in an ice house alongside other slabs of dead meat. As he sat there in the back of that warm, stuffy courtroom, the judge droning an endless stream of silly syllables, people all about him yawning and sniffling and fidgeting and stretching, he decided maybe Dr. Darling was not the friendly, harmless young man he'd taken him for all along. Maybe he was just another dirty-faced little white boy looking to give him a hotfoot.

At night, when he went home weary, he usually went to Lucindy's. He'd begun to think of it as Lucindy's now, not Fudge's. He was never too weary to cook, whenever Lucindy would allow him. She didn't always. She told him he looked tired. She told him to rest, and she prepared the meal as Hen sat at the bone-white table watching her skinny legs and her crooked nose, how it crinkled up when she tasted the soup. After they ate, they would sit around the hearth warming, Napoleon feeding logs to the fire from his great stack behind the cabin, Belle putting her husk dolls to bed, Lucindy often as not knitting or spinning fleece into wool on her little wheel, Hen relaxing in unaccustomed luxury. For two weeks they heard nothing from Means or McKay, no cargos coming or going, and Augustus stayed busy hauling his freight. Though many of the white merchants were loath to deal with him, Augustus had told Hen, they couldn't resist the lure of his rates, which were lower than those of Nelson Turnbull, his chief competitor. How he could afford such low rates, Augustus never explained to him, and Hen never wondered. Now and then on those cold December evenings, Hen would smoke a pipe before going home to his cold little shack down below. One night Lucindy told him to stay.

"Ain't no sense you heading down there in the dark and cold, trying to get a fire set, worry 'bout that chimney of yours falling in. Bring that ol' mattress up here, stick it in the corner over there, you stay warm. Be good to have another man in the place, 'sides Napoleon, though he think he man enough for sure." Napoleon was already in bed, as was Belle. "We move that chair round to the other side, there be plenty of room."

So Hen did. After that Hen had little reason to visit his shack, the shack he'd pieced together, and replaced after the fire, on the site Yellow Charlie had chosen when Hiram Appleby had moved too close to their first spot, and he didn't return after the first few days, having taken his few necessities. Those he stowed at Lucindy's where they took up no room at all—a basin and a blade, a strop and a shirt and vest, a plate and a spoon. He didn't miss his shack. In fact, he felt unusually content for a while, unusually at peace, and he didn't know—didn't bother to worry it out—if it was on account of the comfort of staying there, with Lucindy, or if it might have had to do with quitting the place where he'd lived with Yellow Charlie.

One night Lucindy said, "Fetch another log, Hen—I don't believe I feels like turning in just yet." Hen allowed as how he didn't either. The children were in bed. He fetched the log, placed it on the fire. It was a few days before Christmas, and Lucindy seemed low.

"Surprise we ain't got hardly no snow yet," he said, after they'd stared for a while into the fresh blaze. "None to speak of."

"Sure enough. Probably get some 'fore long. 'Fore Christmas."

They stared a while longer. "First Christmas without Fudge," they both said in unison. Then they both shook their heads in unison, and tried to smile.

"Ain't got him no marker yet," he said.

"No," she said. "I can't..." She let the thought trail off.

After a while, Hen said, "Can't what?"

"Can't decide what. Can't even decide what it is I can't decide what about. We needs a marker, I suppose, make sure that man never get forgot. He too good a man to get forgot. But I just can't see my way clear to marking what's up there in that grave. That ain't even him, what's up there, what they throwed back in that hole."

Then where he at, if that ain't him? The question occurred to Hen, but he didn't speak it. He thought about the empty blue sky, the morning by the Praise House.

Lucindy rocked her chair once, then stopped, and they stared a while at the fire. "I been thinking it was on account of Miss Eva," she said after so much time had passed he'd thought she might have fallen asleep. The sound of her voice startled him.

"What was?"

"Just everything. Everything done happen to Fudge. And me. You remember? We was sitting there talking, the three of us, and Fudge, he done make a joke about Augustus hanging the po' child out to dry, and then I...I made another joke."

"I remember. It was a funny joke."

"No," she said, "wasn't funny. It was mean and hurtful. Po' child."

Hen shrugged, though not so she could see.

"Maybe it was a little bit funny," she allowed, "but we never should of joke about something like that in the first place, po' little white child hanging herself up in there."

"Or getting herself hung up in there."

"Ain't that what started the joking in the first place?"

"Reckon so." Hen shook his head at the fire.

Again there was silence, somber and mournful, the crackling of the fire, the moan of the low wind outside. After a while, she said, "I can't even remember what he look like," in a voice both pitiful and frail.

And Hen, after another while, said, "I can. That was one ugly man."

Lucindy thrust back in her rocker, slapped at its arm, and let loose a howl of laughter, which kept growing, so infectious that Hen succumbed and joined in. They slapped at knees and thighs and arms of chairs and howled.

"One ugly man!" hooted Hen.

"Can't eat no soggy cracker!" Lucindy howled.

On Christmas Eve came a cargo, a single young brown man with three toes shot off, the letter 'W' branded crudely on his cheek. He was an able fellow, cautious but unafraid, shy but alert, and he and Augustus hit it off. His name was David. Augustus, Hen and Napoleon worried and fretted—this was the first delivery since the narrow escape with Randall and Hubbard, the first since Augustus had confirmed that the law was on alert—and they wondered if letting David pass the day resting at Lucindy's would be safe, but it was far too cold to consider the dug-out, and they were at a loss as to where else to turn. An idea stirred in Hen's mind, the memory of an abandoned cabin, Jacob Black's cabin, they might use, but by the time the idea began to blossom, David was sound asleep, Napoleon keeping watch in the cold air with the ram's horn.

And so Hen let the idea, the abandoned cabin, go back to sleep again.

That night they bundled up to deliver the cargo to the Deer Run station, for the air was frigid, the ruts of the road hard as rock, the creeks half-frozen and hard to cross. David rode on the seat up beside Augustus, Hen in the back with Napoleon. Hen didn't mind. It was warmer in the box among the rags and straw. Napoleon declined to cover his ears, the better to listen for hostile sounds, and his ears stung for days afterwards. The journey passed without incident.

On Christmas Day, the next day, the snows came. Upon returning in the early dawn, Augustus had gone to his place, where they'd left him unhitching his team. Hen and Napoleon had gone home to sleep, and sleep they had, through the morning and into the early afternoon. Hen had squeezed his mattress into the children's room for the occasion, so that Lucindy wouldn't disturb him. Napoleon had whittled a fine likeness of a horse from a solid chunk of oak, stained it with lampblack, and was anxious to give it to Belle for Christmas. He awoke earlier than Hen. When Hen arose and looked outside, three or four inches of snow had already fallen, a shock to the eyes in its startling whiteness, more still coming down. He walked outside to leave his sputtering mark. Lucindy had brought in some evergreen boughs to make the cabin smell fresh, and Napoleon had a warm blaze going. Lucindy had procured a goose to roast for supper, and, as Belle was scrubbing the bone-white table, her skinny arms working, her small back hunched in earnest, Lucindy and Hen were consulting over spices—there were parsley and fennel and sage—and side dishes—there were turnips and potatoes and apples—when Napoleon came in with an armful of logs, which he dropped to the hearth with a clatter.

"Somebody out there," he announced.

Through the falling snow, Hen made out two horsemen, then another emerged like a ghost from the veil of white down through the trees, and another, four in all, at an easy walk, rifles upright, butt plates resting on their thighs, barrels pointing upwards toward the invisible sky. At Augustus', one of the riders dismounted, pounded on the cabin door, then burst inside. Another circled the place, while the other two sat on their horses in front.

"Ain't nobody here!" cried the man emerging from the cabin.

"Ain't nobody been here neither, not lately!" said the one who'd circled the cabin. "Got a empty horse stall!"

The four fell in, heading single-file up toward Fudge's, hooves silent in the snow.

They arranged themselves big and close around Hen and Napoleon in the doorway. Just inside, Belle crouched behind Lucindy. The men's hats were festooned with snow, as were their shoulders and thighs, the horses' rumps and manes. Hen didn't recognize Sheriff Mills until he spoke: "Afternoon, Black Hen—you seen any runaway niggers up hereabouts?"

Hen shook his head. "No, sir. Reckon I ain't."

The sheriff shifted his weight in the saddle, repositioned his rifle on his leg. On his gun hand a bare finger protruded from a leather mitten. He looked around at his fellow riders, one of whom wore a wide-brimmed, low-crowned black hat and a silver badge, a man Hen had never seen—the marshal up from Pittsburgh, he guessed. The other two he didn't know. "I know these here niggers," he said. "I know all four of 'em—they're our niggers, been here for years."

"Don't mean they ain't hiding somebody," said the marshal.

"Mind if we take a look, Black Hen?" the sheriff said.

Hen didn't move or speak. The marshal dismounted, as did one of the other riders, shouldering their way inside, tracking in snow and mud. Hen backed off, bringing Napoleon with him, the young man's face frozen hard.

"Where's the niggers at, boy?" said the marshal. "Hear tell you been moving runaways up here abouts."

They stood inside the door, Hen, Napoleon and Lucindy, Belle clutching her mother's apron, as the marshal and the other man began to rummage through the place. Looking for hidden cubbies, crawl spaces, concealed doors, as it was apparent that no one else was there. In the bedrooms they tore the bed clothes and mattresses from the beds, ripping them apart, throwing them to the floor, shoving the beds aside, stomping on the floorboards, in the kitchen they upended the shelves, sending bowls and crockery crashing to the floor, kicking aside the little rag rug to examine the floor underneath, stomping all the while. With long knives from beneath their garments, they pried at the stones of the hearth, to see if any would yield. When the marshal roughly flung the chairs aside, shoving the bone-white table, Hen said, "Careful with that there table—that was her mama's table."

The marshal stopped, regarding Hen with narrow eyes. The snow from his black beard was melting, dripping down his long, black coat beside his badge. "This here table?" he said.

Hen nodded.

"Where you hide the niggers at?" the marshal said.

"Ain't hide no niggers," said Hen.

Napoleon clenched his fists. Tears streaked Belle's bony cheeks.

"Hold on a minute," the marshal said. From the little pantry, where the other man was searching, came a clatter of crashing crockery.

The marshal stepped outside, returning a moment later with the axe from the woodpile. "Where's the niggers at?"

"Ain't hide no niggers," Hen said.

The marshal swing the axe into the bone-white table, splinters flying. Again and again he brought the axe down, mighty, grunting blows, till the table was shattered and splintered.

The marshal dropped the axe. "Ain't nobody here," he said to his companion, who'd been standing and watching alongside the blacks. "Let's clear on out." In the doorway, he paused, turned, surveying the remains of the table wrecked on the cabin floor, the general carnage. "Have yourselves a happy Christmas now, you hear?" he said, a smile on his lips.

As they rode off, Hen heard the sheriff. "Why'd you have to go and do that for?"

The marshal said, "Them niggers is hiding something," and they were still talking as they passed out of earshot, vanishing again into the snowfall from which they'd emerged. Down through Little Brier, all was peaceful, not a soul peeking through a single window. Hen turned. Lucindy was sitting in her rocker, facing the fire. Belle knelt beside her, her face buried in her mother's lap, her back bucking in silent sobs, while Napoleon hadn't budged from where they'd been standing, his face and fists still clenched, his chest still heaving. All around was ruin.

Hen went to Lucindy, stepping over the ruins of her mother's table. "Maybe I can fix it."

Lucindy looked up, her face dry and composed. She stroked Belle's head. She almost smiled. "Ignorant white crackers. Day late and a dollar short, just like they always is."

Lucindy refused to not roast the goose, and they cleaned up the best that they could. Hen retrieved the pieces of the bone-white table, taking them down to his shack where he leaned them in a corner of cobwebs to see what he might be able to salvage from the whole affair. When it came time to eat, Napoleon did so hungrily, angrily, but he alone among the company could muster any semblance of an appetite, Belle unable to touch a morsel.

Augustus showed up well past dark and no one thought to ask where he'd been. He came inside to survey the damage. He knew already, before he entered, what had happened, and no one thought to ask how he knew.

A deputation of Little Brier's leaders arrived, and they too all knew what had happened. Everyone knew, and had known from the moment it occurred. Cornelius Nips was there, Marcus Swan and Hiram Appleby and Solomon McManigle and the Widow Winter and several younger men, and they stood solemnly about, crowded into the little wrecked room, and soon they were pleading to Augustus their case against retribution, for the hot-headed nature of the mysterious young man was known to all. There was no one among them who did not believe it was he who had burned down Kelty's blacksmith shed those months before, and there were few among them who doubted he'd murdered Miss Eva. They feared that retribution by this angry man could lead only to further, more terrible, retribution by the white world, as they all, even those who hadn't lived it, remembered well the awful destruction of Little Brier by the white man's fire. They understood that Augustus also believed in fire, that fire was essentially an angry element, like him, and they understood that fire knew no color. That fire treated all men equally, no matter how rich or poor, how black or white, how good or evil, and that was the source of its hold on Augustus. But they understood better, a fact of life which had been woven into the fabric of their souls at the moment of their birth, like the color of their skin, that in a war of fire, in a war of any kind, only the white man could win.

But they extracted no pledge from Augustus.

This time, Augustus did not debate or argue. Every man knew where the other man stood. This time Augustus only listened, his strong young arms crossed over his chest, his face a stony mask. The elders pleaded with Hen to plead with Augustus.

But they extracted no pledge from Hen. Hen only nodded. He could understand their reasoning and fear, and he agreed with it. He could understand just as well the reasoning and anger of Augustus, and he agreed with it.

That night he moved his corn mattress from the children's room to Lucindy's, to the floor beside her bed, and she did not object, and there he lay awake most of the night, listening to the groans of the ropes, the rustle of the bed clothes every time she tossed in her sleep, the quiet gasps coming out of her nightmares, listening to every breath she breathed.

The day after Christmas they visited Dr. Means. Augustus announced his intention to do so, and Hen made no case for accompaniment, he simply stayed beside the young man till Jupiter was between the shafts and he was on the driver's seat beside Augustus. He'd determined to stay close, though whether it was to deter the young man from retribution or to participate in it, he wasn't certain. Jupiter worked all the harder through six inches of snow, but the Coolbrook road had been rolled and packed, as had the streets of Hartsgrove, where the going was easier. When they reached his door on Cherry Street, the doctor was not in.

Augustus entered the unlocked door to the jangling of the bell. Hen followed. The interior of the little office was dim and unlighted, and Augustus scarcely paused in the antechamber, drawn by the medley of aromas to the inner room, where the plants and herbs hung drying or dried from the twine strung beneath the ceiling around the single tall window. All about gleamed the mortars and pestles, glass jars and bottles, jugs, boxes, books and tins, the rows of small drawers with shiny white knobs, but Augustus made his way straight through the dark and crowded clutter to the plants, where he lingered, eyeing and sniffing each in its turn like a wolf in the gloaming woods.

"Reckon what this here is?" he said, pointing to a plant without turning.

Hen shrugged, unseen by human eyes. "Some meadowsweet maybe?"

"Wonder mightn't be snakeroot.'"

Hen wondered.

"Little this, little that," Augustus mused, sniffing, touching, tasting.

The outer door jangled. Dr. Means appeared, carrying an expression above his red goatee midway between surprise and displeasure.

"Gentlemen? May I help you?"

"Admiring your kitchen," said Augustus, coming away from the window.

"So I see," said the doctor.

"Suppose anybody else been in here admiring your kitchen?"

"No," said Means, "I don't suppose. Why should anyone want to?"

"Maybe stir a little snakeroot up in Fudge's remedy," Augustus said. "Poison the man, why anyone want to. Anyone like maybe that Bullers fella, the little one. Hen and I done heard him bragging about doing in black folk, using 'em to cut up."

"Let me reassure you once and for all, Fudge died of the fever," Means said. "He was under my care. I know." Augustus gave no indication of being impressed. "Let me reassure you even further," Means continued, "that had he had the opportunity, which I believe he had not, Little Bull lacks the requisite knowledge of herbal remedies in all their permutations, nuances and effects to do our friend any harm. The only way Little Bull could possibly have been complicit in the death of Fudge Van Pelt would have been if he'd taken him under his care. He and Vasbinder—and, unfortunately, young Darling, though there's still hope for him—the lot of them in the so-called heroic school of medicine, do more harm to their patients than good. Forever poisoning them with mercury is but one example, bleeding the life out of them another."

"Maybe he smarter'n what you think," Augustus said.

"Regardless," Means said, "opportunity or not, knowledge or not, Samuel Bullers is a doctor. And like all doctors, he took an oath to heal people. To do no harm."

"An oath," said Augustus, "a damn oath—"

"But do the man believe that niggers is people?" Hen said.

Means looked up, as did Augustus; they were the first words Hen had uttered. "That, in truth," Means said, "I suppose I cannot attest to."

After dark they rode into Hartsgrove again, Hen still at the elbow of the younger man, Jupiter still pulling the sturdy red wagon. Napoleon had wanted to come. *Stay home*, Augustus had said. *Watch over your mama*, Hen had said. The evening of the day after Christmas, and the shadows of firelight played on the windows they passed in the dark, empty streets of Hartsgrove. Jupiter's breath plumed out in great clouds, dwarfing the clouds of their own. Hen shivered beneath the blanket he'd wrapped over his old warmus, under the rag he'd wrapped around his ears. A sky full of crystal stars above. They drove the length and breadth of the town, up and down the streets and alleys, from up by the graveyard where the burial place of their friend was hidden in the dark far to the rear of the lot, past the accursed ice house, across to Irishtown where dwelled another downtrodden class of citizens. They drove from Tyrone Road, the long climb east out of town, to the crest of Valley Street at the western edge, Augustus asking Hen the name of this street or that, the occupant of this home or that, Hen answering to the best of his memory, for he had indeed lived much of the town's history, and it was a history that inhabited his bones, which were just as white as any man's.

Augustus pulled up Jupiter behind a thick stand of laurel decked out in snow for the holiday, and he shivered, and he might have said *fire be my only friend*, but Hen wasn't sure, and said nothing in response as the words evaporated along with his breath in the cold night air. They were on Church Street, only a block down from the graveyard where what was left of Fudge lay buried in the cold, across the street near the house where Samuel Bullers sat warm by the fire on his hearth, a house and street they'd passed three times before, a house among the trees, on a deep town lot, a house isolated from its neighbors.

"Anybody come by, whistle," Augustus whispered, and he slipped off across the road, toward the Bullers house, himself a shadow in the faint light from the stars and snow.

Hen watched Augustus as long as he could, till he was lost among the other shadows of the evergreens surrounding the house, then he looked up into the sky again, occupied only by cold, white specks, and he let his breath out slowly, the frosty cloud rising and vanishing, the stars appearing once more from behind the veil. He glanced over at the dark outline of Bullers's house against the trees, the faint firelight limning the window, then he looked up again at the stars, at the revelation of their intensity beside the puny manmade fire, the Big Dipper and the North Star and the stars they called Orion, and the vastness seeped into his heart, and he felt too tiny to be afraid, and he wondered if all that enormity might hide a heaven after all. With such vast thoughts and lofty feelings, he scarcely realized till it was almost too late how badly he had to pee. He was beginning to pee when a snort and snuffle and the clop of a hoof made him move closer to the wheel of the wagon, hiding as best he could, peeing, trying to decide whether or not to whistle, wondering how close was the passing sleigh, the soft tinkling of bells, looking toward the house across the street for any sign of life, the sound of the sleigh coming nearer as Hen moved closer to the iron-sheathed wheel of the wagon, still peeing, and as the sound of the sleigh subsided again, away down another street, he realized his tragic mistake.

Still standing by the wheel five minutes later when Augustus appeared out of the night, Hen shivered, his legs trembling, all the glory of the sky and the stars having forsaken him to his wretched, frail and miserable little self.

Augustus said, "What'd I hear? I hear something?"

"Sleigh pass near. Never come, though."

"Let's go. Seen all's I needs to see. I think we be visiting ol' Bullers again, when there ain't so much tracking snow on the ground." Hen didn't move from beside the wheel. "Come on," Augustus said.

Still Hen didn't move. "Don't touch that brake," he said.

"*Come on*," Augustus said again. "We gots to pull foot."

"Can't move. Done froze my pizzle to the wheel."

"Done what?" said Augustus, looking down.

"Froze my pizzle to the wheel. Peeing on it, standing too close."

Augustus was quiet for a moment. "You in a hell of a fix, ain't you?"

"For sure." Hen's head bobbled slowly. "Froze fast."

"How 'bout I just snap the rein on ol' Jupiter rump, get you unfroze real quick."

"Don't touch that brake." Hen studied the face in the shadow of the narrow brim.

Augustus sat for a moment. Jupiter, having heard her name, tossed her head impatiently. Hen gave a deep breath, eyeing the brake handle through the blinding cloud of frost. The wagon swayed, Augustus stepping down. "See what we can do," he said, moving close to Hen, assessing the old man's predicament with a shaking of his head. "You sure enough got yourself in a pickle this time."

"Sure enough."

"What you gonna do?"

"Been wondering my own self," Hen said. In truth, *worrying* would have been closer to the mark, as he'd never in all his years, however many that may have been, felt more helpless.

"Got me a idea," Augustus said. He unbuttoned his trousers. "Stand back." He began to pee, directing the strong, steady stream toward the wheel of the wagon, where it ran down the iron sheathing toward Hen's frozen part. Hen felt it warming, loosening. "That working?"

Hen nodded in the dark.

"You one lucky old man," Augustus said.

"Lucky?" said Hen.

"Lucky wasn't your tongue got stuck on that wheel." Augustus laughed out loud.

Hen tried to laugh as well, without notable success. There was light enough to see the nearness of their parts, and he felt the splashing wetness from the other man, and fear welled up within him. Augustus chuckled again. Hen had never felt so feeble and so afraid.

Or had he?

Something stirred in his chest, something roiled and rumbled, a memory trying to kick the covers off, and Yellow Charlie was there, standing over him in the dead of that dark, naked night.

Riding back home to Little Brier, Hen sat small and miserable, still feeling the raw stinging from the part of his pizzle that wasn't numb, the front of his britches frozen with another man's piss, the seat sopping wet and freezing slowly from the melting snow in which he'd encased his frostbitten part. Halfway out the Coolbrook Road, having passed Cook's Saw Mill, sitting silent in the night, he said, "You ain't gonna tell Lucindy and them, is you?" Augustus glanced over, not a hint of a grin lingering on his shadowed face. Hen was about to make his case, was about to tell the younger man, *You be old too someday*, but he didn't. He couldn't. He found he didn't really believe it.

As it turned out, it wasn't necessary. "Tell 'em what?" Augustus said.

Augustus' mind had already traveled past the trivial incident of Hen's predicament to more serious matters at hand. Many of which, Hen guessed, concerned fire.

It was late. Hen left Augustus bedding down Jupiter and walked slowly to Lucindy's, his feet numb in his boots as they shuffled through the snow, his groin frozen and painful and wet and shamed. He hoped they would all be asleep. He considered continuing on down to his own shack, but the snow in that direction was deep and unbroken, and the thought of his shack so small and dark and frozen and lonely brought with it thoughts of the grave, and so he opted for Lucindy's instead, warm and alive and, hopefully, sleeping. And so it was. The fire, the only light, was low, and slight snores from Napoleon, Belle's occasional cough, through the open bedroom door. Hen didn't want to awaken Lucindy, so he pulled the little rug over to the wall by the assembly of makeshift boards that had replaced her bone-white table, and he settled in and tried to sleep, listening to the sounds of the others, the random snap and sleepy hiss of the fire, and the heat seeped into his bones and he felt for a while as if he were melting. Sleep wouldn't come, though drowsiness did, the dull ache from his frostbitten part a constant throb, like the ache in his head, the dampness causing an itch he was too weary to scratch, his thoughts drifting and ranging from his humiliation on the wheel to Augustus' chuckles, to Little Bull's house sheltered among the dark, snow-covered pines, awaiting the fire, to Fudge in his cold, cold grave, to Lucindy in her warm, warm bed, and presently he heard a footstep and she was there, a silhouette in the dim firelight. Standing close above him, she asked why he had not come in to his mattress, she asked what was wrong, whispering all the while, and he answered in kind with nods and quiet syllables, and she'd soon pieced it together, feeling his fingers, his feet, how cold they remained, touching his forehead, and she fetched him an old nightshirt of Fudge's, made him take off his clothes and hang them to dry by the fire. She turned her back while he changed, poking the fire with the iron, adding a fresh stick, and she asked him if it hurt. He allowed as how it did, a little anyway. Lucindy made a poultice of raw potatoes, bringing it to him on a clay plate, and she made him show her, and she applied it gently to the red, raw part, murmuring, whispering, *Po' man, po' Henry, ain't nobody ever look after you, is they?* She sat beside him on the floor and finally he slept, his head in her lap, and when he awoke again she was still there, staring into the dying fire.

It was over two weeks before the next cargo was delivered, two good weeks for Hen, a lull, a respite from the tension and angst that had been seething to the surface of his world. He spent those days unconcerned about what might happen next, spent them one at a time, performing his usual medley of odd jobs for the usual medley of white folks who seemed unaware of, or unconcerned by, the tensions. He tried to cobble together a reasonable likeness of Lucindy's bone-white table, using Yellow Charlie's old tools, the few original boards that had survived, and whatever he could salvage wherever he could, searching in vain for the piece that was marked with Fudge's blood. He spent the evenings of those days in the comfort of Lucindy's home—which, despite his misgivings, was beginning to feel like his own—with the family, cooking the evening meal, sitting afterwards by the hearth, dozing, watching Lucindy spin, watching the children at their own amusements. He saw little of Augustus during those days, though he spotted him once or twice leaving the widow Barber's, once or twice harnessing his Morgans for a haul. He spent each day not worrying about any retribution Augustus might or might not decide upon. He spent each day relieved that he'd heard no news of Little Bull's house being torched.

  He found himself relieved too that McKay had yet to deliver another cargo of risk—and as he thought about it, about the next time, the option that had come to his mind earlier came again—the other place, safer than Lucindy's, the cabin in the woods, a place where the next cargo might be more safely stowed away.

  He decided he should take a look. The January thaw came early, and on a morning that felt like spring he walked at his leisurely pace through the woods due east, toward Beechwoods, on a trail he'd blazed over forty years before, but hadn't trekked more than a handful of times in the last thirty. As a youngster he'd hired out to an old settler named Jacob Black, a grim codger who shared certain traits with Yellow Charlie, in particular a dislike of neighbors, a love of loneliness. Hen had helped Black clear a sizable lot, helped him erect a solid cabin in a site beyond the hollow, miles from the nearest settler, well off the nearest road, in the middle of nothing but splendid wilderness. Black had been dead for years now, his cabin abandoned, and Hen wished to assess its condition.

On a Wednesday afternoon in the mid-January young Jacob McKay sought him out at Clover's where he was sweeping the back room: another cargo was on the way.

That night he told Augustus and Napoleon and Lucindy about the cabin.

"Suit a cargo fine for a day," he said. "Dang site better'n a hole in the ground."

"Can't be staying here, that's for dang sure," Napoleon said.

"Got four walls a roof and a fire, should answer good," said Augustus. "Where 'bouts is it? How you know 'bout it?"

"Old settler name of Black," Hen said, "Jacob Black. Hired me when I was a pup, 'bout Napoleon's age. Straight over through the woods past Beechwoods, two, three miles maybe."

"White man name of Black," said Napoleon with Augustus' smirk.

The cargo consisted of a young couple and their baby, and when McKay introduced them at the trailhead behind Lucindy's, Hen couldn't help but think of the cargo a couple of months before, Jemmy and Liza and the little girl, Lulu, who Napoleon had rescued from the creek. This child was a little boy, Pompey, younger than Lulu, for he'd just embarked upon toddling, tottering precariously about the soggy leaves of the forest floor—the Christmas snow long gone by now—anxious to stretch his small legs after the night's long journey. The boy's parents were younger too than the other couple, Lewis no more than eighteen, his wife, Siby, even younger, scarcely older than Napoleon. And they were smaller in stature; Lewis had the body of an otter, sleek and quick, while Siby was scarcely more than a warm sip of water.

Hen, nodding toward the child, said to Napoleon, "You better keep a good holt on that one come creek-crossing time."

Siby's eyes, already her largest part, got bigger. "Why you say that?"

"While back," said Augustus, "child done fell in the creek we was crossing—Napoleon, here, he jumped in slick as a fish and pulled her out again."

Napoleon only nodded grimly, refusing to allow his smile to show through, though Hen detected his chest puffing out.

"You keep a holt of this one for sure," Siby said. "He the reason why we here. He gonna have a good life, a free life, ain't that so, Lewis?"

"That so," said Lewis. Pompey yawned and reached up for his daddy.

The runaways spent the day at the cabin of the late Jacob Black, and all concerned felt more secure for it, off the beaten track as it was. Before they left, Augustus insisted on dousing the fire and scattering the ashes so as not leave the place looking as though it had been occupied in the last twenty years, should a hunter happen by.

Pompey commenced the next leg of their journey that night in his daddy's arms again, though he didn't stay there for long, going in turn from his daddy to his mama to Napoleon, as the child grew more familiar with the boy. Napoleon used all his tricks to keep Pompey amused, buttons and string, googly eyes and funny faces, songs and rhymes, for the night was quiet and light—a half moon in a clear sky—and the child was loud and easily displeased. He had not yet mastered the art of the whisper.

An hour later, the child was growing increasingly rambunctious. The Black cabin had proved itself so comfortable that he'd slept by the fire for most of the day and was well rested, too well rested, not the least bit sleepy. When Napoleon had exhausted his bag of tricks, Siby took Pompey, tried holding him and rocking him, crooning a lullaby, but that too was to no avail, the child struggling rudely to free himself from her grasp. Lewis took him and tried counting stars, pointing at patterns and constellations, looking for a face in the moon. Pompey grew more restless than ever. He grew louder as well, frustrated that his demands—spoken as they were in gibberish—remained unmet, asserting his authority with volume, interpreting the lack of volume in return to be a confirmation of his authority. Augustus turned with a warning to those in the box behind him: find something to amuse the child, find a way to quiet him. Slavers were known to be in the area through which they were passing.

"Ain't nothing for him to do," Siby said in a whiney, pleading voice. "He just bored."

Pompey agreed, with a new burst of gibberish. Four deer fled from the edge of a clearing, white tails in the moonlight disappearing into the black woods.

"He be bored right back to the plantation, he keep it up."

"Come, Pompey," Siby said, reaching for the boy. Pompey slapped his mother's face, then giggled at the look thereon, her eyes and her mouth going big.

"Pompey!" said Lewis.

"He don't mean nothing by it," Siby said. "He just a baby."

Napoleon tried to take the child, who struggled away, fleeing to the rear of the box. There he began to shriek, finding excitement in the way his voice at the top of his lungs could knife through the still night air.

Napoleon retrieved him, causing all the more flailing and shrieking. Augustus reined in Jupiter and Lovejoy and turned around on the seat. "Hush up that boy!"

Hen watched, a sinking feeling in his chest.

The boy hushed, suddenly still, surprised by the unexpected stop, by the harsh words from the loud man up front. It was then that Napoleon held up a finger.

"Shhh," he said. "Listen."

All were quiet, all listening, even Pompey.

"Hear that?" Napoleon said.

"No," Augustus said. "I ain't hear nothing."

"Horses coming," Napoleon said, "coming fast."

Augustus cracked the reins. "Behind us?"

"Not for long," Napoleon said.

Augustus urged his team to a brisk trot over the unforgiving, rutted road, the speed of the wagon and newfound height of the bounces a fresh source of pleasure for the baby, held fast by Napoleon. Pompey giggled and burbled in delight. Hen held his breath, held onto the seat as well, the others in the box holding tight. Within minutes, Augustus found what he was looking for, a place to hide, pulling off the road, across a gentle gully and behind a thick stand of pines on the hillside down from the road. Lovejoy tossed his head and nickered, both horses stamping their feet, as Augustus dismounted, taking Jupiter by the headstall, stroking the foreheads of both of his animals. "What you hear now?"

He needn't have asked. Rapid hoof beats in the distance, drawing quickly closer.

Pompey, who'd been holding his breath with the rest of them, decided the sudden stop, the lack of motion, was not to his liking. He protested with a loud burble. Napoleon, hushed him, stroking his head, holding him faster. The child swung a tiny fist at him. Napoleon took his arm and tucked it away in his grip. Hen watched. His heart had finished sinking, settled now somewhere in the dirt, for now he realized the child was doomed—he realized they all were doomed. Pompey protested his imprisonment with a vigorous squall. The hoof beats by now were clear and close. Pompey's protests grew louder and his mother said, "Give him over here—I take him," and Napoleon shook his head, and Augustus said, "Keep that boy quiet now—everybody, quiet *now!*" The clatter of the hoofs, quite loud, slowed suddenly to separate and distinct hoof clops. Pompey struggled against Napoleon, freeing a fist and hitting, wanting only to be free, but his vehement vocal protests were stifled by Napoleon, who clasped his hand over the child's mouth—he had no choice, Hen agreed. *Shhh*, Napoleon hissed, silently, *shhh*, like the slow leaking of a bellows.

They couldn't see the horsemen on the road above them. They could hear them slowly passing by, so slowly it seemed they must have stopped to walk their horses back and forth near the place where the wagon had left the road and crossed the gulley, back and forth, perhaps looking for tracks or signs. For a moment or two there was silence, not a clop or a breath, no sound in the woods either, not a sound in the world. Everyone in the wagon held their breaths, willed their hearts to stop beating, their blood to stop rushing. Napoleon held the unhappy child in a bear trap of a grip, his hand over his mouth. Presently the clopping resumed. Voices of men were heard. The words could not be made out, but two men spoke, then a third, and Hen was certain the gruff tone belonged to the marshal up from Pittsburgh. The wait, probably no more than a minute or two, seemed endless. Finally a horse whinnied up above, a rattle of hooves like a rearing. Then the clopping resumed, up and down the road once more, then the voices again, then the clopping began to move on, up the road, progressing agonizingly slowly away, toward the outer edge of earshot.

After a few minutes, Hen began to breathe. Augustus stirred from the side of the horses, Lewis and Siby in the box. No one spoke. Only Napoleon, and Pompey, remained still. Siby reached across the box and touched Napoleon's arm. Still Napoleon didn't budge. Siby reached for the boy and Lewis crawled across and they both reached for the boy, and Napoleon only rocked back, still clutching Pompey, whom Siby finally pried from his grip, felt his limpness and cried out. Lewis fell back in the box as though struck. Napoleon curled in a circle. Hen watched. Augustus peered over the side. Siby clutched the small limp body to her chest and began to rock, began to cry, her cry mounting, becoming a wail.

The keening of the wail reached the stars. It was unlike anything the woods had ever heard. They all gathered around her, astounded at the size of the sound, at all that it held, at the smallness of the creature from which it issued forth, all of them around, Hen and Augustus and Lewis and Napoleon, his eyes clenched shut, his black skin pale as a ghost, and the riders down from the road up above, the three white horsemen, rifles in their hands, disbelief in their hearts.

11: January 14, 1858: The Great Escape

Why Yellow Charlie?

Why, at this time and place, would his old rescuer, overseer and vanished master come into Hen's mind? It wasn't as though his mind was otherwise unoccupied. They were in the box of Augustus' wagon, all of them, Hen, Augustus, Napoleon, Lewis, Siby and the body of the little boy, Pompey, the wagon driven by the marshal who'd arrested them. The other two white horsemen rode on either side, staring straight ahead down the dark, starlit road. Hen recognized them, he thought, as the same men who'd accompanied the marshal when they'd wrecked Lucindy's home; only Sheriff Mills was absent from that Christmas day party. The black men were in irons. The road back to Hartsgrove was without end, it seemed to Hen, who had escaped into a trance of sorts—as seemingly had all of the captives, for not a word was spoken. Indeed, when Lewis had tried to speak to Augustus not long after the capture, the marshal had loudly intervened, telling the riders to *shut them God damn niggers up*, making it clear that communication among the captives would not be tolerated. Not that Hen—or any of the others, except perhaps Lewis—was in any mood to attempt to talk at any rate. Napoleon in particular seemed as lifeless as the little boy, a limp corpse himself, curled on his side, staring with vacant eyes into a dark corner of the box, while Siby, the mother, clutched the little boy to her own frail chest, as if trying to keep him from going cold, rocking back and forth slowly, oblivious to the jolts of the wagon on the hard frozen ruts of the road. Hen could see the vacant eyes in the starlight, all but Augustus', hidden behind the stone slits of his face. Lewis's eyes bobbed about like acorns in the water. Hen was freezing. Periodic shivering spasms overtook him, what was left of his teeth chattering, and he pulled his warmus closer about him, pulled his hat down tighter on his head, tried to burrow more deeply into the pile of rags against which he rested, until the rider on his side lowered his rifle and told him to keep still or he'd blow his damn black head off. Just off beyond a clearing four curious deer, little more than shadows, watched the passing procession then returned their mouths to the ground. The only sounds were the clacking of hoofs, the creaking of tack, the groaning of wagon boards and squeaking of wheels. Hen, in his trance, looked heavenward at the stars and warded off the shivers, riding the jouncing course like a leaf upon the water. He tried to think of Lucindy and the warmth of her hearth, tried to remember the sweet taste of the orange upon his tongue, tried to go to his spot on the bank of the creek with the sun on his cheeks, but each image was fleeting at best, soon vanquished by Yellow Charlie. Why Yellow Charlie? The man was dead and gone. He'd been gone for decades had stayed that way, until his recent resurrection in Hen's memory. Now here he was again, filling the doorway of their dark little shanty, dwarfing it, his yellow face and greasy beard glimmering in the gloom, the fingers of his enormous hands like writhing, wriggling serpents. The immensity of the man. The insistence of the serpents. The unaccountable enormity, inhabiting every nook and cranny, every distant corner of the shack, every distant corner of Hen's waking consciousness, every speck of his being. The way he sat in the woods, Yellow Charlie, cross-legged on the ground like an Indian among the weeds and dead leaves, and laughed and laughed when he thought no one was watching, even, the last time, when he knew Hen was there, after he'd realized that Hen had crept up behind him, and was looking at the marks he'd burned into the handle of his axe. Hen couldn't read them. He couldn't read. He remembered the marks though, and years later, long after Yellow Charlie was gone, he'd scratched them in the dirt with a stick so that Lucindy could tell him what they meant—Lucindy, like Fudge, had gone to the colored school in Harrisburg, had learned her A-B-C's—and she'd looked at them first one way, then another, and finally said they might be a *Y* and a *C,* maybe for Yellow Charlie? It made sense, Hen figured, a Y and a C for Yellow Charlie—he must have been marking his tool. But still Hen found it mystifying, for he hadn't suspected that Yellow Charlie could read or write. He'd never left a clue. Now here he was, Hen, freezing, headed to jail, battered and bruised by the pummeling of the wagon, the body of a little boy beside him growing cold on the road to oblivion, a sky full of stars above him stretching to eternity, and all he could think of was Yellow Charlie.

Why Yellow Charlie?

Dr. Nevers had been a tall man with wide shoulders, over which he draped a buckskin cloak that he flourished like a gentleman's cape of silk. He wore a beaver hat and a dappled fawn skin vest. Darling remembered the doctor's hands—large hands with knobs for knuckles—and his hair, which was black, and which he wore long and straight in the manner of the Indians. Darling was six when his father died, and he associated with Dr. Nevers a feeling of fear, or, at the very least, a feeling of utmost timidity, for Dr. Nevers made no concession to youth or immaturity, and his eyes were the color of cold iron. He also associated with Dr. Nevers the muted screams of his father from behind the closed door of the bedroom upstairs, and, ultimately, he associated with him the passing of his father from this life. When Dr. Nevers descended the stairway from the bedroom—the sickroom—following his final operation on Darling's father, gloom descended with him, and the whole house seemed to darken.

In his hand he carried the bag he'd fashioned some years before from the hide of a cougar, in which he carried his surgical instruments, and beneath his arm was a mysterious parcel wrapped in dirty rags, a parcel he'd not carried with him when he'd ascended the stairway an hour before. He paused at the bottom of the stairs to speak with Darling's Aunt Penelope—his mother was still upstairs—and with two ladies of the church. Darling heard the words *dressings*, *lobelia* and *capsicum*, though he made no sense of them whatever.

Dr. Nevers bowed and took his leave. Darling followed. He watched him secure the cougar bag amongst the other gear behind the saddle, and he watched him mount his horse holding the mysterious parcel in his hand. Once in the saddle, he placed the parcel under his arm, snapped the reins and rode off. Darling followed. Not once had the doctor looked in his direction, and Darling wondered if, had he looked his way, he would even have seen the invisible little boy.

Dr. Nevers rode his horse at a pace such that Darling had to run to keep up. He was a good runner. Josh Sandt was a better jumper, but he was the better runner; in wrestling, they were evenly matched. It was a warm day in late April, the sun warm upon his face, and the new leaves on the dogwood at the corner of Prospect were white as fat snowflakes adrift in the air. Dr. Nevers did not turn uphill on Prospect toward Main and his office, as Darling had expected he would. Instead he kept riding straight, toward Water Street. Darling ran after him. It felt good and right to emerge from the gloom, to be running in the sun.

At the end of Pine, Dr. Nevers did not turn onto Water Street. He crossed it instead, into the trees by the side of the road, where there was no path, but the undergrowth was light enough to allow a horseman to pass. It allowed Darling to pass as well, and he continued to follow the doctor down the wooded embankment to Potters Creek, just above where it met the Sandy Lick to create the Red Bank. Here Dr. Nevers pulled up and looked around. His horse lowered his head to drink from the creek waters.

Nevers didn't see the boy crouched in the laurel thicket. He saw no living things but the horse beneath him, the sparrows and robins and blue jays, and he heard nothing but the birds chattering, the light rapping of a woodpecker. He unwrapped the parcel, and, twisting in the saddle, stowed the rags behind him. He looked at the naked object in his hands. Then he brought it back with his right hand, and flung it as far as he could toward the creek. Darling watched it sail, how it caught the sunlight in a golden, red arc, and he saw that it was a leg, and he watched as it fell with a splash that was gone in an instant from the place where the waters converged.

Asleep on the cold planks of the jailhouse floor, Kathleen and Darling were awakened by a clatter and ruckus in the office, the rattle and clank of chains. The door to the corridor came open and Jenkins stepped in, followed by three black men in irons, and a white man with a badge and a rifle. It was the middle of the night. The lovebirds stood, the blanket and pillow falling in a heap at her feet, hands still clasped as they watched the procession with curious, sleepy frowns, as though watching a dream come to life.

"Black Hen?" Darling said in a raspy voice.
"What's she doing in here?" said the man with the badge.
"You better get on home, Miss," Jenkins said.
"Wait," said Darling as Jenkins took her by the elbow.
"What kind a hotel you running here?" said the marshal.
Darling said, "It's late—she must be escorted."
The marshal said, "Hell, I'll see she gets to home all right, she don't mind riding in a wagon with a couple runaway niggers—and one dead little pickaninny."

Napoleon moaned. Darling recognized him, the boy who was Fudge's son, and he watched as he began to weep, a curiously soft, high-pitched wail which continued unbroken as Jenkins pushed him into the cell kitty-cornered from Darling's, then deposited Black Hen in the cell beside Darling's, Augustus in the one across the corridor. For the first time in all the weeks of his stay, all four of the holding cells were occupied.

Jenkins had turned up the camphene lamp on the little stand, and when he and the marshal departed, taking Kathleen with them, he neglected to turn it down again. Darling stood, still grasping the bars, trying to make sense of the scene. The place ablaze in the nighttime was bizarre enough, the black shadows of the bars splayed on the far cell walls, the grooves of the floorboards gleaming, but the presence of two black men standing in opposing cells glaring at him, black and hostile and equal to him in every regard, and the sound of the third, curled on the floor of his cell where Darling couldn't see, crying like an injured animal, was enough to cause Darling to doubt his senses. "Henry," he said. "What's going on?"

Hen didn't answer. He turned away from the young white doctor, peering into the cell across the corridor where Lucindy's little boy lay moaning on the floor. "Napoleon," he said, softly. "That's all right. That's all right."

Augustus too turned away from Darling, looking into Napoleon's cell. "Napoleon," he said, "sit up, boy. Hush up. Sit up. Listen up. I know you wasn't intending it, but you done that child a favor. He better off where he is now, he far better off, than where he'd a been, back in them chains. Ain't no life in chains—better off where he's at now."

Napoleon fell quiet; Darling could almost hear him listening. No one spoke.

"Better off dead than back in them chains," Augustus said.

Darling put it together—*one dead little pickaninny*. Napoleon, stricken. Then—later he would be ashamed for doing so—he put it out of his mind utterly. It was too much. He abandoned the black men, the dead child, their woes and troubles all together, and he let Kathleen come softly into his mind—had she made it home safely? Was she in her bed, asleep? And, after an inexplicable interval, he remembered his proposal of marriage to her. She'd said *yes*—at the memory of the word on her lips, his heart clambered about madly—but now came the doubt: had she actually been awake? Had she even heard him at all? Was he indeed engaged?

Hen too was caught in the familiar wasteland between waking and dreaming, tinged on this occasion with a hue of undeniable strangeness. The death of the child—a bouncing, living, breathing creature one moment, a limp and lifeless thing the next—sent a haunting echo through his mind, and the aftermath, the dreamlike journey back to Hartsgrove, seemed in his memory to have been without a sound. And the ghost of Yellow Charlie, back once again, along with the echo of Augustus's words: *better off dead*.

Neither Hen nor Darling heard Augustus's question from the first time, a slow twisting off of the lid to their consciousnesses, which fully opened the second time he said it. They both looked up and saw Augustus standing at the front of his cell, peering across at the young, white doctor, the underside of the brim of his hat gleaming yellow in the lamplight. "Why did you skin our friend?" was the question.

"Me?" said Darling, realizing the foolishness of the response even before Augustus sneered. Darling rubbed his eyes. "Yes. How shall I put this? How shall I explain?" Neither of the two black men offered assistance; the other, Napoleon, was, for all appearances, insensible. Darling went on. "You have to understand… I liked Fudge, very much. He was a good man. I considered him a friend. I like to think he considered me one as well." Darling looked again to Hen for confirmation, but none was forthcoming. "We resurrected your friend—that is to say, we dug him up—to honor him in a way, to allow him to make a contribution to medical science—to allow him to help us, by studying his body, to become better doctors. Better doctors so that we can become better healers for the benefit of all, including folks like you."

Darling paused, gazing at each man's face to gauge the effect of his words. They were still blank, still unfriendly, Augustus at the edge of hostility. Augustus said, "No need to talk down to us, Doc. Not all us niggers are shuffling, fawning, wide-eyed simpletons. *Yowser, mastah, I understand*"—here he raised his voice into a high-pitched imitation of a cornfield nigger—"*yowser, yowser, and I wants to thank you very kindly, I wants to thank you for digging up ol' black Fudge and skinning his ol' black hide right off a his lazy ol' black body, so that wo'thless ol' nigger can learn yous how to doctor all us po', ignorant niggers.*"

Darling teetered between afraid and offended. "I hadn't intended to talk down to you. Forgive me if it seemed that I was. But in essence what you're saying is true. Let me try to explain the process of dissection, which is the scientific examination of the human anatomy—"

"We *know* what dissection is," Augustus said. From the cell next door, Hen cocked his head, not at all certain that he was among the *we* who knew what dissection was. "What we don't know is what skinning got to do with it. Near as I can figure, you don't need to take the skin off a body in order to cut it up and study what's inside."

Darling blinked, caught in a lie he hadn't realized he was telling.

Augustus said, "So why did you skin our friend?"

Darling tried to remember. "As I recall, we feared that if he were identified—"

"If you'd dug up a white man, would you skinned him?"

"Perhaps not, I suppose we—"

"No," said Augustus. "You wouldn't of. Want to know why you wouldn't of? 'Cause you'd never of dug up a white man in the first place."

Caught again, Darling said nothing.

Augustus said, "Let me tell you a story 'bout this slave, house nigger on a big ol' tobacco plantation down in Virginia. He was an old man, been the house nigger for years, and the older he gets the worse he starts to feeling the cold—gets mighty cold down there in Virginia, too. So one day his master gone into Richmond on business, and this house nigger, ol' Clarence, he takes a chill. It was in November, cold day, and Clarence, he was going in and out of the big house toting in a load of goods arrived that day, so he figure it be faster if he just borrow the master's coat from the peg in the hallway, just throw it around him for a few minutes till he done going in and out. Well don't the old master's son come in and see Clarence in his daddy's coat and start raising holy hell. So you know what they done? When that old master got back? They didn't whip him—could of whipped him, they done that to their niggers all the time—no, they didn't whip him, figured he was getting too old it might of killed him, don't make no sense dollar-wise killing off your chattel like that. What they done was make him take off the master's coat and hang it back up. Then they make him take off his own vest, and his own shirt, and his wool britches, and his underclothes, till he was naked as a crow. Made him take off every stitch he been wearing on his old wrinkly body, and that's the way they made him go about his business, building the morning fires, polishing the brass, sweeping the floors, everything he done—stark naked, whole day long. You know how that make him feel?"

Darling didn't answer. Augustus repeated, "You know how that make him feel?"

"I can imagine," Darling said.

"*No*, you can't. You can't imagine nothing 'bout what it's like to be a nigger, be a slave." Augustus stared. "Slave ain't got no dignity. Nigger ain't got much more, least in the eyes of white *gentlemen* like you. Only dignity he got is in the clothes he wearing on his back"—here Hen looked at his ragged old britches—"and you make a black man take off his clothes, you make him take off his dignity. You can't do nothing more to humiliate a black man than that—I seen Clarence shuffling 'round that big house all day long, getting smaller by the minute till he was 'bout small enough to creep in a mouse hole, wearing nothing but a pair of old slippers and the tears dried up on his saggy old cheeks. Been better off they'd a whipped him.

"Only one thing worse'n stripping a nigger of his clothes: stripping him of his skin. Ain't no worse a shame than that."

In the wake of the alleged discovery of the little girl's body, the faces of the jurors and of the spectators in the gallery—among whom was neither Kathleen nor Sandt— next morning had taken on a fresh aspect of scrutiny and enmity. The gaze of the half-bearded farmer burned crueler, and Darling could detect not an ounce of sympathy on a single countenance.

The prosecution called Andrew Dodd. Under the inquisition of Smathers, Dodd described how he'd discovered the body of the little girl the previous day. He'd been part of a search party of thirty men, under the direction of Sheriff Mills, and after four hours he'd come across a place where it looked as though the floor of the forest heaved slightly, a rise that seemed out of place on the lay of the land, and that had been swept clean of dead leaves. There they unearthed the body beneath less than a foot of frozen dirt. She was badly decomposed, but it was apparent by the dress that it was the body of a small girl. She'd been buried about a hundred yards up from Muddy Bottom Creek, less than three miles from the farm of Enoch Plotner.

Truby cross-examined, asking Dodd if he'd participated in the search for Molly Plotner that had taken place in November. Dodd said that he had, and that it had been a damn sight warmer, prompting a titter of unfounded laughter in the courtroom. Truby established that the same area where Dodd discovered the body had been searched in November, and Dodd could not account for why the body had not been discovered then, surmising that the man who'd covered that ground—it had not been him— had been less keenly observant than him.

When he dismissed the witness, Truby returned to the defense table, his head lowered. He looked up at Darling, and Darling saw beneath the hooded visage the same evasive eyes that had greeted him that morning, eyes containing distinct hints of distrust and accusation. He was aware, for the first time, that his own counsel had begun to doubt him.

Smathers called Enoch Plotner back to the stand. Plotner identified the blue gingham dress as the one in which he had buried his little girl. All Truby could do in cross was ask Plotner where he'd bought the gingham in question, and Plotner told him his wife had picked it out at Clover's, whereupon Truby asked if, to his knowledge, Clover had ever sold blue gingham from that bolt, or any other bolt, to anyone else. Smathers objected and Truby withdrew.

Lucindy showed up in the morning, after Darling was off at his trial. It was a moment that Hen had been dreading. He'd pledged to look after Fudge's family. Now here was his widow, visiting his son in jail, futures bleak— anything but well looked-after. The evidence of Hen's failure sat slumped and dejected on the bunk in the cell across from him.

Lucindy glanced at Hen, then grasped the bars of her son's cell, severely. "They's talk 'bout a dead child," she said to her boy. "Pompey?"

Napoleon's face twisted oddly, but he didn't make a sound. "Wasn't nobody's fault," Hen said, "wasn't nobody's fault."

Lucindy squeezed the iron bars. "Napoleon!" she cried, "Napoleon!" so loud that he recoiled, his face drained, and when his mother commanded, "Come here! Come here now!" he had no choice but to obey. She seized his hand, then his arm, then the other, pulled him, yanked him close, and she held him as close as she could, pressing him in, trying to pull him through the bars between them.

Hen's eyes closed. He heard the butcher's horn blow from down the street, listened to the clatter of a heavy wagon, heard the squeal of a nearby pig, presumably kicked.

Augustus, leaning back on his bunk, knee raised, said, "That child was found in his mama's arms, so his mama's the one done accidentally smothered him, far as the law knows."

"His mama's little boy," Lucindy said, turning slowly. "He *dead*!"

Augustus nodded, his eyes never more narrow. "Yep. Better off that way."

Lucindy pulled back, bewildered, horrified.

"You free niggers," Augustus said, "you can't seem to grasp a hold of that fact."

Napoleon looked up, said his first sentence in a day. "'Before I be a slave I be buried in my grave, and go home to my Lord and be free.'"

After a while, after Lucindy got through fussing, got around to asking what was to become of them, Augustus said they might all soon be wishing they were cold and dead like little Pompey. He said they'd be charged with aiding and abetting the escape of runaway slaves, bad enough a charge for a white man, but for free blacks, worse—punishment often as not was being sold into slavery, the profit going to the owner of the escaped slaves as recompense.

"Lordy," said Lucindy, holding on tight to the bars of her son's jail cell. Napoleon's eyes went big and white. Hen muttered, "Lordy," as well, but not for his own sake—he could feel no special fear at the prospect, for some reason—but as an offering to Lucindy. Lucindy sat, keeping her grip on Napoleon, who, weary, sat on the floor of his cell, holding his mama's hand. She said, "We gots to get us a good lawyer."

"Any black lawyers hereabouts?" Augustus said. "White ones ain't worth pig shit."

Lucindy said nothing. Hen didn't know of any black lawyers, in Hartsgrove or anywhere else in the universe. Augustus said, "Course I been thinking we got us another option. Been thinking might not be a bad idea we just walk on out a this here cracker box, not wait around for no lawyer or no hearing or no trial or no nothing else."

"You thinks you can just strut on out of here like Sunday morning?" Lucindy said.

"Like a cakewalk," said Augustus.

"A world a fuss and bother," Lucindy said. "Won't nothing ever be the same again."

"Nothing ever be the same again your boy gets sold down the river, neither," Hen said.

Lucindy looked at him, the makings of a smile on her mouth. "Leas' you ain't gots to worry none, handsome," she said. "Ain't nobody gonna plunk down a good American dollar for a beat-up ol' black ass like yours anyways."

It felt good to Hen to throw back his head and laugh.

Sandt had news. Bad news, he was afraid. Kathleen's father had stopped by his store to give him a message for Darling: Please advise the young doctor that the mustard water he'd prescribed had provided no positive effect toward the outcome of his lumbago, no positive effect whatsoever. Please tell him too that Kathleen would not be among his visitors this day, nor any other day. Moreover, he'd further instructed Sandt to tell him that he, Darling, was to keep his distance, was to stay away from his daughter altogether if and when he were ever again to walk among free men. "Also, he wanted it to be clear that the banishment from Kathleen was in no way due to his loss of confidence in you as a physician," said Sandt. "You know, the lumbago thing. It's because of what you did to Molly."

"I did nothing to Molly," said Darling, halfheartedly. "Except perhaps to kill her."

"You know that and I know that. He does not. As a matter of fact, no one else knows that. You and I and Kathleen may be the only ones who do." It was late afternoon, after court was recessed and his drug store shuttered. Sandt kept his voice down to something akin to a whisper, inhibited by Darling's three new neighbors.

"Cyrus," said Darling. "Cyrus seems to be the only other one—outside of ourselves—who believes in me whole-heartedly, without reservation. It's almost as though he were with us that night. It even fell to him to convince Truby, my attorney, to keep up the fight. Cyrus says he will find out what's going on."

"What *is* going on?"

"I don't know. All I know is that someone wants to bury me alive."

"Speaking of buried. Do you suppose the body they found could be that of Molly?"

Darling didn't answer. He shook his head.

"You must escape," Sandt said, then glanced quickly around at the three black men, lowering his voice even more. "There is no way you'll avoid conviction, not now. I could help you—we can concoct a plan, just as we did when we barred the master out. You could escape and remove to Ohio, and set up a practice there—you're young, and could start out anew."

"What about my mother? What about Kathleen?"

"*I* will watch over Kathleen."

Darling stared hard into the eyes of his old school chum. Sandt, instantly regretting his remark, looked away, toward the floor, toward the wispy whiskers clinging to his skinny chin. "Her father said she stayed the night," he said. "Delivered home by a marshal."

It was Darling's turn to look at the floor.

"How *could* she stay the night?" Sandt said. "Here? With you?" A spark of modest anger caused a flush to linger on his face.

"It was not the entire night. And there were of course iron bars between us."

After Sandt had departed, the fact of Darling's imprisonment, the cold, hard bars, again settled over him, settling down into his bones. He gazed, unblinking, into a bleak, blank future. Learning that Kathleen had been banished from his life was crushing news, and would of course in normal times have been most devastating. But the pile was too high and too deep already, and another stone was scarcely noticeable. It could not have taken him to a place any deeper and darker. He was already there.

When he glanced across the corridor, Augustus was once again staring through the slits in his eyes. There was that as well. "Thinking 'bout busting out, Doc?" he said. "Been thinking the same damn thing. Maybe we run into one another out there on the big outside."

Dr. Means arrived early next morning, Saturday, before the prisoners had finished feasting upon their watery oatmeal and burnt biscuits. Hen saw a look of delight on Darling's face at receiving a visitor, then watched the delight turn to surprise when Means only nodded at him, smiled, then turned to the black prisoners. "Gentlemen," he said, "I'm very sorry for your trouble."

Then he turned and winked at Darling. "And for yours too, Will."

"Can't spend no sorry here," Augustus said. "Won't buy us nothing."

"Yes," Means said. "And that is what we shall attempt to rectify."

"'Attempt to rectify'," Augustus said. "That white man talk for you aiming to get us the hell out of here?"

"It is. In a manner of speaking." The wheels, Means told them, were already in motion. He'd contacted people who had contacted other people who in turn had contacted the noted abolitionist lawyer from Pittsburgh, Elijah Griffith, who was expected to arrive in Hartsgrove early in the week and personally enter their not guilty at the arraignment. Others were still being contacted; news of the arrest and impending proceedings was raging like a grass fire among the friends and members of the American Anti-Slavery Society in both Pittsburgh and Philadelphia, many of whom could be expected to arrive as well, and, in the event a quick release was not obtained, they intended to make the case every bit as much a cause célèbre as had been the trial of Passmore Williamson in Philadelphia two years previous.

"A coz-what, Doc?" said Hen.

"Cause célèbre. We intend that news of your trial shall be a rallying-cry to raise the public consciousness and carry forth the banner of anti-slavery, exposing the evil and immoral nature of the institution to this part of the country."

"So we just gonna sit here in jail while you doing all that exposing and carrying forth?" Augustus said.

"Only if we cannot secure your quick release. As I said."

"They saying we could be sold down the river," said Napoleon, everyone, including Darling, glancing at the boy with surprise at the rare words.

"Not if the hundreds of stalwart souls in the American Anti-Slavery Society and their legions of sympathizers have any say in the matter," Means said.

"Nobody ever heard of that crowd 'round here, Doc," Augustus said. "This a far cry from Pittsburgh or Philadelphia."

"Nonsense," Means said. "Why, Dr. Darling, your neighbor, has heard of it—haven't you, Will?"

Means, who'd been standing for the most part with his back to Darling as he spoke, turned expectantly toward his friend. "The American Anti-Slavery Committee?" Darling said.

"Society," said Means.

"See there, Doc," said Augustus.

"Society," said Darling. "Yes. I believe I have heard of their work."

"I believe you ain't heard of nothing," Augustus said.

"I sense a note of hostility," Means said, looking from one man to the other and back.

"Man ain't never heard of slavery," Augustus said.

"The man could become your ally," said Means. "He's sympathetic, fair-minded and of excellent moral character—you should be seeking friends, not enemies."

"Why thank you, Steven," Darling said. "I had no idea you were so involved in all of this…all this, whatever it is you're involved in."

"See that, Doc?" Augustus said.

"We must talk at greater length," Means said to Darling. "I've been intending for some time to discuss these other matters with you—there's more to life than medicine. There are souls to mend as well as bodies."

"And just when shall we talk at length?" Darling said. "I am in jail."

"So you are, so you are."

"So is we," Hen said, "so is we."

"Amen," said Augustus. "Say *amen*, Brother Napoleon."

Napoleon said it, "Amen," though without discernible enthusiasm.

Means embarked upon a renewed bout of assurances and optimistic pronouncements, during which his thumbs finally made their first elevated appearance, much to Hen's chagrin. After he'd made his exit, the prisoners, all four, were quiet, Hen looking from one to the other, his eyes finally settling upon Augustus, who seemed—Hen could not be certain, the man's eyes were so cloaked—to be looking at Darling, his face a mite less hostile. Darling was staring back, his face too wearing a more mellow quality. Hen watched the two men seeing each other as if for the first time, and the knot within his chest began to loosen and ease for the first time in days.

On Sunday the clouds in the sky over Hartsgrove—the bit of the sky that Darling could see from the window of his cell—were dark and ominous, pregnant with unfallen snow. Darling's mother visited him after church, as always, as routinely and perfunctorily as ever, scarcely acknowledging the presence of the new Negro arrivals. Every Sunday afternoon Vasbinder visited as well, and he arrived around noon, after Darling's mother had departed, after Darling had finished his dinner of squirrel pot pie—on Sundays, the prisoners were treated to Mrs. Jenkins's finest efforts. Commanding Jenkins to unlock the cell door of his protégé, he walked in with a smile and a greeting, and without so much as a glance toward the three invisible black men in the neighboring cells, ignoring them to an even greater degree than Darling's mother had. He removed his greatcoat, folded it carefully, then placed it on the bunk against the cold stone wall, nestling comfortably into it like a cushion. A great sigh escaped him, as though he'd achieved a high level of comfort, and meant to stay for the duration of whatever it was that needed endured.

"Cyrus," said Darling. "Have you met my neighbors?"

Vasbinder glanced around the neighboring cells, his eyes skipping over each black occupant like a stone over water, with a scarcely perceptible nod of acknowledgement before turning back to Darling. "I had heard," he said. "I'm sorry you've been deprived of the modicum of privacy you had left to you, but I assure you it will only be temporary. And I'm sorry as well for the other—shall we say 'inconveniences'?" Vasbinder's nose gave a twitch of revulsion, as though smelling an unpleasant odor.

Darling glanced toward Black Hen and Augustus to see if they had seen. Neither man gave a clue. "Dr. Means is working to secure their release," Darling said.

"Mr. Means," Vasbinder said, "the would-be doctor?"

"Yes," said Darling. "There's more to Steven than meets the eye—he is apparently quite deeply involved in the anti-slavery movement." Still, neither of his neighbors—Napoleon he couldn't easily see in the farthest cell—seemed to be taking note of the conversation, for which Vasbinder didn't deign to lower his voice in the least.

"So far as I am aware," Vasbinder said, "slavery has been outlawed in Pennsylvania."

"Perhaps," said Darling, "but the movement desires its eradication throughout the nation, as I understand it, and Steven seems quite devoted to its cause."

"A divided allegiance; that would go a long way toward explaining his competence—or lack thereof—as a doctor," said Vasbinder. "Tubers and roots indeed."

Darling looked at his mentor. Vasbinder's collar was askew, a gravy stain gracing the knee of his trousers, and his face was perfectly at ease.

Darling felt a rush of annoyance. When Vasbinder's eyes blinked simultaneously, an easy affirmation of his sincerity, Darling said, "How can you just sit there?"

Vasbinder frowned suddenly and squirmed. "Excellent question, my dear," he said, reaching beneath the blanket for the lump that he'd finally noticed. "What is this?"

He extracted *The American Eclectic Practice of Medicine* from the place where Darling had hidden it when he'd heard Vasbinder arriving.

The old man's eyes looked up, wounded. "*Eclectic*? Will—"

"Cyrus…never mind. Forget the book—Steven lent it to me, and I mean to read it, someday, if my wits ever permit it. Right now it's the farthest thing from my mind. I've lost my liberty, my lady-friend and my reputation, and you just sit there—at least *someone* is working to restore the liberty of my fellow inmates."

"Patience, my dear—you know that we are as well. Patience, the foremost of virtues."

"Patience, patience, yes, of course. "Every good doctor needs patients aplenty."

"Patience, patients," said Vasbinder, his bushy white mustache making way for a gentle chuckle. "Good one, my boy."

Darling was in no mood for levity. Staring out the window at the first falling flakes, he heard another sigh from Vasbinder on the bunk behind him. "Come sit here beside me, Will."

Darling turned. He said, not unkindly, for unkindness would be like scolding a loyal old dog, "Cyrus, I'm in no mood for sitting. I cannot sit. I am exercising my freedom to pace—one of the few freedoms left to me." At that, he paced across the cell and back to the window again. Vasbinder watched, the smile vacating his face, replaced by a grimmer aspect.

"Will, the restoration of your liberty and your reputation—and perhaps your lady-friend as well—is only a matter of days away."

"It is, is it?"

"It is indeed."

Darling straddled the wooden chair, resting his elbows upon the back, the better to stare at his mentor. "Upon what do you base that supposition?"

"The case against you is nothing but humbug and quack," said Vasbinder. "Hardly the stuff upon which a conviction could be built."

"You honestly believe that?"

"Patience," said Vasbinder, "is the key."

Darling shook his head. "Thank you, Doctor."

"Will, do you remember Mrs. Foulkrod?" Darling remembered. "You'd been riding with me just over a year," said Vasbinder, "when we were summoned that day to the Foulkrods."

Darling recalled the day in July, hot despite the thunderstorms that had barged through earlier in the afternoon, leaving behind a pleasantly pungent odor in the air. The Slabtown Road was littered with twigs and limbs, and larger broken branches. Jacob Foulkrod made saddles and leather goods and lived in a frame dwelling to which several rooms had been added over the years. He lived with his wife and five children; another five had died before reaching maturity, three in childbirth, and they thought—feared—that Adeline Foulkrod was pregnant again. At forty, her last pregnancy had been exceedingly difficult.

"When you were able, without significant assistance from me, to diagnose her condition as ascites, rather than pregnancy, I was never prouder of you," Vasbinder said. Darling remembered detecting the watery accumulations in Mrs. Foulkrod's abdomen by the wavy motion evident when he exerted pressure with his fingers on her sides in an alternating rhythm, just as his preceptor had taught him. The flat, dull sound emitted upon percussion confirmed it, and the Foulkrods were relieved by the diagnosis of abdominal dropsy. They had not desired another mouth to feed, nor the complications of another pregnancy. "That was when I knew you were born to be a doctor. That was when I knew we had chosen the proper profession, the profession in which you would prosper and grow."

Darling nodded. "Prosper and grow—just *see* how I've prospered and grown."

Vasbinder allowed his charge to indulge his self-pity, accommodating it with a weary smile. "I believe I know now what I missed, having never been a father. Watching you grow and mature, Will, has been a blessing. And half the joy of it—this may surprise you—half the joy is not where you might expect. For it is not only in witnessing your triumphs and victories that I find reward, it is also in watching the manner in which you bear your troubles and tribulations. And overcome them. That is, in truth, the essence of seeing you learn and mature."

Darling sighed. It was not the sort of thesis one could gracefully argue. "I will have to take your word for it, I'm afraid."

"How you manage your tribulations can lead to your greatest triumphs."

"I shall have to take your word for that as well."

"You shall not. You shall see for yourself."

"*When* shall I see for myself?"

"In good time."

"How *much* good time?"

"Not much good time, my dear, not much good time at all."

Vasbinder seemed to genuinely believe Darling would not be convicted of this crime. *Was* that what he truly believed? Or was Darling so hopeful, so desperate, that he was projecting that belief onto his mentor solely for the purpose of borrowing it back? Sitting on the hard chair in his cell, staring at his face, Darling allowed himself to believe it. Despite himself, he allowed hope to seep in. He was a boy again, a neophyte, trusting in his all-knowing preceptor.

    Through the cell window, they watched the snow begin to fall more steadily. The topic turned to the weather. As they were talking, Black Hen and Augustus exchanged a few quiet words as well, and Napoleon seemed to be humming to himself, curled on his bunk in the far cell, his face to the wall. Jenkins came in with fresh sticks for the stove, which was soon ticking and crackling and glowing, the warmth radiating out through the cells. Darling saw his preceptor growing drowsy, watching the snow fall, saw his head nod and his eyelids grow heavy. When Vasbinder fell asleep, Darling found himself in the same condition, scarcely able to keep his own eyes open, and he glanced around at his neighbors, who seemed to be napping as well. Finally he gave in, taking the pillow and blanket and curling up on the floor beside the bunk. Before he fell asleep listening to the fire and to the gentle breathing of his preceptor, while the snow fell beyond his window, burying Hartsgrove in a shroud of white, his thoughts returned again to the Foulkrods, and he remembered their relief at the news that Adeline was not pregnant. He remembered how short-lived had been that relief when the ascites had metastasized to her heart six months later, making a widower of Jacob.

Sandt was not in the gallery next morning, Monday, the day the defense began its presentation, but he visited Darling at the jail late in the afternoon. His intent was to cheer up his old chum, to assure him he hadn't been abandoned. Despite the fact that construction on his new home was at a standstill, his new shipment of wares from Philadelphia had not yet been properly displayed upon his shelves, his old stock not properly rotated, despite the customers flowing in and out of his doors in a steady stream, Sandt was nonetheless determined to sacrifice whatever needed sacrificing to make time for friend; of this he made certain his friend was aware.

    Briefly, Darling was happy to see his face. The feeling passed quickly. In truth, it was painful, Sandt's blatherings aside, for all his presence did was call attention to the absence of Kathleen. It was as though an amputation had been performed, and the prosthesis was crude, painful and entirely inferior.

    "How did you fare in court today?"

    Darling shook his head. "Even Esquire Truby was at a loss for words."

    "Old man Gayley didn't laud you in the most lavish of terms?"

    "Oh, he lauded me all right. He would laud me straight into the penitentiary."

The defense strategy included calling to the stand character witnesses, acquaintances of Darling who'd known him before he'd become a doctor, and who were presumably unaware of his interest in dissection. Among them was his old master, Mr. Gayley, who, looking as stern taking the stand as he had at the head of his classroom, never broke a smile. Yes, he knew Will Darling, knew him well. Yes, he was a fine scholar, a smart lad, yes, he seemed to be a leader among his peers. As a matter of fact, he and the Sandt boy had barred him from the classroom one day—other boys had tried, every year, it was a tradition, but none so determinedly, so doggedly, so successfully. Young Darling, for all his intelligence and charisma, displayed a remarkable disdain for structure, regulation and order. When the rules were not to his liking, he tended to disregard them, and play by his own.

Smathers had declined to cross-examine.

"The old reprobate." Sandt sighed. "I must say, it does not bode well. What shall we do? You cannot go to prison for a crime you did not commit."

"I suppose it could be argued that I am in fact guilty. Perhaps not of the crime of which I'm specifically accused, but the same precise crime all the same."

"As are we all," Sandt said, "but selective justice is no justice at all."

"Cyrus doesn't seem at all troubled. He's asked me to be patient. He says the jury will never convict me on the basis of so flimsy a case. Humbug and quack, he calls it."

"Not ragtag and bobtail?"

"Perhaps a bit of both," said Darling.

Sandt glanced around at the neighboring cells, whose occupants seemed otherwise occupied; nevertheless, he lowered his voice. "I still say escape is a plausible option. The Paine County jailhouse is known far and wide as a sieve—the penitentiary would be quite another matter, I'm afraid."

"Escape is the recourse of only the guilty."

"And is that not the way you've just pleaded?" said Sandt. "Just now?"

Darling thought it over, then nodded, reassuring only himself. "Cyrus is convinced."

Sandt said, "And Cyrus has never been wrong?"

His penchant for avoiding haste served Hen well in confinement, as he was able to accommodate it with more equanimity than his fellow inmates, including the white doctor, who were all young, all restless, all pacing and grumbling and grasping of bars. Certainly Hen missed the sunshine upon his cheeks, the crunch of snow beneath his feet, the flavor of pickled pigs' knuckles upon his tongue, and he missed Lucindy, but he revisited them all in his dreams, half-dreams and daydreams. Having no reason to arise and nowhere to go allowed him to extend his familiar state of somnolence indefinitely. He remained as a leaf upon the water.

Dr. Means visited again, as did Lucindy, Cornelius Nips, Solomon McManigle, each in turn, and the conversations raged and flowed and ebbed and raged again, each concern, each memory and mystery, each worry, each outrage and injustice, every grievance, plan and hope, all were rehashed, reworded, restated, repeated again and again and over again. Hen's contribution was seldom more than a nod.

He lay on his bunk and did his dreaming, barely asleep, barely awake. Nights and days were all the same, varying shades of gray and black. Until the fourth night. Late and dark—it was the darkest night of them all—Pompey came back to him, the little fellow alive again in Hen's dream, alive and full of the devil. He slapped Hen's face and giggled. He poked a sharp finger in Hen's cheek, and he started to poke his eye, but Hen ducked, grabbing at the little finger. He missed it. Pompey was too quick for the old man. Leaping from Napoleon's grasp, he tumbled over Hen, poking and slapping and burbling and drooling, being a general nuisance, pestering him to the point of desperation. Hen was at a loss as to why the child was behaving as he was, all over him to the exclusion of everyone else in the wagon, till it came to him that the child was crying for help: He wished for Hen to save him. The child did not want to die. Nor did he want to grow up in slavery, and it was up to Hen to save him. But Hen couldn't; he didn't know how. He was quite at a loss. Pompey drew back and looked with horror into Hen's eyes, horror and fear and disbelief that the old man could not save him, and Hen was about to explain why he could not, why he did not know how to, when he was interrupted by the sudden apparition of Yellow Charlie. Enormous Yellow Charlie, his immense yellow face and greasy beard hovering over all, above the wagon in the star-filled night, impervious to the chill, the fingers of his huge hands writhing and wriggling like poisonous snakes. And the look on the face of the child went from surprise to fear to horror as he was taken up like a fallen leaf in Yellow Charlie's gigantic hands, and he began to burble again, more urgently now, and moan and yell, and—though he could not yet talk, had not yet mastered that skill—Hen could understand what he was saying. He did not want to be taken; he did not want to be saved by Yellow Charlie; he wanted *Hen* to save him, Hen alone, only Hen: save him from slavery, from dying—save him from Yellow Charlie! Only Hen! Hen could understand him, and the longer he listened, the clearer the child's words became—but they no longer made any sense. For some reason, Pompey had begun to mumble *Molly*. This was the word that kept coming from the child's mouth: *Molly, Molly, Molly.*

Hen sat up on the edge of his bunk in the pitch-black cell. The dream vanished. Pompey was surely dead and gone—Hen had failed. In the chilled air, sweat pooled on his chest, and the feverish moans and the mumbling of *Molly* were coming, not from Pompey, but from the cell beside his. From young Dr. Darling.

Hen had never seen a blacker night. He waved his hand in front of his face: invisible. His head was incredibly clear. He was blind. He felt the cold stone of the wall behind him, found the window, put his face near, and was able to discern vague shadows and shapes of the outside world, assuring him his sight remained, though when he turned to peer next door, to the cell where Darling continued to thrash and moan, there was nothing again but darkness.

He eased himself to the foot of his bunk, touching the bars between his cell and that of the young doctor. "Doc," he said, his whisper harsh and loud, "Mr. Doc—"

The moans and mumbles ceased, and everything was silent.

"Mr. Doc," Hen whispered again. "You asleep?"

Came the response, oddly deep and disembodied: "Not now."

"You been fussing about—bad dreaming." When Darling didn't answer, Hen said, "You been saying Molly—Molly this, Molly that, over and over."

"I was?"

"You was."

Hen heard a rustle, a stirring; Darling sitting up? The voice was closer: "Molly?"

"Molly," Hen said. "She that little girl? She that little girl you done dug up?"

"I dug no one up," Darling said, then hesitated. "That night," he added.

"Then who that little girl they done found?"

The question went unanswered. Darling's voice had seemed close, but Hen couldn't tell where he might be. Were they inches apart or yards? Darling said, "What time is it?"

"Don't rightly know, Doc. Middle of the night, on towards morning."

"I can't see a thing," said Darling. "I can't see my nose in front of my face." Then, a moment later, he said, "We're both the same color now."

Hen felt his old cheeks lift. "You ain't white and I ain't black no more."

"Or perhaps we're both black. Black seems to be the predominate color of the moment."

"How you like being a nigger, Doc?" Hen chuckled.

"I can't tell. I can't feel a thing. How does it feel to you?"

How did it feel to breathe air? Hen shrugged. "Ain't never felt no other way."

"Want to feel what it's like, Doc?" said the disembodied voice of Augustus, a clap of thunder out of the black. "Want to feel close up what it's like to be a nigger? Here's what we gonna do: We put you in the nigger box. Nigger box, three foot square, got a tin top on it, they stuff you in naked—course they let you keep your skin on, usually—and let you bake out there in the hot sun all the day long. That's what it feel like being a nigger."

After some time Darling spoke. "I've heard of cruelties," he said.

"But you ain't never felt 'em," said Augustus.

"On the whole, I'd prefer to rely on my imagination, if it's all the same with you."

Augustus chuckled. "Your mama, she didn't raise up no fool."

"No," Darling said. "Ada Darling did not raise a fool."

Everything was quiet for a moment, then came a sob, more like a wet snort, resounding in the blackness from a fresh direction: Napoleon. Hen, steeling himself for another wailing binge, impotent to comfort the boy, was surprised when, just as quickly, Napoleon spoke instead, two words strong and clear: "Them cocksuckers," he said.

Hen wasn't sure what he'd heard; it was Napoleon's voice, but not his words, at least not like any he'd ever heard him speak before.

"Them white cocksuckers!" Napoleon said, wet and garbled, snot-like.

"Mind your manners, boy," Augustus said. "We got company. We got one of them white cocksuckers sitting right in here amongst us."

Hen threw back his head and laughed. He laughed at the disembodied voices out of nowhere, at the very idea of a talking blackness, at the way they lived inside his head, and only inside his head. He laughed like the howl of a wolf in the woods, so long and so hard in the darkness that he was never sure if anyone else had joined in.

Beyond the bars of his window the day dawned fiery, red clouds fanning out in layers across the eastern sky. The frost on the window pane was lacy and pink, and through it Darling saw his little slice of town coming awake, watched Mrs. Jenkins carry the chamber pot from her back door to the necessary behind the house, her breath trailing like a vanishing white shadow. He alone in the cellblock seemed to be awake and alert, having slept little since the fantastic incident in the nighttime when Hen had laughed himself—and apparently his companions as well—fairly well to sleep. There had been menace on the face of the words that were spoken, but Darling sensed it was only skin-deep, like their colors, and he felt quite at ease among the black men, having shared those otherworldly moments with them, a bond quite singular and unique.

It was the day the defense rested. In Darling's estimation it rested with a whimper, not with a roar, stifled by the very presence of Levi Smathers. Smathers, his confidence manifest and mounting, was larger than life, strutting like a peacock, his muttonchops bristling, his eyes flashing, his voice booming with eloquence, the creases on his trousers sharp enough to slice flesh. It was the day on which court, absent again both Vasbinder and Kathleen, was adjourned after a brief session to allow counsel to begin preparing their final arguments.

It was the day that Vasbinder came to visit him in his cell for the final time.

He appeared in the corridor that afternoon rumpled and weary, the anti-Smathers in Darling's eyes, ignoring again the black men as if they were invisible. His shirttail had escaped his striped trousers, and his sleeve bore ink stains from a recalcitrant quill used in the writing of a recent prescription. Undaunted however, he expressed the utmost confidence that Darling's freedom was in the offing.

"Poppycock and twaddle," he said, "is the whole of their case."

"I wish I had your conviction," said Darling.

"That is the only conviction you shall have, my dear. You must have faith. You have to believe. Stuff and nonsense is all the prosecution has offered."

"Stuff and nonsense? Or poppycock and twaddle?"

From the edge of the bunk, Vasbinder looked up at Darling standing by the window. Vasbinder's mustache trembled. "I'm often unsure how to regard your remarks, my dear."

"You *truly* believe the jury will acquit?"

Vasbinder placed his thumb beneath his chin, flicking his forefinger through his bushy white mustache, causing a ripple like wind through tall grass. It was a familiar gesture, though Darling had not seen it in some time. "With all my heart," he said.

"And I shall walk out of the courtroom a free man?"

"Free as a starling. Soon, you shall sleep in your own bed, be about your own life's work once again, and all this unpleasantness"—his eyes swept over Darling's black neighbors—"shall be behind you. Rely on it, Will." Again the thumb, the flick, the ripple.

Darling's heart sank.

He had learned much from his preceptor over the years; as well, he had learned much about his preceptor. He knew Vasbinder's habits and attitudes, his likes and dislikes, his politics and religion, almost as well as he knew his own. He knew that Vasbinder's favorite food was fresh fried trout, that he liked his steak well done, that his favorite vegetable was scallions dipped in salt, and he could tell when he'd been eating them by the flatulence that invariably ensued. He knew that he preferred his feather pillow filled plump to bursting and that, since his wife had died, he preferred to lay abed on a Sunday morning rather than rise for church. He knew when his mentor was suffering from constipation by the red, swollen veins on his brow. He knew about the ringlet of Gertrude's hair—his wife's, not the horse's—which Vasbinder kept pressed in a journal and hidden in the drawer of his chest in the parlor. He knew Vasbinder's expressions and gestures, and their meanings, better than he knew those of his own mother, or of his best chum, Sandt, certainly better than he'd ever learned of his own father.

He knew the thumb, the flick, the ripple.

The first time he'd seen Vasbinder employ it was on the occasion of a call to the home of Elijah Knapp on Water Street, during the summer of the first year they'd ridden together. The doctor had diagnosed the youngest son, Robert, with whooping cough, applied his cups accordingly, prescribed a regimen of calomel and Dover's Powder, and administered the first doses. Explaining the diagnosis and treatment to the elder Knapps, Vasbinder engaged the same gesture, thumb on his chin, finger flicking through his mustache. As they mounted their horses and rode away later, he instructed Darling on the lessons to be learned from the case, as he did after every call. This particular case had been difficult, as the chest cavity of the little patient had been too narrow to rely upon the inconclusive sounds emitted by the percussion and auscultation, the febrile condition too arbitrary. As a result, Vasbinder could not be entirely certain, he told Darling, if the boy was indeed suffering from the whooping cough, and not the croup, with which it was often confounded, and which would affect the prescribed treatment accordingly. Since that date Darling had noticed that Vasbinder employed the gesture—the thumb, the flick, the ripple—only when he was unsure of his diagnosis, unsure of himself.

Now Darling stood in his cell, hearing the assurances of his mentor, watching the bushy white mustache ripple like tall grass in the wind. The thumb, the flick, the ripple.

Darkness fell. Jenkins came and asked if Dr. Vasbinder wished to extend his visit for another half hour, as he was about to leave for that period of time to take his supper at his home, and fetch back that of the prisoners. Vasbinder replied in the affirmative, for he was quite comfortably ensconced upon the bunk in Darling's cell, growing drowsy and enjoying the company of his charge.

Darling had already noted that Jenkins had, again, neglected to lock the cell door.

Vasbinder's sleep was sudden and deep, the sleep of a weary old man.

Darling was weary as well. He was weary of playing the puppet, weary of the political machinations and orchestrations grinding on behind his back, weary of God's and Cyrus's mysterious ways. During the course of his musings on Gertie, the horse that he loved and missed, it had occurred to him that he was just as pitiful a creature as she, just as enslaved by his own limitations. This epiphany had arrived even before the arrival of the black men, imprisoned for the crime of hating slavery; it had arrived even before he'd begun to consider real enslavement, the kind imposed not by one's own limitations, but by the laws of man.

Darling opened the door of his cell and stepped through, closing it softly behind him.

Standing in the corridor, a free man—however tentatively—he found himself face to face with Augustus, grasping the bars of his own cell, beside his own cell door, which was still quite locked. Black Hen stood likewise in his cell, Napoleon on the edge of the bunk in his. Each man stared at Darling, each black face inscrutable. No one mentioned the keys they knew to be hanging in the office. No one spoke at all. Vasbinder, meanwhile, still reclining on Darling's bunk, muttered an odd snort of a snore, then settled back into his sleep, his lips smacking twice. Darling sighed and nodded, started to gesture, started to speak, did neither, turned and departed, out of the corridor, through the office and out into the cold night air of Hartsgrove.

There would be a price to pay. There was always a price to pay. Since the day he'd followed Dr. Nevers from the gloom of his house into the bright April sunshine, Darling knew that there always had been, and always would be, a cost associated with freedom. You could not run in the sunshine without paying the price.

12: January 19, 1858: Love, Dirt and Fire

There was a hint of wood smoke in the cold, clean air over Hartsgrove, delightfully foreign after so many weeks in confinement, as was the crunch of the frozen dirt beneath his boots. Pulling Vasbinder's greatcoat more tightly around him against the chill, Darling strolled east on Main Street, resisting the urge to dash. Encountering Howard Kunselman wobbling between the bar of the Union Hotel and the Peace and Poverty Tavern, Darling nodded. "Howard," he said. "Fine evening for a stroll." Kunselman staggered to a standstill, his hollow old face placid and imperturbable but for his eyes, which repeatedly widened and squinted. Darling continued walking, continued resisting the urge to haste. When he was certain he was hidden once more in the shadows, he crossed the street toward Sandt's. Though the windows were shuttered, there was a small light within. Making his way around the side of the building, Darling rapped lightly upon the back door.

He figured he had fifteen minutes at best before Jenkins returned from his supper and raised the alarm. Even if Vasbinder awoke before then, Darling doubted that he'd alert anyone. Though he couldn't imagine his mentor's reaction—shock, anger, surprise, resignation, perhaps a modicum of satisfaction?—he couldn't imagine betrayal in that mix.

Sandt opened the door in his apron, the wispy whiskers on his skinny chin dropping in surprise. "Will! My God—"

"Hide me."

"But—"

"It was your idea," Darling said. "Here I am."

"Yes," said Sandt. "Here you are in the first place they'll look."

"Then let us remove ourselves to, say, the last place they'll look."

"In the back of the wagon," Sandt said, pointing toward the shed.

"I'll be out shortly."

Darling climbed into Sandt's Dearborn behind the canvas curtains, burrowing beneath the pile of woolen wrappers and burlap sacks, where he waited. Soon, he heard another voice.

"Will! Will Darling! Can you hear me?" Vasbinder. "Will—if you can hear me, come out. It's not too late. You're making a grievous error."

He heard Sandt come to the door and he listened to the two men talk, though he was unable to make out a word. Presently the conversation concluded and he heard footsteps—presumably those of Vasbinder—retreating along the frozen dirt, then there was nothing but silence. Though it seemed longer in the blackness of the nest in the wagon, it was probably only minutes before Sandt came and, without a word, hitched up his horse to the wagon. Not until they were on the move did Darling peek out.

"What did Cyrus want?"

"He wants you to return. He wants his greatcoat back. He told me to tell you, should our paths chance to cross, that it was not yet too late. That you're squandering an opportunity for legitimate freedom for an impromptu, ill-advised adventure."

Darling pondered the alternatives. "Which would you choose if you were me?" he said. "An opportunity for freedom, or freedom?"

In the darkness, Darling could make out the vapor of Sandt's breath white and ghostly on the blackness of the air, the shaking of his head. "I can still head toward the jailhouse."

"Take me to Irishtown," Darling said. He found suddenly that the solving of the mystery of Molly was not the primary mission on his mind. His singular focus was the solving—and the abolishing—of the absence of Kathleen O'Hanlon from his life. Sandt, however, soon made him listen to reason: it would be exceedingly imprudent to go to Irishtown—the second place they'd look. He must first go into hiding, allow matters to sort themselves out.

From riding the circuit with Vasbinder, Darling knew of an abandoned cabin just beyond a secluded hollow off the Beechwoods Road, less than five miles from town. They rode first to Cook's Saw Mill, procuring a load of scrap timber, twigs and splinters for tinder, and pieces of boards left to rot in the yard. The night was cold, and Darling would need fire.

The cabin had belonged to an old pioneer named Jacob Black. It consisted of one-room, and was built of logs with a clapboard roof, a puncheon door and floor, and a single window that was nothing more than a hole in the wall, glassless and open, the greased paper that once covered it having long since vanished. The original fireplace and chimney of mortar and sticks had been improved before the cabin had been abandoned, and Darling judged that the stones and mortar could safely withstand a fire. He was surprised, upon closer inspection, at the condition of the place, far less deteriorated than he might have expected. He and Sandt unloaded the wagon and built the fire, unloading too a number of wrappers and sacks which they placed on the floor before the hearth for Darling to use as his bed. After these arrangements had been concluded, the two men shook hands in a somber, conspiratorial manner, and Sandt departed into the black and frozen night. What was next?

He settled himself before the fire. He had no idea what was next. For the longest time his thoughts raged, leaping and snapping and crackling in tune to the fire, rest as elusive as any given flame. Soon the notion settled itself upon him that while he was no longer behind bars, he was, nevertheless, far from being a free man. There was the matter of the mysterious machinations taking place beyond his ken, working to bring about his ruin. And there was the matter of the less-than-invisible machinations working to keep him from Kathleen. Awareness of the matters, however, failed to give him any purchase. He was unable to devise a plan. Lingering as well in his mind was the dilemma of the three black men, his erstwhile fellow inmates, for try as he might, he could not shake off a feeling of concern. The bond had been made. He trusted that daylight would clear his mind and bring with it the wherewithal to function once again as a free and free-willed man, an intelligent being capable of meeting his adversity and addressing it in such a way as to effect a positive outcome. Sandt would get word to Kathleen, and within a day or two, three at most, he would see her again. Somehow. Then the three of them—somehow— would plot the best way forward. To address the mystery of Molly and attempt to solve the conspiracy against him? Or to flee, to relocate in a less hostile place and begin anew? Even that much, the answer to the most basic and fundamental question at hand, quite eluded him.

Each time his mind began to loosen its grip, to let go, to allow some manner of ease to overcome the anxiety, the fire died down toward ashes and the threat of frozen blackness jolted him awake again, and he roused himself from his nest to rekindle and feed the flames. As the fire rose up once more, so too did the unrest in his mind.

It was a decidedly uneasy night.

He was a free man, shackled to his fears.

The cellblock was oddly quiet without Darling, an oddity in and of itself, as the young white doctor had seldom made much noise to speak of. But they had talked, and that must have been it, Hen thought, the talk between Augustus and Darling, mostly, although Hen himself had contributed a word now and then when he'd felt that a nod wouldn't answer. Now that Darling was gone, Hen and his companions had little to say to one another—no one wondered why Darling had not freed them as well, no one would have expected him to—and Hen reclined on his bunk for the most part, waiting, not exactly sure what he was waiting for beyond some vague notion of Dr. Means, Elijah Griffith and the American Anti-Slavery Society coming to the rescue. That, or perhaps Augustus' plan to escape, even more vague a notion. Augustus slept soundly, as if restoring himself, breathing heavily, a breathing that never quite crossed into snoring, and when he wasn't sleeping, he often seemed in a trance of sorts, sitting on the edge of his bunk, his strong black arms at his sides, hands gripping the edge, his face raised, his eyes closed—though Hen had to admit it was difficult to tell when his eyes were closed or when they were open, such was their appearance to begin with. Napoleon for his part slept a good deal too, though it seemed a sleep of refuge more than restoration, and when he wasn't sleeping he sometimes hummed to himself, or sang softly a tune from his childhood. Hen recognized *Pop Goes the Weasel!* The night was decidedly more illuminated than the dark night before, the night of the voices in the blackness, as Jenkins had left the camphene lamp on the little stand bright and burning the whole night through. It was as if he thought the light could prevent another escape, as though the reason Darling had walked free was not because he'd neglected to lock the cell door, but because the lamp had been too low.

Not much of a fuss had been raised. As if prisoners strolled free every day. Not long after Darling had departed, the old doctor had awoken and looked around the cell, rubbed his eyes and looked again. He'd glanced quickly around the rest of the cellblock, skimming over the three invisible black men, only confirming that his young friend, Darling, was not in one of their cells. Then he'd scratched his head and flicked a forefinger through his bushy white mustache. He'd started to leave, then turned, going back into the cell and stooping to look under the bunk, the stoop causing the violent departure of a fart from his body. Then he'd left for good.

A few minutes later, Jenkins had returned, a stricken look on his pale old face, and had gone to each cell door, yanking at each in turn to ensure it was locked, mumbling to himself all the while. Then he'd turned up the lamp and left, walking wearily out of the corridor.

The ruckus didn't come until morning. Hearing a noise in the office, Hen glanced outside at the gray of the sky, judging it to be too early for their breakfast, and the door had sprung open, several men striding in. He recognized Sheriff Mills immediately, then another familiar brute whose name he couldn't recall, and a familiar deputy, then the forlorn figure of Jenkins trailing behind. There was one other man in the lead, a man it took him a moment to place, till the curled mustache and barrel chest asserted themselves and Hen realized he was gazing, for the first time in months, at Captain Alcorn.

The men scarcely glanced in the direction of Hen or Napoleon, heading straight for Augustus' cell. Alcorn unfurled a rolled-up poster. "See? See? It is him—no doubt of it."

Mills looked over his shoulder, glancing from the poster in Captain Alcorn's hands to the face of Augustus Hamilton, which was meeting their scrutiny with its own.

"There's a resemblance, I'll give you that," said the sheriff.

"Resemblance?" said Alcorn. "By God, he's the spitting image. They're one and the same. Says right there, eyes like a Chinaman—gentlemen, meet Simon Minkins, escaped out of North Carolina. Wanted there for murder, for the murder of his owner, Robert Bane."

"They both got squinty eyes," said the sheriff, "but looky here—says 'has got a scar on his back and right arm near the shoulder, caused by a rifle ball.'"

"Take off that shirt, boy," Alcorn said, "and let's have a look at that scar."

Augustus didn't budge. His head back, he looked down his nose at the congregation of white men there, eyes all but closed, nostrils flaring like a bull before charging.

"Take it off, boy," the sheriff said. "Or we come in there."

Hen glanced at Napoleon. The boy showed no outward signs of fear, watching intently.

"You Simon Minkins?" said the brute whose name escaped Hen.

Augustus stood up slowly. "Simon who?" Slowly, he unbuttoned his shirt, and when he was done, he took it off just as slowly, glaring—presumably—at the white men. The muscles of his chest and arms were compact and sculpted, glistening a deep chocolate brown.

"Turn around, boy," Alcorn said. "Get a move on."

Taking a deep chestful of air, Augustus turned, slowly. Hen saw Alcorn's fists clenching, his jaw tightening. The right side of Augustus' back was smooth as a new saddle; on the left there was a gash of a white scar running from just below his shoulder blade nearly to the tip of his shoulder. "See there!" said Alcorn, pointing.

"That's on his left side, not on his right," the sheriff pointed out.

"Ain't really on his arm, either," the deputy said.

"Sure as hell ain't his right arm anyways," said the brute.

"They just wrote it down wrong," Alcorn insisted. "They must of meant the *left*."

"Maybe," said the brute, "from where the man that drawed the picture was looking at him it was on his right, but on Minkins's left."

"That's just plain dumb," the sheriff said.

"My name is not Simon Minkins," said Augustus. "I'm Augustus Hamilton, free Negro out of Connecticut, and I got my certificate to prove it. If you haven't put a match to it yet."

"I saw that certificate," Captain Alcorn said. "Ink's barely dry on it." Hen saw the blood in Alcorn's face, glowing like coals in his eyes. Alcorn, Hen figured, was looking at the man he believed hanged his daughter, Miss Eva. Hen couldn't help but wonder if he was.

The white men argued on, the deputy pointing out that the scar resembled a knife wound more than a gunshot, as Augustus put his shirt back on slowly and sat back on his bunk. The sheriff said they couldn't ship a nigger to North Carolina based on evidence so flimsy, and Alcorn, rolling the poster back up, insisted they present the case to the magistrate and allow him to decide. Mills offered that it might be worthwhile to send for Minkins's owner and let him identify Augustus first hand. When Alcorn pointed out that the owner was dead, his throat cut in the night by the man sitting before them, the sheriff said that anyone from the Bane family would answer just as well, and Alcorn insisted they call for the marshal in Pittsburgh, and they argued down the corridor and out the door, leaving the black men in silence.

It was a long time till anyone spoke. Hen never did. Napoleon finally stood and went to the bars between his cell and Augustus'. Augustus still sat on his bunk. Napoleon said, "'Gustus—'Gustus." The other man looked up. "You that Simon Minkins?" Napoleon said.

"Simon who?" said Augustus.

He heard her voice in the grayness of the new dawn—"Will! Will Darlin'!"—certain he was only dreaming it. He was certain until the crude door burst open and she was flying across the floor, launching herself upon him, embracing him, kissing his face, her own face wet with tears, and with the other, unmentionable, secretions. *Snot* was too mean a word, for she was the most beautiful apparition ever to land upon him.

He shared the fluids gladly, willingly, freely. He was crying as well, never more joyous.

In the doorway stood Sandt, a stricken look upon his long and ghostly face.

Kathleen was oblivious to the man, but Darling could not be. Ever so reluctantly he sat up, ever so conscious of the feelings of his friend, who was equally in love, he was sure, with the girl now smothering him with kisses. Kathleen refused to loose contact, and Darling looked up sheepishly at his old school chum.

"She came to me," Sandt said, "she refused to be denied—"

Kathleen said, "When the word come you'd busted out—"

Sandt said, "She insisted—"

Kathleen said, "I was afraid you were gone for good and—"

Darling said, "What about your father and—"

"The devil take him!"

"She wouldn't take no—" Sandt said.

"Are they looking for me?" Darling said.

"All over town," said Sandt.

"The devil take the lot of them!" said Kathleen.

"My place, your mother's place—they're all over Irishtown," Sandt said.

"I was so scared you'd left altogether—" Kathleen said.

"Were you followed?" said Darling.

Silence. Sandt turned in the doorway to look out. Darling stood and lifted the burlap he'd hung over the hole that passed for a window in the log wall, peering through. Kathleen stood as well, making her way to the door beside Sandt, and, as Darling joined them, they stepped outside, into the cold, frosted air. All was perfectly still. There was no sign of life, but for the young blue roan hitched to Sandt's Dearborn wagon standing like a statue, white clouds of breath silently escaping his head, his ears up, listening. The snow-covered ground was gray in the early dawn, the stubbly brush, bristly, stark and black, reclaiming the once-cleared acre around the cabin. Beyond, the tall pines were lost in shadow, not yet able to rise to the level of green. The roan gave his bridle a shake, snorted, and the stillness descended again.

"No," said Sandt.

They listened a while longer. "I'm hungry," Darling said.

"I brung some bread," said Kathleen.

The loaf of soda bread was the whole of their provisions. There was neither butter nor knives, but the chunks broken free and devoured before the fire were perhaps the most delicious Darling had ever tasted. Sandt found a pot in the back of his wagon and they melted snow on the fire to drink. Kathleen attached herself to the side of Darling as they sat in the make-shift bed, while Sandt sat like an Indian a few feet off, awkward and self-conscious.

"What now?" said Sandt when the loaf was gone.

Kathleen squeezed his arm, her head resting against his shoulder, as if that were enough.

"I must have time to think," Darling said. "But I scarcely know where to start. I don't even know whether to stay or to flee."

"Why, we're staying, sure we're staying," Kathleen said, sitting up. "That pack of ignorant maggots'll not drive us from our home."

"No," said Sandt, "of course they won't."

"I shall have to talk to Cyrus," Darling said.

"Why?" said Kathleen.

Darling was a bit confounded. "Why…to seek his counsel, of course."

"Why?" said Kathleen.

"Cyrus would counsel you right back into your cell," Sandt said.

Darling shrugged. "Only because he was so convinced I'd be acquitted. Because he so believed in my innocence. When very few did, I might add."

"Does it not strike you a wee bit odd," said Kathleen, "how so very convinced the man was of your innocence from the start?"

"Cyrus? No, of course not. Why, he's like a father to me."

"And is your mother not like a mother to you?" Kathleen said. Darling didn't answer. "Your own mother's convinced you're guilty as a coon."

"I did think it odd, now you mention it," Sandt said. "I thought all along it was almost as though Cyrus were with us that night. Almost as if he *knew* the coffin was empty."

"What are you saying?" Darling said. "What are you implying?"

Sandt shrugged his lanky shoulders. Kathleen said, "I'm just wondering if the man knows more than he's let on, is all."

Darling frowned, not pleased with the directions his thoughts were taking him. "All the more reason to speak with him."

How that might be accomplished was the subject of the conversation that ensued. Little headway was made. In the end they concluded it would be best for Darling to lie low for a few days, a week perhaps, to allow the initial tempest to blow over.

Sandt said, "We must be getting back then—I have patrons, and my doors must be open. We shall visit again tonight, and bring with us some provisions."

"Very well," said Darling as Sandt stood.

Kathleen didn't move. "Kathleen," said Sandt, extending his hand, "we must go."

"I'm going nowhere." She took Darling's arm, squeezing it to her chest.

Sandt, his pale face half frowning, glanced at Darling, then back to Kathleen. "Is it wise to stay?" When she said nothing, he looked again at Darling. "Is it wise to let her to stay?"

"To *let* me stay?" Kathleen said.

Darling shrugged, his heart at the back of his throat. To his mind there was nothing the least improper for the girl to whom he was engaged to stay with him; moreover it was his first cause for joy in weeks. Of course, his friend didn't know they were engaged. He wondered, in fact, if the girl to whom he was engaged knew that they were engaged. From the floor, they both stared up at their friend.

"Very well, then," said Sandt. A flush overcame the pallor of his face, and he turned and walked to the door. At the threshold he hesitated, almost turned, but didn't. They watched his shoulders slump and pass through the door. They heard the groan of the wagon and the snort of the roan, the soft cry of *gee* from Sandt, and the sound of the wagon wheels on frozen snow fading off through the woods, leaving them alone.

They built up the fire and rested, reclining in their nest on the floor, holding hands shyly, staring at the rough roof of the cabin where the light winked through in slices here and there between the boards. They put their dilemma aside, letting it rest for a while as well, and Kathleen told him the latest gossip, the latest news of her family—her own escape from her father, who'd been doing his best to hold her captive—their friends, even his mother and her falling out with Mrs. Stormer, the result of an argument concerning the testimony of Little Bull. Though her belief in his innocence might be in doubt, said Kathleen, heaven help the person who impugned her boy Will.

Eventually, in the drowsy heat of the fire, they settled into slumber.

They awoke at the same time, no longer side-by-side, but face-to-face, entwined, as close as they could be, their eyes opening together, inches apart, and Darling was immersed in a green aura that seemed to engulf him, soul and all. What happened then was nothing as he'd imagined so many times before. There was no awkwardness, no darkness, no embarrassment or shame, there was only light and anticipation, easeful tension and the certain flow of nature. It was mutually intuitive, the most natural thing in the world, yet beyond the limits of his imagination.

When it was over, they held each other so closely he could feel her heart through his skin, in perfect counterpoint with his own. He felt it racing, then slowing, then settling into a mellow rhythm, the slow mellow rhythm of living. And once again they drifted into sleep.

Not a word had been spoken.

Lucindy brought Belle to see her brother. Though Hen had never observed lavish displays of affection between the two, he was not surprised at the tears that washed down the little girl's face, at the dampening of Napoleon's own eyes, as they embraced the best they could, the iron bars between them. Belle removed from her neck the string with a chicken foot attached for good luck, and gave it to her brother, who put it on. Then they set about playing. She'd brought with her a new top, a whip-top that Marcus Swan had carved for her, and she and Napoleon sat on the floor at the front of the cell and played, taking turns spinning it on this side of the bars or that, as though the bars weren't there, counting to see who could make it spin the longest, laughing at each failed or feeble attempt, and Hen and Lucindy watched the young man who had ended the life of a child, the young man who might well be sold into slavery, playing like a boy without care. Augustus, reclining on his bunk with his hands behind his head, seemed oblivious.

Hen wished he could touch Lucindy. Then, as soon as he recognized the wish, he frowned at the very idea. Where had it come from? He'd never wished such a thing before, though maybe that was because there had been nothing—such as these bars between them—to prevent him from touching her before, if he had so wished. Except perhaps for Fudge. Hen frowned more deeply, easing back to the edge of his bunk. He couldn't recall ever touching her. She'd touched him a few times, her hand on his knee as she spun this story or that, and, most memorably, applying the poultice to his wounded part, but beyond that... Once, when she'd slipped on the ice at the edge of the creek, hadn't he helped her up? At Fudge's funeral, he'd tried to wrap his warmus around her shoulders—hadn't he touched her then? Had he ever touched her arm? Had he ever held her hand?

"How you doing, ol' Hen?" Lucindy had turned from her children. He rose, shambling slowly to the front of his cell.

"Ain't gots nowheres to go," he said. "Ain't in no hurry to get there, neither."

"Good thing you ain't," she said.

The children played on, Belle's laughter at a particularly wayward wobble of the top by her brother causing a coughing spell at which they both laughed all the harder. Lucindy grasped the bar, her hand just inches from Hen. "I been thinking," he said. "I done come up with a idea."

"You ain't got nothing else to do in here."

"You know the sign, the one Fudge carved, shape of a boot, hung up over his shop?" She nodded. "That sign still up there, last time I looked," he said. "Reckon I could fetch it down, lacquer it up good, and set it up there in the graveyard for a marker for ol' Fudge."

Her eyes even wider. "We could carve his name on it, 'cross the heel and toe."

Hen nodded. Her eyes narrowed. "You in the jailhouse, Hen—how you gonna fetch that boot down and fix it up there in the graveyard when you all locked up in here?"

His nod continued as he thought for a moment. "Soon as that there Anti-Slavery bunch spring me loose, I march right in there and fetch it down."

She laughed. "Lordy, Hen, I love the way you thinks." She reached through the bars.

And there it was. Lucindy holding his hand. Hen felt the warmth of it enter through his cold fingers and sweep in an instant up his arm and swell throughout his whole body. He saw, to his surprise, Augustus was standing, grasping the bars, gaping in their direction. Hen felt the sweat break out. Had he ever held her hand before? Had he ever held anyone's hand before? His mother's? Surely his mother had held his hand, at least before his living memory, but, just as surely, Lucindy never had.

"Lordy, Hen," she said again, "if you ain't got the clammiest paw I ever done felt!" Smiling, she withdrew her hand, wiped it on her black wool dress, then reached again for his. "Ain't you never held a woman's hand before?

Hen said nothing. He thought no, no, he'd never held a woman's hand before. And no, no, he'd never had a wish come true before.

Images of shoveled dirt came into Darling's mind. They were not dreams, for he had come awake to change positions and rescue his arm that had fallen asleep, and he'd noticed that it was darker, that it must be getting late in the afternoon, though he was not yet fully alert. When he closed his eyes the images resumed again: fresh, clean-smelling earth falling from shovels. Almost by an act of will, these images were replaced in turn by visions of newly plowed furrows on a clear spring morning, gleaming plows and sweating horses, birds in a scramble through the air; but these were fleeting and elusive and soon the shoveled dirt was back, growing blacker, thicker, muddier.

When he sensed that Kathleen had come awake as well, he told her about them. It was the smell, he guessed. The fire had unloosed in the cabin the smell of clay, which in turn had unloosed in his mind the images of shoveled dirt, which, he theorized, was the way his mind had chosen to remember his father's funeral. For that was the most vivid memory of his childhood, the sight of the fresh, reddish-brown earth falling from the shovels of the two men filling the grave of his father that late April morning, the dirt good and clean, and the green of the grass and the new leaves, the singing of the birds, the scent of apple blossoms.

"Shoveled dirt?" Kathleen said.

"Yes," said Darling. They'd stretched and shifted and rearranged themselves, and now were lying close again. "Isn't it amazing how the mind works?"

"Amazing is one way of putting it," she said.

"You know, I wonder if that was a reason this dirty business of the resurrections came to me so easily, and not just my curiosity as a doctor. Perhaps my mind is fixing them with the unburying of my father—with the restoration somehow of life."

"My mind was full of rainbows," she said.

"Rainbows?"

"Yes—rainbows. After what we... After... Afterwards, my mind was full of rainbows and cherry blossoms, pretty things. You had dirt on yours."

"Well, yes... It's complicated."

"Had it been Josh, he'd have been reciting romantic poetry. Not shoveled dirt."

"*Had it been Josh?*"

"You know what I mean."

"Was Josh a consideration? Was he an option to you?"

"That's not at all what I meant."

"It sounded to me as though that *is* what you meant."

"Is that what you want me to mean?"

Darling sat up. "Is that what you want me to want you to mean?"

With jerky motions, Kathleen retrieved bits of her clothing from the nest and began putting them on. Darling retrieved his as well, and they stood and finished dressing, their backs to one another. When he was fully restored, Darling walked outside.

It was nearly dark and quite cold. The tall pines surrounding the cabin were fading into indistinguishable silhouettes, black against a darkening sky. From some distance off through the woods came the howl of a hungry wolf. Darling realized he was hungry too. Kathleen joined him without a word, placing her hand upon his shoulder, an apology, or close enough, and he put his arm around her waist, and they stared for a while at the place in the tree line where the trail from the road came out, though in the dusk they couldn't be sure precisely where it was. Here he was, a free man. A free man in hiding, his stomach empty, his provisions gone, his supply of firewood nearly exhausted as well, his love at his side, just as hungry and cold, and entirely dependent upon him.

"He's not coming back, is he?" she said.

"Who?" said Darling. "Your Josh?"

Though he was a generation or two removed, Darling was well versed in the hardships and privations endured by the first settlers, for Vasbinder had heard them first-hand from many of the original pioneers who'd been his patients in their aging, dying years, and he'd passed them on to his charge. Jacob Black—in whose cabin Kathleen and Darling were now in hiding—who'd passed away seven years previous in his eighty-second year, was one of them.

Their lives had been lonely, difficult and perilous. Here and there in the vast wilderness smoke curled up from an isolated cabin, while nearby in the woods lurked the savage Indian, the bear, the wolf, the panther. The deadly rattlesnake sometimes slithered to their very threshold to find the sun. Mortality was always near-by. There were no doctors, no neighbors, no settlements. Their cabins were rough and crude, without modern comforts and luxuries, for they possessed only the things that could be carried with them on horseback over the coarse trails through the wilderness—a little bedding, clothing, cooking utensils, a few articles of table wear. But, according to Vasbinder, according to all of the history passed down by word of mouth—for most of it had yet to be written—they had no regrets or second thoughts. Their hearts were happy despite the hardships, for their very environment, their proximity to nature, was ennobling. The tall pines and sheltering hardwoods, the forest and hills themselves, seemed to point toward heaven and bring them closer to God. Songbirds flitted from branch to branch warbling gloriously all the days, while the wild flowers in the spring and summer bloomed at their very doorsteps. Courageously they clawed out a foothold in the wilderness, engaging year-round in the relentless labor of field and forest, expanding the patches of sunshine surrounding their simple cabins, until one day they heard in the forest the ring of an axe, signifying the arrival of a new neighbor. It was only through their toils and tribulations that the comforts and blessings of civilization were now available for the present generation to enjoy.

Standing in the old settler's footsteps before the old settler's cabin in the wilderness, coldness and blackness encroaching, his love shivering beside him, having apparently been forsaken by their friend, their supply of firewood dwindling, stomachs aching and empty, Darling felt far from ennobled.

He felt in fact the stirrings of desperation.

They could scour the nearby forest—the snow wasn't too deep—gathering fallen branches for firewood. There would be fuel enough. But what use was heat without food? Without nourishment for another day, they could easily lose the ability to even walk out of the woods and give themselves up.

Indecision seized him. Already the hunger was gnawing; already he felt too weak to think. Standing in the deep dusk, Kathleen at his side, he didn't know if he had strength enough even to go into the woods for firewood, much less to walk out to civilization. Would Sandt come, or had he truly abandoned them? Should he wait or should he walk? What about Kathleen? Should he take her or leave her and send someone back? Did he have strength enough left? To do what?

The weight of the indecision made him even weaker, filling him with despair. He closed his eyes and pointed his face upward. A simple prayer passed through his mind. *God, please help me. God, please show me the way.* He took a deep breath, the clean, cold air laced with the sweet smoke from their fire. He waited for a sign.

He heard a cluck.

Before him, not fifteen feet away, stood a chicken.

A chicken. Darling blinked his eyes and shook his head, but when he looked again, it was indeed there, engaged in a hesitant waddle beside a scraggly bush. It was indeed real. Not a wild turkey, not a rabbit or squirrel with all their elusive quickness, but a fat, domesticated bird out of nowhere.

It clucked and ducked. How far was the nearest farm? He looked at Kathleen. They both looked toward heaven, then down once again at the chicken, which clucked and gabbled impatiently, looking up at them indifferently, with something like disdain.

Darling had strength enough left for one final sprint.

When Jenkins took away their supper plates, he left the camphene lamp burning high and hot on the little stand in the hallway. Augustus waited half an hour. Then, breaking his trance, he stood, stretched, donned his brimless black derby and walked to the corner of his cell, as close as he could to his two fellow inmates. "Napoleon," he said, "put on them boots. Lace 'em up good. Hen—get that old warmus of yours on." Augustus took a deep breath. The command in his voice left no room for doubt or debate.

"Why?" said Napoleon.

"Get 'em on, boy," Augustus said.

He took his thin wool blanket and rolled it up like a whip. From the corner of his cell, the camphene lamp on the little stand in the hallway was but a few feet away. Reaching beyond the bars, he began to flick the blanket, like a whip, toward the lamp.

The first time he hit it, it wobbled. The second try missed. The third caught the lamp squarely. It toppled from the stand to the wooden floor with a crash and a clatter, the great splash of camphor and sulphuric acid exploding into a curtain of fire.

"Turnkey!" Augustus shouted. "Mastah Turnkey! Fire! Fire!"

Napoleon yelled, "Fire! Fire!"

Hen nodded at breakneck speed.

Jenkins appeared, Augustus and Napoleon still yelling, the old man recoiling in horror at the sight of the flames. "Get us out of here, Mastah!" yelled Augustus. "Gonna get burnt alive! Get us out of here! Quick!"

"Get us out of here!" shouted Napoleon.

Hen watched the old man teetering on the brink of indecision, on a very high, perilous brink. Augustus said, "We help you put it out! Unlock these here doors, we help you!"

Napoleon screamed, "Help! Unlock us! Help!"

Hen caught the old man's eye. "You ain't gonna let us roast, is you?" he said quietly. The fire on the floor was crackling, snapping, crawling, spreading.

The old man skirted the flames, skimming the bars of Hen's cell to Augustus', the farthest, and unlocked the door. Augustus burst through and made for the door to the office.

"Raise the alarm!" shouted Jenkins.

Augustus was gone. Jenkins made his way to Napoleon's door, fumbling the key into the lock. Hen could see the tremble in his hands, the

Old Grimes Is Dead

sweat pouring into his collar, as Napoleon burst through the door, nearly knocking the old man over. Jenkins called, "Wait—wait there!" as Napoleon vanished through the door, then he glanced sheepishly at Hen, as if realizing the folly of the words.

"What happened?" he said, unlocking Hen's door.

Hen shrugged. "Lamp done fell and broke."

He hurried out behind Jenkins. "They're gone!" said the old man, bursting into the empty office. "Them damn lying niggers is gone!"

"Damn lying niggers," Hen said.

"You ain't going nowhere—you grab that pail there and start hauling water!"

"Yes, sir, hauling water."

Jenkins ran in a shuffle to the door. "Fire! Fire!" he shouted up and down Main Street, "Fire at the jailhouse!"

Hen saw the fire behind them, growling, menacing, bigger, meaner. He took the pail from the corner by the desk, noticing that someone had been using it as a spittoon, and walked out front to the pump by the street, above the trough, where he commenced to pump the handle. Augustus and Napoleon were nowhere to be seen. Jenkins's cry had brought men running, pouring from the doors of the American Hotel, Garrity's, the Peace and Poverty, from this place and that, cries of *Fire! Fire at the jailhouse!* resounding from every direction. In the uproar he heard the words *fire engine*, and saw men heading past the jailhouse toward the town stable on the corner of Hamilton where the fire engine was housed. Men arrived just as he had pumped the first of the water into his pail, sloshed it about to clean it for some reason, then refilled it. He was elbowed aside by a burly man in denim and a beard. "Move aside, nigger!" he said. "I'm pumping!" A line of men with pails had formed. Hen carried his inside, and from the doorway of the office saw that the hungry tongues of the blaze reaching inside the cells. He pitched his pitiful bucketful of water, which the flames shrugged off like a gnat.

Other men rushed in behind him, man after man, pail after pail. Hen carried his empty pail back outside, to the end of the line where he stood for a moment or two as the tumult in his stomach was suddenly set loose, making its way to his limbs, buckling his knees and causing the pail to fall from his trembling grasp, where it bounced and rolled in the dirt. Down the street, half a dozen men wheeled the fire engine out of the stable. Hen wobbled away, bracing himself against the clapboard wall of the jailhouse to keep from collapsing. It was the fire he'd seen in the cells, where he might have been, where he could have been, where he *should* have been. The fire eating him alive. When he could, he took a chestful of smoky air and walked away. Other men were still rushing from here and there, carrying pails, men who scarcely glanced at the old black man strolling down the street.

Nevertheless, Hen turned up Spring Alley before he reached Mill Street, making his way toward the Coolbrook Road, and Little Brier, via a route where he was less likely to be seen. Here, beyond the hubbub, the houses were quiet, most of them closed up against the cold night air, the orange reflection of many a hearth fire on windows. Fire. Hen's legs felt like wet straw, his heartbeat throbbing from his toes to the roots of his hair. Another spasm of fear roiled through him. He saw Jenkins perched on the brink, deciding whether to let him out or let him burn, let him live or let him die, and he felt a flush of anger at the gamble with his life taken by Augustus without even a word of warning, and he decided he didn't know who this Augustus Hamilton—or Simon Minkins—was at all. The flush of anger, foreign and unfamiliar, served to quell the fear. And it occurred to him too that Fudge had been right in his dislike of the boy, and thinking of Fudge made him think of Lucindy, and he wondered where Augustus and Napoleon had gone, and though he figured the law would be calling soon to Little Brier, he had no idea where else to go.

At the corner of Spring and Mill he encountered a rotund man, a deerskin thrown over his nightshirt, standing by the street as he attempted to decipher the distant clamor down on Main. At that moment, Hen's knees buckled and he nearly pitched forward; the anger, wrestling the fear, had it in a headlock. Seeing Hen, the man in the dark seemed to frown, and he watched him walk past, Hen sensing his eyes upon him the whole way down Mill. Neither man spoke. Hen waited for him to call out, to raise the alarm, the fear and the anger holding their breath. He resisted the urge to hurry, however. He avoided haste as a general rule. He pointed his feet toward Little Brier, toward Lucindy.

13: January 21, 1858: The Price You Must Pay

The sodden branches from the forest floor burned well enough, albeit with more smoke and sizzle, but with heat enough to enable a drowsy sense of well-being. Darling and Kathleen slept again, late that evening, their stock of wood piled high and deep, their stomachs sated with roasted chicken, their souls sated with the love of one another. Tomorrow was a day they would face only after this day was done.

They'd discussed that very morrow as they'd roasted the chicken on the open fire and feasted. If Sandt failed to show again, as they expected he would, Darling had proposed to walk into town—alone—at dusk, enter it after dark, find their erstwhile friend, confront him, persuade him, do whatever he, Darling, had to do, with or without Sandt, to procure provisions enough to enable them to remain in hiding for at least another week. Nonsense, Kathleen had said, that would be too risky. She would go. She was not a wanted fugitive, and the sight of her would not cause the alarm to be raised. He'd not argued beyond an initial protest, but had fallen silent, and they'd left it at that, resolved in her mind. Resolved in his as well, though in an entirely different direction.

He awoke when he sensed the night was at its deepest. He eased himself out from under her arm, her lips kissing at the air as she slept. Gently, he brushed the black hair from her face to gaze upon it for a moment in the dancing firelight shadows. Leaving their nest, he quietly placed another stick upon the fire, then another for good measure. Then he stood, donning Vasbinder's greatcoat. He tiptoed to the door and through it with one last glance at Kathleen, easing it shut behind him, then off into the dark, cold woods.

He reached town within two hours, he calculated. He was not that far removed from playing hide-and-go-seek behind the bushes, trees and shanties in the streets and alleyways of the town, and in the blackness of the night he felt confident in his ability to move about invisibly. He hoped the authorities would speculate that he was miles away by now, and that Constable McClay would be engaged in his normal custom of spending a good number of his duty hours dozing or playing cards with Jenkins before the sheriff's hot stove. Adrenaline and determination sustained him.

He entered Sandt's house on Coal Alley, standing in the foyer for a moment or two, feeling the heat soak in. Then he lighted the candle sitting on the little stand—he knew the place as well as his own house—and mounted the steps. He paused by the door of the bedroom at the top of the stairs and listened to the snoring from behind the closed door. Not only was Sandt's father a sound sleeper, he was too deaf to hear the cannon roar at the muster grounds. Darling opened the door of the other bedroom, holding the candle aloft. Sandt, as he expected, was sitting on the edge of his bed in his nightshirt. A sound sleeper his friend was not.

Darling stood in his greatcoat, flame held high, an angel of the night. "Why hast thou forsaken me?" he accused in his best biblical voice.

Sandt's eyes were wide and white in the candlelight, until he looked at the floor. "I hast not forsaken thee."

"Hast to."

"Hast not."

"Hast to."

Sandt looked up again. He was reluctant to look into the light, to look into Darling's eyes. "I intended to return in the morning. The wagon is loaded. See for yourself."

"You promised to return yesterday. We nearly perished."

"Perished. Please."

"Why did you not come back?"

Sandt's eyes came out in the open. "You know why."

He did, of course. And the realization, the accusation by his friend, had its intended effect, a pang of remorse filtering through him. The remorse was not for loving Kathleen, not for defeating his rival, but for flaunting his victory, for glorying in it, for his total disregard of the feelings of his friend. Of course he was far from willing to admit to such a thing. "Kathleen has made her choice," he said simply.

Sandt nodded, back again toward the floor, with an indeterminate grumble.

"We must get on with our lives," Darling said. "There are more important things afoot."

"What could be more important?"

My life and liberty. My reputation and livelihood. These things Darling thought, but was loath to utter aloud for their sheer conceit. "The mystery of Molly Plotner, for one thing," he said instead. He set the candle on the nightstand and sat beside his friend. He sat at a distance, near the foot of the bed. Perhaps Darling had won the heart of Kathleen, breaking Sandt's in the process, but Sandt was nevertheless a free man, a wealthy and prosperous man, while he, Darling, was a fugitive, and a poor man to boot. He could not arouse within himself a great deal of sympathy for his old school chum, for which he felt vaguely guilty.

"Do you ever have the feeling," Sandt said, "that we are mere pieces on a playing board?"

"Every day," said Darling, though he offered nothing more.

After a while, Sandt said, "Kathleen's still there?" Darling nodded, though his friend didn't see him. After another moment, Sandt said, "I'll bring you there. Now."

"What provisions have you prepared?" Darling said.

"Jerked beef and biscuits, hard-boiled eggs, some dried hominy. Potatoes and turnips."

"No saddles of venison?" Darling loved saddles of venison, smoked and salted.

Sandt shook his head.

"I'll take food enough for a few days," Darling said. "You needn't bring me. Don't come out until you feel as though you are ready."

Sandt didn't reply. He sat, elbows on his knees, slumped, staring at the dark floorboards, bony shoulder blades poking up beneath his nightshirt. Darling started to touch his friend, but his hand stopped an inch or two short. He couldn't bring himself to lower it all the way.

Leaving Sandt's, he crept through the shadows, from tree to tree, his sack of provisions on his back, down Prospect Street. He intended a reunion with Gertie; there was a serviceable old stable behind the cabin of Jacob Black, only half collapsed, sufficient to keep her safe from the elements. His only fear was that she would be so overjoyed to see him she might raise the alarm with her whinnying and hoofing.

At the corner of Pine he hesitated. Instead of heading toward his home, he walked another block and turned onto Water Street, toward Vasbinder's. Why, he wasn't certain. What he was looking for, he didn't know—positive encouragement, an inkling of a plan—but he supposed it amounted to hope. What he expected to see was a darkened home, perhaps a glimmer of a night light squeezing through a curtain, the same as all the other homes in the sleeping town, but what he saw was quite unexpected. The parlor was as bright as of an early evening.

He could not resist. Against his better judgment, he slipped onto the porch, rapping lightly on the door. After what seemed too long, Vasbinder appeared. His eyebrows arose in surprise and he placed a finger to his bushy white mustache, shutting the door in Darling's face. Darling hesitated, uncertain of the meaning. A moment later Vasbinder opened the door again, this time to a darkened interior.

Without a word, he embraced Darling. Through the wrapper Vasbinder wore over his nightshirt, Darling felt dampness.

"I thought you'd fled," Vasbinder said as he disengaged, holding Darling's shoulders, staring into his eyes, his own eyebrows engaged in their earnest tics of sincerity. "I was certain I'd never see you again, this side of the promised land."

"Are you perspiring?" Darling said.

"Oh," said Vasbinder. "Come in, come in, before we catch our death. No, my dear, not perspiring—I've been bathing myself in mustard water. I've been suffering pains in my limbs and in my back—a dreadful nuisance. In my loins as well."

"Cyrus—are you all right?"

"It shall pass. It's just all this business—you should *never* have absconded—it's getting to be too much for an old man."

"The cell door was open. The temptation was too great."

"A mistake! A grievous mistake. You were on the verge of walking out a free man."

"How can you be so certain I would have been acquitted? How?"

Vasbinder issued a quavering sigh. "Let us sit," he said. In the dim room—lighted only by the lamp turned low in the foyer—he made his way to his rocking chair, at the foot of which sat a basin, the mustard water. Darling sat in the wingback chair near the coal stove hulking in the shadows, radiating a warm, pleasantly acrid scent, an easy sizzling noise. The old man settled in his rocker, kicked off his slippers, placing his feet in the basin with a modest splash. "A most eventful evening," he said. "First the fires, and now a visitation from a wanted fugitive."

"The fires?"

"Yes, of course, you could not have heard. Two fires—both the jailhouse and the house of Samuel Bullers. The blaze at the jailhouse was brought under control, but with the resources all committed there, Little Bull's house was a total loss."

"What of the prisoners? The Negroes who were jailed there?"

"Jenkins has come under some criticism for having let them just walk away. It would seem they've simply vanished."

"What was he to do? Let them burn?"

Vasbinder shrugged, or so it seemed to Darling in the darkness. He asked where he was hiding out, and Darling told him. His mentor recalled the old pioneer well, having been present at the death of Jacob Black, under his care at the time for neuralgia of the heart. Darling told him about Kathleen O'Hanlon joining him, how they'd been forsaken by Sandt, and the miracle of the chicken. That particular miracle, however, passed without comment.

"So, Kathleen, the pretty Irish girl, is with you at the cabin?"

"Yes," said Darling. "Entirely of her own choosing. She insisted."

Vasbinder nodded his head. "That explains quite a lot."

"What do you mean by that?"

"I'll wager you scarcely resisted." Even in the dark, Darling could see the nod of his mentor's head evolve into a resigned shaking. "Ah, young love. Nothing like it. Can you imagine, Gertie—my wife—and I used to dance, here, in this parlor, scarcely any room at all, but we danced. To what you may ask—scarcely room for an orchestra either—why, to the sound of our voices. We sang, she had the most lovely voice, we sang *Pine Creek Lady* and *Gentle Annie* and we danced and danced. Oh, we were so very young. I supposed I, too, might have suffered such a thoughtless lapse in judgment in order to be with her. Young men tend to think less with their brains than with their nether parts."

"I had no idea at the time that I would be with Kathleen," said Darling with a hint of indignation. When his mentor, unconvinced, did not respond, he continued. "The reason I fled was that I could not—cannot—face a prolonged period of imprisonment. Pure and simple. The idea of bars between me and the world."

"Hogwash," said Vasbinder. "A verdict was days away."

"And supposing I had not been acquitted, Cyrus? To me, and to Josh, and to others as well, the outcome seemed in some doubt."

"And if you had been found guilty? What makes you think you would have gone to prison? Hulse was just as likely, with your profession, your standing, to have sentenced you to probation. And if he had not? Three years is the maximum term. Three years! Why a young man can waltz for three years! Three years is nothing! A trifle!"

"A trifle?"

"A trifle!"

For the first time in his life a chasm, a yawing gap, loomed between him and his mentor. It was an entirely new sensation, and it encompassed, in an instant, the concept of forging ahead all on his own after the bridge has collapsed, after the bulwark has crumbled. Darling felt his heart reverberate in the stillness of his chest. "Cyrus, I must return to the cabin before daylight."

"Forgive me, my dear."

"Forgive you?"

"Yes. I'm not feeling well, and perhaps I'm taking it out on you. But the essence remains. You've taken a molehill and made of it a mountain. They'll be hard-pressed to forgive you now, after you've made them the fools."

"If I can find out what happened to Molly," Darling said. "If I can discover the truth, I believe it will clear my name. Exonerate me completely, as a matter of fact."

"Will," said Vasbinder, but the thought trailed away. "There is another thing you are too young to know—life is full of mysteries that remain just that: mysteries. Not everything in this world is knowable." There was a lull, the stove in the corner whispering its quiet hiss. "Having said that…" Vasbinder shook his head in the shadows. "Having said that, I must say I am quite displeased with the honorable Levi Smathers, who has, in my opinion, proved himself most unworthy of the title of 'honorable.' In fact, henceforth I shall cease to use it."

"That should certainly fix his wagon."

Vasbinder stared at his charge, Darling fully expecting to hear that he was often unsure how to regard his remarks. Instead Vasbinder said, "Some serious horse-trading was undertaken to avoid our prosecution in the Van Pelt case, and an honorable gentleman would have seen it carried forward to the Plotner affair as well. *Especially* in that case, given that—"

"Given what? What horse-trading?"

His mentor dropped his hand on the arm of the chair, waving the conversation off. "Never mind. You're hearing the ramblings of an old, sick man. You needn't concern yourself with the minutiae of political maneuvering."

"Then with what should I be concerned? What would you have me do?"

"You have two options: The first is to turn yourself in. If you were to surrender, show genuine remorse, plead temporary insanity, throw yourself on the mercy of the court—Hulse might be persuaded toward leniency. You might be no worse off than you were before—which, as I have repeatedly stated, is not so bad off at all."

"And the other option?"

"Flee," Vasbinder said. "Be gone. Leave these parts behind you. Take Kathleen with you if you will, and start anew somewhere far from here. You're young enough, accomplished enough, you could quite easily start a new life."

"Without my mother? Without my life here, my patients, my friends? Without you?"

There was a moment of silence as the rocking chair creaked. A coal popped in the stove. "If that is the price you must pay, my dear. If that is the price you must pay."

Hen walked in the dark and the cold, ducking frequently behind a tree or into the brush by the side of the road when he heard an approaching horse or wagon. Or when he had to pee, which, despite the extraordinary circumstance of this given evening, was no less often than usual. He was cold and his feet were frozen, but he found he could turn to his anger—as opposed to quickening his pace, a tactic to which he was fundamentally opposed—for a modicum of heat, enough to see him through. Anger was not a feeling with which he was familiar, or comfortable, but it had arisen out of the fear, had banished the fear altogether, and it served to keep the shivering at bay. The anger, and perhaps the memory of the fearful flames with which it was associated, the hot, blazing, devouring, too-close-for-comfort flames. As he thought of Augustus' gamble with his life, his dislike of the brash young man took firmer root, and, as well, the anger began to branch out on its own, an invasive new species of plant overtaking a fertile field. If nothing else, Augustus had introduced him to the notion that black men could harbor hatred toward white—a concept new to Hen—and that was the direction in which his new-found anger unfurled, as vague and wide-ranging as the angry black clouds begrudging the sky overhead, defined only by the white snow cover below.

Hearing horses, he again ducked into the woods where he watched a party of armed men gallop sternly by. When the road was clear, he resumed his trek, refusing to pick up his pace, ignoring the *Move it, Hen!* he heard somewhere in his mind, same as he'd always ignored it.

He was warmed by a burning anger toward Jenkins, the nerve of the man, stopping, hesitating, *actually having to decide* whether or not to allow him to burn to death, but that was only an ounce of the anger he felt. There was plenty to go around: for Sheriff Mills clapping irons on his wrists, for the marshal smashing Lucindy's bone-white table, for Dr. Bullers skinning his friend—here young Dr. Darling seemed somehow to have earned redemption of a sort—for all the white big bugs, the judges and slavers and stone-throwers and politicians and merchants—here the exempt included Dr. Means, Silas McKay, Jim Bundy. The white race was divided into two distinct groups: those he knew to be friendly, and the rest, the faceless, *white* faceless, masses who held him and the rest of niggerdom in chains and perpetrated unspeakable acts of cruelty: The nigger box! Whippings and cat-haulings and brandings and mutilations! Hen found his forearms aching from the clenching of his fists.

He looked at his clenched fist curiously; had he himself ever committed an act of violence? He thought not. He'd never wrestled for sport, even when he was younger, when it was a most popular diversion on summer afternoons in Little Brier. He could not remember ever having raised his hand in violence. He tried to remember, but his memory could reach back only so far, his early years lost to him, the years before Yellow Charlie had walked into the woods and vanished.

Yellow Charlie. Yellow Charlie was there, suddenly, along with Augustus among the ranks of the white faceless masses on the wrong side of Hen's divide. Yellow Charlie fueling the anger. He was furious at Yellow Charlie for removing him from his life, enraged at him for taking that life and making it his own. Somehow, Yellow Charlie joining those ranks ignited his anger even hotter, to encompass the biggest, whitest, most contemptible white face of all: that of God. Hen stopped, looked up at the black clouds, considered it, then shook his fist at the sky.

A bit mollified, he resumed his laggardly pace, so hot now that he opened his warmus to let the night air cool the sweat on his chest. He walked along the frozen ruts of Coolbrook Road, past the lane into Little Brier, another half mile north to the well hidden trail through the woods that led to Fudge's cabin, the trail seldom used by anyone other than Silas McKay. Emerging at the north edge of Little Brier, he saw Fudge's cabin was dark. Augustus' as well. Down across the settlement, much of it visible in the dead of winter through the bare tree skeletons, scarcely a light could be seen. Moving closer, he saw that the snow around Fudge's cabin had been trampled, as though by a horde of horses and men.

He took off his old floppy hat and scratched his head. He listened, and all that came was the soft sound of a breeze high in the limbs of the trees. No wolf, no owl, no human voice.

Lucindy's door had been ripped from its hinges. He stepped inside. The place had been wrecked, again, only this time they'd finished the job. The windows were smashed, not a shelf remained on a wall, furnishings wrecked, floors covered with rubble. The crane had been torn from the fireplace, and the hearth was cold; no fire there for hours. He felt the anger surge again, but this time it collapsed just as quickly beneath the weight of a crushing dread.

He made his way outside, over the trampled snow to Augustus'. Just as wrecked.

The red wagon was gone from the stable, the horses gone as well.

The heart of the settlement was quiet, desolate. Nearly every window was dark. He saw a gleam from Cornelius Nips's.

Answering the door, Cornelius said, "Brother Henry, Lordy, praise God almighty!"

As soon as Cornelius had finished his hug, Hen said, "Where Lucindy at?"

Cornelius shook his head. "Gone," he said. "She lit out. She done left me something for you though." Retrieving it from his mantle, he handed Hen a piece of paper folded over, sealed with candle wax. Hen stuffed it in his pocket. "Want me to read it?" Cornelius said.

"I read it later."

Cornelius said, "Since when you can read? You can't read no more'n that frying pan over there can read."

"Maybe I can read good enough."

"You can't read. Stubborn old fool."

Hen felt the paper in his pocket in his throbbing hand. How he longed to have Cornelius read it to him. "When she leave?"

"Good hour before the posse show up," Cornelius said. "You lucky you so dang slow, you miss the whole circumstance—they looking for you, looking real hard."

"Who she leave with? 'Gustus, he show up?"

"Only Napoleon and Belle. They done took 'Gustus' wagon, all right, but 'Gustus, he ain't in it. Nobody seen him. He never show."

Hen turned to walk away. "Them white ruffians be back, Brother Hen," Cornelius said from his doorway. "You best be sure, they be back."

Hen was sure too, but he found he couldn't care less. He was suddenly too weary, too old, too spent. He was empty. The anger had burned itself out. Before it did, it had consumed not only the fear, but everything else that was in him, leaving nothing but a hollow shell where the absence of Lucindy now echoed. He walked up to her cabin, went in, made his way to the bedroom where her bed was shattered on the floor. Curling up in the ruins, burrowing into the tangle of bedclothes, he pulled the letter from his pocket, broke the seal, unfolded the paper. Even in the dark he could see the wondrous, mysterious markings all up and down the page. He touched them with his fingers, every mark, to the far corners of the world, but it was no use. Try as he may, press and rub as he might, he couldn't make them mean a thing.

When Darling rode Gertie out of the woods and into the clearing around Jacob Black's cabin, pink clouds fanning out low in the eastern sky, Kathleen came running even before he dismounted, reaching him as his boots touched the ground, tears flowing freely down her cheeks. "Oh, Will, oh my God, Will, Will," she cried over and over, thrusting herself into his arms, throwing him off balance, trying to squeeze the life out of him, the two tipsy and wobbling, a dainty dance on the crusty snow beside the horse.

Darling, laughing, holding on, was taken aback as her joy turned to fury, for just as quickly she was pounding her fists upon his chest. "Don't you *ever* do that to me again!" she cried, the lovely face now red with anger. "If you ever leave me like that again, I'll kill you!"

Then she kissed him again, and squeezed him. "Oh God, Will, I was so scared!"

"Easy, girl." He couldn't keep from smiling, and the more he smiled, the angrier she became. He took the sack from behind Gertie's saddle, holding it up. "Breakfast."

Her eyes lit up. "I'm famished!"

Over biscuits and hard-boiled eggs by the fire, coffee made with melted snow, he told her about his visit to Hartsgrove. Sandt had apologized for being detained, he said, having intended to come out first thing this morning; he didn't tell her the real reason Sandt hadn't showed. He wasn't certain if she was aware of Sandt's true feelings, and he did not want her to be, a want that made him feel vaguely guilty.

"What about your poor mother?" she said. He told her he hadn't wished to disturb her; the house had been peaceful and dark, and so he'd left her to her rest. Kathleen hit him again. "She's your *mother*. Surely you left her a note?"

"I hadn't a pencil."

"Will Darlin'. Sure, she'll kill you if I don't do it for her."

He told her about his conversation with Vasbinder, that in hindsight he wondered now if his mentor ever truly believed he'd be acquitted at all, that his lack of concern instead seemed to be based on a belief that three years imprisonment was insignificant, a "trifle."

"A *trifle*!" she said. "I can't believe he said that at all."

"He did. He said my only two options now are to turn myself in or to leave altogether. Relocate, live the life of a fugitive from justice far, far away."

"Rubbish. Your *only* option—*our* only option—is to find out who really took Molly. Once we've found that out, everything else will sort itself out."

"He thinks we'll never know," he said. "Not everything in this life is knowable, says he."

"Rubbish. Makes me wonder what *he* knows."

"He alluded to horse-trading with Smathers, with secret arrangements and deals—he said I shouldn't be troubled with them. The 'minutiae of political maneuvering.'"

"Makes me wonder," Kathleen said.

It made Darling wonder too, but it was a wonder he was pleased to set aside. He was tired from a long night, and worry and wonder could wait on the shelf. There would be time enough later for that. Now, he was with Kathleen. Now, he was in love. Sandt was out of the picture—for now. The love of his life nestled close to him. They were warm and well fed, without obligation to parents or patients or books, comfortable and rested, alone, together, safe and free.

Now, the hours stretched before them like an infinite feast.

By late afternoon they'd made love and slept, ate a lunch of jerked beef and stale coffee, made love again, walked in the woods in the unusual warmth of the bright January afternoon, then returned to lie before the fire. Their conversation meandered pleasantly. Having been so recently hungry, she told him some of her earliest memories of the Hunger in Ireland—the degree of which she was far too young to appreciate at the time, its severity only instilled upon her after the fact—and of the endless gray ocean she'd crossed as a child, when her mother had still been alive. He shared with her the story of Dr. Nevers and his father's amputated leg, wondering if that incident had had any bearing on his decision to take up the practice of medicine, which in turn led to stories about riding with Vasbinder, his stern and earnest instruction. Which in turn led to his telling her how his preceptor, in one of the early lessons, had taught him the art of auscultation and percussion, how to tap the fingers just so upon the patient's chest, one or two fingers laid flat. Here he felt obliged to demonstrate upon the chest of Kathleen, explaining that the entirely denuded state of the patient's chest was preferable in all instances, although, as Vasbinder had put it, the delicacy of females under certain circumstances might bar such exposure. The pinkness of his preceptor's face, particularly when taken with the whiteness of his mustache, was a wonder to behold, Darling told her, when Vasbinder first demonstrated the technique upon the vast, heaving bosom of Mrs. Giles, equally pink, with naught but a flimsy piece of linen between them. Darling was certain, though, that present circumstances would in no wise serve to bar the entirely denuded state.

They made love and napped again, and when he awoke, sunlight slanted in low through the window—from which he'd removed the burlap to allow in the fresh, cool air—illuminating their nest. Her face was close, her eyebrows curled into the tiny knot above her nose, her green eyes intently examining his cheek, focusing like a child studying the workings of a butterfly.

"Do you ever shave at all?" she said.

"Now and then. Once a month whether it's necessary or not."

She stroked his cheek lightly. "I've seen fuzzier peaches."

"Have you ever tasted a fuzzier peach?"

"Never," she said, licking his cheek. "Nor one more tasty."

She nestled close, breathing with him. A surge of mild curiosity unsettled him briefly, wonder at how he could feel so content given the totality of his troubled circumstance, but he brushed it away as he might a flea. For a moment or two then, the curiosity distilled into vague and guilty stirrings at the happiness he felt; what was the price? He'd left behind two of his closest friends, Sandt and Vasbinder, each to his own misery, each desolate and joyless in his own particular way, misery caused, in more or less degree, by Darling's own happiness.

"What was that?" she said.

"What was what?"

"I heard a whinny."

"Gertie?"

"It came from the other way."

They listened; nothing but the mourning of a dove. He relaxed. Then came a distinct snort not of Gertie's making, followed by a call. "Will! Kathleen!" It was Sandt.

"Jesus!" she whispered, as the scramble for clothing commenced.

Darling muttered, "What the devil!" struggling into his pantaloons, realizing they were backwards, righting them, pulling them up, standing, furiously trying to work the buttons through the holes. Sandt called again, much closer, and they could hear the hooves in the crusty snow drawing near to the door of the cabin, the squeak and thump of dismount. "Josh?" called Darling, helping Kathleen to fasten her skirt behind her, handing her her shawl.

The door came open as she finished fastening her blouse, her face crimson, and Sandt hesitated, looking at them. He leaned against the doorjamb, deflated.

"Josh," Darling said sternly. Sandt's emotional state notwithstanding, there were limits, limits the man had clearly crossed. "Have you no respect for the privacy—"

He never finished the sentence. Sandt held up a hand.

"I've come with news," he said. "It's Cyrus."

"He was found in his parlor late this morning. I thought you would want to know."

14: January 21, 1858: The Axe Man Cometh

Hen touched the letter in his pocket. It was the only precious thing he'd ever owned. During the course of his long trek through the woods, he'd maintained constant contact with it, walking with one hand, and when he'd stopped to rest and to pee, not infrequently, he'd unfurled the thing to touch the little lines and loops again and again. The secret those markings held had filled his mind all the way up to the top but still it swelled, ready to burst, aching to erupt into the light of day—and wretchedly unable to do so.

Not unlike his need to pee. He was growing increasingly unable to satisfactorily empty his bladder, feeling always bloated and uncomfortable, and he tried again, peeing in fits and trickles, watching the chimney smoke rising from the cabin in the clearing.

Upon first seeing the smoke, the lazy black stream curling into the cloudless sky, he'd been crestfallen. All afternoon as he'd walked, the letter and only the letter had busied his mind. He'd been fortunate to have even thought of the cabin in the first place, and had not considered the possibility that someone might be there, nor certainly what to do in the event that someone was. Now that someone was, now that he should consider what to do, he was still unable to do so. His thoughts constantly circled back like a lost duck to the letter in his pocket.

He buttoned his britches back up, his bladder still unsatisfied. He'd been standing, watching the cabin from just inside the edge of the woods for some time now. The dusk was growing deeper, bright sunshine still sweeping the blue of the sky overhead, leaving the shadows to deepen in the pines where he stood, to lengthen across the clearing surrounding the cabin. A short while ago, a rider had arrived, a young white man who looked familiar, who he tried to place, but through the shadows he couldn't be sure. Now as he watched, someone else emerged, and walked across the clearing, coming toward him.

It was young Dr. Darling. Hen hid.

It had been a warm afternoon for January but now the sun was low and it was colder, yet Darling wore only a shirt. He did not seem to notice the cold. He did not seem to notice his surroundings at all, and Hen thought that he could be standing in the open and the young man wouldn't see him. He watched as Darling engaged in the most uncommon of antics: He raised his arms in the air where they trembled, his smooth young face twisted in anguish. He issued elongated grunts, as if of constipation. He punched at a low limb, knocking loose bits of needles, bark and twigs, then he kicked at the air, too hard and too high, falling to his backside on the pine needle floor of the forest. Then he seemed to go limp. Another anguished, quiet moan. Hen thought there were tears, too, and when Darling rolled over to smite the ground, Hen stepped into the open behind him.

He said, "Gots the miseries, Mr. Doc?" launching Darling from the earth as though he'd been goosed.

He looked at Hen and shook his head once, twice, like a dog shaking water from its fur. "Black Hen? What in the devil are you doing here?"

"Just standing still mostly. What you doing here?"

"That's none of your—I was—what are you—never—" Taking a breath he seemed to go limp again. "Black Hen," he said. "What *are* you doing here?"

"Come here to hide out," said Hen. "Same as you done, I suspect."

"The same indeed." Darling nodded. Kept nodding.

"Only I ain't punching at no dirt, kicking up no fuss."

"Yes, that." Darling sighed, quite audibly, even over the distance between them, some twenty feet or more. He walked toward Hen, then sat on a fallen log. "Come. Sit beside me."

Hen did, ambling slowly, sitting softly. He kept a discrete distance between himself and the young doctor on the log. "You gots some miseries, does you, Mr. Doc?"

"Can you call me Will?"

Hen shook his head. "Don't reckon."

Darling gripped his own knee and squeezed it. "You remember Cyrus?"

"Cyrus," Hen said. "Cyrus, Cyrus."

"Cyrus Vasbinder. My mentor. My preceptor. The man who taught me medicine, the man who became as a father to me."

"No, sir. Don't reckon I does."

"The old gentleman with the bushy white mustache who visited me in jail."

"Oh. Him."

"He's died. Apparently just after I visited with him. Perhaps *because* I visited with him, or, at any rate, because of me, because of my actions in some way or other."

"He just old, Mr. Doc. Maybe that the onliest reason he died."

Darling thought about it a while, the shaking of his head winding down. "'The windowless chamber of death is the destiny of us all,' Cyrus always used to say. If I had a penny for every time he said that..."

"That just mean we all gonna die, don't it? I already knowed that, didn't you?"

"Of course. It's just that... What I mean is... I don't know what I mean. I miss him. And here I am, in hiding, unable even to attend his funeral, unable to even help him at his ending in any way."

"So that why you crying and carrying on?"

Darling considered the question for some time. He said, "No. It isn't. To be perfectly honest, I believe I was carrying on for myself. Out of frustration."

"For you own self?"

"Yes. Because I am unable to cry for Cyrus. Unable to muster a single tear."

When Darling returned to the cabin with Hen, Sandt and Kathleen were sitting in silence at opposite ends of the hearth, both staring into the fire, a silence and opposition that Darling found entirely satisfying, if with a modicum of vague guilt. As the two men entered, Kathleen and Sandt looked up from the fire with frowns of profound surprise. "Have you met Black Hen, my erstwhile fellow prisoner?" said Darling.

"He followed you home and you wish to keep him?" Sandt said.

Sandt's quip was roundly ignored and he took to sulking, or resuming his sulk, while Kathleen stood and asked the old black man if he was hungry. Hen reckoned he was not, holding forth the sack of provisions he was toting, and he was told to make himself comfortable—he apparently had to be told, as he'd given no indication of moving beyond the doorway where he stood, floppy hat in hand—and Darling joined Kathleen in their nest of wrappers and sacks, Sandt across the floor, reclining against the pile of branches and sticks for the fire. Hen set his sack on the floor in the far corner, gingerly lowering his old bones down beside it. It was a while before he leaned back against the wall. For the longest time it was quiet as they stared into the fire, as if they were incapable of rounding up all the urgencies stampeding through their minds into conversational corrals. Finally Kathleen wondered who were Cyrus's relatives, who was his next of kin. Sandt thought the old doctor had none, but Darling was aware of a brother-in-law—Gertie's youngest sibling—who lived, he thought, in

Meadville. When Darling wondered when the funeral would be, Sandt said he could find out, and Kathleen said for what purpose, they couldn't attend at any rate, and Darling wondered when Sandt intended to find out, and Sandt said, "Why? Are you anxious for me to leave?" That brought the silence around once again, silence from which Hen had never wandered. From the dark corner of the cabin he watched the white folks as if watching bears going about their business in the woods. It occurred to him that here, right here in this very cabin where he and the white folks were living their lives at this moment, was the place where the child Pompey had lived the very last day of his, and he thought he should tell them. But he did not.

Sandt put another stick to the fire. Darkness had finished descending and Darling draped the burlap back over the hole in the wall, cold air creeping in through the cracks and crevices all around. The fire popped and sizzled, a spark sailing out to the middle of the cabin floor, where they all watched it fade to black. The dank smell of clay from the earth beneath the cabin floor mixed with the acrid scent of smoke. When Darling supposed they should be thinking about making some plans, no one seemed anxious, or able, to do so.

After a few moments, Kathleen allowed that the plan was clear: Find Molly, clear Will's name, resume their lives, plan the marriage.

Darling, despite the delight he felt at hearing those words on her lips, glanced at Sandt, wary of his reaction. Sandt, however, remained composed. "Let us see," he mused, "where would we be if we were Molly Plotner?"

"Be home in my bed with my dolly," Hen said, a voice so unexpected the other three flinched. Hen thought of Lucindy's bed, wrecked and cold, of Belle's husk doll he'd spotted in the darkened ruins. He thought of the letter in his pocket and touched it again.

"I as well," said Kathleen, squeezing the hand of Darling.

"In order to be there," Darling said, "you would have to be alive."

"Not necessarily," said Sandt. "Or, to put it another way, not necessarily."

Another silence, thoughts burrowing this way and that. Darling said that now that Cyrus was gone, only three sources remained from which they might seek their answers: Enoch Plotner, Little Bull and Levi Smathers, the great man himself.

"Smathers?" Hen said. "He the white big bug with the black cheek whiskers I seen in the courtroom? The one gots the ghost living up in his house?"

"He would indeed be the white 'big bug,' I suppose," Darling said, "but I was unaware of any ghost."

"He lives in a haunted house?" said Kathleen, eyes wide.

"'Gustus done said so," said Hen. "Done told me he heard that

Smathers fellow gots the ghost of his little girl, the one got burnt up in the fire, still living in his house with him. Up there in Bootjack."

"Such folderol," said Sandt.

"Cyrus would say poppycock and twaddle," Darling said.

"Or bobtail and ragtag," Sandt said.

"No, no," said Darling. "Ragtag and bobtail—the other way 'round."

"Say folks hears her crying and wailing on nights when they's a full moon," Hen said. "Other times too, day and night."

"Yes," Sandt said, "and they see fairies dancing about on the lawn."

"I've *seen* fairies dancing," Kathleen said, "with my own eyes!"

"At any rate," Darling said, "I would be very much surprised if the ghost or the fairies or whatever have anything at all to do with the political horse-trading to which Cyrus alluded."

"And you think this horse-trading that might have took place between Cyrus and Smathers," Kathleen said, "you think it could lead us to Molly?"

"Most unlikely," Sandt said.

"We shall never know until we learn the particulars," said Darling.

"So we should start with him then, with Smathers," Kathleen said. "Sure that Enoch Plotner fella—and the liar, Little Bull as well—they've already done their party piece in court. They're unlikely to change a word of it."

"And just how do you propose to get the truth out of the man?" said Sandt. "Or, for that matter, to even approach him, to even approach any of them at all, in any manner whatsoever? As wanted fugitives."

"Sure only the one of us is really wanted," Kathleen said. "And he is *really* wanted," she added, squeezing his hand once again. Darling watched Sandt's eyes as they rolled.

They thought it over, grist grinding in the mills of their minds. Darling said, "Perhaps we would do well to sleep on it," and the moment the words came out, the awkwardness set in, at the presumed sleeping arrangements necessitated by the situation. Did Sandt indeed intend to stay the night? Did Black Hen ever intend to move from his rigid pose in the corner? What did he intend to do? Black Hen's circumstance was entirely different from Darling's, the only similarity superficial at best—both of them running from the law. "Black Hen—have you made any plans of your own?"

Hen had not. His plans were in his pocket. He pulled out the letter from Lucindy, unfolding it once again. In his dark corner, the markings were all but invisible. He realized that not only had he made no plans—beyond hiding here—but that no plans *could* be made until he learned what Lucindy had told him to do. He reckoned it must be in her letter, her telling him what to do, just as Fudge had always told him what to do down through all the years. And even though he wanted to keep her message to himself, there was simply no way to do so, he realized, no way short of going to school. "No sir," he said. "Ain't yet, anyways."

Darling said, "What is that you're reading?"

"Truth be told, Mr. Doc," Hen said, "I ain't too good at the reading—was thinking maybe you could read it for me."

"Of course," Darling said. He watched the old man struggle stiffly to his feet, with a passing feeling of vague guilt; he should have gone to fetch the thing himself.

Hen handed it over. "Oh dear," said Darling. He held it this way and that, pulling it up close to his nose. "I need more light." He stood and moved to the fire, holding the letter as close as he could. "It seems to be terribly smudged and faded," he said. "Some words entirely obliterated. What on earth happened to it? How old is it?"

Hen didn't answer. He stood where he was, beside Darling's nest, his heart fluttering down toward the clay beneath the floorboards. Kathleen joined Darling by the fire. Sandt went over as well. Hen watched the three young white folks pouring over his piece of paper, his treasure, spread out on the hearth between them. "Oh dear," Kathleen said.

"What is this exactly?" Darling asked Hen, "a letter?" Hen nodded, though Darling never turned to see him.

Sandt said, "There—there, the first word has to be *Ham*."

"It is in the salutation line," Darling said, "where it would probably be *Hen*."

"*Hen*, of course," Kathleen said.

"That word down there looks like *Panama*," said Darling, pointing.

"*Panama*?" Sandt said.

"*Canada*," said Kathleen.

"That strikes me as a *P*," Darling said, "not a *C*." He looked up at Hen. "I'm afraid it's all but illegible."

Illegible was not a word with which Hen was familiar, but he knew immediately what it meant, and his fingers trembled. "Can I have it back, Mr. Doc?"

"Of course," Darling said.

"Is that *have* or *love*?" Kathleen said.

They studied the letter a few minutes more. Was it *wait* or *waif*? *Maker* or *marker*? *Sorry* or *furry*? *Augustus* or *Orange tree*? Finally, they gave up, Darling returning the letter to Hen. "I'm sorry," he said.

"What happened to it, anyways?" asked Kathleen. "How did it get so smudged?"

Hen didn't answer. He retreated slowly to the dark, cold corner of the cabin, to the dark, cold corner of his life, burying his guilty fingers deep in the ragged graves of his pockets.

Sandt stayed, as did Hen. Kathleen shared with them a few of the sacks from her nest, which, along with a few pliable boughs, made comfortable—if the term could be applied in so crude a circumstance—sleeping places for the two men. They settled in. They would need their rest, of that much they were certain, although no one, Darling foremost, was entirely certain for what purpose it would be needed.

For a while Darling tried to sleep, Kathleen curled close beside him. He was aware of Sandt's back, which his chum had purposely presented toward the pair, and for the longest time Sandt's presence inhibited Darling's rest, though not, apparently, Kathleen's. After a while he too drifted off. He was awakened some time later when Hen opened the door to a rush of cold air and went outside, then again when he came back in, and once more, a short time later, when he went out again and returned. The old man was going outside to pee. Darling was not annoyed. He didn't mind being awakened. Being awake was being alive, and for some reason, this night, more than any other night of his life, being aware of being alive seemed a fine and fitting thing to be, although the very thought of it, the gladness of being alive when his friend, his mentor, his preceptor was not, brought about once again the vague feelings of guilt. Where was Cyrus now? Or had he simply ceased to be? He thought of Hen's story, the ghost of Smathers's deceased little girl in his mansion in Bootjack, and it brought him more fully awake. He did not believe in ghosts. He remembered the reputed ghost that had haunted Mortimer's Pool when he was a child, and how the ghost had turned out to be an old, unbalanced recluse of an Indian, averse to being seen by white men, or by anyone else. He wondered: How could anyone believe in ghosts? Why? Presumably someone actually heard this so-called wailing and crying from Smathers's mansion, the ghost of the girl; was it wind? A wolf in the woods? Was it morbid imagination? Whatever it was, Darling was sure there was an eminently logical, earthly explanation.

A little later still, in the heart of the night, he fell into a troubled semi-slumber. His last visit to Cyrus—the last moments of Cyrus's life—played itself out, over and over. For some reason Darling's mind, in its somnolent state, insisted on getting it right, insisted on replaying every movement of both him and his mentor, every gesture, every word of conversation in an endless, repetitive loop, till the memory became dream, the dream memory. Cyrus's exact words—*some serious horse-trading was undertaken to avoid our prosecution*—fixed themselves in his mind—*the minutiae of political maneuvering*. The words in turn brought back the memory, the image of his father and Cyrus laughing alongside the other men, the other politicians, cigar smoke encircling their heads at the front of the room in the brick schoolhouse, before the master's desk—only now, suddenly, he recalled the source of their amusement at long last: a stud bull. For the price of the services of a stud bull on the farm of a political rival's supporter, an opposing candidate had been bought; he would step aside. *Hippocrates*—he even remembered the name of the bull. And he wondered, even as a feeling of relaxation began to overcome him (for the wonder was not an urgent one): What was the name of Enoch Plotner's new ox? He began to sink, to fall loose, to evaporate. Only then, when his mind had gotten it precisely right, only then, did he finally fall into an easy sleep, and abandon his mind to its workings.

In the dark, on the cold hard floor of the drafty cabin, a horror in the guise of Yellow Charlie visited Hen. The thing he decided to call a dream—for he'd been half awake at the time—had begun pleasantly enough, with the memory of Lucindy not so long ago applying the poultice of raw potato to his frostbitten pizzle, so soothing and healing and wondrous. In his dream, however, it had been even more than soothing and wondrous, for, in his dream, quite unlike the actual event, quite the opposite of it in fact, he had not merely surrendered himself to a state of helpless, needy infancy, had not merely allowed himself to be cosseted; in his dream he'd begun to take on a lustful aspect and his manhood had begun to stir and come alive beneath Lucindy's startled touch, beneath her widening eyes. It was a strange, foreign and frightful feeling, as lust was not a mode with which Hen had ever been familiar. Never. Neither he nor Lucindy, in the dream, had known what to do next, his manhood rising up, both of them staring at it in wonder, as they might—as they had—at a baby's first steps, or at the wonder of the aurora borealis unfolding across the northern sky. Lucindy had begun to speak to him then, with both words and gestures, kindly expressions of love on her face, explaining to him what was happening—a simple, easy explanation—but Hen could not comprehend what she was saying. He could not decipher a single word that left her lips and his desperation grew, until Yellow Charlie was there, quite suddenly and terribly, wielding his own calcified manhood like a weapon, an instrument of torture and destruction, and Lucindy had begun to cry out, excitedly, putting forth exactly what she and Hen had to do to save themselves from this fresh, old horror. But Hen could not understand a word of her instruction.

He sat up in the corner of the cabin so suddenly that he swooned for a moment, and the swirling motion of the swoon was the dream fleeing his mind in glittering shards and pieces like embers fleeing a fire, vanishing into the night. But before it was completely gone, he was finally, in a moment of great clarity and release and relief, able to understand the very last thing she said, though, for the life of him, he couldn't decipher its meaning: *horse-trading*, she said. It didn't make a lick of sense. Then she repeated it. *Horse-trading. Plotner's ox!*

Darling sat upright in the room little illuminated by the dying fire, causing Kathleen to stir beside him in their nest. *Horse-trading. Horse-trading!* His unconscious mind had done his work for him. The pieces had fallen into place, the puzzle had been assembled for him, as if by a fairy who had visited in the night. *Horse-trading. Slave-trading. Horses, slaves, bulls, oxen—little girls, dead and alive…*

"Horse-trading." This time he said it aloud. He could see his breath.

"*Horse-trading!*" came to life in joyful puffs. "*Plotner's ox!*"

Kathleen sat up beside him, her eyes wide and alarmed in the dim firelight. Across the room, Darling heard—scarcely seeing—Sandt rolling upright, Black Hen stirring as well.

"Of course!" Darling said. "She's alive!"

No one else spoke. In the darkness three faces were watching. "Don't you see?" Darling said. "It all adds up!

"Why do you suppose Cyrus so readily believed my story—he knew she was alive! And why do you suppose Enoch Plotner didn't search for his little girl—he knew she was alive! And how, how do you suppose Plotner procured his new ox? *How?*

"Black Hen—Black Hen! Tell me this: Do you believe in ghosts?"

"No sir, no, don't reckon I does," came the grumble of a voice from the darkest corner. Hen had come awake, though he was still sweating and chilled from his nightmare of Yellow Charlie. "Reckon I does believe in goats, though."

"Neither do I!" said Darling. "Neither do I!

"By *God* if she isn't alive!"

They waited. After Sandt left, Darling paced the little floor before the fire, full of steam and zeal, Kathleen was up and down, pacing beside him, reclining again, in an endless shower of chatter, as Hen only watched and listened from his far chilly corner. Yellow Charlie lingered. Yellow Charlie refused to quit him this time. Finally Hen quit—grown weary just watching—and walked outside, across the clearing, through the scraggly brush to the pines where he'd waited the day before, the last place he'd stood with hope in his pocket. The early morning air was cold, his hands and feet numb, but scarcely as numb as his mind and his heart. The sky was overcast, a blank, gray slate, fittingly, no lines, no shapes or colors, no direction. He watched a squirrel worry its way up a tree, going home.

He reckoned he would go with them, the young white folks. He hadn't been invited, but he hadn't not been invited either. Sandt had ridden his blue roan into town, intending to return with it hitched between the shafts of his Dearborn wagon, in which they intended to journey to Bootjack, there to seek out the mansion of Levi Smathers and learn what there was to be learned. Hen had no plans. Yellow Charlie had none either. He couldn't return to Little Brier, he couldn't go anywhere else. Lucindy was gone, he knew not where, but wherever it was, he suspected there was no place for him there, either.

He couldn't begin to follow or fathom the entanglement of people and things and events that Darling and the others devised in the cabin before he'd walked out, the devious schemes that they calculated must have played out. A farmer had bartered his daughter for an ox, was the gist. The old man who'd just died had forever stained his legacy by being the broker. Another doctor had perjured himself for access to cadavers, and someone had gone so far as to procure the corpse of an orphan girl to rebury in Molly's stead. But of all the rumor, speculation and guesswork, only one piece snagged in Hen's mind and stuck, like a splinter festering in his finger: Why would Smathers, Darling wondered, a childless widower, have wanted to procure for himself another little girl in the first place, particularly in that manner? The suspicions came out and they filled up the air, the rotten miasma of a dead skunk. They suspected it was something darker than love or loneliness, much darker, as an above-board adoption or indenture could have accomplished as much. Why the subterfuge, why the secrecy? Kathleen's face had blanched and she'd looked at Darling with a trembling lip. As the others engaged in veiled and delicately worded speculation, not wanting to put a name to the worst of their fears, Hen could only recall the words Dr. Means had used to describe Levi Smathers: *Horrid. Evil.* He'd spoken of dark hints and rumors that the evil of that man went beyond imagination. Hen felt the stinking breath of Yellow Charlie on his neck.

Sandt drove the Dearborn, Darling, Kathleen and Hen concealed in the box, the canvas curtains rolled down the sides. The journey commenced in silence, the wagon jolting rudely over the path through the woods to the Beechwoods Road. When the jouncing abated and finally permitted, Kathleen said, "What shall we do if she's there?"

"We shall bring her out," said Darling, stoutly.

"And what shall we do if she isn't?" said Sandt.

There was hesitation in the air as Darling pondered the problem. "We shall not bring her out," he said, just as stoutly.

Hen nodded. At last, he thought. At last they were making some sense.

None of them had ever seen it, but the mansion was easy to find, being the only building within a hundred miles that might be fitting of so grand a title.

House was the next grandest and of those there were plenty, along with the usual cabins, shacks and shanties. Smathers's estate was situated on the edge of Bootjack, one foot in the town, one in the country, at the place where Main Street became the Tionesta Turnpike—a grand enough name itself for a packed dirt road only slightly wider than most—and continued on its windy, hilly way northwest, through ever-thickening forest. A three-story structure of yellow clapboard with gabled roofs and elaborate blue cornices and trim, it was visible only because it was elevated on the hill that rose up from the road, for along the front for a hundred yards ran a tall, impenetrable fence. In the middle of the fence was a gate, beside which stood a small building the size of a privy.

Sandt drove his Dearborn up to the gate. A guard stepped from the privy, which, for the moment, became a guardhouse. "Can I help you?"

Sandt said, "I am here to see Congressman Smathers."

"You got an appointment?" said the guard.

From his hiding place in the back behind the curtains, Darling thought the guard sounded old, tubercular and black. Sandt said, "No—nor should I need one to meet with my own congressman."

"Move on, then," said the guard.

"I demand to see my elected representative."

"That and a nickel'll get you a haircut."

"You are very impudent. What is your name?"

"Move on," the guard said.

"Very well, Mr. Move On," muttered Sandt, "we shall just see about that." Flicking the reins on the roan's rump he pulled away. When they were well up the road, he said, "The nerve. I've a mind to report that fellow."

"To whom?" said Darling, sitting up. "Please bear in mind that we have no real wish to see the congressman. Only to see the inside of his house."

"Still," Sandt said. "There's a principle."

"Was he an old Negro man? He sounded it. He sounded sickly as well."

"He was young, white and healthy as a horse."

Before Darling could argue—he still believed he was right, that Sandt was merely being contrary—Kathleen said, "Never mind the guard—what shall we do now?"

Sandt said, "I doubt that the fence could conceivably enclose the whole of the estate. Why, it would have to run for miles."

Around the bend, beyond the spot where the fence left the road and commenced the climb up the hill through the woods, Sandt stopped to allow Darling, Kathleen and Hen to disembark. The three followed the fence into the woods, as Sandt headed back to argue with—and to distract—the guard.

Down by the road on the lee side of the hill, the snow was deeper and difficult to negotiate, but by the time they'd made their way a hundred yards up, the going was easier, only a few inches deep at the most. They heard the sound of an axe ringing on wood, coming from inside the fence, where there were trees aplenty as well. "That might well be Smathers himself," Darling said softly. "I understand he likes to keep fit by chopping his own wood. Or so Cyrus told me on several occasions."

They continued to follow the fence, up behind the estate where the woods grew even denser, the undergrowth so thick in places they had to detour around and down into the woods before making their way back to the fence. The fence remained tall, strong and apparently impenetrable, though the pristine, white-washed façade by the roadside had given way to weathered boards. They made their way as quietly as they could, speaking only in whispers, and when a grouse exploded into the air out of a thicket beside them, Darling and Kathleen nearly jumped from their skins—Hen was as unperturbed as ever. They stopped to catch their breath. Darling calculated they must be directly behind the mansion by now, quite opposite the road, where he wondered if Sandt was still arguing with the guard. He doubted it, as a good half hour or more must have passed since they'd parted company. More likely he was waiting already around the bend where he'd dropped them off, at their planned rendezvous.

"It would seem our friend was wrong," Darling said. "Again. As usual."

"Joshua?" said Kathleen.

"Who but? It appears to me that the fence does indeed encircle the entirety of the estate. And then some."

From the trunk of a birch tree, Hen peeled off a piece of white bark. Down along the weathered gray boards of the fence, the trees seemed to grow ever closer, touching the boards in places. Darling suggested they might do well to seek an alternative method of entry, perhaps the overhanging limb of a tree which they could climb, make their way over the fence and drop inside in that manner. Kathleen thought the lay of the land—rough and uneven—might eventually yield a place where the gap between fence and ground might allow them to burrow underneath. Both looked at Hen, who said nothing, both wondering if the old man was up to either climbing or burrowing. Hen rolled his piece of white birch bark and stuck it in his mouth to chew. He looked at the fence, sized it up, touched it in several places, picked a likely spot, stood back and stomped it hard with his boot. The board split down the middle, giving way to splinters, a rabbit springing from a nearby burrow and scampering across the crust of the snow. Darling and Kathleen exchanged glances, then looked at Hen. "Good job," Darling said. Hen nodded.

They pried the board loose, then the one beside it, and stepped through. They could still hear the sound of the axe chopping wood, from over close to the house. Inside the fence, the woods of the estate had been tamed; the trees remained, tall and stately, along with thickets of laurel and rhododendron, but all traces of rude undergrowth had been cleared, leaving a long, broad, undulating, snow-covered lawn. A copse of blue spruce trees graced a spot where a fresh stump protruded, this year's Christmas tree. Perhaps two hundred yards away, the spires of the mansion rose above the crown of the hill. That was where they headed.

There were no faces peering out from the windows, as far as they could tell, and the axe man—Smathers himself?—was around the far side of the house, where he remained unseen. Staying behind trees, thickets and outbuildings—a stable, a small barn, a corncrib, a privy or two, the servants' quarters—as best they could, they made their way to a decorative portico enclosing a back entry. The door was unlocked.

They found themselves in a well stocked pantry, shelf upon shelf of tinned goods, stacks of crates and sacks and barrels of provisions. Outside, the axe still rang, steady, rhythmic thumps. From inside they heard a noise, footsteps, the rasping of broom, and looked out to see in the dim interior light a Negro woman, a servant, sweeping the hallway. She was old and frail, shaking with palsy. Beyond, a large fire burned in the great fireplace of the parlor, where the walls were papered crimson and green and the tin ceiling was high and ornately impressed. In the other direction, a wide stairway, beside which stood a grandfather clock, pendulum winking glints of gold. It was quarter past twelve.

When the old lady swept her way into the parlor, Darling and Kathleen tiptoed out and up the stairs, Hen trailing behind on the flats of his feet.

Upstairs the hallway was wide and austere, elaborate gas lanterns affixed to the walls at regular intervals. Several bedroom doors stood open in each direction. A smaller stairway led to the third floor, and that was where Darling pointed, where they made their way.

Upstairs, on the third floor, the hallway was narrower, and the doors along it in either direction were closed. It was even darker, the only illumination coming from a small, diamond-shaped window at the end of the corridor, toward which they walked. Hen and Kathleen followed Darling, who stopped at each door, carefully examining each latch. When he found the door, the only door, that was latched from the outside, he stopped and held up his hand.

Lifting the latch, he opened the door and they entered, Darling followed by Kathleen, then Hen. There was a small cry and the sound of little bones thumping on wood, as a child scrambled beneath the bed. "Molly?" said Darling.

The child didn't answer. There was the sound of a snuffle, the smell of urine.

Darling dropped to his knees to peer under the bed. Two wide and frightened eyes peered back from the darkness. "Molly?"

It was as though he could hear the child holding her breath.

"Come here," said Darling, "come to me. It's all right."

Kathleen knelt behind him to peer in. Hen remained in the doorway. Outside the thumps of the axe resounded at greater intervals, slowing, like a dying heartbeat. Hen crossed the room to look out the window.

The child crouched further back. Darling couldn't be certain it was her. "Come," he said. "Don't be afraid. No one will hurt you."

Still she didn't budge. Darling sang, just above a whisper:

But poor old Grimes is now at rest, / Nor fears misfortune's frown. / He had a double-breasted vest— / The stripes ran up and down...

When he stopped, they could hear a faltering echo of the tune from under the bed, a small, uncertain hum. "Molly—come," Darling said softly.

The child crawled out. It was her.

He picked her up. She was dressed only in underclothes. She seemed lighter than before, a wisp of smoke. He held her close, then reached for a blanket from the bed and began to wrap her in it, but then he stopped. Seeing her damage, he held her up before him. Kathleen saw. Hen saw. Molly clenched her eyes shut, as if in shame. Tears squirmed out.

There were bruises on her cheeks and one eye was purpled.

Deep yellow and blue bruises on her ribs and skinny thighs.

Blood dried rusty red on her underpants.

Darling quickly wrapped her up and held her. Kathleen came to them and hugged the child as well, blinking back the tears she refused to cry.

From the window, Hen looked down and saw the man with bristling cheek whiskers bury his axe in the stump. He saw Smathers release the axe, retrieve a handkerchief from his pocket and mop his neck. He watched him take a deep chestful of air and raise his sweating face toward heaven where the sun was trying to break through the bleak cloud cover, and thank God he was alive. Hen turned and walked from the room and down the hallway.

He descended both staircases slowly, shambling at his given pace toward the front door. The old Negro woman was on her knees in the parlor, scrubbing at a stain on the carpet. She looked up at the old black man walking by. She wasn't sure. She was nearly blind. Her mouth fell open. She uttered not a word. As Hen walked out the front door, she shook her head, shaking the vision away, and bent once more to her work, trying to scrub away the stain.

Hen walked around back. Smathers had moved off a few paces from his woodpile, where his axe remained lodged in the stump upon which he split the wood. He stood with his hands on his hips surveying his estate, his back to Hen and his work, his breath issuing upwards from his body in great, soughing plumes. Hen jerked the axe from its home in the stump. He studied it in his hands. There were markings on the handle. He couldn't read them, but he could tell—because he'd memorized those particular markings—that they were not a *Y* and a *C*. They were not. But they could have been. They might have been.

Axe in hand, he walked toward Smathers. Smathers, hearing Hen approach, turned, and, seeing the old black man's grip on the axe, his color peeled away from his face like the skin from an orange.

He was not Yellow Charlie. But he could have been.

He might have been.

ABOUT THE AUTHOR

Dennis McFadden, a retired project manager, lives and writes in a cedar-shingled cottage called Summerhill in the woods of upstate New York. His short story collection "Jimtown Road," won the 2016 Press 53 Award for Short Fiction, and his first collection, "Hart's Grove," was published by Colgate University Press in 2010; his third collection, "The Signal Tower," was a finalist for the 2020 Brighthorse Prize for Short Fiction. His stories have appeared in dozens of publications, including *The Missouri Review, New England Review, The Sewanee Review, Crazyhorse, The Antioch Review, The Massachusetts Review, Ellery Queen Mystery Magazine, Alfred Hitchcock Mystery Magazine, The Best American Mystery Stories* and in the inaugural volume of the new series, *The Best Mystery Stories the Year 2021*, edited by Lee Child. In 2018 he was awarded a Fellowship at the MacDowell Colony.

Made in the USA
Middletown, DE
15 October 2022

12739192R10149